The Thracian Idol

Andrew Clawson

© 2024 Andrew Clawson *All rights reserved*. No part of this book may be used, reproduced or transmitted in any form or by any means, electronic or mechanical, including photocopying, recording, or by any information storage or retrieval system, without the written permission of the publisher, except where permitted by law, or in the case of brief quotations embodied in critical articles and reviews.

This book is a work of fiction. The characters, incidents, and dialogue are drawn from the author's imagination and are not to be construed as real. Any resemblance to actual events or persons, living or dead, is entirely coincidental.

Get Your FREE Copy of the Harry Fox story *THE NAPOLEON CIPHER*.

Sign up for my VIP reader mailing list, and I'll send you the novel for free.

Details can be found at the end of this book.

Chapter 1

Corsica

Skin tore from his fingers as Harry Fox dangled thirty feet above jagged rocks. His feet kicked at the sheer cliff face, failing to find purchase, while the twisting and turning loosened his grip. He slipped further down the crumbling stone, gravity pulling at him with each ragged breath. The climbing rope around his waist fluttered uselessly in the stiff breeze. He cursed. Forget to check one anchor and look what happens.

He could have sworn the piton had been sturdy. Harry closed his eyes. *Look how that turned out.* One instant he had been reaching for the cliff edge above him, ready to haul himself up and over it; the next, his climbing anchor had broken loose and he was dangling by one hand on the side of a cliff.

Why was that monk even buried up here? Harry pushed the thought aside. First, get to the top of the cliff. Then worry about who to blame.

His nose scraped against the vertical rock face. Harry held on, his jaw clenched. He moved his other hand up, fingers inching over the surface, feeling for any crack or cranny. A beat later they snaked into a crevice and locked tight. Fire burned in his shoulders as he took a breath and pulled, hauling himself closer to the cliff edge, his screaming arms already weakened from a day of climbing. Dusty air filled his nose and lungs. No footholds were in reach, so Harry shifted his weight to one arm, jammed his fingers in as far as they would go—which wasn't far—and heaved. Up he went, precious vertical inches higher, until he could reach the edge of the plateau above so his forearm lay across the ground. He pulled and kicked until, with one last surge, he vaulted up and over the edge, twisting and rolling away from the sheer drop behind him.

An orange sky looked down on Harry as he lay on his back, chest heaving. It was still weeks before spring would arrive; the scent of the macchia filled his nose. The wild scrub covered the island and bathed Corsica with the vibrant scent of rosemary, narcissi and other wildflowers. A Corsican welcome to this inhospitable cliff three stories above flat ground. A cliff hiding the tomb of a long-forgotten Christian monk.

Overextended tendons protested as he got to his feet and moved back toward the edge, looking at the ground far below. Ancient rubble lay across the hillside, remnants of a staircase carved into the hillside that had long ago fallen loose. Scorch marks blackened the cliffside he'd ascended. Harry kicked a loose rock over the edge. It landed a few seconds later with a small, distant *crack*.

He backed up slowly and turned around. Another jagged peak soared above; the narrow plateau he stood on was merely a waypoint for anyone wishing to reach the top. Not that anyone had climbed this forlorn peak in years. With nearly five hundred named mountains in the single range stretching across Corsica, this one was hardly on any mountaineering bucket list. Which was exactly what Harry had wanted to hear. Three months spent scouring history books for clues, digging through church archives across France and Germany, never knowing if what he sought still existed, and here he was. A destination hidden for centuries. The final resting place of a monk unremarkable in every way, save one. A monk with a secret Harry intended to reveal.

Abbot Agilulph had served in the First Abbey of Aachen in the late eighth and early ninth centuries. He had been an otherwise unremarkable servant of God, and then Agilulph's life had taken a dramatic turn when one particular man had read the abbot's religious treatise. The reader had felt as though God himself had spoken through the writings of Agilulph, and he had been so moved he'd bestowed upon Abbot Agilulph and his entire abbey patronage sufficient to make their abbey a bastion of scholarly study. Agilulph had become the man's personal clergy, the only one to hear the man's sins and guide his soul. A weighty responsibility.

The man Agilulph served? Charlemagne. King of the Franks and Lombards, and later the Holy Roman Emperor. The man often referred to today as *the Father of Europe*, a man canonized by an antipope and to whom several current monarchies could trace their lineage. Charlemagne changed the course of history, and in his lifetime he trusted Agilulph on all matters as he built an empire, making Agilulph one of the few people outside Charlemagne's family the king trusted with his life. And also, Harry suspected, with much more.

Harry removed a folded sheet of paper from his pocket. He studied the cragged mountainside ahead of him, eyes narrowed. Three months searching for the information on this piece of paper had taken him from Brooklyn to a church in Northern France, to a monastery outside Berlin, and to several other churches and museums across each nation. All based on whispers heard by a woman who knew everyone in the world of black-market antiquities, a world filled with lies and half-truths. What began as a rumor took shape during his journey, and had culminated in Harry finally uncovering the evidence in a musty church basement in a French village. That evidence had brought him to this Corsican mountainside, a stone's throw from an ancient village where centuries ago a boy named Agilulph was born.

According to a battered record book Harry reviewed in that rural French village, Agilulph outlived his benefactor, serving in Aachen's abbey until his death, after which the abbot's body was returned to his home village for burial. Not unusual, but it was a footnote in the entry that caught Harry's eye. The monk whose records memorialized Agilulph's return commented on the large number of royal guards who escorted Agilulph's body home. An incredible sight, the monk wrote; there had been so many guards that the entire village came out to watch them pass. In addition to the guards, skilled craftsmen accompanied the group high into the mountains to bury Agilulph in an undisclosed location. No one explained why the abbot would be buried in such a place, why such secrecy had been maintained throughout the burial and why the townsfolk were forbidden, on pain of death, from visiting the grave. The entire event was cloaked in an impenetrable veil of mystery.

Impenetrable until one of the craftsmen felt compelled to unburden his soul in the village church. Who heard his confession? The monk who recorded this event in the church's ledger. Harry had paged through the Latin entry and discovered the monk had also broken his own vow of secrecy, recounting the craftsman's tale not only in words, but in a drawing. A drawing Harry now held in his hands. It was an image that Harry believed would not only reveal Agilulph's secret, but also save Harry's family.

The monk had sketched a face in profile. The face of Charlemagne, a face with large ears, a prominent nose and downturned lips below the laurel crown atop his head. A classic and contemporary image of Charlemagne. Harry expected to find this same image somewhere on the mountainside, if the craftsman from so long ago was to be believed. But where to start?

The paper went back into his pocket as he approached the mountainside. Cold wind kicked up as Harry blew warm air into hands scraped raw from his climb. Trickles of blood mixed with the climbing chalk coating his palms. He wiped them on his pants before reaching out to the irregular rock face in front of him. Plenty of places here to conceal a carving. He leaned back, trying to see around one part of the wall that stuck out further than the others. He leaned back a little further. *That could work.*

The outcropping was deeper than any other. Wide too, and so deep he had to pull out his flashlight to see inside; the rock was angled so as to cut off any sunlight trying to break through. Lichen and dry moss covered the rocks. He rubbed at the growth, got nowhere and then ripped off a handful. More and more fell away until a pile of debris lay by his feet. Not that Harry noticed. He was too busy staring at Charlemagne's face.

The same image as the one in his pocket, carved here into the mountainside. His breath came faster, the cold darkness of this hidden nook turning it to clouds as his hands ran across the rocky surface. There must be a way in. A lever, a hidden door, a spring to trip. The craftsman's tale had said so. It *must* be here.

Harry shook his head. *Take a breath. Focus.* Think for a second and the answer often presented itself. He looked up. He took a step back. His heart sank. He'd found the door.

This wasn't a mountainside in front of him. It was a massive *boulder*. Judging from the faint toolmarks surrounding the boulder and the mountain behind it, this boulder concealed the entrance to a cave. A cave with something very valuable inside.

He moved back to the cliff edge, grabbed a trail rope hooked to his backpack three stories below and pulled it up to the plateau where he stood. Out came several plastic bags of a mixture used by commercial companies to mine, quarry, or otherwise move massive amounts of stone through controlled explosions in short order. The bags contained ammonium nitrate fuel oil, or ANFO.

The high explosive wouldn't detonate without a booster explosion, so it had posed little danger while strapped to Harry's back. Add in the gel explosive sticks he had stored separately in his bag, however, and it was a different story. Harry held the sandwich-baggie-sized ANFO pouches in one hand and the gel sticks in the other as he knelt beside the massive boulder and shoved them as far back as he could, repeating the process on the other side before cautiously placing a small battery-powered detonator under each one.

Harry moved as far to one side of the plateau as he could before pulling out the transmitter and turning on the power. He scanned the mountain for a long minute, searching for any sign of movement. Nobody in sight. Sending out an apology to any wildlife below, he pressed his back to the stone, closed his eyes, and pressed the detonator.

A massive *boom* filled the air. The rock face cracked and shook, vibrations rattling his body as Harry flattened himself against the wall. He'd used only half the explosive. The booming noise faded and the ground stopped shaking. Harry counted to one hundred for good measure before slipping the pack over his back and picking his way around a debris field of rocks and dust. He stopped in front of where Charlemagne's face had been.

Only a gaping black hole remained. An entrance, just as the confessing craftsman had said. Harry flicked his flashlight on and aimed it inside, peering through a million tiny flecks of light as the dust settled.

Harry stepped over a fallen rock as he took one step in, and then stopped. The scratched Latin words in the ancient record book came to mind: the confessions of a craftsman with no understanding of what his words revealed. He'd questioned why they had carried the monk to a mountain cave when the local graveyard was hardly full. Why every man on site was sworn to secrecy on pain of eternal damnation. But those weren't the words that made Harry's skin tingle now.

What need have we for such devious devices in a tomb? The dead cannot walk.

That was what had convinced him this mountainside cave was what he sought. A resting place for more than merely a monk with the king's ear. This tomb held a greater secret, and a greater treasure.

Musty air filled his lungs as Harry's flashlight beam played over the dusty interior. He was warmer now that he was away from the biting wind outside. The cave had a rough floor leading into darkness, with smooth walls and a rounded roof overhead, free of stalactites. Several steps inside brought him clear of the newly fallen rubble, none of which appeared to have come from the inside walls. The cave structure didn't appear to be compromised, yet he still paused after a few steps and waited.

Shadows darted across the walls as his light moved. The dust had settled enough for him to see ahead. The beam flashed over a wall, then came back. He stepped closer. "Latin." His word echoed in the still air. "That's Latin."

Letters carved into the cave wall at eye level. *CAROLUS MAGNUS.* Charles the Great. Another inscription on the opposite wall read *KAROLUS IMPERATOR AUGUSTUS,* the title given to Charlemagne when he was crowned Emperor of the Romans by Pope Leo III in St. Peter's Basilica.

Harry pressed on. The hair on his arms rose as he walked, his steps tentative. He'd seen what happened when you rushed after a relic, so even though nothing about this cave stood out, that's exactly what gave him pause. Nothing in his line of work was this easy. He glanced back as a bird's cry sounded outside the cave entrance. Someone following him? He shook his head. Nobody could have trailed him this far up the mountain unseen. Even if they had, all those rocks he'd just blasted over the edge of the cliff would make them think twice about climbing up here.

He turned back, lifted his flashlight higher, and stopped cold. Another cavern loomed ahead. No, not a cavern. An alcove, carved out of the stone, barely high enough for a man to stand inside. Additional openings on either side, both man-made, both dark. Harry stopped between the two side caves, with the rear alcove in front of him. His flashlight beam revealed a rectangular chunk of cut stone resting in the center of each room, three identical blocks tucked away in this cave hidden inside a mountain. No, not chunks of rock. *Sarcophagi.*

"Three of them," he said in the still air. "To conceal the monk. That's what he was talking about."

The craftsman's question came to mind. What sort of *devious devices* did he mean? Harry crept toward the rear alcove on the balls of his feet, checking every inch of the floor before he moved. Charlemagne hadn't been satisfied with hiding this monk high up on a mountain behind a massive boulder. He'd hired stoneworkers to erect an additional layer of protection. Protection meant to keep people out.

Three identical sarcophagi placed in three identical alcoves. Identical, that is, except for the single-word inscriptions written above each entrance.

DESIDERATA to the left. *HILDEGARD* straight ahead. *FASTRADA* to the right. Three names. Three names he recognized. "Those are Charlemagne's wives." Not a complete list, as the king had

had upwards of ten wives or concubines, producing nearly twenty children among them.

"Agilulph was a monk," Harry said to himself. "What does a Corsican monk have to do with Charlemagne's wives?" The monk had come into Charlemagne's life during his early years, which would have been while Charlemagne was married to his first wife, Desiderata.

He moved toward Desiderata's alcove, one cautious step at a time, until he stood on the threshold. His light revealed an unmarked tomb and nothing else. No carvings on the walls, no inscriptions on the lid, nothing on the floor to warn him death waited for any who entered. He looked down. He looked up. He squinted against the light. "That's odd."

A pair of lines had been cut into the stone above him. It looked like a doorframe, though one without any sort of door to hold. Harry leaned into the space without crossing the threshold. Nothing of note. He leaned back and it hit him.

"He was a *monk*. Monks can marry people. Of course."

Three months of scouring Charlemagne's life had taught him a lot about the man. Including who had presided over his marriages. "Agilulph officiated one of the ceremonies." Harry stepped back into the cave. "The marriage to *Hildegard*."

The trusted monk had married Charlemagne and Hildegard the same year Charlemagne's marriage to his first wife was annulled. That marriage to Desiderata was politically motivated, though what she offered in terms of wealth and power didn't stand up to what Hildegard brought, so Charlemagne had found a sympathetic church leader to annul his marriage. Soon afterwards, Agilulph had entered the picture and joined Charlemagne and his new bride in marriage.

"It has to be Hildegard."

Concern kept his feet glued to the ground. Concern he could be wrong. Concern his haste could get him killed. "One way to check." He walked back to the entrance, picked up several rocks, and came back to Desiderata's tomb. The rocks were roughly the size and shape of baseballs, and Harry Fox had been known to throw a fastball or two in his day. Now he needed a target.

Desiderata's sarcophagus hid a trap, he suspected. Just as Fastrada's had to. But why? This was Agilulph's final resting place, and the only one of the wives Agilulph had a connection with was Hildegard. Leaning into Desiderata's alcove, but stepping no farther, he scanned the area. The floor was of a uniform color all around; natural, flat rock that was part of the mountain. No tell-tale cuts or openings in the wall in which to hide projectiles, no tripwires or switches. Nothing other than the stone sarcophagus.

His light flashed slowly over the stone block. Its lid rested atop the base, with a narrow opening between the top and bottom. Vertical lines decorated the interior of the lip. No, not designs. Harry put one hand on the cave entrance for support and leaned in as far as he could. *What in the world?*

The vertical lines weren't a design. They were small tiles, lined up like dominos between the sarcophagus lid and base, running the entire length in either direction. Harry stood straight, tossed a rock in his hand up and down, getting a feel for it, then took aim and fired.

A direct hit on the domino-like rocks, spraying them in every direction and sending the rest collapsing in both directions. A rumble sounded before his makeshift baseball landed. Harry blinked as his nose was nearly sheared off by the gigantic stone door that crashed down from inside the cave wall and hit the floor.

The rush of air and the rumble of stone tumbling was a physical blow, knocking him to the ground. Translucent curtains of dust cascaded from the ceiling, turned to flashing specks in his flashlight beam. Only after the last echoes faded did he get to his feet. *I knew it.*

Hildegard it was. A look at the cave mouth found nothing amiss. He paused at the threshold to Hildegard's alcove. The same little stone dominos stood between the lid and base of her sarcophagus. Harry stepped over to Fastrada's alcove and found it identical in every way, down to the domino tiles on the tomb. Turning back, he eyed the sarcophagus in Hildegard's tomb. The queen's body wouldn't be in there, not unless Charlemagne had had it moved from her actual tomb in France.

The breath stuck in his throat as he stepped into Hildegard's alcove. He paused. Nothing happened. Harry exhaled, steeled himself and went for the tomb. This lid was thick, at least two inches of solid stone. His only bet was to manhandle it open far enough to reach inside. He might or might not find a body, but he believed he would find something else.

The stone was surprisingly cold on his fingers. He leaned against the nearest corner of the lid, which he could slide over only a few inches. He flexed his fingers, bent at the knees, and gritted his teeth. Slow and steady would get this lid off, not slamming into it over and over. One hand slipped as he pushed and nudged a stone domino off-center.

Ancient rocks grated in the walls. Harry twisted on a heel and dove toward the exit just as the first stone domino slipped free, activating Charlemagne's deadly trap. The second stone slab shot down and smashed to the floor with utter finality, clipping the heel of his boot as he landed and rolled clear.

Harry lay flat on the shaking ground, heart hammering in his chest as echoes bounced off the walls. How long he stayed down he had no idea, though his chest still thumped as though his ribs would break when he sat up and came nose-to-stone with the door that had nearly sealed him inside for the next thousand years. He blinked. *I was wrong. How?*

He rubbed grit from his face. Fastrada was the only one left, so what he sought must be with her.

Harry stepped into her alcove and fired a half-dozen rocks at the small dominos surrounding her sarcophagus. The tiles went flying. The door stayed up. He hurled another few rocks into the chamber for good measure, none of which activated anything, then walked cautiously over to stand beside the tomb. The floor didn't fall from beneath his feet. No spears flew out. There was nothing but his dry footfalls sounding inside the small alcove. Harry let out a breath and reached for the tomb lid. Hands on the edge, legs bent, he pushed against the stone, slowly at first before leaning into it, boots scraping on the floor as he levered every ounce of strength to move the gigantic lid.

It budged. Inches at first, but he kept pushing. Rock ground against rock until he pushed it clear and the lid crashed to the ground. Harry stared at the yellowed teeth of the long-dead monk.

Agilulph looked at him from vacant eyeholes. A skeleton clad in what used to be a simple woolen tunic and cowl, both now faded and dry. A single rope encircled his waist, while unremarkable shoes covered the bones of his feet. Harry took it all in with a glance, then reached into the enclosure. He didn't touch the monk's skeleton or the clothes. What he lifted from atop Agilulph's chest was no less ordinary on the surface, yet inside it lay riches beyond measure.

Harry held Agilulph's bible. Not just any bible, but the bible spoken of by a craftsman who had poured out his soul to a Corsican monk, a craftsman who never suspected his words would serve as a map for Harry Fox. A map that would lead him to his vengeance.

Animal skin, still smooth even a millennium after it was harvested, crackled as he opened the cover. Scratched Latin lettering filled the pages, so small as to be nearly unreadable. Harry didn't bother reading any of it. Finding the inside cover blank, he flipped to the rear cover. His eyes widened. *It's true.*

A message covered the back page. Not scripture. A personal note. About a peace brokered and an alliance formed. Along with the spoils accompanying the accord.

Harry moved to close the book when a phrase at the top of the page caught his eye. *Eam in dominum suam.* It meant *her home.* Understanding dawned. That was the connection, why the sarcophagus labeled *Fastrada* had been correct. Fastrada had been from this same Corsican town. She was a native, like Agilulph. That was the link. And it gave Charlemagne a perfect way to hide the truth.

He flipped the book shut, slipped it into his backpack and offered a silent apology to Agilulph for desecrating his tomb. There would be time to review the note in detail later. For now, however, this was what Harry knew: Charlemagne would likely have claimed he wanted to keep the monk's burial location a secret from the enemies who wanted to unwind an alliance he had built. An object symbolized the accord. An object Charlemagne had gone to great pains to bury. An object Harry could locate using Agilulph's bible.

Harry moved quickly back to the cave entrance and stepped back into the bright sunlight, almost blinding after the cave's dim interior. Harry closed his eyes, lifted his head to the cold sun, and breathed deeply.

"*Non muoverti*," said a voice in coarse Italian. *Don't move.* Harry's eyes flew open as he started and then froze. Having a gun jammed into your neck tended to do that. The gun pressed harder. No message needed this time. *Walk.*

Harry followed orders. He started to turn once, but a harsh command to look ahead stayed that. He could tell that the man behind him was tall. Two things happened as they approached the plateau's edge. Harry realized his climbing rope had vanished, and he could hear voices coming from the ground far below. Harry cautiously leaned over to look.

Three other men stood below. One of them touched his flat cap and stared up at him. "*Ciao.*"

Harry noted their common clothes and dusty shoes. They looked like a crew of street cleaners, not mountain thieves. He responded in Italian. "Is this how you introduce yourself?"

Flat cap shrugged. "When the time calls for it." He raised his other hand. Harry couldn't fail to note the pistol it held. "What have you been doing up there?" the man asked.

"Exercising," Harry said. "It's a nice day."

"We heard an explosion," flat cap said. "I worried you were injured."

"You followed me here from the village?" Harry had taken care to check for anyone following him from the rustic town below. Not carefully enough, apparently. "Why?"

Flat cap smiled. "The village has ears, my friend. It hears your whispers. Your questions about the mountain. About a monk." His voice dropped. "And a *king*. Whispers that draw attention."

Harry groaned inwardly. "It's nothing," Harry said. "An old legend."

"A legend that causes explosions. Who brings dynamite to these mountains?" Flat cap tapped the side of his head. "A man with secrets to hide."

A rapid-fire burst of Italian ensued. The man holding Harry at gunpoint described the three alcoves inside the cave. Only one remained, he said. The man had seen Harry take something from it.

"What did you take?" flat cap asked.

"A finger bone. For good luck."

Flat cap grinned. "You are a funny man. Let us see if you are so funny with a bullet in your leg."

"Wait." Harry glanced over his shoulder. The man behind him didn't seem put off by the thought of shooting him. "I found an old bible." He paused. "And another book," he lied. "I'm not sure what it is."

Flat cap beckoned. "Toss them here."

"Are you crazy? They could be damaged."

"Toss them or my associate shoots you."

Hard to argue with that. "Fine." He looked back at the gunman. "Don't pull the trigger, okay? I'm getting the books."

The man backed up a step. He didn't lower the gun. Harry slipped his backpack off so it hung from one shoulder, reached inside and removed the bible. "I'm giving this one to your buddy," Harry called down to flat cap. He shoved the bible into the gunman's hands before anyone could argue. The gunman kept his pistol on Harry as he held the book.

"What is it?" flat cap called out from below.

As the gunman opened the bible, Harry set down his pack, reached into it and rummaged through it, making a show of hunting for the second book. He seemed to have trouble getting it out, though neither flat cap or the gunman took note; the gunman was engrossed in inspecting the bible, and flat cap was craning his neck, watching him. Harry finally removed an object from his bag and straightened up. One hand stayed closed. The other held the object over the side. "Ready?" Harry called. "Here it comes."

Flat cap had no chance to argue before Harry knelt, stuck his arm over the edge, and released what he held. Flat cap and his two men below all moved toward it, the pair huddling around their boss as he reached up and grabbed it. He caught it with the sound of rustling sand. "It is a plastic bag," flat cap said after a moment. "What did you—"

He never finished. Harry pressed the detonator in his hand. Fire erupted, rocks disintegrated and the trio of Corsican thugs below no longer existed. Harry turned and smashed his fist into the gunman's forearm to send the pistol and the bible flying, then ducked as a jab brushed his cheek. He threw one of his own in return but missed. The gunman caught Harry with a punch to the gut, doubling him over and sending him staggering closer to the cliff edge. The gunman reached for him.

Exactly as Harry hoped. The blow to his gut hadn't truly connected; Harry had faked his pain to lure the gunman closer. He grabbed both of the gunman's arms now, pulling on them as he bent low and used his body as leverage to flip the man up, over and into the air. The man screamed, and Harry straightened again a moment before the cries ended abruptly on the rubble below.

Harry scooped the bible up, slid it back into his pack and slipped the straps over his shoulders before leaning over to peer at the rocks below. There was no other way off this mountain. Harry got down on his backside, turned over onto his stomach and slid himself slowly feet first over the edge, digging his fingers into the lip of the rock and lowering himself until he couldn't stretch any further. His toes barely scraped the top of the biggest rock on the slope below him. Harry grinned. *I'm out of here.*

Chapter 2

Brooklyn

A soft chime sounded in Harry Fox's office, tucked behind the showroom floor. He looked up from the ancient bible on his desk with a frown. *Did she forget something?*

Only it wasn't his last customer, an heiress whose hobbies included stocking her Upper East Side home with museum-worthy pieces to impress her friends. His surveillance system showed a different woman standing outside his door. Someone much more interesting.

"I'm in the back," Harry said into the speaker. A button released the industrial-grade lock on his reinforced front door. "Wipe your shoes."

The woman in front of his shop flipped him the bird. A grin creased Harry's face when he stood, back cracking as he stretched the knots out. All this adventuring took a toll on a guy.

Sharp *clicks* sounded from the showroom as his visitor approached. Harry's eyes narrowed when she came into view. "You didn't wipe your shoes."

Sara Hamed stopped inside the door. She looked down, stepped inside his office, then wiped her feet on the hardwood floor. "Better?"

"You're the worst."

Sara tossed her handbag on one of the visitors' chairs in front of his desk as she walked around, brushing him out of the way before falling into his desk chair. "My feet are killing me," she said. "I guided three tours of our new acquisitions today. Do you have any idea how long scholars enjoy standing and talking about Egyptian artifacts?"

Harry's eyes remained narrow. "I have an idea."

"Very funny." Her gaze fell to the object on his desk and she started. "You have it out?"

"I'm trying to understand what Agilulph is saying. At least I was, until you barged in."

Sara leaned over the ancient bible. She did not touch it. "I thought you had a client coming?"

"Come and gone."

"How many pieces did she buy?"

"Enough to keep the lights on for a few months." And to pay the mortgage for several centuries. Lucky for Harry he didn't have a mortgage. "Apparently word is getting out. A number of her friends have been in touch, looking for new trophy pieces."

"Perhaps I can retire."

"The Anthropology Division curator would have a heart attack if her Egyptologist left after three months."

"Laurel de Voogt is capable. She'd manage." Now Sara reached for the bible, gently gripping the front cover and opening it. "It's blank."

Harry pulled her arm away. "Look at the rear cover." Her mouth opened when she saw the ancient script. "What do you think?"

"Incredible. I can't believe you found it."

"It's what I do."

"Your humility knows no bounds." Her voice was lower when she spoke again. "Does anyone else know this artifact exists?"

What she really meant was *Is this going to get you killed*. "Not any longer."

Her arched eyebrow suggested she had thoughts about that. "Tell me. The truth."

He did. At least the highlights, including what had happened to the men who tried to rob him.

"You know better than to ask too many questions in a small town," Sara eventually said. "And where did you get explosives?" He started to respond when she cut him off. "Actually, don't tell me."

One side of his mouth curled up. "I was never really in danger."

Her face made it clear what she thought of that. "Against my better judgment, I believe you. Don't make me regret it."

He knew enough to keep his mouth shut. Instead, he gestured to the rear cover. "Interested in reading the story?"

Sara moved closer to the desk. "Ancient Latin. Agilulph was a monk, so he would read and write the language." Her eyes flitted back and forth as she read. "This is Agilulph's recounting of Charlemagne brokering an alliance between his empire and the Abbasid Caliphate. The agreement with the caliphate's supreme ruler—Caliph Harun al-Rashid—stopped an ongoing conflict between the two powers and united them against common enemies. The Abbasid Caliphate was one of the few opponents capable of defeating Charlemagne." She looked up at Harry. "Peace with the caliphate allowed Charlemagne to focus on other conquests. That's how he became the *Father of Europe*."

"Keep reading," Harry said. "The agreement wasn't only signatures on a contract. What do kings do when they make agreements?"

Her gaze returned to the page. "Exchange elaborate gifts," she said after a moment. "Such as an elephant."

"I'm not interested in elephant bones."

Sara read on. "Charlemagne received exquisite chess pieces, perfume, a candelabra." She stopped, then looked up. "And a water clock, in which al-Rashid placed the keys to the holy city of Jerusalem. That's what you're after. Charlemagne's clock."

"Pretty hard to find a better lure than the keys to Jerusalem."

Sara didn't blink. "Are you certain this is what you want to do?"

"He destroyed my life. He forced my mother to abandon us. He may not have killed my father himself, but what he did led to the murder."

What was in her head, he couldn't say, and right now he wasn't sure he wanted to know. Sara knew all about Olivier Lloris, how decades ago the French industrialist had forced Harry's father to turn away from his wife and raise their son to believe his mother was dead. Three short months earlier Harry had reunited with his mother, and learned that a man he'd never heard of had done all of this to him and his family.

Harry couldn't let it go. That's why he needed Agilulph's bible. To exact his revenge.

"Whatever you're planning won't change the past," Sara said.

"This is about the future. About making sure we live on our terms, not his. Olivier Lloris isn't the kind of guy to let things go. He needs to know I'm different. Guys like him never hear *no*. It's time he did."

At the same time that Harry had reunited with his mother, Sara had left her university teaching role in Germany to accept a position at the American Museum of Natural History. It was a step forward in her career as an Egyptologist, and it had also brought her to New York. Where Harry lived.

She only shook her head. "I won't try to change your mind."

At least she knew that much about him by now. She also knew what he did, knew at times his activities were a lot closer to illegal than legal, and she still stuck around. Sara Hamed the scholar was slowly becoming Sara Hamed the realist. The world was gray, not black and white. Harry did his best to save artifacts and preserve history. An imperfect man in an imperfect world.

He pointed to the book. "Agilulph makes vague references to either people or locations. I can't make heads or tails of it. Anything make sense to you?"

Sara looked back down at the book, then did the oddest thing. She closed it. "Can we do this later? I have an event this evening and I need to go."

Harry almost fell backward. A museum event was more important than this artifact, more important than the story it told?

He cleared his throat. "Right. Later is fine. Tonight, if you're not too tired. Or tomorrow."

"I'll call you." A wan smile momentarily crossed her face as she stood. "I understand why you're doing this. I might do the same in your situation. You mustn't forget what happened a few months ago. We nearly died in—"

The doorbell chimed. Harry turned to the security monitor and found

Joey Morello standing outside his door. "Joey?" Harry frowned. "I'm not expecting him."

"I should be going." Sara grabbed her bag and headed for the front door, Harry trailing behind after he released the lock. "I'll see you and the book later."

Every question on Harry's lips stayed there as Joey walked into the shop. His face lit up when he saw who was inside. "Sara, what a surprise." Joey opened his arms for a hug. "It's good to see you."

Any frost in the air dissipated. "You too, Joey." She returned his embrace. "I was just leaving."

Joey almost stopped himself from glancing at Harry. "Too bad. We need to get together soon. The three of us. I want to hear all about the museum."

"I'd like that." Sara squeezed Joey's hand before heading outside. She didn't turn to look at Harry as she walked out.

Joey lifted an eyebrow after the door closed. "Bad timing?"

Harry pulled his gaze from the closed door. "No." He waved a hand. "She's just sorting through some stuff."

"Would that *stuff* be your adventures?"

"I wouldn't call them that. More like a vacation, really."

"Any trip with more than one corpse involved isn't a vacation." Joey inclined his head to the glass display cases surrounding them. "How's business?"

"Steady. I might have to hire someone if word keeps getting around."

"I hear the high rollers near Park Avenue are discovering this place."

Harry didn't bother asking how Joey knew. A guy like Joey stayed alive by keeping his ear to the ground, and Joey had plenty of people to keep him informed. "My only problem is they want more exotic pieces each time. Getting new inventory is the challenge."

"Good thing you know your way around an ancient temple." Joey winked. "Did any of my pieces sell?"

"A couple," Harry said. "I'll have the money for you next week. Once I finish with the accounting."

"I appreciate it." He rubbed a thumb over the cleft in his chin. "You don't have to sell them for me if you don't want to." A pause. "You know that."

Harry did. A year ago, he never would have considered saying no to Joey Morello, who was his boss. You didn't turn down a request from your boss lightly. Certainly not when he was the head of the New York mob. "I know," Harry said. "I'm happy to do it." He gestured to the showroom. "You gave me this place. It's the least I can do."

"You earned it," Joey said. "And I'm serious. You ever don't want to move money through here, tell me. I have other places to clean it."

Selling Joey's artifacts wasn't about profit. It was about dirty money. The sort a mob boss made from illegal operations and which needed to be laundered. Harry's legitimate business could do that. "How are your new businesses doing?" Harry asked.

"A work in progress," Joey said. "I bought into an online casino and sportsbook. The taxes are ridiculous, but people still love to gamble. My piece of a new wind energy farm near Buffalo is turning a profit already." His face darkened. "The boutique bank is another story. You wouldn't believe how much red tape I'm wading through to get that set up."

Joey hadn't worried about red tape before in his life. Same as his father hadn't. Mob bosses had other things to worry about. Things like staying alive. "I can only imagine," Harry said. "Glad to hear it's all coming together."

Joey smirked. "My father will turn over in his grave when I pay my tax bill." Joey waved a hand. "Enough about business. I was passing through the neighborhood, so I wanted to drop in, see how you were doing. Corsica can be a tough place. I know some guys in that town." His voice took on a reproachful tone. "You should have asked for help."

"And have your friends get a cut of the profits?" Harry shook his head. "No thanks. The only guy I pay tribute to is you."

Joey wagged a finger. "Not anymore. This is your business, not mine."

"I do it out of respect."

Both men chuckled. It was the line Harry's father had always used when talking about the late Vincent Morello, Joey's father. Vincent, who had given Fred Fox a second chance at life. "Some things don't change," Joey said. "Including you Foxes finding trouble."

"Like I told Sara, it was no trouble."

"Humor me."

Harry took a breath before launching into a recap of his trip, this time leaving nothing out. "I have an idea about where to look for the water clock and keys," Harry finished as they stood in front of his desk. "Agilulph's message vaguely references what may be several locations."

"What does Sara think?"

"She hasn't had a chance to review everything yet."

Joey looked at the book. "Is that because you keep putting yourself in harm's way, or because you're still working with me?"

"Sara loves you."

"I know." Joey winked. "The problem is my professional side. She knows what I do. If Sara ever settles down with a guy, she won't want him to have ties to the mob."

"Settle down?" Harry looked around the office. "Did she say something to you?"

"You can be pretty dense for a smart guy." Joey shook his head. "I know she didn't move into your place yet, but it's definitely on her mind." He pointed at the book. "Or she's worried about your quest to find Charlemagne's relics. Maybe she doesn't want a guy who's always trying to get himself killed."

"This is about protecting my family." A beat passed. "And her."

Joey held a hand up, palm out. "I'd do the same thing. You can't let this Olivier chump get away with what he did. He finds out you're an artifact hunter like your father, maybe he thinks it's an opportunity to add to his collection by using you." One of Joey's fingers pointed at Harry's chest. "There aren't many guys with your skill set running around."

"The only relic he's getting from me is a live grenade. Without the pin."

"If I can do anything to help, ask. I have acquaintances all over. I bet a few of them know people who know Olivier Lloris." He turned to leave.

"I appreciate it, Joey. And I will." Harry's phone buzzed in his pocket an instant after Joey walked out the door. His heartbeat accelerated when he saw who was calling. "Hello, Rose."

"Harry, my dear. Back for so long without a call?"

"Forgive me, Rose. It's been hectic."

"You are forgiven." The sound of metal grating on metal came through his phone, followed by the crackle of burning tobacco. Harry could almost smell the cigarette smoke floating from the end of her long-stemmed holder. "What did you find?"

Harry told his story for the third time today, focusing on the artifact. "I'm not looking to sell it," he said. "At least not yet."

"Even a man with his own antiquities shop will come to me eventually. I will be here."

Rose Leroux was the biggest fence in New York. She was right: Harry would need her eventually. She'd moved his relics long before Fox & Son Antiquities had existed. However, Rose could do much more.

"There is another matter," Harry said. "One you're well positioned to assist with. Does the name Olivier Lloris mean anything to you?"

Silence ensued. "Perhaps it is best if you tell me why you want to know," Rose finally said. "For your sake. And mine."

If anyone else said that, Harry would have thought they were afraid. Anyone except Rose. Rumor had it the last person to cross her was at the bottom of the Hudson. Harry believed it.

"Olivier was the person blackmailing my father, the reason Dad didn't contact my mother for two decades. He's the reason my family stayed apart. I need to earn his trust. Then it's time for payback."

"I see." Ice clinked as a drink was poured. As far as Harry knew, Rose never drank anything but martinis, no matter the time of day. "The answer is yes. I am familiar with the name."

"Have you worked with him?"

"I never reveal the names of my clients," she reminded him. "Not even to you."

"Fair enough," Harry said. "If I wanted to make him aware that a Frankish bible with ties to Charlemagne is for sale to the right buyer, could you make that happen?"

Silence. Of course she could. She was Rose Leroux.

"Would you do that for me, Rose? I'll send you photos of the artifact."

"I will contact the appropriate people. Olivier knows how to contact me if he has interest."

That was as much confirmation that Rose had worked with the man as Harry would get. "Thanks. I appreciate it."

Now the sound of what might have been several olives falling into a martini glass filled his ear. "Harry, are you certain this is wise?"

"No. But I'm doing it anyway."

Rose sighed. "If Olivier discovers you provide the same service your father once did, he may come after you. Either to force you to retrieve artifacts for him, or to keep you from speaking out about what he did to your father."

Nobody could ever accuse Rose of not being perceptive. He scratched at the stubble on his cheek. "Now why don't you tell me the real reason you're warning me?"

"The warning is for my safety, not yours. Three months ago, I made what many would consider to be an ill-advised decision, a decision involving you. The fewer reasons I give people to connect our names, the better."

"Do you regret it?"

"Not at all. I am simply being cautious. In our work, caution keeps one alive."

Three months ago, Rose had helped Harry fabricate evidence to bring down Altin Cana, boss of the Albanian mob in New York. His crime family might no longer exist, but that didn't mean those in Rose's professional circles would take kindly to hearing that their fence had played such a direct role in putting the Cana mob boss in jail.

"All I need is to get Olivier's attention," Harry said. "Nothing else. Your name will never come up again unless it's to move the artifacts I have for him."

Rose took another puff on her cigarette. "It sounds as though you are determined to do this. In that case, you should be fully aware of who you are facing."

"You know more about this guy than just his name."

"Olivier Lloris is a successful French industrialist. No doubt you've heard the rumors about how he arrived at his place in life. The untimely death of his former partner. The alleged painting forgeries. He is not a man to trifle with."

"You act like I haven't dealt with his kind before. He's a good painter who faked a couple of canvasses, and he pushed a guy out of a boat."

"That is exactly why I am warning you, Harry. Unsavory characters abound in your world; some foolish, others deadly." Her voice roughened. "I have dealt in the world of fraudulent paintings for years. The people who deal in such goods are more deadly than you realize. The potential for vast profits is more than incentive enough for people to kill."

"Did Olivier kill someone over a painting?"

"Perhaps. Perhaps not. I have heard stories. Nothing proven, of course."

Harry scratched his chin now. "I appreciate the warning. I'll be careful."

"Thank you." Another pause. "Olivier was born into poverty in one of Paris's least desirable banlieues. The local elementary school now bears his name, as does the library and at least one health clinic."

"That's what rich people do to make themselves look better."

"Yes. I tell you this so you understand there are many people who view Olivier as a force for good."

"I'll keep it in mind."

Rose seemed to have made her point. "I will be in touch. Until then, I suggest you consider obtaining more unique artifacts of interest."

"Why?"

"Olivier Lloris is never satisfied. He always wants more."

Chapter 3

Paris

Moonlight glinted off a bronze Roman gladiator's helmet. A jagged scar cut through the intricate carvings on the headpiece, testament to an opponent's power. The strength needed to slice through a quarter-inch of solid bronze would have been tremendous. Unfortunately for the gladiator who wore this piece two thousand years ago, his adversary had possessed it.

Olivier Lloris ran a finger over the gash in the helmet. *I wish I could have been there.* The roaring crowd, the thunderous applause. The finality of the battle. All of it captured in this weathered, beautiful piece, proof that while time moved on, men's true nature never wavered.

Cars moved slowly along Avenue Montaigne outside his window. Olivier's private residence in the Eighth Arrondissement put him close to Paris's main business district, while keeping the city far enough away to afford privacy. The sort of privacy that came with a wine cellar, an expansive balcony and a sprawling yard protected by tall privacy fencing. The sort of home a leading industrialist maintained in the city. A stately, spacious dwelling with sufficient room to display his extensive private collection of rare antiquities from across the globe.

One by one he took in the artifacts from various cultures and time periods, a museum-worthy collection. Roman artifacts like the gladiatorial helmet in front of one window and the ceremonial wine goblet covered with intricate carvings beside it. A goblet crafted for the Roman emperor Valerian, which Olivier felt complemented the Etruscan fresco displayed on a pedestal nearby. The objects on display never failed to impress his guests, though their enjoyment was not why he collected. Olivier sought relics because of how they made him feel. A poor boy from government housing now able to connect with cultures across time and distance, able to physically touch the past in ways others never would. He'd come a long way.

The phone on his desk rang. Olivier crossed the room with quick, purposeful steps. Only a few people had that number. He pressed a button to connect the call. "Yes?"

"Good evening." It was Lucas Mendy, his attorney. "I read the profile yesterday. Impressive."

A Parisian magazine had run an article on Olivier and his private collection, complete with photographs of several pieces and an interview with the industrialist. Olivier had ensured that his charitable efforts featured prominently. "What did you think?"

"That you are a buffoon. I told you not to do it."

Olivier bit back a caustic remark. "I'll thank you not to speak to me that way."

"Why? Because no one else will? Check social media. A few commenters are already asking about the provenance of certain artifacts."

"Internet comment sections are where the dregs of humanity dwell."

"And if they're correct? Your collection is incredible. It's also private for a reason: so that these people do not have access."

"They still don't. I only shared a few photographs of what I own." Olivier looked to one side of the room. "I didn't let them see *everything*. Despite your suggestion, I am not a buffoon."

Lucas grumbled. "It still invites questions."

"From whom? Understaffed law enforcement agencies with investigators who are both ill-equipped and uneducated?" He waved a hand as though Lucas could see him. "Stop wasting my time."

"You won't be so dismissive if the authorities knock on your door."

"I have provenance for all of my pieces." A lie, and Lucas knew it. "Regardless, the authorities have more pressing concerns."

"Let's hope they do." Lucas let out a long breath. "You pay me for legal advice, Olivier. At least consider pausing on your acquisitions. Let some time pass. The press will move on. Anyone interested in questioning your private collection will eventually find other topics to worry about."

"Perhaps."

"Excellent. I will be in touch if I hear anything relevant."

Olivier waited for Lucas to hang up, then gently pressed the button on his desktop phone to confirm the call had ended. Then he waited. For his muscles to untense. For his jaw to unclench. For the visceral reaction that came from an *employee* challenging him to stay out of the public eye. Lucas Mendy knew his way around a courtroom. He should stay there, where he belonged.

Mahogany shelves lined one wall of the expansive room. Marble pillars stood at either end of it, while spotlights illuminated pieces on display. Olivier went to the far pillar, to a Greek terra-cotta bowl decorated with an image of Achilles in full battle gear. Olivier touched the marble pillar, pressing a nearly invisible button so that, with a soft *snick*, a section of the wall came out. A concealed door swung open when he pulled it. Floor lighting activated as the door opened and Olivier slipped through, closing the door behind him. Only when the door fully closed did the overhead lights come on.

A world of his treasures appeared. Each object in its own display case, complete with lighting to accentuate the unique characteristics. An Egyptian sarcophagus crafted three thousand years before stood to one side, near a statue of Zeus that had existed when Plato walked the streets of Athens. A sculpture of the Virgin Mary with an infant Jesus carved by Donato di Niccolò di Betto Bardi, better known as Donatello. Other relics in the room included a Greek sculpture of Medusa, fossils of the jaw and skull of a Tyrannosaurus Rex, a second-century bronze statue of Alexander the Great and a marble sphinx from Cleopatra's time.

Paintings adorned the walls, including original works by Picasso, Cézanne and Vermeer. All obtained in various ways through Olivier's unique skill—an almost otherworldly ability to mimic the style of other artists. The skill that had propelled him to his place in life today. That, and a willingness to do whatever was required to succeed. He hadn't always been the most successful tire producer in the nation. At one time Olivier's enterprise was small, supplying local shops and stores. The competition nearly drove him out of business. Until his competitor's facility burned to the ground in a terrible, timely fire. But that was in the past.

This was his. His private oasis, shown only to a select few he invited into his world, a world where Olivier ruled supreme. It was hard to imagine the little boy with nothing could have ended up here. Yet he had.

He nearly jumped when the cell phone in his pocket vibrated. A familiar number on the screen. "What is it?" Olivier said.

"An opportunity."

Olivier's stomach fluttered. It always did when he received these calls. His personal antiquities dealer, a man who catered to an ultra-exclusive clientele. Who never asked if the paperwork was in order. "I'm listening." *Lucas Mendy could go to hell.*

"An associate of mine would like to speak with you."

Olivier frowned. "I don't deal with strangers."

"Her credibility is impeccable." Benoit Lafont had connections to all aspects of the international antiquities trade, from museum directors and renowned scholars to criminal enterprises. In short, he knew everyone. "I have worked with Rose Leroux many times. You may trust her."

Olivier sensed an odd wind in the air. "It's unlike you to give another dealer access to a client. Aren't you worried about her cutting you out?"

"She would never do such a thing."

Benoit lived his life in the shadows. If he trusted this woman, Olivier would as well. "What does she have?"

"Keep your phone nearby," Benoit said before clicking off.

Olivier had one foot outside his hidden display room when his phone buzzed. A blocked number. "Who is this?" he demanded.

"Good evening, Mr. Lloris." A cultured voice, female. Possibly

French at one time, but years and the world had turned it into a mixture of accents he couldn't identify. "Mr. Lafont told you to expect my call."

"Ms. Leroux." Olivier closed the secret door behind him.

"I understand you are a discerning collector," Rose said.

"I am."

"Then you will be interested in what I have to say." She paused, and what sounded like a cigarette lighter flaring came through the phone. "I have been retained to find a new home for a unique piece. One with ties to a Frankish king."

"There were many Frankish kings."

"*The* Frankish king."

Olivier's hand tightened on the phone. "Charlemagne?"

"A book written by his personal spiritual guide, a man named Agilulph. It is a bible, and it contains firsthand accounts of Charlemagne's conquests from a man who witnessed them."

"Where did you get it?"

"Are you concerned about the authenticity?"

Benoit's assurance came to mind. "No, Ms. Leroux. Merely interested in the story behind the piece."

"It came from Agilulph's tomb, recently discovered."

"I haven't heard of such a discovery."

"The expedition was a private undertaking."

A looting, in other words. "I see." Olivier turned to look out over the city lights. "Do you have images of the artifact?"

"Check your phone."

The device dinged as she spoke. A series of pictures had arrived via text. Olivier scrolled through multiple shots of an ancient bible written in Latin. The final image was of the inside rear cover. "The last picture is blurry," he said.

"Intentionally. That handwritten message from Agilulph contains information my client does not yet wish to share."

Olivier's back stiffened. "Why not?"

"The writing contains information of great value. I am not at liberty to say more."

"I do not purchase items I cannot view in their entirety." A lie.

"As you wish. Good day, Mr. Lloris."

"Wait." He took a breath. "Perhaps I have been hasty. I understand you deal in only the highest-quality relics. How much is your client asking?" She named a price just short of outrageous. "I am willing to offer half that amount."

"Others will pay that and more. Last chance, Mr. Lloris."

Olivier Lloris spent his days with some of France's savviest businesspeople. Years of experience told him this woman wasn't bluffing. "The price is outrageous." He didn't hesitate. "I'll pay it."

"You will have your item within a week. Check your phone for payment details."

The line went dead. Olivier barely had time to sit before payment instructions arrived on his phone, which he sent to Lucas Mendy for handling. The man immediately responded with his thoughts on Olivier acquiring another artifact. Olivier reminded him who worked for whom. That handled, he dialed Benoit Lafont's number. "Tell me about Rose Leroux," Olivier said when his antiquities dealer picked up. "I just purchased a piece from her."

"She is trustworthy. Experienced. Discerning. I have never heard a collector speak poorly of her."

"I know all of that," Olivier said. "Or else you would not have put her in touch with me. What else do you know?"

"Nothing concrete." Benoit hesitated. "Rumors, mostly."

Olivier waited, tapping a finger on his desk. "What sort of rumors?" Benoit fumbled for words. "What aren't you telling me?"

"Rose Leroux is associated with the New York mob."

Olivier's finger stopped mid-tap. "How closely?"

"Closely enough that you should be aware of it."

Benoit was one of the few people who knew the extent of Olivier's connections to certain Sicilian entrepreneurs. When Olivier first did business with them years ago, he hadn't realized how their interests could impact his own. They didn't like it when Olivier did business with other mobsters. In the view of his Sicilian friends, that was profit they had lost. And they weren't the sort of people content with sending sternly worded emails.

"Why didn't you make that clear before I agreed to buy from her?"

"Would it have stopped you?" No, and Benoit knew it. "I will call her to make certain everything went well," Benoit said. "And to remind her that certain parties may not take kindly to learning of your acquisition. Rose will understand."

"She'd better."

"Olivier, I am saying this as a friend. I know you would never threaten Rose Leroux. You are not that sort of person." Another lie, and they both knew it. "However, she does not know you as I do. It would be wise to remember this."

Again he bit off a caustic remark. "Call her. Make certain she keeps this quiet." Olivier's finger resumed tapping. Benoit was right. Offending his Sicilian contacts could make life difficult in unexpected ways. "Have her call me. Right now."

Olivier hung up, and his phone buzzed less than a minute later. "Ms. Leroux."

"You wished to speak with me?"

"Yes. You will appreciate that a man in my position must be careful. I have friends who may not look kindly upon my dealing with you."

"That is not my concern."

"No, but it *is* your concern to maintain relationships with clients of means. Such as myself. I expect this transaction will remain private?"

"I treat all my clients with the same respect, Mr. Lloris. Our business will remain between us. You have my word."

As good as he could hope to get. "Thank you." A question sprang from his lips before he could stop it. "Ms. Leroux, without compromising your client's interests, what else can you tell me about the message inside my new bible?"

"Nothing."

Olivier sensed a message behind that single word. "Nothing?"

The flare of a lighter sparking sounded in his ear. "In the spirit of our new relationship, I can share one detail. Given it may prove useful to your interests in the future."

"How so?" he asked sharply.

"The message suggests this may not be the final artifact tied to Agilulph and Charlemagne." Rose's next words sent a charge through Olivier's body. "There may be additional items in play. Items my client intends to recover. Items on which the tides of history changed."

"Such as?"

"Wait and see, Mr. Lloris. Wait and see."

Chapter 4

Brooklyn

Frigid wind slipped down Harry's neck as he walked, hunched over, hands in his pockets. His upturned coat collar was little defense against the Brooklyn winter. *I should have worn a scarf.*

His pace quickened as he walked under a streetlight, the lamp overhead flashing to life as he passed. Steam wafting from the tailpipes of stopped cars twisted between his legs as he cut across the street toward a bar not far from his house. A couple walked out as he approached; Harry grabbed the door and slipped into the establishment's warm embrace. A song explaining why they called it the blues played as he unzipped his coat, scanning the crowd until he spotted an upraised hand in the back. Harry grinned. *She's catching on.*

Two women watched from their seats around a table as he approached. One bore a passing resemblance to him. The other, an uncanny one. "Hi, Mom."

"Hello, dear." Dani Doyle hugged her son. "Great to see you."

"Evening." Nora Doyle nodded at her half-brother. "You're late."

"We can't all have government jobs," he fired back. "I had a client stay late."

Nora grumbled. "I hope you made some money at least."

"I did." He checked his watch. "And I'm five minutes late. Take it easy."

"She's kidding," Dani said. "We only ordered a moment ago."

"I got you a beer," Nora said. "You're welcome."

"Despite outward appearances, you're a peach. Don't let anyone tell you different." He turned to his mom before she could offer a riposte. "Thanks for making the trip into the city."

"Of course," Dani said. "Gary is working late again. The Cana prosecutions are filling his hours lately." She winked. "I suppose he has you to thank for that."

"What am I, chopped liver?" Nora said. "My team brought him down."

"I know," Dani said. "Though I imagine your father has not let you forget your hard work."

Gary Doyle was the assistant district attorney in charge of prosecuting the Cana crime family. Nora Doyle was not only his daughter, but the head of the New York district attorney's Anti-Trafficking Unit, a team of law enforcement officers working to stop the flow of illegal artifacts and antiquities through the city. An impossible task that kept her almost constantly busy. More so than ever before, thanks to the informant she'd cultivated inside the criminal underworld. A man with close ties to the Morello crime family. Her half-brother, Harry Fox.

Nora fell silent as their drinks arrived. "Dad has enough trouble without crossing me."

"Has she always been this much fun?" Harry asked.

Dani failed to hide her grin. "You have no idea." She continued before Nora could get a word in. "How is Sara? I'm looking forward to seeing her new exhibit on the Library of Alexandria."

"Busy," Harry said. "Creating a destination international exhibit makes for some late nights."

"I hope she's getting enough sleep." Dani paused. "Is she?"

"Probably," Harry said. "I don't call to check." He sipped his beer as Dani glanced at Nora. "You could just ask me, you know."

Dani put on a *Who, me?* look. "Ask you what, dear?"

Harry rolled his eyes. "If she's moved in yet. I'm not dense." He glared at Nora. "Don't."

"Make a joke at your expense?" Nora asked. "Never crossed my mind."

"I'm certainly not prying," Dani said. Then she lifted an eyebrow. "Much."

"Sara still lives in her apartment by the museum. I have my place. I'll tell you if anything changes." He inclined his glass toward Dani. "Did you find a home for the new horse?"

Dani Doyle volunteered at an animal rescue organization in the suburbs, and her current project was to find a new home for an abandoned farm horse.

"I did," Dani said. "A farm across the state line in Connecticut took him. Now he has a stable full of horses to be with and plenty of room to run."

"His name was Oscar, right?"

"Good memory," Dani said. "You know, a cat would be excellent company in your house."

Harry shook his head. "No chance. I'm not exactly what you'd call a pet person."

Dani sighed. "Neither was Fred. I never convinced him. Perhaps I'll have better luck with you."

Harry winked. "About the same luck as you had in our Scrabble game last week."

Dani did not laugh. "A misstep, that's all. Next time you won't be so fortunate."

Nora Doyle cleared her throat. "Is there anything else you two have been doing that I should be aware of?"

"Nothing urgent," Dani said. "Harry and I engaged in several heated games of Scrabble last week at his house. It did not end well for me."

"I haven't played Scrabble in months," Nora said. "Since we got together for a holiday in the summer."

"You're welcome to join next time," Harry said. "A family tournament."

Nora went still at the mention of *family*. She still wasn't fully on board with the new concept, no matter how hard Harry tried. "How kind of you," Nora said. She turned to Dani. "Dad and I had a good time at dinner earlier this week. We missed you."

"Harry and I had a spontaneous trip to the art museum. It was such fun. I'm glad you and your father were still able to connect."

Dani either wasn't picking up on Nora's tone, or she simply didn't care. Harry had been in enough arguments with Nora Doyle before he knew they were related. They never ended well. "Would you like to come over to my place for dinner next week?" Harry asked. "Mom and I had plans. It would be nice if you could come too."

Nora visibly started. "Dinner? At your place?"

"Yeah, dinner. In between bringing down mob families and recovering relics, I still need to eat."

"Is that so?" Her words came to him on an icy wind. "I never guessed."

Harry brushed the cold aside. "Is that a yes?"

"Please, Nora." Dani spoke softly. "I would like you to join us."

Nora gave her version of a *harrumph*. "I suppose. What about Dad?"

"You two have ensured his calendar is full for some time," Dani said. "I'm sure he'd come if he was able. Even so, it will be nice to do this again, just the three of us." She put one hand on Nora's, the other on Harry's. "I love catching up with both of you."

"His charm can wear thin," Nora said.

"As can yours, dear." Dani frowned at her daughter. "Mine as well."

Nora didn't laugh, but her frown vanished. "That's the truth. Yes, I'd like to come over. At least there are decent delivery restaurants in his neighborhood."

"Delivery?" Harry touched his chest. "Not a chance. You're in for a culinary experience." Nora rolled her eyes and didn't respond.

"How's the shop doing?" Nora asked. "Busy?"

"Very." He peered at her over the rim of his glass. "Thanks for asking."

"The demand for antiquities didn't go anywhere, even if one of the suppliers did. I'm wondering where all the people who relied on Altin Cana for their artifacts will turn now."

"If you're asking did they come to me, the answer is no." He sipped his beer. "My clients are the kind who pay taxes."

Nora opened her mouth to say something, but Dani held up a hand. "Nora, that's quite enough." Dani gazed at Nora for a long moment before turning to Harry. "That's wonderful," she said. "Though she's correct. Collectors without concern for where their artifacts came from won't disappear. What if they come to you?"

"He'll tell them he no longer provides that service." Nora looked at Harry when she spoke. "He's legitimate now."

Nora knew that was partially true. She said it to drag Harry across hot coals their mother couldn't see.

"I am," Harry said. He kept his voice even. "Everything is legitimate. Including my tax bill." He turned to Dani. "An interesting artifact came into my shop earlier this week. A bible tied to Charlemagne."

"Amazing," Dani said.

"How did you find it?" Nora asked quickly.

"Through hard work," Harry said. "It's an important piece."

"Oh, no." Dani's shoulders dropped. "Is this tied to Olivier Lloris?" Her words barely made it across the table. "I want you to let it go, Harry. He's caused us enough trouble already."

"It is," Harry said. "And you know I can't do that. We've talked about this." Mainly Harry had talked and his mother had argued, but he was resolute. Olivier Lloris had to be dealt with. "The bible came from Italy."

Dani interlaced her fingers on the table. "I hope it was an uneventful trip."

Harry shrugged. "Nothing I haven't dealt with before."

If she believed him, he sure didn't see it on her face. "I won't try to talk you out of abandoning this effort."

"Good." He turned and spoke to Nora before their mother could change her mind. "How's the expanded team coming along?"

"Taking down Altin Cana brought us more funding than I expected,"

Nora said. "We're hiring several new agents. The reinforcements are welcome, but now it seems as though all I do is push paper. Managing more people keeps me at my desk too much."

"You haven't called me for assistance lately."

"Amazing we can function without you, isn't it?" Nora almost grinned at her own joke. Almost. "It's actually been quiet. I think after what happened to Altin Cana most of the black-market buyers are lying low. They're still out there, though. That's why I asked about your business," she said to Harry. "Not because I think you're doing anything illegal." A pause. "Because I know they will try to find other places to acquire relics."

"If they do, it won't be from me." He glanced around the bar. Nobody was paying them any attention. "I get an occasional call from people asking if I do custom requests. Which I do not."

Nora ran a hand through her hair. "Let me know if you hear anything. At least I can keep an eye out for any names you give me, see if they pop up on my radar somewhere else."

"Why don't you make Gary do all the extra paperwork?" Harry said.

"I'd love nothing more," Nora said. "He's too busy right now. Maybe once all the Cana family criminals are sentenced." Harry glanced over to find Dani looking at Nora as she continued. "I don't see much of Dad at work," Nora said. The glass twirled. "I did get a minute with him yesterday." She looked at her mother. "Is anything going on with him?"

"What do you mean?" Dani asked.

"He seemed off. No, not off. More like distracted. He barely had time to talk when I stopped by, and I could tell his mind was elsewhere. He wouldn't admit anything was bothering him when I asked."

"Your father rarely talks about his work," Dani said. "Likely because I've never invited the conversation."

"I didn't think he'd have told you anything," Nora said. Then she turned to Harry. "But maybe he told you?"

"Me?" Harry tapped his chest. "No idea. I doubt he'd come to me with anything. That's what you're for."

"That's what I thought too." The glass rotated once more. "Thought I'd ask."

"Do not let your father off so easily," Dani said. "If you have a question, march into his office and demand answers."

Nora shook her head. "There's something else on his mind. He'll tell me about it eventually."

"Perhaps not," Dani said. "We are both adept at keeping secrets, for better or worse. Just ask him."

"I will. I've seen him act like this when he has a new case that may need my team's involvement. Dad likes to be in control. Antiquities aren't exactly in his wheelhouse."

"I'm certain you will be among the first to know if your father has a new case," Dani said. "You're the expert."

A phone on the tabletop vibrated. Nora's. "Speaking of Dad," she said as she picked it up and looked at the text. "He wants to see me tonight. In the office." Nora downed her drink. "Looks like I may not have to ask him after all."

Harry finished his drink. "I should be getting home. Need to practice the incredible meal I'll make for you two."

Both women stared at him. "Really?" they asked together.

"No," he said. "Sara's coming over. I want to hear about the new exhibit she's putting together." He laid some bills on the table. "That, and I want her take on the bible I found. She sent me a message earlier. Apparently, there's something on her mind." He stood. "Something that may help me understand what the bible truly says."

Chapter 5

Brooklyn

Harry's head snapped up as the first deadbolt turned. A second deadbolt shot open, then someone leaned on the doorbell and thumped the front door.

"It's me," Sara shouted through the closed door. "A little help would be nice."

"Hang on." Harry leapt up but failed to make it to the door before Sara threw it open. "I was coming," he said.

"Not fast enough." She pushed past him, the bag on her shoulder filled to overflowing with papers and a laptop. "Please tell me you have dinner ready. I'm starving."

"It's on the table," Harry said.

Sara dumped her bag beside the table, washed her hands quickly at the sink, and dove straight into her meal. Harry sat down across from her and ate with her in silence, waiting until she had nearly finished eating before he said a word. "Rough day?" he asked.

"The new exhibit materials will arrive any day now," she said. "It was easier to find them in Egypt than it has been to get them over here. The governmental forms never end."

A small portion of the Library of Alexandria treasure Harry and Sara had unearthed several months ago was now coming to the American Museum of Natural History, the first stop on an international tour.

"It'll be worth it in the end," Harry said. "Though I expect you've had enough for today."

"You would be correct." Sara finished the last of her food, then sat back in her chair and pulled her auburn hair back with a sigh. "How was your day?"

"Fine," he said. "I appreciate you coming over tonight. I know it's easier to just stay at your place."

"It is," she said. "It is."

"Lots of work to finish tonight?"

"Too much." Lines creased her forehead. "None of which I intend to do. I'm exhausted."

"You've been working too much. You deserve a night off."

"It's not only the Alexandria exhibit. I still need to plan for what comes *after* this exhibit. Securing another display is also time-consuming."

"Even for a celebrity like you?"

"Very funny. You would be amazed how quickly the world moves on." Sara looked toward Harry's bar, studying the wine selection.

"Want me to open a bottle?" Harry asked.

"I would love for you to do that," she said. "Except I have too much work tomorrow."

"Anything I can do to help?"

"Put more black-market antiquities dealers and hunters and all the associated crooks in jail for me."

"How would that help?"

She rubbed one eye. "That's what takes up so much of my time beyond the exhibits. I am the point of contact for new exhibits brought in… Part of what I aim to do with each exhibit is demonstrate to guests the proper way of collecting artifacts. How to do it respectfully, in a way that celebrates and honors the past, without corrupting it for our personal benefit."

"You mean without becoming the British Museum."

An old joke sprang from Sara's lips. "Why are the pyramids in Egypt?"

"Because they're too heavy to carry to the British Museum," Harry answered.

"It's not only the potential exhibits I must sift through. Several of our major donors are part of the problem as well. Luminaries of New York society whose personal collections are incredible. They don't collect for their own enjoyment. They collect to show off, and what better way to do that than to have pieces on display in our museum?" She leaned across the table, her words gaining steam. "Do you have any idea how questionable their artifacts can be? The provenance is nonexistent, and they don't even have the decency to be ashamed when I mention it."

"They didn't get rich by being nice."

She sighed. "Here's one example. A collector's personal secretary offered to loan us a collection of Greek influenced artifacts, many from Pompeii. I reviewed their inventory, then called the auction houses where most of the pieces were purchased. Do you know how many had provenance to prove ownership?" She held a closed fist in the air. "None. Not a single one. For all I know, this collector stole every artifact."

Harry didn't blink. "The only part that surprises me is you're surprised. Don't let it get you down." He reached out and put his hand over hers. "You're doing the right thing. Making the city a better, more enlightened place. Focus on that and forget about the rest. Leave the shady characters alone for now." She didn't say anything, so he plunged on. "You mentioned something about the message inside Agilulph's bible?"

"Yes." She perked up. "Except I can't talk about it, not yet. I'm not certain and I don't want to influence your research."

He swallowed. "Right. Thanks. I appreciate it." So much for that. "You know, if you really need a new artifact for your museum, I know a moderately successful relic hunter who could help."

"No." She looked down at the table. "I forbid it."

"I'm joking." He put his hands out, palms toward her. "Mainly." Now he crossed his arms on his chest. "But why not? You have a recovery specialist on staff or something?"

"A what?" She looked up. "No, I don't have a recovery specialist on staff." Sara aimed a finger at him. "You are a dolt. A wonderful, exasperating dolt." Harry shrugged as she continued. "I am surrounded by artifacts of questionable provenance and collectors of ill repute. The very last thing I need is another person circling my exhibit who could in any way cast doubt on the process."

"That's not nice."

"You work with the authorities in an undercover role. You are courageous, intelligent, daring and reckless." She jabbed her finger at each trait for emphasis. "Which is why I cannot have your assistance. Not now. I need this to be entirely above board."

"I am above board."

"*Mostly* above board," Sara said. "I know it wasn't always the case." Now she put her hands up to ward off any protest. "How we arrived at where we are today is in the past. What matters is where we go next. There will be a day in the future when I will need a man with your skills. A *moderately successful relic hunter* will prove vital to my goal. Which is providing a world-class museum experience. However, that day is not now."

He grumbled for a beat. "You could have just said no."

"I'm not finished." Sara met his frown with one of her own. "Harry, it's not just about the exhibit and provenance and suspicious characters. Of which you are not one," she said quickly. "It's about safety. Your work is dangerous. Even so, I still come with you on the occasional excursion because I love our adventures, and I love being with you."

He did his very best not to react. "You do?"

"I take it back. You are a complete dolt, full stop." She leaned back in her chair, running both hands over her head. "You get results no one else can in a dangerous business. That's the other part of why I'm saying no. You've already risked enough for me."

"I'd do it again."

"You may now add *sweet* to your list of traits." She winked. "But don't tempt fate. The number of unsavory characters I come across in my new job makes me think twice about you being out in the field again. These people are well-spoken, rich criminals with no qualms about hurting others. Including people like you."

"I can take care of myself."

"I know you can. But I don't want you to get hurt, and I need you to stay out of this for me."

Harry lifted an eyebrow. "I'm trying to help."

"I need to stand on my own two feet." Wind rattled a nearby window. "That's the main reason. That, and every time you go out there's a risk. There's no guarantee you'll return. I can't do that. It's not fair to you."

"I like my job."

"It's not fair to *me*, either. Your past cannot be changed. That doesn't mean you need to continue making those decisions." A moment passed. "There are more people counting on you now. Your family." Another long moment. "And others."

It took him longer than usual to find his voice. "Change is hard. I can't stop being me."

"Don't stop being you. Keep growing."

Harry almost laughed. *That's what you get for getting mixed up with a smart lady like her.* "I'll try," he said. "And to be clear, you are doing a fine job standing on your own. There's only one internationally recognized scholar at this table."

"Who became that way through teamwork. I wouldn't have the acclaim without you."

"I barely did a thing," Harry said. "And does that mean we are going back into the field together? I wouldn't want our team to break up."

"Let me finish with this exhibition and we'll talk," Sara said. "I trust you to do the right thing when we search for artifacts. Trust me to do the right thing when it comes to the museum."

"Deal."

They fell into a companionable silence, Sara kneading a knot in her neck, Harry leaning back and closing his eyes. Amazing how a full day of doing nothing but office work and dealing with clients took it out of him. Or maybe this sort of day never really got him going in the first place. He liked making money, sure, but was he cut out for decades of deskwork? Hard to say.

Sara put her hands on the table. "Thank you for dinner," she said, casting one eye across the room at her bulging shoulder bag. "I'm beat. This work will have to wait until morning."

Harry didn't have a chance to respond before his cell phone buzzed. "It's Gary Doyle," he said. "Wonder what he wants."

"The Canas are his problem now. You have a business to run." She stood and looked down at him from beneath drooping eyelids. "Don't stay up too late." With that, she headed up the stairs and out of sight.

Harry connected the call. "Evening, Gary."

"Good evening, Harry. My apologies for calling at this hour."

"No worries. Trouble with the Cana prosecution?"

A dry laugh. "None to be concerned about. Every prosecution brings a new set of challenges. This one is no exception. I'm calling about a different matter. Have you seen the news reports about the earthquakes in southern Bulgaria?" Harry had not. "They happened near the base of the Balkan Mountain range."

Harry's ears perked up. "Balkans? This doesn't have anything to do with Stefan Rudovic, does it? He's dead."

Stefan Rudovic had been Altin Cana's relic hunter. Someone had once described him as a poor man's version of Harry Fox, but Stefan had been nothing of the sort. He had nearly killed Harry and Sara more than once, though eventually his scheming had backfired in a hidden temple outside of Luxor, Egypt.

"No," Gary said. "This involves questions I cannot answer."

"And you want my input?"

"Are you alone?"

"Yes. Sara's upstairs getting ready for bed. I'm the only one down here."

"The earthquakes occurred near an ongoing archaeological dig site."

Harry stood up. "Where?"

"Near what used to be the capital city of ancient Thrace."

"A region variously ruled by the Persians, Greeks, Macedonians and

Romans. Thrace had a rough go of it throughout history."

"I'll take your word on that," Gary said. "A region filled with history is how my contact phrased it."

Harry couldn't help himself. "Why do you have a contact on an archaeological dig?"

"One step at a time, Harry. The main dig focused on an ancient village and was organized by a Bulgarian university in coordination with representatives from various European institutions. Including representatives from international law enforcement."

The dots started to connect in Harry's mind. "Something happened at the dig site. Something that made one of those people call you."

"Not bad, Harry. The earthquake dislodged part of the mountainside near the dig site. There was a small landslide."

"I didn't know landslides came in size small."

"Nobody was hurt, thank goodness, but the displaced rock revealed a new area of interest."

"Does Nora know about it?"

"Not yet. I only learned about it this afternoon while I was dealing with Cana prosecution issues. You're the first person I've told."

"Why not tell her? The only reason they'd call you is if this has something to do with artifacts trafficking." His breath quickened. "What did they find?"

"I'm discussing it with her later," Gary said. "But I felt you should hear this from me first."

"Hear what?"

"That I need your help."

"*My* help?" Harry's chair rattled on the floor as he sat back down. "What kind of site is this?"

"A king's tomb." Papers rustled. "King Cotys the Fourth."

"Who?" Gary repeated the name. "I've heard of him," Harry said. "But barely."

"I never heard the name until today. Thrace had many kings."

"At least four named Cotys," Harry said. "But then again, nobody cared about a boy pharaoh named Tutankhamun until they found his tomb. What's inside?" An alarm bell that had been ringing in the back of his mind grew louder. "Hold on. Why are you telling me all this before you tell Nora? She's technically my boss when it comes to this sort of thing."

"She is also overseeing an expanding team. If she is to succeed, she must focus."

The hairs on his neck rose slightly. "You're protecting her."

"If I ever said you were not perceptive, I take it back. Yes, I'm protecting her."

One of Harry's hands clenched. "Gary, what's going on?"

"A royal Thracian tomb was uncovered," Gary said. "An undisturbed tomb containing burial goods and treasures of a king." Now Gary sighed, and for an instant he no longer sounded like a New York prosecutor. He sounded like a father worrying about his daughter. "Two bodies were found at the tomb today."

"It's a tomb. I hope you found dead people inside."

"Fresh bodies," Gary said. "And one of them may have been murdered."

Chapter 6

Brooklyn

Harry got up again and began pacing the room. "How?"

"How what?" Gary Doyle asked.

"How did they die?"

"It appears to be an accident of some sort. Or not."

"Which is why you don't want Nora involved. It's dangerous." Harry stopped pacing. "What does a Thracian king have to do with antiquities trafficking in New York?"

"Nothing."

"What aren't you telling me?"

"One of the deceased was a roommate of the New York governor's daughter."

Harry swore to himself. "How in the world did you get involved with this? You don't work for the governor."

"It wouldn't be unusual for a city mayor to aspire to become governor."

Harry chided himself for not making the connection. Gary Doyle worked for the mayor of New York City. That the mayor had designs on the governor's mansion shouldn't surprise him.

Gary continued. "The governor's daughter attends college in London. The deceased man was a roommate of hers."

Harry shook his head. "Forget it. I'm not interested in helping."

"I thought you might say that. I understand. I'll let you get back to your evening."

"Hang on," Harry said quickly, then kicked himself. He knew better, yet he took the bait. "Tell me the rest of the story."

"Everything I know is preliminary. The bodies were found yesterday."

"Who's the other dead guy?"

"I'm not certain," Gary said. "Information is a bit chaotic, as was the dig site. Right now, my contact in Bulgaria is trying to confirm his identity."

"Maybe one of them was killed, maybe both. Maybe neither." Conflicting or nonexistent information wasn't unusual in the field. "Tell me what the earthquake uncovered."

Gary coughed. "Harry, before we go on, I need to make something clear. I'm sharing this information with you for a reason."

"Nora's busy, and it's dangerous." He didn't add *not necessarily in that order*.

"Both true. As is the primary reason I'm telling you this. It's because you are very good at what you do. The best I've ever known."

A new voice sounded from Gary's end of the phone. "Hi, Dad."

"Is Nora with you?" Harry asked.

"She is," Gary said. "One moment. We may as well do this now." There was a crackling sound. "Harry, you're on speaker."

Nora barked at her father in her normal tone. "Why are you talking to Harry?"

"Your dad and I were just talking about Bulgaria," Harry said.

"What's in Bulgaria?" Nora asked.

Gary Doyle spoke up. "A matter I intended to discuss with you shortly."

"Why did you need to tell Harry first?" Nora asked. "He works for me. Off the books."

"I felt it was the best course," Gary said. "You're here now, so listen."

Harry sat back as Gary recapped the discussion so far. Nora kept quiet until the end. "I don't like you keeping me out of the loop," she said once Gary finished. "Don't you trust me?"

"You already have enough on your plate," Gary said. "And I trust you.

This is tailor-made for Harry's skill set. My duty as your superior is to position you for success. I'm doing that now."

"I can handle it, Dad."

"You are feisty, focused, and organized. You have a need to control situations to the point that you can overextend yourself. Harry has experience in this sort of assignment. I'm giving you a direct order to let him handle it. And as for you, Harry, demonstrating your ability to succeed without the need for close oversight is critical."

"I'm not controlling," Nora said. "I'm thorough."

Harry laughed. "You can be a royal pain in the rear."

"Stop agreeing with each other," Gary said. "That's an order."

Nora grumbled something Harry couldn't hear, but she didn't argue. "Fine," she eventually said. "I'll do what you say. Now tell us about Cotys the Fourth."

Harry interrupted. "I want to hear about the area first. You said two people may have been murdered. Are they digging in a war zone?"

"No," Gary said. "The dig site is between towns. There are roads in the area, though the site itself is in the countryside."

"Do you have any law enforcement contacts in the area?" Harry asked.

"International agencies," Gary said. "Not local. I'll connect you before you leave."

"*If* I leave." Gary didn't respond. "What did they find inside the cave?"

"An elaborate tomb," Gary said.

"Any safeguards or defense mechanisms inside?"

"None so far, though further inspection of the tomb is on hold due to the deaths. I did learn of a message inscribed on a wall in plain view."

Harry and Nora responded as one. "What message?"

"A message above the coffin. The tomb has statues of Cotys the Fourth around the interior, though it's more spartan than I would have imagined. There are some tributes to the king, summaries of his victories and passages extolling his virtues. But of all the imagery and writing inside, only one appears to have been composed by the king himself. It focuses on his son."

"I don't know anything about Cotys the Fourth," Harry said. "Or any other Cotys for that matter. Is his son important?"

Gary cleared his throat. "Thrace was subjugated by Rome during Cotys's reign. Many Thracians were mercenaries who either sold their sword to the highest bidder or outright enlisted in the Roman armies. A military life was often the only choice for any son after the first in a wealthy or well-connected family."

"Because only the first son inherited his father's estate," Harry said. "The army offered other sons a chance at fortune and glory."

"Correct," Gary said. "Cotys the Fourth had several sons. The one mentioned in his tomb is not the oldest. This son took the military route, though at some point it went horribly wrong and he went from soldier to gladiator."

A connection sparked in Harry's mind. "Hold on. A Thracian gladiator?"

"Seeking fortune and glory," Nora said.

"I know a story," Harry said, "about a Thracian who became a Roman soldier, then eventually a gladiator. But he wasn't a prince. At least not that anyone was aware of." Harry's knuckles whitened on the phone. "Is it him, Gary? Is that who you're talking about?"

"I was only given a name," Gary said.

Harry swallowed on a dry throat. "Spartacus."

"Yes," Gary said. "The king's son mentioned on his tomb wall is named Spartacus. According to the message, Spartacus fought the Romans in an attempt to free Thrace from their rule. He led an army to several victories in an ultimately unsuccessful war." More paper shuffling. "That's all I know."

Harry ran a hand over his face. "What's known is that Spartacus was an enslaved gladiator who escaped captivity and led an uprising against the Roman Republic. What began with fifty escaped gladiators grew into a ragtag army of over one hundred thousand men, women and children.

Spartacus's forces defeated several Roman legions before eventually being destroyed when Rome sent an overwhelming force against them."

"Hang on," Nora said. "You're telling me nobody knew Spartacus was a prince?"

Harry shook his head. "If it's even the same guy."

"Which is why I called you," Gary said.

"I thought you called me because the New York governor's kid lived with one of the dead guys."

"That's part of it," Gary said. "The other is this Thracian king's tomb with a possible reference to Spartacus inside. A message unseen for over two thousand years. I assumed it would pique your interest."

Pique? On any other day Harry would be on a plane the next morning. "It's not much evidence to go on."

"I expect you've taken trips based on less," Gary said.

He had a point. "True, but I have another matter occupying my time."

"The antiquities store?" Gary asked. "You will eventually have to restock your supply. Call this a scouting excursion. Though you won't take anything home from the tomb, I assure you."

"It's a personal matter," Harry said, leaving it at that.

To his credit, Gary didn't ask. "It's your decision, Harry. I understand if you aren't interested in this sort of opportunity." Harry bit his tongue to prevent himself from taking another bit of Gary's bait. "Please keep this to yourself," Gary said. "I'll notify my contact in Bulgaria we can't help."

"Wait." The word slipped out before Harry could stop himself. "Nora, what do you think?"

"You want my opinion?"

"Don't sound so surprised."

"Shocked is more like it," Nora said. "Honestly, I'm surprised you'd even consider passing this up. This is exactly what you do."

"I own an antiquities store."

"Which won't stay in business for long if you don't keep on top of the market."

He grumbled to himself. "Normally I'd say yes. But I can't. I have another matter to handle."

Gary jumped in. "I would consider it a personal favor. Ask Nora how often I say that."

"Once a year," Nora said. "And only to Mom."

Harry stopped cold. *Mom.* This wasn't just his boss and her boss. This was his half-sister. And Gary, who was a nice guy, as far as guys who married your mom went. This was new. He frowned. New and confusing.

"Say I decide to go," Harry said. "What are you looking for me to do?"

"Figure out the truth about the tomb. Follow your instincts."

"I'm not a cop."

"No, but you're perfect for this. And I trust you."

Gary Doyle, hardened prosecutor, was laying it on thick. Funny thing, though. It worked. "Three days," Harry said. "That's how long I can give you. And I do it my way, understood? No interference."

He could afford three days. Sara was refusing to share her thoughts on the message inside Agilulph's bible so far, and he hadn't deciphered where the message suggested he go next. Perhaps a few days away was in order. Not to mention what waited at the dig site.

Why not? "Agreed?" Harry asked.

"Agreed," Gary said.

Nora cut in. "Seeing as I'm irrelevant here, I'm going home."

Gary chuckled. "Your sense of humor is always appreciated." Nora shouted a goodbye to Harry as her footsteps faded away. "She has your back as much as I do," Gary said once Nora was gone. "Never doubt that."

He didn't. "Where am I flying to?"

"Check your email. Is tomorrow too soon to leave?" Harry said it wasn't. "Good man. I'll get you a first-class seat. Can't have you arriving tired."

Harry shook his head. "At least you're keeping up with my travel expectations."

"You usually travel this way?"

"My old boss also believed in my arriving well-rested."

"Vincent Morello took care of those he valued," Gary said. "Or that's what I've heard."

"You heard right. No expenses spared. Mainly because of loyalty to my dad. I can thank him for all those nice flights. My dad and I never had to worry about Vincent pinching pennies."

"I wish I could have met your father."

"You do?" It slipped out before Harry could stop himself.

"Yes. Any man Jennifer—or Dani, forgive me, I'm struggling with that—chose to be with must have been an excellent man."

"He was."

"Dani still won't speak about him. In many areas of her life, she's entirely open and forthcoming. So I respect her privacy, even though I am curious about your father. He certainly led an interesting life."

"Not by choice."

"I am sorry for your losses. All of them."

"Thanks."

"It's challenging to realize your misfortune led to my marriage. Guilt is a new emotion for me when I think about my relationship with Dani."

Harry shrugged. "No reason to feel guilty. Not like we can change the past." Gary didn't respond immediately, so Harry threw out a line. "How did you guys meet, anyway?"

Gary was quiet for a moment before continuing. "Your mother was Jennifer Shah when I met her. I was a newly minted attorney, full of idealized goals and eager to change the world. She was, in some ways, a woman of mystery." Harry lifted an eyebrow. "She didn't talk about her past. Not the day I met her. Not on our first date. Not when I asked her to be my wife. I accepted it, because that was Jennifer." He paused again. "And to answer your question, the library. I met your mother at the Ninety-Sixth Street Public Library in Manhattan."

"Didn't you wonder why she never talked about her past?"

"At first. Then I accepted it. Dani made it clear from the very start that she had been involved with someone before, but that was all she would say. No details, no hints, certainly nothing about a child. She gave me a choice early on to accept that boundary or walk away."

"Couldn't have been easy for a guy like you to let such a big topic go. Finding the truth is what you do."

"It was the easiest decision I ever made." Humor tinged his next words. "And if you believe all attorneys are interested in finding the truth, I have news to share. Regardless, your entry into our lives and her pulling back the curtain slightly on what happened before we met has made life interesting."

Harry had never considered that before. "I'll bet it has."

"I see the change in her. A shift, as though light is shining in places it couldn't reach before. That light is because of you, Harry. No matter what happens, thank you for making that possible. Dani needs you in her life. You have no idea how grateful she is to have you back."

Of all the things Gary Doyle could have said, Harry expected this the least. "Same for me," he said. "Guess I'll have to dial it back in Bulgaria. Take fewer risks." Not just because of his mom. And not just because of his stepdad and half-sister, or even Sara for that matter. There was a Frenchman Harry still needed to handle.

"Be yourself, Harry. It's gotten you this far."

Gary Doyle had a point. "You know Gary, you're not half as bad as Nora says."

"One of the nicer things anyone will say about me today." Beeping sounded in Harry's ear. "Check your phone," Gary said. "I just sent a photo of the message in Cotys's tomb. Anything catch your eye?"

Chapter 7

Brooklyn

One aspect of the message stood out. "It's not very long," Harry said.

"I'm sending the translation now," Gary said.

"No need. I read Latin." He scanned the few short lines. "I've never seen anything like this before."

"How so?"

"First, it's brief. Kings love to boast about themselves. Cotys says only three things about his own life. That he ruled wisely, defended Thrace, and secured his nation's future through an alliance with Rome. That's it. Then he talks about his son." Harry stopped on the name. *Spartacus.* "The events Cotys claims his son was involved with match up with historical accounts. Fighting to free Thrace, leading an uprising, winning several battles."

"That's what my initial reports noted as well," Gary said. "The brevity first and foremost."

"He had an entire cave wall to work with," Harry said. "Not as though he was short on room. Hang on." He zoomed in on one side of the cave wall, part of it outside of where the message had been written. "There's something else on the wall. It's not part of the message." He tilted his phone. "What is that?"

A rudimentary drawing was carved into the wall adjacent to Cotys's message. A flat line running horizontal to the floor, with a half-circle in the middle above it. Additional short, straight lines shot out from the curving half-circle at regular intervals.

"My report offers several suggestions," Gary said. "We can't be certain the image and the message are connected. It may be—"

"—a sun," Harry finished for him. "It's a rising sun." He squinted. "Or at least I think it is."

"That was one possibility," Gary said. "Any suggestions as to how it relates to the message?"

"It doesn't," Harry said. "At least not directly. I'll check for ties between Spartacus and a sun on my flight tomorrow."

"I'll send you anything I learn in the interim," Gary said. "Your airline ticket and hotel accommodations in Bulgaria will be over shortly. I'll have my contact meet you at the dig site."

"Who is this contact?"

"His name is Taxiarchis Limnios," Gary said. "He goes by Tax."

"That's a new one."

"He's Greek. Tax works for his nation's Department Against Smuggling of Antiquities, which partners with Interpol to protect cultural property." A pause. "I'm sure you're familiar with their efforts."

Harry pretended not to notice that last part. "What's a Greek cop doing in Bulgaria?"

"Greece borders Bulgaria. They share an interest in protecting cultural property. The Bulgarian authorities invited Tax to assist when they discovered the tomb."

"Can I trust him?" No chance of that happening, not yet. But at least let Gary think he might.

"As much as you trust anyone you've never met."

"Interesting response."

"Normally I would say to trust him," Gary said. "Then again, I'm not normally talking to my wife's son." The word "stepson" did not make an appearance. "So I'll say trust your instincts. Something tells me you have a better feeling for that than I do."

"I'll give him a chance," Harry said. "At least a bit of a chance. It doesn't help that I know you're not doing this entirely out of the goodness of your heart."

"I've been clear about that part," Gary said. "The governor may yet be the mayor's best ally."

"You'd better remember this if your boss moves up in the world."

"I'll remember it no matter what," Gary said. "I'm not sending you into more than I know you can handle. Nora and I talk, and I'm not the only one who thinks you're the best. Actually, her complimenting your abilities helped convince me."

"She doesn't seem thrilled to be left out of this."

"That's her nature. She needs to prove herself. I know better. She truly believes she can do anything but doesn't think anyone else believes it." Here Gary's voice warmed. "And you know what? She can."

"I'll buy her a beer for talking me up," Harry said. "One more thing. I don't need anyone looking over my shoulder."

"I'm here to support you in any way you need. Even if that means leaving you alone."

"Good man."

Harry promised to keep Gary in the loop before clicking off. He immediately dialed another number. Gary Doyle might have the official connection to Bulgaria that provided Harry's entrance ticket, but Harry knew Gary didn't have the only line on information about Cotys's uncovered tomb.

"Harry Fox. To what do I owe the pleasure?"

Harry couldn't help but grin. "Evening, Rose. I'm in the market for information. Figured you were the person to call."

Rose Leroux knew everyone, and everyone trusted her. If a Thracian king's tomb had just been uncovered in Bulgaria, Rose would know about it.

"I don't normally share information with my competitors."

"I can't hold a candle to you." It was true. "And you know my store doesn't handle the…specialized merchandise you do."

"Not even for your best customers?"

Harry opened his mouth. He closed it. She had him there. "Not often, at least." He didn't bother lying to her. If Joey asked him to move a relic with less-than-complete provenance through his store, he probably would. Probably. "But that doesn't change the fact that I'm not your competition. I don't compete with you."

"Not yet, perhaps. But do not underestimate yourself." Metal scraped on metal, the familiar sound of Rose firing up a lighter. Harry could almost smell the smoke. "What information are you seeking?"

"Anything you know about a Thracian king's tomb in Bulgaria."

"Near the site of a recent earthquake?"

"I knew I called the right person."

"I thought you were an antiquities dealer now, Harry. A man who left the field behind."

"Don't believe everything you hear."

"I do not. And, if you are interested, I approve. Yours is a rare talent." More tobacco crackling. "Why do you ask about the tomb?"

Rose Leroux and Harry Fox had worked to undermine one of the most dangerous mobsters in the city. They'd both be dead if that ever got out, which meant Rose was one of the very few people Harry trusted with his life. "Someone asked me to do them a favor."

He told her everything. Gary Doyle's request. The governor's daughter. The two bodies. Rose listened silently until he finished. "Quite an opportunity," she said thoughtfully.

"Opportunity to get myself killed, maybe."

"It wouldn't hurt to have the likely next governor owe you."

"True."

"What can you tell me about the Bulgarian tomb?"

"Allegedly it is the tomb of King Cotys the Fourth, a Thracian who battled but ultimately acquiesced to Roman rule."

Rose proceeded to describe the tomb, referenced the message on the wall, and generally made it clear a person with firsthand knowledge had detailed the find to her. She even knew about the two bodies.

"It is possible they died by accident," Rose said after her tale. "Except you would be foolish to believe that."

"You know something I don't?"

"No. Merely experience talking. I recommend you be careful with your trust."

"Always," Harry said before switching gears. "Any update on Olivier Lloris?"

"Nothing official. Unofficially, I understand he has been making discreet inquiries about what may be available beyond the bible."

"He's taking the bait."

"Some would call it hook, line and sinker." Another inhale on her cigarette. "Mr. Lloris is clearly interested in future acquisitions tied to this artifact. That they are shrouded in mystery only adds to the allure." Another pause. "That he hasn't contacted me directly is odd. Men like Olivier are not often patient. I will be surprised if he does not reach out soon."

"Let him stew," Harry said. "I have to spend a few days in Bulgaria." He snapped his fingers. "One last question. Have you heard of anyone else who's interested in Cotys's tomb? Unofficial interest?"

"No, I have not heard of anyone interested in the tomb. Yet. Of course, if the tomb contains more than the bones of a forgotten king, that will quickly change."

"I'm leaving tomorrow." No need to give other relic hunters enough time to get interested in the tomb. Interest—and competition—brought trouble. "I'll be in touch."

"I have friends in that part of the world," Rose said. "If you require assistance, do not hesitate."

He thanked her and clicked off with the secure feeling that came with knowing New York's biggest fence would have his back if he needed her. Harry fired up his computer, staring at the screen with his hands over the keyboard. A sliver of moonlight hung in the sky outside a nearby window, yet sleep was far from his mind. Not with this new adventure on the horizon. An adventure in Bulgaria, a land about which he knew nothing, involving a Thracian king about whom he knew only a tiny bit more. Time to fix that.

An hour of research later, his head was stuffed with facts about King

Cotys and Thrace. He'd never have guessed Thracian leaders had all belonged to what was now called—no joke—a *mystery religion*. The Thracians hadn't called it that, but when he found a reference to the *Sanctuary of the Great Gods*, Harry dug further.

A temple on the island of Samothrace had been constructed to honor the gods of this secretive faith. Could it relate to the tomb in Bulgaria? Not that he could tell. Several more dead ends of this nature convinced him that enough was enough. Thrace had existed in one form or another for over two thousand years. Its history was incredible, enough to bury him in research for years if he let it.

Harry closed his laptop. He'd learned long ago that to be a successful relic hunter, you needed information. But to be the best, you also had to get out in the field. In this case, fly to Bulgaria and see this tomb for himself. Then he'd figure out what else he needed. He tried and failed to suppress a yawn. He was wired, on edge, and exhausted, and his bed was calling louder with each passing minute. Harry picked up his phone. One more issue. Then he could rest.

The phone rang twice after he dialed. A familiar voice answered. "Harry, how are you?"

"Hey, Joey. I'm fine. You have a second?" Joey said he did. "I'm headed out of town. For my other job."

"Working for the government sounds more dangerous than working for me."

"You got that right. It's only a few days. While I'm gone, would you do me a favor and keep an eye on Sara? Quietly?"

"I can have two of my guys tail her all day, and have two more in a car outside her apartment all night."

"You need me to send you the definition of discreet?"

"I'm joking, Harry. No problem. I'll have a couple of guys watch her. *Quietly*. Should they be looking for anyone in particular?"

"Just have them keep their eyes open. I don't have any reason to think she's in danger. It's more a gut feeling. Of not wanting anything to happen. I've made a few more enemies lately." Talk about an understatement. Fortunately, most of them had gone somewhere they couldn't hurt Sara. Unless you believed in ghosts.

"I know what that's like." Joey ran the New York mob. Of course he knew. "Don't worry about Sara. She'll be safe."

"Thanks. I'll let her know a couple of shadows will be around while I'm gone. Don't want her going after them when they're only trying to help."

Joey said to call if he needed anything before Harry hung up. His eyelids felt ready to drop shut, so he headed for the stairs and his bedroom. Sara was lying still when he walked in and lay down beside her. Appearances, though, were deceiving.

"What are you planning?" Her voice cut the darkness.

"Nothing," Harry said quickly.

"I don't believe you."

He almost laughed. *Can't fool her.* "I'm going to Bulgaria."

She didn't so much as move. Yet he sensed a shift in the room, a jolt of energy.

"I'm listening."

He told her everything. Cotys IV's tomb. The earthquake. Two bodies and a message on the wall. She listened in silence, and that silence stretched on after he stopped talking.

"It's only a few days," Harry said.

"What about Agilulph's bible? I thought you wanted my opinion."

Darn. "I do," he said quickly. "Whenever you're ready to share it."

"What if I'm not ready within the next three days?"

He almost suppressed the sigh. "Don't be like that."

"I'm not being *like* anything. You have a new business to run. Why race off to Bulgaria and leave it unattended?"

"My business is fine and you know it," he said. "You're not thrilled about me going back into the field."

"I never said that."

"I'm not dense." She made a noise approximating disagreement. He ignored it. "Keeping you safe is the most important thing I do. My going to Bulgaria doesn't put you at risk. Heck, I'm barely putting myself at risk."

"Two corpses would suggest otherwise."

"It could be an accident. Nobody knows."

"If you believe that, you are denser than I suspected."

"Very funny." Also very true. "I'll be back in three days. Gary is part of my family now. Helping him out goes a long way."

"You helped uncover lost documents from the Library of Alexandria. Gratitude from people with influence is not lacking in your toolkit."

Harry shrugged, though she couldn't see it. "Never hurts to have more friends."

"I don't agree with your decision." He opened his mouth to respond, then listened to the tiny voice shouting at him to keep quiet. It proved wise. "However," Sara continued, "I understand."

"Understand what?"

"Why you're flying to Bulgaria. I'm a bit surprised it took this long."

He nearly sat up. "Took this long for what?"

"For you to decide to do what you've always done. It's who you are, Harry. Nothing will change that. Not my coming to America, not reconnecting with your mother, not starting your business. Which is how it should be. It makes you who you are."

A strong urge to hug her came over him. An urge, he knew, that should be ignored right now. "Thanks."

"I may not agree with it, but I'll support your decision. I only hope your mother and sister support it as well."

"What they think matters. But they're not you, Sara."

A car engine rumbled outside. Clouds moved, letting stars shine and then wink out again. Sara eventually responded.

"You should still tell your mother. Gary Doyle doesn't run their household. She does. Get her support and the rest will follow."

Chapter 8

Brooklyn

Harry rolled out of an empty bed not long after the sun came up. The only trace of Sara was a note on the table. Three words: *Call your mother.*

First, coffee. The pot had almost finished brewing when his phone buzzed with a text from his mother. *Are you at home? I'm on my way over.*

Harry grumbled to the walls. "Sara's behind this."

He sent a response confirming he was at home and that Dani could come by. Ten minutes later his doorbell rang.

Harry opened the door without a smile on his face. "It takes you an hour to get here. I only texted you ten minutes ago."

Dani Fox didn't blink. "Sara told me you'd be here. My message was a courtesy."

He grumbled some more as she hugged him. "You two are bad news," Harry said. "How's a guy supposed to have any privacy around here?"

"He's not." Dani stepped back. "You need to shave."

Harry rubbed his chin. "I will before I go. How much did Gary and Sara tell you?"

"Everything. That's why I'm here. Is that coffee I smell?"

Only after they were seated at his table did he respond. "I gather you have thoughts on my trip to Bulgaria? I bet Gary's sorry he ever asked me."

"Why would he be sorry?"

"You didn't come here to tell me about Bulgarian cuisine."

Dani sipped her coffee. She sipped it again. "I came to tell you a story.

Two stories. The first one is quite short." Her coffee mug settled on his table without a sound. "Once there was a mother who believed in her son. She knew he could do anything he put his mind to. Care to guess their names?"

He shook his head. "Thanks, Mom."

"Now that we're clear on that, the second story." Dani picked up her coffee mug. It went halfway to her lips, then changed course and went back on the table without her taking a sip. She reached for her necklace—not the amulet one Harry's father had given her—and twirled the etched blue glass in her fingers. "This one is about me and Gary."

Harry lifted an eyebrow. "Did Gary send you with a message?"

Dani eyed him across the table. "Do you know how Gary and I met?"

A question he'd considered many times. He'd never asked. Hearing how his mother came to be with a new man after abandoning—no, not abandoning: after *sacrificing* her entire life with her family. He'd thought about it. He didn't speak about it. "No," Harry lied. All stories had two sides. He knew Gary's. Not hers. "No idea."

"Have you wondered?"

"I've wondered lots of things." He looked out the window at a dark sky that offered no solace. "Some I've thought about more than others."

"I know this isn't easy, Harry, but I'm not hiding anything for one more second. Including how I met Gary." She leaned closer and her voice dropped. "He's a good man, Harry. Let me tell you why."

Harry motioned for her to go on. He didn't look at her.

"I spent six months in Pakistan after your father helped stage my death. I left the United States as Dani Fox and returned as Jennifer Shah. I had no contact with anyone I knew as Dani."

"Other than sending letters to Dad through the imam."

"Yes. I had enough money to survive for a time, but I needed a job. I was hired at a neighborhood library to help with community programs and handle some administrative duties. After several months a position above me opened, then it happened again. Soon I was the program director, overseeing local outreach efforts and educational programs, pretty much anything we did to connect with our neighbors."

"Did Gary come in to borrow a book?"

"Hardly. Gary reads law books and sports biographies his friends give him. Beyond that, he chooses something active. Don't ever challenge him to a golf match. He's ruthless." The last few fallen leaves whistled past on a frigid breeze outside his window. "We offered a language course at the library teaching English as a second language. It was one of our most popular classes." Her face darkened. "Unfortunately, not everyone supported the library's mission."

Harry had heard this sort of story before. "Somebody showed up who didn't like immigrants."

"There is no shortage of people with such feelings in the city," Dani said. "I had been the program director for about six months when a man walked into one of our English language classes with a knife. He berated the students with all manner of invective, but his ranting is what likely saved everyone. I was down the hall in my office and heard the commotion. I ran to the room and saw what was happening. The intruder had his back to the door." The invisible clouds darkening her face seemed to lift. "The staff break room was next to the classroom. There had been a potluck meal that day, and one dish had arrived in a cast iron pan."

Harry sat straighter. "You didn't. Did you?"

"If the question is did I use a cast iron pan to subdue the intruder, the answer is yes. I grabbed the pan and smacked him on the head. Not hard enough, though. He fell after I hit him, then jumped up and came at me with the knife. I was ready to bash him again when a student tackled the man from behind. The intruder cut the student with his knife before I smacked him on the head again. This time it knocked him out."

"Was the student okay?"

"He needed several stitches, which made me feel terrible, but that's all. We were lucky. If the intruder had had a gun or if he'd attacked immediately instead of shouting at the students, it would have been much worse. That is when I met Gary."

"Was he an assistant D.A. back then?"

"Yes. He was assigned to prosecute the case. I didn't realize what that meant for me. I gave a short statement to the police when they arrested the intruder, then told them I wanted nothing else to do with it."

"You didn't want them looking into your background."

"I did not. My new identity may have held up under scrutiny, but I couldn't risk it. I declined to be interviewed by the D.A.'s office several times, but the A.D.A. overseeing the prosecution refused to take no for an answer. He proved tenacious in his efforts to convince me to testify."

"It was Gary."

"Yes. I told him time and again I didn't want to be involved for personal reasons."

"Hang on. This intruder attacked a classroom full of people. Why did they need you to testify so badly? He had a ton of witnesses."

"Everyone hid when the intruder barged into the classroom. I hit him the first time and knocked him down in the classroom doorway. I was out in the hallway when he came after me and cut the student." Dani's eyes narrowed. "The intruder's attorney claimed his client was trying to run away when I hit him."

"That's a lie."

"And defense lawyers never lie, do they?" Harry rolled his eyes. "The attorney claimed his client had made a mistake and was trying to lay his knife down when I hit him, and the student who intervened was cut because of the student's aggressive attack on a man who was trying to surrender."

"That's ridiculous."

Dani shrugged. "I agree, but without my testimony there was no one to refute that story other than that one student. Two competing versions of the story, and only two witnesses. Gary explained to me how unpredictable juries could be. With my testimony the intruder would almost certainly have been convicted. Without it, there was a chance he would be found not guilty. Gary was not offering a plea deal, and the attacker decided to take his chances with a jury."

"Gary needed you to testify."

"A straightforward decision for any witness who wasn't living under a false identity." Here Dani looked past Harry, over his shoulder and into the past. "Gary handled it well. He never spoke down to me, never told me I was making a mistake. He was unrelenting but unfailingly respectful. Not every person in his position would have been the same. He could have leaned on me with all the weight of his office. What would he have uncovered if he looked too closely at my background? Perhaps he doesn't dig very far. Perhaps he does. Gary had the resources to make my life very uncomfortable. He didn't do that."

"What happened?"

"He took the case to trial without my testimony."

"Which risked having the jury not convict this guy."

"Yes. The man deserved to go to jail for a long time. He could have walked free. Fortunately, Gary is good at his job. The jury convicted the man on all counts. He's still in jail."

"Gutsy of him."

"Courageous," Dani said. "Though with the benefit of hindsight, I believe his motivations were not entirely unselfish."

Harry rolled his eyes. "Gary was interested in you."

"It was wholly unreciprocated." She turned her gaze back on him. "At first. I only wanted to be left alone. Gary was puzzled as to why I wouldn't testify, and he eventually realized I wouldn't say why, no matter how many times he asked. He assured me I would be protected, that it would only take a day."

"What made him stop asking?"

"I asked him if he thought he could get a conviction without my help. He said he could, and that's when I finally told him the truth."

"That you weren't Jennifer Shah?"

"No. I never told him my real name. I explained I couldn't let anyone dig into my past because I'd been through some terrible experiences I wouldn't discuss, no matter what. It must have been the way I said it, or the look on my face, but Gary accepted it." Dani's face had been gradually brightening as she spoke. Now a vibrant smile lit up the room. "And a day after the verdict he asked me out for coffee."

"You still never told him the truth?"

"Not when we were dating, not after we were engaged and married." Dani sat back in her chair. "Are you two getting along?"

"As much as a guy can with the man who married his mom."

"Stop it." Now Dani leaned over, reaching out to put her hand atop Harry's. "He's not your father. No one will ever replace Fred. Gary is my husband and Nora's father, and even though this isn't how I wish my life had played out, here we are. Give Gary a chance."

Harry turned his hand over under his mom's and gently squeezed her fingers. The other hand reached up and brushed across his amulet. "Okay."

"Okay?"

"I'll take your word for it that he's okay."

"You are as hard-headed as your father."

"And my mother." Harry dodged, almost avoiding her gentle swipe at his shoulder. "Gary seems like a good guy."

"I told Gary the Bulgaria request was your decision, and yours alone. He assured me he wouldn't pressure you to go. Did he?"

Harry lifted a shoulder. "Not really. Besides, it's not like I don't want to go. I enjoy this kind of work."

"Which is the only reason I allowed him to make his request in the first place."

"He asked your permission?"

Dani tilted her head, one eyebrow going up. "Gary would never approach you without my permission. He's far too intelligent to cross me."

"Gary said I'd be doing him a favor."

"Which doesn't matter," Dani said. "What matters is what you decide. I only help guide Gary's decisions. Which is exactly what I want for you. To be your own man and make your own decisions." Now she pointed at herself. "I trust you'll do what's right. For *you*, not me. Your father was the best man I ever knew. I know he taught you well."

Harry held his coffee cup for several breaths, then took a long drink and looked at the table. "He did." He looked up and found Dani watching him intently. "Do you think I should go?"

"You should do what you think is best."

"I want your opinion. Honestly."

Dani didn't hesitate. "In that case, no. I would prefer if you stayed here. However, I'll support you no matter what. I trust you'll act with caution in Bulgaria, and I cannot wait to hear about your trip when you return."

"You'd rather I didn't go?"

"Yes. Because I can't stand the thought of you in danger. Because I love you."

"Thanks, Mom. Love you too." Another slug of coffee. "I'm going."

Dani shook her head theatrically. "Why do I bother?" She patted his hand again. "Promise me you'll be careful."

"I'll be careful," Harry said. "And I know. Last thing I want to do is deprive you of spending more time with someone as special as me."

"Your humility is impressive. No, doofus, I'm not talking about me. I'm talking about Sara. That lovely girl didn't move from Germany only for a new job."

"Come on, Mom. She loves this job."

"Harry, do you realize the sacrifice she made to come here? Moving to a new country where they don't speak your native language is an enormous challenge. That she undertook it to, at least in some measure, be closer to you—that should speak volumes." Dani pointed a finger at Harry's chest. "You should consider her feelings about the trip."

"She'd want me to go," he said quickly.

Dani wasn't buying it. "You know that? Don't make selfish decisions, Harry. The truth—does Sara want you to go?"

Harry frowned. "She didn't say no. Sara worries. A lot. She's getting better, but what I do makes her nervous."

"It makes me nervous."

"Want to know something? It makes me a little nervous too. Nervous in a good way, the sort of nerves you want to feel. I can't wait to see what's out there. A tomb with a message about Spartacus." He leaned closer. "I have a chance to see it in person."

Harry stood from his seat, turning to look out the window. "I'm not only going for me. I'm also going to keep her safe."

"This is related to Olivier Lloris?"

"Not yet. But it could be."

"How?"

"Who knows what I'll find? Not that I plan on keeping it." He paused long enough to let her consider. "People like Olivier want what others don't have. This trip may also give me a way to tempt Olivier. I don't know what will draw him in. I only know I can't miss the chance."

"I see your mind will not be changed. Given that, will you tell me your plan?"

Harry couldn't keep one corner of his mouth from going up. "I think there's more than just a tomb in Bulgaria. Much more."

"What else could be in the tomb?"

"The truth behind a legend."

Chapter 9

Balkan Mountains, Bulgaria

Wind raced down the snowcapped mountains. The bitterly cold air brought tears to Harry's eyes. He ran the back of one gloved hand over his face as he followed his shadow toward the muted hubbub at the dig site's base camp. He had an appointment with a Greek man. His only friend in the country. A man he'd never even met.

Harry ducked his chin against the wind and looked at his phone. A snapshot of Taxiarchis Limnios, agent with the Greek Department Against Smuggling of Antiquities. Currently partnering with Interpol to protect the cultural property at King Cotys IV's tomb. Hopefully Tax intended to let Harry get on with the search as he saw fit, away from everyone else. People milled about, most with their heads down, hands jammed in pockets, breath fogging the air for an instant before it was whisked away on the wind. Nobody looked like the man on his phone.

Harry didn't have time for this. It was too cold. "Hey, buddy," he called out in English to the nearest person. A security guard, judging from the uniform. "Where can I find Tax?"

The man studied the picture on Harry's upraised phone. He responded in English, with a harshness on the consonants that rattled Harry's ears.

"Big tent." He pointed to the biggest tent.

"Thanks," Harry said. He noted a steady flow of people headed toward the parking lot. "Where's everybody going?" Harry asked the guard.

"Food." The guard pointed at a bus now rolling onto the dig site. "Hot food."

It looked like whoever was running this place had sprung for a better meal than usual. Harry checked his watch. It was lunchtime. "Grab it while it's fresh," Harry said. The guard didn't blink, so Harry patted him on the shoulder. "Stay warm."

The people headed to the tent had one thing in common. They all looked like academics. No one set off his radar, or looked at him for too long. In fact, nobody looked at him at all. The lunch bus had their eye.

He waited at the big tent for another bespectacled person to walk out before he ducked through the opening. The first person he spotted looked familiar. "Tax?" Harry called out.

"You must be Mr. Fox." The man who approached Harry stood not much taller than him. Not unusual, but the man was also nearly as wide as he was tall. He looked to have swallowed a barrel, and the ready smile on his face suggested he had enjoyed every bite. The big pistol strapped to his waist, however, made it clear that while Tax Limnios wasn't outrunning anyone, he didn't need to.

Harry pulled off a glove and stuck his hand out. "*Yassas*," Harry said. *Hello.*

Tax replied in his mother tongue, unleashing a torrent of Greek that bowled over Harry like a wave. The Greek antiquities man fell silent, an expectant look on his face.

"I don't speak Greek," Harry said. "English?"

"Works for me," Tax said without hesitation. "Gary told me you work for his team. Undercover." The lines on Tax's forehead deepened. "Interesting."

Where to start? Harry shook his head. At the end was his preference. "I handle jobs his main team can't." If Nora Doyle ever got wind he'd said that, there would be hell to pay. "Like this one."

"You are a lucky man, Mr. Fox." Tax stuck his arms out to either side. "Look where it brought you. To the edge of history!"

Harry could get along with a man who thought that way. "An edge that seems to be more dangerous than most dig sites," he said. "What do you know about the two bodies?"

Tax looked left. He looked right. He reached up with one hand and stroked the bushy mustache sitting on his upper lip. "Little." Then Tax leaned closer. "Which you must keep to yourself."

"Won't breathe a word," Harry said.

"One of the deceased is a college student from England."

"The New York governor's daughter's roommate," Harry said.

"He died not far from here. White foam was on his mouth. A witness saw him fall to the floor. He could not speak, but grabbed his throat, then died."

"White foam? Was he allergic to anything?"

"Not that I know of," Tax said. "Except perhaps the wild mushrooms found in his pocket."

"Mushrooms? Did he forage in the mountains and eat a poisonous one?"

"The coroner will tell us," Tax said. "Perhaps it is something else."

"Some kid eats bad mushrooms and now I'm in Bulgaria to study a king's tomb. You can't make this stuff up."

"The world is strange, my friend."

"What about the other corpse?"

"Since I spoke to Gary, we received more information. The second person died in a landslide."

Harry's head went on a swivel. "Here? Are we safe?"

"Yes, my friend." Tax clapped a hand on Harry's shoulder. "We are safe near the camp. It is in the mountains that rockslides can get you. The second man walked too far out on his own. The earthquake moved many large rocks. One of them crushed this man."

"Just bad luck?"

"Perhaps a coincidence."

Coincidences were for suckers. "You sure? It wouldn't take much to send a few rocks down a hill and onto some guy's head. Are we certain it was the earthquake?"

"I am certain." Tax tapped the side of his head. "I know when to question, and when to believe. The second man's death was an accident."

"I'll still keep my eyes open."

"Then you are a wise man," Tax said. "What else do you wish to know?"

"What can you tell me about the tomb, and when can I go inside?"

Tax gave Harry a sly wink. "A man of action. You should speak with the dig's historian."

"You have confidence in him?"

"As much as I do anyone here," Tax said. "He can tell you about the site and what they have found. After that, you may go inside. I have secured access for you today. The cave will be all ours, but you may go in alone."

"You're not coming?"

"I would like you to see it without my thoughts interfering. I will keep watch at the entrance."

Harry inclined his head toward the small cannon on Tax's waist. "Appreciate it. Nobody's messing with that piece of artillery."

"This little pistol?" Tax's hand moved faster than Harry thought possible. One instant the gun was holstered at his side. The next, it gleamed with the polish of a thousand cleanings in Tax's grip. "It is nothing. An accessory for my belt."

"Looks like a .44 Magnum to me. You could stop a bear with that thing."

"Or a grave robber." The spark in Tax's eye was not entirely friendly. "Provided you hit him, that is."

"Could you? Hit him, that is."

"I have not missed one yet." Tax laughed and the gun was back in his holster before Harry knew what happened. "Now, you must speak with the historian. Then, the tomb."

Tax ambled to the tent's entrance, put two fingers to his lips, then unleashed an ear-splitting whistle that might have caused another landslide miles away. Seconds later, a man ducked through the doorway and Harry found himself listening intently as the dig historian regaled Harry with information about King Cotys IV. Harry had read that the Thracian king had believed in a form of democratic governance, but he was surprised to learn that Thrace had been a tribal land, not unlike Greece's city-states. He also wouldn't have pegged Thrace as a thriving center of artistic creation in the ancient world.

Harry thanked the historian, then waited for the scholar to leave before turning to Tax. "I'm ready."

"Follow me, my friend."

Tax led Harry into the sunlight, passing two men who nearly ran into them. Harry listened as one of them, a brute whose bald head gleamed even in the weak winter light, asked Tax where the historian was; Harry tuned out the answer as he studied the terrain. Rocky and unforgiving were two words that jumped to mind. Cold was another. His breath frosted the air as he looked over the snow-dusted slopes, mountain peaks, and valleys stretching into the distance beneath low-hanging clouds. Green trees covered in a dusting of white stood far ahead on the mountains.

Tax turned from the two men back to Harry. "Now, for the big reveal."

Harry looked back over his shoulder as they walked. The big guy who'd asked about the historian caught his eye. Why, he couldn't say, but the guy gave off a vibe Harry didn't like. The man returned Harry's gaze for a beat and then turned to his partner as the tent flap fell shut.

"Who are those two guys?" Harry asked.

"The supply men?" Tax shook his head. "I don't know their names. They are important for the camp site."

"Why?"

Tax's face brightened. "They bring the food. Who is more important than the man who brings your food?"

Harry shook his head. *Stop being paranoid.* He pushed the unease aside. "Where's the cave entrance?"

"We must climb."

Tax offered nothing more as he set off toward a patch of rugged trees not far ahead. Weathered gray rock crunched underfoot as the ground turned from soil to stone. Evergreens more gray than green sprouted from an unforgiving landscape, while snow covered the mountain peaks of this stretch of the Balkans for miles in either direction. A boulder roughly the size of an American sport utility vehicle waited beyond the trees, forcing them to detour around it. Fresh marks in the stone told Harry a story.

Harry pointed at the boulder. "Did that come down in the earthquake?"

"Yes," Tax said. "Very close call for the trees. And that is one of the smaller rocks that fell."

Harry touched the rough stone as they passed. A chill went up his arm. "Smaller?"

"Follow me."

Tax moved quickly for a man of his bulk, navigating the treacherous ground with ease. Harry had to double-time it to keep up. They passed another car-sized boulder before veering to the right as loose soil underfoot threatened to send Harry spilling onto his backside and back down to the camp. Eyes down, he didn't realize Tax had stopped until Harry nearly ran into the man.

"Up there." Tax pointed at a ledge Harry hadn't seen until now. "We must go around. The path is on the far side."

A nearly vertical wall of gray stone loomed out of the ground ahead. The ten feet of jagged stone ended in a flat plateau; Harry couldn't see if anything was on top of the plateau or not. Broken rocks littered the ground around them. Harry picked one up and found one side clean. "This only broke off a few days ago."

Tax spread both hands out to encompass the area. "This is what remains of the rocks that covered the entrance."

Harry looked back toward camp. Their trip had covered a hundred yards at most, though the rapid change in elevation put them a good twenty yards above the tallest tent. Darkening clouds covered the sun and stole what weak light it offered. Only a handful of people could be seen walking in the vicinity. Most were off getting something to eat.

He turned to find Tax disappearing around the path ahead. By the time Harry caught up they were stepping onto the flat plateau. Harry stopped short. The scene of destruction in front of them grabbed his attention with two hands and didn't let go. "Holy smokes."

Tax looked back. "What is smoking?"

"It's an expression," Harry said. "I had no idea it was this bad."

"You mean the landslide?" Tax chuckled. "It would have killed anyone nearby. The falling rocks revealed this chamber. The original dig site is down near the main tent. This area had not been explored."

Harry stepped past Tax and moved cautiously toward the hole. And that's the best way he could describe it: a hole blown into the side of the mountain.

Tax pointed to a pile of stones. "Those are some of the stones that covered the entrance. The Thracians used them to cover this natural cave. Then they built a second wall, this one of much smaller stones. They built it to look rough and natural, which the archaeologists believe was to make it more difficult to notice."

"Smart move." Harry took a harder look at the pile of rock Tax pointed to. "Even if the outer layer of small stone fell off, trying to move those bigger ones would be tough."

"We used a bulldozer to move them," Tax said. "Ready to go inside?"

"Thought you'd never ask."

They made it two steps before the radio strapped to Tax's belt squawked. "One moment," Tax said. He pressed a button on the device and loosed a torrent of rapid Greek. The man on the other end responded in kind, and Tax's grin vanished. He barked a response, then jammed the device back onto his belt. "I must go back down," Tax said. "There is a problem with the government."

"Anything serious?"

"No," Tax said with a scowl. "The government is dumb. Too many people want to know about the site. Only authorized officials are allowed to visit here. I must deal with an official who wants to come inside and is not allowed. This will be fun."

"Can we come back after you're done?"

Tax pointed to the cave entrance. "You stay. Go inside, look around. I am told you are a great explorer."

"Don't believe everything you hear."

"Harry Fox, the man who found Alexandria's lost library." The scowl vanished. "You will be fine." Now Tax wagged a finger in Harry's face. "Do not break anything," he said, mirth in his voice. "I would have to arrest you."

"You sure?"

Tax pushed him toward the cave. "Go, go. I will be back after I handle this, what do you call them, this clown?"

"That's what I call them."

"Then good. He is a clown." Tax pointed at Harry's belt. "Do your batteries work?"

Harry pulled the flashlight off his belt and flicked it on. "Good to go."

"I will see you soon."

With that, Tax turned and moved off, heading downhill and around the edge of the plateau. Harry took a long look at the camp site below. Off in the distance a knot of people huddled by the front entrance, marked by a group of sawhorses with giant spotlights and a roaring generator. One man had a fist in the air, waving it wildly. The barrel that was Tax moved toward the man on a collision course.

That guy has no idea what's coming. Harry looked over the entire scene once more. Nothing drew his eye. He turned, a loose rock skittered away underfoot, and as he moved to the dark hole in this mountain, his heart accelerated. Snowflakes blown down from the peaks skipped through his vision, one landing on his nose as the cave entrance beckoned. Harry stopped beneath the jagged entrance and peered inside.

He couldn't see a thing because his breath fogged the wintry air. A gust of wind raced across the open cave mouth with a deep *whoosh*. He peered into the cave. The cave may have peered back. Harry grabbed the flashlight off his belt and flicked it on. No light. His throat tightened, the cold air now even colder. What the heck? He tried the power switch again.

This time its light flooded the darkness. A mess of footsteps led in and out of the cave, hundreds of prints in the dirt showing how many people had been in and out of here in the past few days. Harry straightened his back, took a breath, and walked into the yawning mouth; he followed his light as the cave wrapped him in a chilling embrace. He was prepared for the chill. What he didn't expect was the silence.

All noise vanished after only a few steps. Harry stopped when he reached the edge of the weak natural light. He lifted his flashlight, aimed it dead ahead and found what he was looking for. His eyes widened, but he didn't move. Instead, he turned his light to the left and right. That's when he saw the cables.

Thick electrical cables ran the length of each side, tucked against the stone. The cave walls curved inward as they rose, forming a sloped ceiling at least twenty feet overhead. Harry turned his light back to the cables, twisting to follow them back to their source. He found it just outside the cave entrance.

"I walked right past it," he said to the darkness. Heading back to where he'd entered, Harry reached out and found a switch fastened to the wall. He flicked the switch up. Light flooded the cave.

The cables were attached to a solar-powered generator. Flipping the switch activated portable lights mounted on tripods in each corner of the cave. The interior lit up like a construction site, which is to say there were spots of retina-searing brightness alongside murky shadows in which an explorer could get lost. Harry kept his flashlight handy, yet all in all, it seemed not a bad place to work.

Dust motes flitted about on the still cave air. The familiar sensation that came with millions of tons of rock above his head was reassuring. Harry looked ahead to the rear wall. He touched the amulet around his neck. The hair on his arms stood up.

An inscription ran across the rear wall. "Cotys, fourth of his name."

Harry read the Latin letters again, then turned his attention to the star of the show: a stone sarcophagus big enough to hold a basketball team, sitting below the inscription. The lid was sealed and would remain so until a preservation team could assemble and investigate it.

His gaze flicked to the carvings on either side of the stone box. The first side featured imagery of Cotys in flowing regalia with a crown atop his head; the opposite side showed him as a warrior, sword in hand and the same crown on his head. Cotys as the educated leader. Cotys as the battle-hardened protector. Two images, one king.

In both depictions, Cotys sported a beard that would make any grizzled frontiersman jealous; the beard nearly as impressive as the drooping mustache on Cotys's lip. Harry smirked. A mustache to give Tax a run for his money.

The details of the carvings cried out for closer inspection, but that would have to wait. The inscription that had brought Harry across an ocean came next. He turned now to a few sentences engraved on the wall near the carvings of Cotys, an awfully short bit of writing for a king's grave.

The inscription said three things about Cotys's life. That he had ruled wisely, he had defended Thrace, and he had secured his nation's future through an alliance with Rome. That was it. Then it talked about his son. *Spartacus.* The message celebrated his fight to free Thrace, his leadership and his battlefield successes. Harry went back to the beginning and read it aloud.

Cotys, fourth of his name, wise ruler of Thrace and defender of his people who secured Thracian prosperity by allying with Rome.

Cotys, father of Spartacus, brave warrior who fought to free Thrace. Spartacus led a victorious uprising against Thrace's enemies, battling valiantly to the end.

Spartacus rose in Thrace's time of need, bringing honor to his name with no concern for the danger he faced. Spartacus ascended to glory, a beacon to all Thracians in their darkest hour.

The Thracian Idol

His words faded in the quiet chamber as a carving beside the inscription drew his attention. A flat line running horizontal to the floor, with a half-circle in the middle above the flat line. Smaller lines shot out from the curving half-circle at regular intervals.

The rising sun carving he'd seen in the photos Gary provided. Nothing in his research tied the image to Spartacus. Odd, given Cotys IV had included it inside his tomb. Kings didn't leave imagery in their final resting place unless it had meaning, so this clearly meant something. Standing in this cave within arm's reach of Cotys's bones, Harry had an idea.

He turned back to the wall and stepped closer, reaching out and finding the cave walls cold when he touched them. That chill running up his arm now didn't come from the cool stone wall under his fingers. His muscles tightened a fraction and he stuck his other hand out, tracing the sun's contours, running a fingernail along the grooves. What if this wasn't merely a carving? It was too simple. Too small. Too *common*. This man had ruled a nation. He wouldn't have been laid to rest for eternity with a just couple of wall carvings and a few lines of text to accompany him. There had to be more.

Call it a hunch, or call it plain stubbornness, but Harry could feel it. This wasn't Cotys's entire message. Not by a long shot. *But what now?* If those carved lines were any guide, the answer lay right in front of him.

Harry narrowed his eyes. The sun etching looked off. A half-circle at the horizon had lines emanating outward to represent rays or warmth or light; straight lines, all the same length. Or *nearly* so. One sunbeam had a decoration on the end. Two tiny lines coming from the tip, both pointed back toward the sun. It looked an awful lot like an arrow. Harry blinked. A directional arrow, pointing to his right. To a dark corner of the cave.

Harry went to the closest portable light and slid it around so the beam illuminated that corner. It revealed a new treasure. "Why is there a rope here?" he asked the still air.

A braided rope had been wound in a circle and hung on a stone outcropping. There was nothing else around it, no tools, no markings on the wall. Just that single rope, tied at one end into a loop. The thing looked ancient, old enough to have been left by the Thracians who had built this tomb. Interesting, but why?

"What good is a rope in this cave?"

The cave walls responded. The answer was literally on the wall. Cotys had chosen his words carefully.

"It's about Spartacus," Harry said to himself. "About him coming to Thrace's rescue. Rising to the occasion, ascending to glory. Rising, ascending."

Harry craned his neck toward the roof of the cave. It was, of course, pitch black, so he twisted the portable lamp upward. The breath left his lungs. "That's a hook."

A rusted metal hook hung from the cave ceiling twenty feet overhead. A hook that rope could reach if Harry threw it high enough. And if he aimed it just right, he could catch the looped end on the hook so the rope would hang straight down. A way to *ascend* inside this cave. And was there a dark patch on the wall near the hook? Almost like a small opening?

Harry lifted the rope off the outcropping, hefting it in his hand. He ran the length of it between his hands, testing. The fibers held strong, or seemed to after so many centuries. It should hold his weight. Probably.

Dragging the rope until he stood beneath the hanging hook, Harry took hold of it near the looped end and started swinging it in a circle, gaining momentum until he threw it skyward toward the hook. The loop brushed against the hook but didn't catch. Harry jumped out of the way as it slithered back to earth. Harry cursed as he gathered it up and started swinging again, round and round, then threw it again toward the hook.

It caught. One tug, two tugs, and still it held. Harry pulled and started climbing before his self-preservation instincts could kick in. Fibers frayed and metal creaked with each pull as he went higher. He never looked down, reaching and lifting until the cave's stone ceiling was only inches above his head. And now he could see it: what had looked like a spot on the wall below the ceiling was far more.

It was an opening. A black void in front of his face, big enough for a man to walk through. In fact, someone already had. There was a handhold just inside the opening. Close enough that he could grab it to haul himself through, if he could swing himself over to it. Harry gritted his teeth. The rope had held so far. It would stand up to a few swings.

Legs dangling, he kicked toward the opening, then away from it, using his weight to swing back toward the opening with one arm outstretched. His fingers brushed the metal handhold, then he lost it.

Back away from the opening he went, kicking for distance until the rope had stretched to its limit. Harry swung himself back at the opening with enough speed to propel him into the opening. Or at least he thought so until a *snap* filled the cave.

The rope broke and he dropped like a stone. He reached for the handhold, too far away with him falling too fast to solid stone bel—

He got it. Aching fingers latched onto the bar and held tight. Dangling from the opening nearly snapped his forearm as his legs flew out. His shout echoed inside the stone chamber as he threw his other hand up to grab the bar. He kicked one leg up to clamber over the lip of the opening and up to safety. He flipped over, the stone cold on his neck as he gasped for breath, his chest rising and falling. He'd made it.

Made it where? The question made him sit up like a shot. The flashlight came off his belt and fired to life. A natural cavern stretched out ahead for perhaps twenty feet before the ground disappeared. He stretched his arms out on either side, fingers nearly touching the walls.

Harry got to his feet and moved deeper into the cavern with cautious steps. A wall lay ahead, and the roof in this small space dropped sharply down to block his path. Only when he was nearly at the wall did he see the stairs cut into the rock, stairs leading down in a treacherously steep route deep into the mountainside. A path on roughly hewn steps only a fool would walk down.

A fool like him. It's not as though he had another choice. The rope had broken. How else was he getting out of here?

He moved to the first step. An instant before his foot touched the stone, he spotted it: Latin writing, carved into the wall to one side at eye level. A sixth sense, honed in jungles and ancient temples and on sturdy castle walls, made him go still. Cotys would have protected this tunnel. Harry turned his light on the lettering and read it aloud.

Honor Cotys. Do not tarnish his name.

How could Harry do that? His light swept over the steps leading into darkness below, then across the walls and ceiling, even the floor behind him. No other writing, no marks or engravings. Only this single line of text written where it was hard to miss. Though Harry nearly had.

Harry knelt and leaned out over the edge of the first step to check the vertical front of it. The stone steps were as smooth as hand-hewn stone could be, which is to say not very. He stood and blinked. Think, Harry. Those sentences held the clue. *Honor Cotys.* How did you honor a person? By acknowledging their greatness. By speaking highly of their deeds. Somehow, he needed to traverse these steps without walking all over Cotys's name.

"The *fourth*. Cotys was the fourth of his name." How could Harry honor the king if his only option was to walk down the steps? By avoiding every fourth step, perhaps?

Hard to tell without stepping where he shouldn't. If that even mattered. The message might have an entirely different meaning. He believed in himself, always had, a belief that one day would undoubtedly get him in real trouble. Except he didn't think it was today.

First step first. He leaned down to inspect it, feeling gently for any hidden crevices or disguised holes, an indication it was more than it seemed. Finding nothing, he pressed on it. Gently at first, then harder, until he was trying to push through the stone. Still nothing. It was a step, that's all. A wide step, at least three times as wide as modern ones. He stood and put his weight on it. Nothing happened other than he was now one step closer to whatever lay below.

He took another step down: same result. Then another. Harry knelt to inspect the fourth step. He tapped the stone with his fist, lightly at first, then with more force. The sound made him stop. He rapped on the step beneath his feet, the third one down. A dull *thud* sounded. He tapped the fourth step again. No thud this time.

"It's hollow." He tapped different parts of the fourth step, with the same result each time. Harry reached across it, down to the fifth step, and got a solid thud once more. "This one is hollow," he told himself. It appeared as though a narrow strip of stone had been laid down to make it look like the step was normal, at least until someone stepped on it, which was when the funny stuff probably started.

The next set of four steps repeated the process. Three solid steps followed by a hollow one. Harry suspected falling through one of the fake steps would do more than send him careening down the steep incline. The tumble could break his neck, though he suspected he'd be dead before the tumbling started. Spikes, or maybe flames? He shuddered. He'd seen that and more, all of it deadly.

The staircase curved around as it descended, taking him on a path that by his estimates led back to ground level. As he rounded the last turn, he leaned around the wall and aimed his light ahead, expecting to see the rear side of the cave wall behind Cotys's tomb, the one with engravings on it. He found light instead.

One second his flashlight showed a dusty stone floor. The next, brilliant light exploded in the darkness. Harry snapped his eyes shut against the onslaught and instinctively backed away.

Onto one of the false steps.

He froze, his foot barely touching the hollow stone. A look down revealed a hairline crack had appeared on the surface. Bracing one hand against the wall, he slowly lifted his foot, not breathing or even blinking as his boot came off the stone to leave only that single crack running through it. The fake stone held.

Dust billowed as he exhaled. *Too close.* Harry looked back up at the shimmering light that had blinded him. He thought he was ready for it this time, eyes narrowed, senses alert. He had no idea what it was.

Harry's chest went still. This wasn't natural light. It was *golden*, bathing the entire room, a cave that hadn't seen light for two thousand years.

"Aquila." The word sprang to his lips. "It's an aquila."

A majestic golden eagle stared back at him with unnerving intensity. An eagle that had sent shivers down men's spines two thousand years ago as it stood at the forefront of a Roman legion. Broad wings spread out as though the great bird were readying to take flight, and though the golden wingtips were scarcely a foot apart, the brilliant metal burned bright under Harry's flashlight. The eagle stood mounted on an outcropping, this one far too smooth and straight to be natural. Cotys had carved this into the wall specifically to display the aquila.

Harry checked the floor and found it unremarkable. Only then did he move to the golden eagle. Another check found the ledge it sat atop was only that, not the trigger for an attack. The rock surrounding him seemed to press closer as Harry reached for the eagle, picking it up with only a hint of hesitation, and when nothing tried to kill him, he moved his light all around to get a better view.

An exquisite piece of craftsmanship, it wasn't overly large, yet power emanated from the piece like almost nothing he'd ever seen. Entire armies would go still at the sight of the aquila, for behind it came the greatest fighting force in the ancient world, five thousand Roman soldiers ready for battle. A nearly undefeatable force that trampled entire nations. A force that had been decimated by a ragtag group of slaves led by Spartacus.

He turned the aquila upside down to reveal two engraved letters on the bottom, one on each foot.

L. G.

Lucius Gellius. It had to be. The Roman general who had led a legion against Spartacus during the Third Servile War. A legion twice defeated in battle by the slave army.

He barely believed it. He was holding an actual aquila, one that could be traced to a specific legion in history. None was thought to have survived to the present day. This was the only one of its kind in the world.

This was big. And it was far too dangerous to take the aquila out of the cave now. He had to come back when there were no witnesses. He only trusted one person in Bulgaria—himself. Not Taxiarchis Limnios, a man he'd only met today and whom even Gary Doyle didn't fully trust. Harry would come back here tonight—alone—and retrieve the aquila. Only then would he consider whom to tell. Probably Gary Doyle. Beyond that, no one. A discovery of this magnitude could easily prove deadly to the finder if word got out to the wrong people.

Speaking of which, he needed to do that. Get out. He'd been in here long enough. If Tax came back and found the misplaced rope and Harry nowhere in sight, he'd think the worst, and he wouldn't be far off. Harry returned the eagle to its perch before the truth hit him. *How am I going to get out of here now?* The rope had broken, and jumping twenty feet down to a stone floor was asking for a broken ankle at best.

He frowned and turned his flashlight toward the wall. There had to be another exit that didn't risk a broken neck. The wall in front of him was nothing but smooth rock. He flipped his light to the other side of the pedestal. He stopped. *That's more like it.*

A section of the wall about the size of a shoebox had been cut out. A stone handle was just inside the opening. A handle that would be directly behind the carved image of Cotys with a sword in hand that was in the cavern. Had that carving concealed a door? It must have, though he'd missed it earlier. It would save a lot of trouble if he could slip through a hidden door to get back here to the eagle. He reached for the handle, hesitating an instant before grasping the cold stone and pulling. It didn't budge. He pulled harder, fired off a few choice words, then switched gears and shoved it forward.

Stone gears grated and rumbled. His teeth rattled for a beat before dust wafted across his face from a far corner of the chamber. The corner concealed a hidden door. The door hung open now, and when Harry poked his head around the opening, he found himself staring at the spot on the wall from where he'd removed the rope only minutes before. The door had been concealed in the darkness, hinged inside the wall so that you couldn't see the opening even if you stood directly in front of it. Harry stepped through, then pulled the door shut behind him. It closed on squeaking hinges, locking so tightly the lines vanished and he couldn't see the door outline even knowing it was there.

No sign of Tax. Harry walked around the cave, scuffing out his footprints near the hidden door. He picked up the broken rope and erased his footprints from around it before bundling it back over the outcropping so it looked like nobody had touched it. Nothing he could do about the frayed length dangling overhead. Hopefully Tax wouldn't notice, and when Harry came back tonight with his own rope, he could pull that piece of evidence down. Then he could figure out how to bring Tax into the loop about his find. Harry didn't intend to keep the aquila for himself. He only needed to figure out who he could tell: someone who wouldn't have him thrown in jail. Or worse.

He hurried down the mountainside toward camp. Just in time, too. Tax came out of the main tent, and Harry hustled down to deter him from suggesting they head back to the cave right then.

"I'm done for now," Harry said before Tax could speak. "Amazing place. I need to research the carvings before we go back in. I can get back in there, right?"

"Why, yes." Tax looked Harry up and down. "Did you fall?"

"What?"

"Your clothes." Tax pointed at Harry's shirt, then his pants. "They are dirty."

Harry looked down. His clothes were caked with grime, his arms and boots as dusty as the tomb's floor. He looked up and laughed. "I like to get close to whatever I'm looking at. Easier to see the details."

"I see." Tax said he did, but Harry suspected the Greek found him odd. "What are your thoughts?"

Harry crossed his arms on his chest. He stared up at the cave for several long, silent seconds. "I think there's more to find," he finally said.

That was true. "Although I'm not sure what it is." Not even close to true. "I'll have a better idea tomorrow. Am I allowed back inside in the morning?"

"I will see to it that you are."

Harry turned back to face the camp, but Tax lingered, his eyes still on the cave above.

"Is there anything I should see now?" Tax asked.

Harry almost felt bad for him. Almost. "Not right now. Let me dig into this and tomorrow we'll check it out together."

Tax's face fell, though he recovered quickly. "Very well."

Harry started walking toward the base camp, and Tax followed. "What happened with the government people?" Harry asked him.

The familiar scowl reappeared under Tax's mustache. "Permits. Always with the government it is permits, and each permit has a fee."

As they walked down to the tent, Tax offered his thoughts on government officials all the while, his words hot enough that no mention was made of returning to the cave today. Harry let him go until the steam ran out. By then they were passing the main tent.

"Glad it worked out," Harry said. "Excavating archaeological sites is expensive work."

"Not nearly as expensive as keeping the treasures here where they belong."

Harry chose to ignore that one. He stuck his hand out. "Thanks for your help today. Until tomorrow morning?"

Tax clasped Harry's hand. "Tomorrow morning."

He said Harry could arrive any time after the sun rose, which in truth sounded horrifically early, but Harry said he'd be there. Movement caught Harry's eye as he turned to leave. A figure moving alongside one of the smaller tents set up at base camp. A dark figure. Harry stopped, looking hard at the shape. The outline of a man he recognized. One of the men Tax said handled the camp food supply. The one who had asked about the camp historian. As Harry watched, the man stood and turned to look across the camp site. Did his eyes linger on Harry? Hard to say, but it seemed as if they did. Before Harry could get a better look the man pulled a phone from his pocket and walked out of sight, the device pressed to his ear.

Harry turned on a heel and headed for his vehicle. Enough questionable characters had populated Harry's life for him to know when someone deserved close attention. That food guy and his buddy were near the top of the list. He couldn't say why other than they set off his radar, a warning system that had kept him alive through some serious scrapes. Was he off base? Maybe. Should he ignore his instincts? Not a chance.

Dirt and pebbles crunched underfoot as he headed for the exit gate. Harry tucked his chin down low, hands jammed in his pockets, leaning against the stiff breeze as he passed an opening in the metal fence. Harry stopped and twisted to look back at the camp site. Something wasn't right.

The clouds of vapor coming out of his mouth vanished as his breath died in his throat. A man stood by the main tent, staring directly at Harry. Another man he knew. The second food guy.

The man didn't look away. Instead, he raised an arm in greeting. Harry did not lift his arm in return. He turned and he walked off the dig site, mind churning with questions. He would find some answers tonight. Others would have to wait; those answers could prove dangerous.

Chapter 10

Bulgaria

A shard of moonlight illuminated the slumbering dig site; and the moonlight highlighted a shadow that moved near the fencing surrounding the site. If anyone had been there to listen, they would have heard boots crunching over wild brush, breath coming fast, and a colorful English curse word when the shadow ran into an unseen boulder.

Harry rubbed his shin. Stupid rocks. The mountainside shrubs and wild grass covered the landscape thickly enough to hide both him and any rocks he could run into. It made for slow going, but he needed to get around the fencing and into the dig site unnoticed by the two guards at the front gate. Both were more interested in staying out of the elements than in scanning the upper reaches of the site for intruders. They hadn't poked their heads out of the small shed by the gate since he'd first crept up the mountainside a half-hour earlier to make his way around the fencing. Harry's car waited behind a row of thick trees, well off the road where no one could spot it. His path back would only be more challenging with a heavy golden eagle in tow. A burden he would be happy to carry.

Bare tree limbs swayed as he approached the far end of the camp's perimeter fence. A single lamp atop the last steel fencepost hardly pushed back the darkness as Harry skirted its pool of light and made his way toward the camp. The terrain funneled down toward several smaller tents. It would be impossible to access the tomb entrance without passing behind them, although all of them were dark and apparently empty. Tax had told him earlier today that nobody lived on site; the only people here at night were the front guards.

Flashes of moonlight came and went as black clouds lumbered across the dark sky. The length of climbing rope looped across his torso kept Harry vigilant for snags and obstructions as he moved, keeping the tents between himself and the guards, staying on the balls of his feet and moving slowly. Too slowly for his taste, but it was not yet midnight and the first camp inhabitants wouldn't arrive until after dawn. Enough time for Harry to get the aquila and figure out who he should trust.

A half-open tent flap snapped in the wind as he knelt behind the last structure before the open ground ahead. The guards turned only periodically to look toward the tomb entrance. Chances were they wouldn't see him if he stayed low to the ground. Taking that chance could work in his favor. Or get him shot.

Harry took off. Crouching low, moving as fast as he dared, he crossed the uneven terrain toward the path. Pain arced up his calves as the ground sloped sharply upward. A few missteps had him throwing his hands out for balance as he moved, his footsteps booming in his ears like thunder, surely loud enough to get the guards' attention. He paused on the hillside and looked back. No movement from the guard shed. He forged on, passing the sheer wall of stone and looping around until the tomb entrance was in front of him.

His boots left tracks in the recently fallen snow as he entered the mountainside. Once he was well into the cave, he donned a headlamp and turned on its low red light.

The tomb walls came to life in the reddish glow. Two images of Cotys, the inscription, the tomb. All just as he'd left it. He unwound his new climbing rope, looped it around his torso and over his head, and then he tripped.

His foot landed on something hard. Harry jumped back as though it were a snake. One hand balled into a fist before he realized. *It's only the broken rope*. He was standing beneath the hook latched to the ceiling, the one he'd used to climb to Cotys's hidden exit. The chunk of rope must have fallen after he left. He picked the fragment up and buried it inside the rest of the ancient rope he'd used earlier.

He leaned back, holding one end of the new climbing line in one hand as he began whirling it in larger and larger circles. The end of his rope had a knot looped in it, which he threw up toward the hook above. It caught on the first try. He tugged, found it secure, and began climbing hand over hand until he could swing over to the hidden opening, making it easily this time. He unhooked his rope and looped it over his torso once more before following the red light on his forehead down the stairs, avoiding every fourth step. The tunnel didn't seem so narrow this time around. The eagle of Lucius Gellius, however, shone just as brightly.

A small shoulder bag tucked beneath his jacket held the eagle perfectly. The strap dug into his shoulder to remind him of the weight he now carried. One hand went for the recessed door handle, then paused in the air, not pulling the handle, not doing anything. Harry pulled his hand back. A thought that had been buzzing at the edge of his mind finally came into clear view. *There must be more.*

The message from Cotys focused more on Spartacus than on the king himself. Spartacus was the larger focus, as Spartacus represented Cotys's ideal Thracian, a man possessing the type of strength and steadfast determination the nation required to stay alive in the face of overwhelming Roman power.

Harry looked at the eagle tucked in his bag. A symbol of Roman power, immensely important, yet the voice in Harry's head said there was more to find. He'd learned not to ignore that voice. His hand went to the amulet around his neck. *What do you think, Dad?*

Fred Fox would tell him to trust his gut, right up until he shouldn't. Right now, his instincts said there was time. He could afford to look around.

He looked at the pillar on which he'd found the aquila. He stepped close and scrutinized it, clearing the dust off with his hand. Letters carved into the flat surface. Latin.

Travel the golden river to the high fortress. At the temple of the false king follow the Thracian son to honor the next triumph, safe below Bendis.

The Latin letters told a story he could read. Understand? Not at all.

He could decipher it later. Harry snapped a photo of the message with his phone, waited for his vision to clear, then yanked the door handle. A *whoosh* of air accompanied the hidden door as it opened. He was adjusting the shoulder bag as he stepped through the door, which is why it didn't register at first. Only when he reached back to pull the door closed behind him did his mind catch up with his ears. Voices. There were people in the tomb. A tomb now filled with red light.

Harry went still as the words stopped. Two red lights turned on him, a ghostly face beneath each, crimson eyes reflected in his light. Two men were standing in the middle of the tomb. One of them held the length of broken rope in his hands.

That man spoke. "There you are."

Harry knew that voice. *The food guy.* The bald one he'd overhead speaking to Tax earlier today. Harry didn't hesitate. The way to convince people you belonged in a place you didn't was simple: act like you did.

"You're not supposed to be in here." Harry barked the words and leveled a finger at the big bald guy. "Don't touch anything."

Neither man moved. "Why are you here?" baldie asked.

"I'm with the Greek government," Harry fired back. "I'm supposed to be working here. The food team isn't." Harry pulled himself up to his not-overly-impressive full height. "Who's your supervisor? I need to ask them what's going on."

Baldie's mouth curled into a sneer. "You are the one who will answer."

The words kicked at Harry's brain. Why did this guy have a Russian accent? "I'm supposed to be here," Harry repeated. "Now get your boss on the phone." He pushed his luck. "You two trying to rob the tomb?

That's a fast way to get tossed in jail."

Bad idea. "You are the thief," baldie said. "What is in your bag?"

"Tools," Harry said. He waved a hand at the guy and reached into his pocket. "Enough of this. I'm calling Tax."

"Stop." The smaller man this time, a guy who not only had hair, but was faster than he looked. No sooner had the word come out than a blade appeared in his hand. "Answer the question. Or end up like the last one."

Harry gulped. *That's no kitchen knife.* And was the *last one* the dead roommate tied to the governor? Sounded like it. "What's the matter with you?" Harry said. "Put that down."

"You are a treasure hunter," baldie said. "Where is the treasure?"

The smaller guy angled his head. "What is that on your neck? It looks like gold."

Harry reached up and felt his amulet, now hanging outside his shirt. It must have come out during his climb. "It's fake," he blurted out.

Both men were sneering now. "We will take it. It is a king's treasure."

Harry blinked as the men moved toward him. Baldie was a lot bigger than he'd realized, but he could have been King Kong and it wouldn't have mattered. Not when they were after his father's amulet. Harry reached toward his neck. "You want it? Here, take it. It's brass, you morons."

They hesitated. Only a breath or two, but enough for Harry to step close enough to pull the shoulder bag over his head, whip it around and connect with a deadly *thunk* on the side of short guy's head. He went down in a heap. Baldie didn't have time to react before Harry had the bag back over his head and his trusty knuckledusters on his hand.

"The bag." Baldie spoke between two upraised fists. "It is the bag I want, not the necklace."

Harry didn't say a word; he just flicked his headlamp from red light to white and charged. Baldie's guttural roar reverberated around the tomb as he covered his besieged eyes and loosed a wild haymaker. Harry ducked easily as a meaty fist whooshed harmlessly overhead, then fired his armored knuckles up at baldie's head. The jab landed smack on baldie's nose. Cartilage cracked, blood spurted, and the big goon hardly moved. Harry fired another jab at his gut, again with no effect. Baldie growled, firing punches rapidly as Harry juked and dodged all of them—except one. That caught him flush on the cheek. He stumbled back, went to one knee, then jumped up and backed out of the way.

Baldie came at Harry with his fists up.

Harry had been in more than a few boxing gyms in his day. A kid who looked half-Pakistani growing up in an Italian neighborhood had to if he wanted to survive. Experienced fighters were easy to spot if you knew what to look for. A couple of punches was all it took. In this case, one punch. Baldie knew how to throw them, and when he came bouncing in at Harry, light on his feet and his head moving, Harry had seen enough. Fighting smart was better than fighting hard. Definitely against a brute like this one.

Harry turned and ran. Strength hurt, but speed killed. At least he hoped so.

Harry ran for the hidden door. It hung slightly open: the rope he'd dropped in his surprise at seeing the two intruders had prevented the door from closing. The door flew open as he smashed into it, careful not to kick the rope away as he slowed on the other side, listening for and hearing crashing footsteps. Baldie was close on his tail.

Harry flicked his headlamp from white to red light and dashed toward the stairs, stopping at the bottom. He looked back to see baldie bull-rush through the hidden opening, knocking the thick stone door aside as though it were hollow. He shouted in that incongruent Russian accent and gave chase. Harry darted up the first three stairs just seconds ahead of baldie, then pretended to stumble and leapt over the fourth step up. He hesitated again as baldie reached the steps, then went full speed ahead, deftly repeating his three-steps-stumble-miss-a-step maneuver.

Harry was up and over the second false stair when it happened. The sound of baldie's pounding feet and his growling threats were suddenly cut off, and the cavern echoed with a shrill cry that ended abruptly.

Harry stopped and turned to look back down the stairs. The fourth step from the bottom had vanished. The hole in its place was wide enough to swallow a man, even one as big as baldie, and when Harry made his way to the newly created hole he froze in astonishment. The edges of the hole were smooth, meaning the design was clearly intentional, and the bottom of the trap, maybe ten feet down, bristled with cruel metal spikes. Harry didn't look too long at what used to be baldie.

One long, cautious step took him over the deadly hole as he headed back to the bottom of the stairs. He flicked the white headlight back to red, pausing to listen for any sign that baldie's partner had woken up. He heard none. The chase with baldie couldn't have taken more than a minute or two—possibly enough time for the other guy to get up, possibly not. No noise was good news, so Harry headed for the open door. He'd close it behind him. Baldie's partner had either vanished or was lying there, and if he had any brains he'd be long gone before the sun came up. Harry could walk back into the cave later that morning with Tax and "discover" the hidden access route, and together they would find baldie in his grave. How did he get there? Harry would only shrug. A thief with treasure on his mind who had ventured one step too far.

Harry slipped through the hidden door. He knelt to retrieve his climbing rope. Light exploded across the tomb.

"*Ne dvigaysya!*"

Harry didn't speak Russian, but he didn't need to understand it to know what that meant. He needed to get out of the light fast.

He darted for the tomb exit. If he could get outside, he guessed this second guy wouldn't risk being spotted on the mountainside chasing Harry toward camp. Harry's presence in the tomb at this odd hour could be explained away. The two alleged food supply guys, not so much. Whoever they really were, they wouldn't want attention. He needed to get out of here and get closer to camp, and then he was home—

A gunshot erupted. Fire flashed, metal whined through the air and a volley of sparks exploded off the cave wall mere feet behind Harry.

So much for avoiding attention. This guy was either crazy or desperate. Harry skidded to a halt as another shot blasted through the tomb, a bullet shrieking past his head. Escaping through the tomb entrance wasn't happening. Harry flicked his headlamp off, took two more steps toward the tomb exit and the gunman near it, then reversed course and barreled toward the hidden door concealing Cotys's treasure room. There, he scooped up the rope and pulled the door silently shut behind him.

His headlamp came back on, the eerie red light washing over smooth walls, an empty pedestal, and the broken step ahead concealing a fresh corpse. The red light matched the growing fury in Harry's gut. Who were these guys? How did they know there was more to this tomb—and Harry's interest in it—than everyone else did? He might be able to get at least one answer tonight—if the gunman in the cave hadn't run away yet.

Up the stairs he went, skipping the false ones, not sparing a glance down at baldie's skewered corpse. He slowed to a quick walk in the overhead tunnel, then moved silently to the edge, where he looked down on and heard a thoroughly confused gunman talking to himself in Russian, likely wondering how the guy he was after had vanished through a stone wall.

The corner of Harry's mouth turned up. *Now walk over here where I can see you.*

More muttering, closer this time. Harry crouched at the lip of the entrance, eyeing the floor twenty feet below. Not a bad drop if you planned ahead. The Russian grumbling grew louder, and a moment later the gunman walked into view, his head moving left and right as he studied the walls. He did a complete circle and looked in every direction but up. *Keep walking, keep walking...now.*

Harry jumped. No shouts, nothing but the soft *whoosh* of a man leaping off a perfectly solid floor into thin air and a two-story fall. He flew feet first at the gunman. He did not miss.

Harry's boots crashed into the gunman's back. The gun went flying; the gunman went down flat onto the stone floor. Something cracked, perhaps a rib or two, and the gunman wheezed as the air left his lungs.

Harry bounced off and rolled to the side, jumped up and grabbed the nearby gun, standing tall as he aimed down at the shooter.

The guy didn't budge. Harry crept closer and nudged him with the toe of a boot. No response other than the slow rise and fall of his chest. The guy wasn't dead. Being knocked out two times in one night wouldn't do much for his cognitive abilities, and it definitely hadn't helped his aim. Harry turned to study the pockmarks in the stone wall, evidence of this man's appalling marksmanship. Harry shook his head. He'd been lucky this time. Next time he'd be more careful. He grinned. *I always say that.*

The door he'd vanished through remained resolutely shut. His plan could still work. If baldie's partner had any sense, he'd run as far from this cave as possible, leaving his dead partner for someone else to handle. Harry could still rediscover the roof entrance tomorrow, Tax at his side, and let Tax find the corpse. It could still work.

As Harry obscured the footprints their battle had left, he saw only one real victim in this scenario. Or, more accurately, a whole bunch of victims: all the people in camp who would go hungry when their food delivery men failed to show up in the morning.

Tax stared at Harry through narrowed eyes. "You intend to climb up there." Tax's index finger extended toward the ceiling of Cotys's tomb. "On that rope." Now the digit aimed at the climbing rope around Harry's shoulder.

Harry shrugged. "Looks sturdy enough to me." He did glance down near Tax's feet, now standing on the spot where Harry had crashed into the shooter last night after his leap from above. A shooter who had apparently done the smart thing and vanished.

Tax's mustache danced a caterpillar-like jitterbug on his lip. "I do not think this is wise."

"I'm not worried." Harry took the rope off his shoulder. He did not look at the pockmarked wall to one side where the bullets had hit last night. The wall wasn't smooth to begin with, making the bullet marks difficult to spot. "Besides, you'll catch me if I fall. Won't you?"

Tax's eyes grew round. Harry winked. "I won't fall. Now stand back."

The pre-knotted rope looped around and around as Harry got up a head of steam before flinging it toward the hook above. It caught on the first throw. Again, Tax had no reason to suspect his American guest had more experience at this than it appeared. "I'll go up first," Harry said after making a show of tugging on the rope to check that it held. "Coming up with me?"

Tax and his mustache frowned as he tugged the rope. "Yes. I will follow you. If it holds."

"It'll hold." Harry's suspicion about Tax had been correct. Overweight as he was, the guy wasn't the sort to spend all day behind a desk. Or on the ground, in this case. Not when there was an ancient tomb to explore. "You want to go first so I can hold the rope steady for you?"

Hidden lips may have curled up. "I know how to climb a rope, Harry."

"Good man." That settled, Harry grabbed the thin mountaineering rope and hauled himself skyward. Seconds after reaching the top and swinging himself into the opening—with a practiced grace this time—Tax had scaled the rope with an agility belying his size and had hold of Harry's outstretched hand, pulling himself safely into the passage's entrance.

"Take one." Harry removed a pair of headlamps from his coat pocket and offered one to Tax. "Ever find a hidden path in a tomb before?"

Tax strapped the lamp onto his head. "No." He touched the on switch and the bulb flared to life. "Nobody has."

"I have." Harry turned his own light on. "That's why I'll go first." Harry made it several steps before he realized Tax wasn't following. "What's wrong?" he asked.

Tax's face was that of a man who had stumbled into an underworld he didn't quite believe in. "Do you believe it is dangerous?"

"If you were King Cotys and you wanted to hide something so badly you made a tunnel like this, would you leave it unprotected?"

Tax considered the question. "I would not."

"Neither would I. Yes, I think it could be dangerous. That's why I'm going first. Stay behind me. If anything happens, get out and come back with an ambulance."

He turned and left Tax to chew on that one. "There are steps," Harry called over a shoulder. He stopped at the first one, waiting until Tax stood close behind him. "Look." Harry pointed at the writing on the wall as though seeing it for the first time. "It says '*Honor Cotys. Do not tarnish his name.*'"

Tax gently shouldered Harry aside for a better look. "What does it mean?"

A suitable period of false contemplation before Harry revealed the solution. Tax offered to go first and Harry looked at him yet again through fresh eyes. Brave guy. "It's my theory," Harry said. "I'll test it out." He didn't quite make it to the first false step before he stopped again. "Hey, Tax." Harry put a heavy dose of concern in his voice. "We're not the first ones to use these steps."

Harry leaned over the broken step near the bottom and began *tap tap tapping* each false step to confirm it was hollow. Baldie's corpse elicited a suitably horrified response from Tax, who quickly recognized the man as the camp's provider of food. Drawing back, a look of horror on his face, Tax declared that he wanted to go back. Harry convinced him to press on. That led them to the empty pillar with writing on it and the hidden door.

Harry acted appropriately shocked at each finding.

They made their way back to the cave's exterior, where Tax asked Harry to stand guard while he went back to gather reinforcements from the camp and notify the authorities. The sun snuck out from behind steel-gray clouds as Harry stood at the tomb's threshold and watched Tax hurtle down the hill. He turned his face toward the meager warmth for a beat before his gaze snapped back to the panoramic view of the Bulgarian mountainside. One of those people milling below might not be who they seemed. Was the man who tried to shoot him down there, waiting for another chance? Probably not, but in this sort of game, Harry only had to be wrong once.

His phone buzzed. A message from Sara. *Are you okay?*

He smiled slightly, despite himself. Sara was worried about him. She might not like the fact he'd agreed to this wild goose chase—a theory now disproven, though he wouldn't rub it in—and she might be up to her eyeballs in work, but she still cared. An urge to respond in kind overtook him. His fingers flashed as a message took shape, then hovered over the *SEND* button. Sara was different from most women. Heck, different from all the ones Harry knew. Sara didn't want to hear how much he missed her. She knew he did, same as she missed him.

He deleted the message. An obvious replacement leapt to mind. Two short sentences, followed by one more. Perfect.

He fired it off. The cryptic message carved under the aquila would make Sara happier than anything he could come up with. A new mystery to solve. And proof he'd been correct about visiting Bulgaria.

Not that he'd rub it in.

A response arrived faster than expected. *Can you talk?*

He said it would have to wait until he could get away. The questions came rapid fire now, most of them mirroring Harry's own thoughts, formed on the way back to camp this morning. *No rivers are made of gold. It may be mineral deposits in it or nearby. No high fortress I know of in Thrace. Temple might tie in with fortress.*

All thoughts he'd had, but none he could verify right now. He needed time to research the possible meanings. There would be plenty of action to come after that.

Harry looked up from his phone. Tax was on his way back, and it looked like half the camp was trying to follow. The Greek man had to stop and wave his arms about before the crowd following him turned and walked back down the mountainside, many with shoulders slumped. A trio of people continued walking forward with Tax. Harry decided on the spot he wouldn't reveal anything to them. No telling who they really were, even if Tax trusted them.

"These are the only archaeologists on site this morning," Tax said when he and his entourage made it to Harry's side. "They will oversee this new find."

Harry shook hands with a man and woman he'd never seen before. They started peppering him with questions until he raised a hand to quiet them.

"One second," Harry said, then lowered his voice and leaned toward Tax. "Who's the other guy?"

Tax looked past Harry to the third new arrival, a man in dusty clothes and sturdy boots who was carrying two thick coils of wire around his shoulders. The guy was not much bigger than Harry, but he walked as though the heavy load he carried didn't exist. Harry's eyes narrowed as the newcomer walked right past him without speaking and headed up to the tomb's entrance without as much as a glance in any direction.

"The camp electrician," Tax said. "We need more lighting."

"Good idea." Harry began making his own way toward the tomb's entrance, Tax at his side. "What do you want to know?" he asked the two archaeologists on his heels. The sooner he got through this, the sooner he could get to the real research that needed to be done.

Without waiting for them to respond, Harry entered the cave and pointed at the hidden entrance overhead, offering them an explanation of what they saw and how it had happened that would align with what Tax would say. The two were curious about what had initially made Harry look up at the hook in the ceiling. He shrugged. Better to leave that part alone.

Deftly changing the topic, he asked whether they wanted him to show them the deadly stairs. They practically shoved him through the hidden door in response, nearly tripping over the electrician kneeling inside the door, connecting wires and lights to help their search.

Harry didn't blink when light filled the hidden passageway. If he'd turned to look, he would have seen the electrician using a flashlight to illuminate the interior, then adjusting cables and going through the process again. If Harry had paid attention, he might have seen the electrician snap photographs of the inscription with his phone before continuing with his work. But Harry didn't notice, because who paid attention to electricians until the lights went out?

No one looked when the electrician stood and walked out of the cave. He stopped a distance from the entrance, pulled out his phone, and made a call. His voice was low when he spoke. His words, Russian.

"Boss, I have news. There is a hidden passage inside the cave." He gave the name of the dead food supply guy, then the name of the missing supply man. Their real names. "No, I do not know where he is. There is writing in the passage. I am sending it now."

A moment passed. Only after a voice sounded in his ear did he speak again, a short reply. "Understood. I will send anything else I find. And I will not lose the American."

Chapter 11

Paris

"Do I have five euros? Five? Do I have five euros for this incredible piece?"

The auctioneer's bow tie hung slightly askew as he belted out numbers in French. "Five euros?" His hand shot off the podium. "Five. I have five in the back—thank you, madam. Do I hear six euros? Six, for this exquisite chalk-on-paper landscape?"

Only a salesman or a relative of the artist would describe the artwork as "exquisite." One day in the future this artist's drawing might elicit such a description. Today was not that day.

"I have six euros from the gentleman in the back." The auctioneer nearly jumped at that bid. "Do I hear seven? Seven for this lovely work by"—and here he consulted a sheet of paper—"Miss Emilia Jennings of the elementary one class?"

A woman whose laugh-lined face was tucked beneath a hat of the sort Queen Elizabeth II had favored spoke up. "I bid seven."

"Going once. Going twice." The auctioneer's hammer—a tiny bell borrowed from the front desk—dinged with gusto. "Sold, for seven euros. Congratulations, madam."

The biannual art auction fundraiser at the local elementary school in this banlieue outside Paris was now truly underway. Parents and grandparents seated at desks meant for small humans offered bids for pieces of art created by their littlest family members. The muted shrieks of children out on the playground could be heard, at least when the janitor pushing a whirring floor polisher wasn't right outside the classroom now serving as an auction house. Works created with enthusiasm and occasionally even actual talent went from auction block to desktop in short order, all in the name of raising funds to purchase new art supplies for the classes.

The precocious works sold in short order. All of them, that is, until the very last one. This piece the auctioneer had intentionally put at the end. Perhaps the artist's mother was running late and this was the one day she had time off to attend. Or had not remembered to come at all. Young Wendie did not have a father listed in her records. Her mother was the only contact, although one rarely seen.

"Here is our final piece of the evening, ladies and gentlemen." The auctioneer placed said piece on the less-than-sturdy display stand. "A magnificent recreation of da Vinci's *Mona Lisa* done in green and yellow paint. Quite an original interpretation." He risked a look toward the audience. "Do I have one euro?"

Silence. The parents whose children played with Wendie at recess and after school looked around. Wendie's mother was not there.

"One euro for this fine work of art." Hope laced with a tinge of sadness filled the words. "All purchases support the art program for our wonderful students. Do I have one euro?"

A voice sounded from the last row of tiny desks. "Ten thousand euros."

The auctioneer blinked once. The yellowish light cast by the overworked sodium ceiling lights reflected off his teeth. "I did not see you, Mr. Lloris. Welcome."

Olivier Lloris dipped his chin in acknowledgment. "It's a steal at ten thousand."

The bell dinged. "Sold to Mr. Lloris for ten thousand euros."

With that, all the proud new owners stood and prepared to settle their bills with the auctioneer. A small stack of money had accumulated on his desk when Olivier collected his purchase.

"An excellent piece," he said as he took the small painting. "Would you see that the funds get to her parents?"

"Of course," the auctioneer said. "Her mother will appreciate it."

The envelope Olivier handed over overflowed with hundred-euro notes. "See you in six months."

Olivier felt eyes on him as he walked out, trying to meet each in turn and offer a smile or kind word. The parents and grandparents here tonight cared about the children, and despite the well-worn clothes on their backs, they shared what they could to make sure the children's school had an art program. Olivier's attendance at these auctions was not widely broadcast, a practice he preferred. His purchase tonight would remain private.

Brittle leaves crackled under his feet as he walked out of the small school and slid into the back seat of the waiting sedan. Olivier dialed Benoit Lafont's number as the vehicle pulled into traffic and accelerated back toward Paris. A ringing sounded before Benoit's cultured voice filled the air. "Good afternoon, Mr. Lloris."

"I don't have my bible yet."

"Ms. Leroux indicated it would take at least a week for delivery," Benoit said smoothly. "Is there reason for concern?"

"I don't like buying from someone I don't know." He hurried on before Benoit could respond. "I know you vouch for her. What I want to know is where she found the book and what else she has available."

Silence ensued. A strategy Olivier knew well. "You're going to tell me that's a bad idea," Olivier said.

"That is outside my purview," Benoit said. "However, as I mentioned earlier, Ms. Leroux's connections include the organized crime families in New York."

"I'm not stealing from her."

"Of course not. Though I assume you have made inquiries as to what else she possesses that you may wish to purchase?" Olivier's own silence was answer enough. Benoit sighed. "It is my experience that people in her business are not fond of others looking too closely into their affairs."

Olivier almost laughed. "Do you think I'm afraid of her?"

"Wise men act with caution in such matters. You, sir, are most certainly a wise man."

Benoit Lafont was also no fool. "I have been discreet, Benoit. She doesn't know of my inquiries."

"With all due respect, I would not count on that."

"I want to know what else she has," Olivier said. "And I want to know how she found it, and who is out there recovering artifacts no one else can find. I must know."

"You are in the position to purchase anything they locate," Benoit said. "As well as anything for sale at the auction tonight. I noted a Picasso will go under the hammer. You are interested?"

Olivier waved a dismissive hand. "I am. Don't change the subject." The asphalt rumbled beneath tires bearing his name. The same tires on millions of cars across Europe, an army of rubber with one purpose: to enrich Olivier Lloris. A barren tree threw spindly shadows through his window when his driver stopped at a traffic light. Sunlight snuck through the clouds for an instant. "Benoit, perhaps you're correct."

Benoit was never caught off guard. Almost. "Mr. Lloris?"

"You're right." Olivier's words picked up steam. "Moving outside one's orbit can be dangerous."

"A wise observation."

"Don't flatter me, Benoit. Enough people do that." Again, Benoit chose silence. "Reach out to Rose Leroux," Olivier said. "Openly. Inquire as to when she'll reveal any other artifacts tied to Charlemagne. The items she said her client intends to recover. Items on which"—and here Olivier's voice tightened—"the tides of history changed, as she put it. For those, I am an interested buyer."

"Of course, sir. You will hear from me."

Olivier clicked off. He wanted answers. If Benoit wouldn't provide them, Olivier would handle it himself. He pulled up another contact and made a call.

The phone did not ring for long. *"Signore."*

Olivier slipped into passable Italian. *"Buon pomeriggio."* Good afternoon. He switched to English, a common language between Olivier and the man on the phone. "Are you free?"

"A moment." The phone went silent for several beats before the voice returned. "That is better. What do you wish to speak about?"

"Information."

"Are you buying or selling?"

"We are old friends," Olivier said. "This must stay between us."

Carmelo Piazza may have left Sicily at some point in his life, but if he had, he didn't talk about it. His father had been an underboss in a local Cosa Nostra clan, one of nearly a hundred loosely affiliated groups who controlled territories on the island. Carmelo had followed in his father's footsteps, but his ambitions outstripped those of the old man.

Carmelo Piazza was now the boss of his clan, and through alliances and intimidation had become one of the most influential bosses on the island. He had built a network of contacts stretching across the oceans, including friends in Manhattan. If any of them could tell Olivier Lloris who was finding new artifacts, it was Carmelo.

"You know I collect antiquities." Olivier started with the truth. He intended to stay with it. "A new relic appeared on the market recently. I purchased it. Does the name Rose Leroux mean anything to you?"

Carmelo did not respond. He didn't hang up either, so Olivier waited.

"I'll take that as a yes," Olivier eventually said.

"You may continue."

"Rose Leroux sold me a bible that was once owned by Charlemagne. She hinted there are more relics to come, relics tied to that great king." The streets around Olivier were growing heavy with people as they drove closer to the heart of Paris. "I want to know who is finding these relics."

"Are you worried they are fakes?"

"No."

"Then what is your interest?"

"I want to know where the relics were found. Such a site interests me. As does the sort of person who can locate such pieces."

"You want to steal anything else there is to find, or you want to hire this person to do that for you."

Maybe both. For now, however, Olivier wanted the information. He didn't like not knowing all the players in this game. "Right now, all I want is a name. Can you get it?"

Carmelo grumbled in that Sicilian dialect Olivier could not decipher. "Rose Leroux is a woman to be respected," Carmelo eventually said. "Never manipulated, threatened or lied to."

"It almost sounds like she scares you. If that's true, I want to know why."

"Rose Leroux is the biggest fence in New York," Carmelo said. "She has many friends."

"Who does she work with?" Olivier asked.

"Everyone. Including the Morello family."

Olivier's eyebrows lifted. "Vincent Morello?"

"Joey Morello. Vincent's son. The new head of the family, and the *capo dei capi* of the New York families."

The boss of the bosses. "Damn."

"You see why I do not wish to discuss this."

"Is Rose protected?"

Carmelo chuckled. "Only a fool would cross Rose Leroux. She works with everyone, and everyone profits. I would rather betray the pope than her."

"I'm not interested in a fight. I want to know who is finding artifacts for her."

"Several people, though not as many as before. There are fewer suppliers of undocumented antiquities in New York than there used to be."

"How so?"

"The Albanian mob ceased to exist earlier this year. Altin Cana's family. They were one of Rose's best customers. Now it is the Italians, mainly the Morello family."

Joey Morello ran an empire. Men like him didn't dirty their hands, literally or figuratively. "Who gets the artifacts for Joey Morello?"

"I do not have that information at this time."

"But you can get it."

"Perhaps. It would require an intermediary."

"How long will it take?"

Carmelo didn't answer. Olivier's hand clenched into a fist as they slowed for yet another red light in the stop-and-go traffic that never seemed to lessen in Paris.

"I propose a new agreement," Carmelo finally said. "Consider any information I provide to be a token of my appreciation. For our friendship, and for future endeavors. Free of charge."

"I'm listening."

"I can get the information. I would also be unhappy if Joey Morello discovered I made inquiries regarding his business."

"I won't tell him."

"Why are you risking your health and my reputation for this name? You can bid on any artifact that comes to market without it."

Because Olivier didn't appreciate a glorified shopkeeper in New York baiting him with the promise of more artifacts to come, and forcing him to follow her timeline. Because, above all else, Olivier hadn't gotten where he was today by letting anyone stand in his way.

"That is my business. I'll wait for your call."

He clicked off before Carmelo could respond. The auction house where he hoped to add another Picasso to his private collection came into view. "The side entrance," Olivier said to his driver. "I have no wish to deal with anyone right now."

"Of course, sir."

Olivier straightened his tie. First, the Picasso. Then he would get to work on learning who had found these incredible new relics, after which he would speak with the seller. If they didn't want to work with him, well, Olivier could be quite persuasive.

His phone buzzed as the car slowed to a stop outside a side door to the auction house. A message from Carmelo. Olivier read it, then read it again. *Vindication.*

Olivier would have his answer soon. Carmelo's source was already at work uncovering the name he needed. The name of a person Olivier intended to speak with very soon.

Chapter 12

Bulgaria

"Are you in danger?"

Harry leaned back in the hotel room chair and took in the textured ceiling overhead. "Only of falling asleep and missing my flight. I'm wiped out."

"Get more coffee." Sara Hamed clearly had no time for his nonsense. "But first, tell me what you found."

He ran a hand across eyes that seemed to have a fine layer of sand over them. "A hidden passageway inside Cotys's tomb. I had to throw a rope onto a hook in the ceiling, climb up, then swing over to an opening that led to a set of steps." He detailed solving the riddle of how every fourth step was deadly. "There was something at the bottom of the steps."

"The message you sent me."

"Along with a hidden door leading back into the tomb." The wind kicked up outside his window. "And a Thracian battle prize."

Her words were breathless. "You didn't tell me that."

"An aquila."

"The standard of a Roman legion? None survived from antiquity. There aren't any left in the world."

"I'm looking at one right now." The golden standard gleamed dully even under hotel room lights. "Damn thing's heavy. Heavy enough to knock out a guy trying to shoot me."

"I assume he missed?"

"I'm quick on my feet."

"I'll finish the job for him unless you tell me everything right now."

He recapped finding the aquila, then returning after nightfall to discover the supply men in the cave before getting the literal drop on both men, sandwiched in between a shootout and his subsequent deception of Tax the next morning.

"Quick thinking all the way," Sara said when he finished. "Do you suspect Tax is involved?"

"I don't trust anybody here right now." He tapped a finger on the golden eagle. "The two supply guys had Russian accents. Not sure what that means, but I don't like it."

"They could be immigrants. Like me."

"Maybe. Maybe not."

"Tax will not be happy when he learns you took the aquila."

"I'll worry about that later. Being shot at is my good excuse."

"You cannot leave the country with it."

"What makes you think I'm leaving Bulgaria?"

"Two men tried to kill you. One of them is dead. The other is missing. You are not the sort to wait around for him to find you again."

All true. And all misdirection. "That's not why you think I'm leaving."

She didn't bother arguing. "No, it's not."

"You think I want to pursue this Cotys mess."

She hesitated, only for an instant. "That's correct; I do."

"The truth is I can't wait to get out of here and come back to Brooklyn. But I have other things to take care of."

"Such as using yourself as bait?"

His face tightened. "I mean finding out if Agilulph's bible is the first step on a longer path. I mean finishing the job Gary Doyle asked me to do because some kid connected to the governor of New York through six degrees of Kevin Bacon nonsense got himself killed in Bulgaria. I mean doing what I have to do to protect my family." *And you* almost rolled off his lips.

"All of which leads to you using yourself as bait."

"I still want to hear your thoughts on Agilulph's bible."

"I'm not yet certain what I think," Sara said. "I need another day. Two at most." She sighed like she meant it. "The museum is so busy. I haven't had the time."

"The world wants more of Sara Hamed."

"All of the world except for you."

"That's not fair. I want to work on Agilulph's bible with you."

Sara's words were heavy with fatigue. "Above all I want you to be safe. Pursuing a vendetta against Olivier Lloris is the antithesis of safe."

"So is following a Thracian king's trail at Gary's behest." Sara had more of a point than he wanted to admit. What was he doing in a Bulgarian hotel thousands of miles from the people he cared about? "I think I've had enough of Spartacus and Cotys. Gary can get out from behind his desk and do this himself."

He expected her to agree. To remind him about the new business he'd left, one being ignored just when things were really taking off. Clients with money to spend and friends to refer.

"No," Sara said. "He can't. You're the only one who can."

It took Harry a second to find his voice. "Hang on. You're defending him?"

"I'm stating a fact. Gary Doyle is not a world-class relic hunter."

Uh-oh. Flattery was never a good sign. "This relic hunter has other projects to focus on right now."

"You mean your antiquities business, which is currently being neglected?" There it was.

"I mean keeping my family and friends safe. Which includes you."

"Am I part of the family or the friends?"

He avoided that grenade of a question. "You're one of the very few people in this world I care enough about to risk everything I have."

"Then why don't you come back and run the business?"

"You just said you wanted me to help Gary."

"Don't tell me what I said. The least you can do is follow through on what you started over there."

His head was spinning. "Hang on. Are you saying you want me to help Gary with this Thracian mess, or come back and run the antiquities shop?"

"I'm saying Gary Doyle is your stepfather."

"Don't call him that," Harry said with an edge in his voice.

Sara wasn't interested. "It's a fact. He's a good man, and he asked for your help. Why? Nora has her hands full, and even if she didn't, she's not you. I'm not massaging your ego when I say very few people in the world could follow Cotys's trail. Gary needs you."

The wind kicked up again and clouds covered the sun over this part of Bulgaria. "What is it you want me to do?"

"Stand up for yourself, to start. You want to tempt Olivier Lloris with artifacts tied to Charlemagne? I don't like the idea, but I'll support you, because you're doing it to keep your family safe. Which should also include supporting Nora. Your sister."

"The last thing Nora wants is my help."

"Don't confuse her pride with indifference. Nora is proud, the same as you are. She's leading a new law enforcement team to preserve antiquities and cultural relics. She's busy, so her superior—your stepfather—asked you for assistance. If you want to support Nora, your mother and Gary, you'll help him."

"That's not what you said when I left." His jaw tightened. "Did Nora talk to you?"

"What Nora and I discuss is not your business." If he had to guess, a smile was now flitting across her face. "If we discussed anything, it was your safety, and how you work to keep others safe while taking unnecessary risks yourself."

"Such as coming to Bulgaria and investigating this Thracian mystery? Because that's what you said when I left."

"That was before you recovered an aquila and a message from Cotys."

The clouds outside his window parted. A shaft of sunlight filled his room. "You want me to follow the message."

"I did not believe you made a wise decision when you left. The evidence has caused me to re-evaluate my position."

"Including on Gary Doyle being such a great guy?"

"He's family, Harry. Be grateful you have one. For however long that may be."

"What if I don't want to *travel the golden river?* Whatever the heck that means."

"Then I say you're fooling yourself."

He opened his mouth. He closed it. "Remind me again who's a world-class relic hunter?"

"You also have a world-class ego and need to be knocked down a peg," she fired back. "Make up your mind. Are you abandoning Gary or are you interested in my thoughts on Cotys's message?" She hesitated. "Along with my thoughts on Agilulph's bible."

The smart move would be to focus on settling the score with Olivier Lloris. To stick to one adventure. But did Harry ever make the smart move?

He couldn't help himself. "Where is the golden river?"

"I thought so," Sara said. "You certainly make life interesting."

"I'll sell more relics next week. After we figure out whether Spartacus is a real prince."

"A question for you. Which Greek or Roman gods did Thracians worship?"

"Whichever ones the Greeks or Romans told them to."

A short laugh slipped out of her mouth. "That was actually funny. But no, the answer is Dionysus."

"Bacchus to the Romans."

"Yes. One of only three gods worshipped in Thrace."

"They only had three gods? At least they could have come up with three original ones."

"Some people would say there hasn't been an original god in three thousand years," Sara said dryly. "Regardless, Thracians honored three gods that scholars have identified as Artemis, Dionysus and Ares. The mother, father and son."

"What's so special about Dionysus? He was the party animal when it came to gods."

"Wine-making, fertility, theater and insanity, among other traits."

Harry wracked his brain. "I don't recall gold being associated with Dionysus."

"Correct. And irrelevant."

"We need a *golden river* to travel for this riddle. How does Dionysus relate to gold?"

"Put that on hold. Thracians were warriors. Agriculture played an important role in their society, yes, but at the heart of their culture, Thracians were always ready for battle. What did warriors need? Arms, armor, and above all, funding. If you wanted to win, gold made it happen."

"You think Cotys is talking about a river that has gold deposits."

"It's logical," Sara said.

"One that leads to or passes a *high fortress*."

"You are not entirely useless."

He almost stopped himself from laughing. "Funny. What river are we talking about here?"

"I spoke with a colleague at the museum whose research specializes in the Roman Republic. The republic began around five hundred B.C. when the last Roman king was overthrown, and lasted until around thirty B.C. when Octavian became the first emperor."

"Octavian, who defeated Antony and Cleopatra."

"Interesting how your many adventures connect in some way, isn't it? My colleague was able to shed light on what Cotys's message could mean."

"Rome controlled Thrace at one point, but that's about it. What would the Roman Republic have to do with gold mining in Thrace?"

"Nothing. And everything. Thrace's history intertwines with the republic, so my colleague is well versed in Thracian history."

"Including where they mined gold," Harry said. "Lucky I have you around."

"I expect you would have unraveled the connection. Eventually." Sara paused. "I'll ask one last time. Are you certain you want to do this?"

He recited an unfamiliar turn of phrase. "Gary is family now."

"Answer the question."

Was there a tiny voice in the back of his head shouting at him to watch out? Yes. Did he plan to listen? Well, that remained to be seen.

"I'm certain," Harry said. "Now, what did your colleague say about Thracian gold mining?"

"Thracians mined gold primarily near bodies of water, where the metal could be retrieved by hand. Various gold deposits in or near water existed in Thrace during Cotys's time. Which could have been a problem for us given the sheer number of possible locations to sort through."

"*Could* have been?"

"My colleague wasn't certain what the line meant because there were so many choices. I recommended she focus on the second portion of the sentence to narrow those down."

"The *high fortress*."

"That phrase presents its own challenge. My colleague had never heard of a high fortress in the region."

"Thrace had mountain ranges," Harry said as he looked out his window. "I'm looking at one right now. There must be fortifications on some of the peaks."

"Nearly all of which have rivers or streams below them in the valleys."

"I didn't say it was a good idea."

"You're not far off. The sentence is misleading. Intentionally so, is my guess. The *high fortress* isn't high. It's *elevated*." She fell silent. The sort of silence Harry knew meant the gears in her head were churning. He kept quiet. "And, to make matters more confusing, it's not a fortress at all."

"Another layer of misdirection," Harry said. "When is a fortress not a fortress, and where is it? Probably best that we get that sorted sooner rather than later. Remember, I still have a shooter on the loose around here."

"Right." She got to it. "The only gold-producing river near a structure fitting the *high fortress* description is the Perpereshka River. It runs through southern Bulgaria, and is less than a day's journey from Cotys's tomb."

One problem immediately came to mind. "How long is this river?"

"Long enough to require a more specific location if you're going to find what Cotys describes. I don't believe he's referencing a fortress. I suspect his message points to a village called Gorna krepost. It sits at the base of a hill along the Perpereshka River. The village has several ruins and archaeological sites within a day's walk."

"Gorna krepost it is," Harry said.

"The name translates to 'Upper fortress,'" Sara said. "It's a literal translation."

"And only part of the solution. We know where to start. Next, I have to find the *temple of the false king*, and go from there." He waited. "Any ideas?" Harry finally asked. Sara sighed. *That's not good*, Harry thought. "I'll even take bad ideas," he said.

"Thracians may only have worshipped three main gods, but they have an overwhelming number of kings to sort through. True kings. False kings. Kings who may or may not have even existed. People identified as Thracian existed for at least a thousand years in a time when record-keeping ranged from exacting to nonexistent. Who was king often depended on where a person lived or even who you were asking – allegiances mattered. My colleague said she is unqualified to provide an answer as to who this *false king* may be."

"Is there someone else you can ask?" Harry ran a hand across his face. "We need an expert with local knowledge. Someone intimately familiar with Thrace. Maybe even someone whose ancestors were Thracian."

"My colleague recommended visiting a professor in the history department of the local university," she said, ignoring him entirely. "It's a department of one, though this professor has published several highly regarded articles on Thracian history. She's a recognized expert on the subject who should be in a much more prestigious posting. I suggest you meet with her about the rest of the message."

"You're forgetting about the part where there's a gunman running around town looking for me?"

"It's possible that the man is long gone. Which leaves you free to locate and meet with this professor—who may hold the key to uncovering what Cotys meant."

She was right. But still. "You're pretty casual about my safety."

"I wouldn't suggest it if I didn't believe you couldn't handle yourself."

He grumbled in grudging appreciation. "What's the name of the woman I need to see?" he asked.

"Her name is Dessi Zheleva."

"You hadn't heard of this Zheleva woman until today. What makes you so sure she'll help me?"

"Dr. Zheleva is teaching at the local university rather than at a larger European institution because of her outspoken political positions. She's vehemently anti-government. What you might call a libertarian." A pause. "Or even an anarchist. She is also what many people would call a handful."

Perfect. As if performing the delicate dance of convincing this expert scholar of his intentions wasn't going to be hard enough. "Are you sure she's the right person?"

"Just talk to Dr. Zheleva. See if she can shine a light where ours is lacking. Call me when you're finished."

"I thought you were busy."

"I am. For this, though, I will make time." She paused for a moment. "You could also be right about the gunman. Stay alert. The man who died chasing you might be related to the shooter and he may still be out there. If that's true, you've made an enemy for life."

He promised to call her soon, and then clicked off. Experience told him to pack his stuff for a quick departure, and after a moment's thought, he took all his luggage with him to the front desk, where he received directions to the local university. Harry kept one eye on his surroundings while walking to his car, while driving into town, and after parking a block away from the school. Nothing grabbed his attention. Nothing to see beyond small-town Bulgarians going about their business.

Harry moved quickly through town and walked up the front steps of the modest university administration building, which the hotel desk clerk had told him housed the entirety of the university faculty. Harry found *Zheleva, D.* listed on the directory. Her office was on the first floor.

He found the door open. "Hello?" Harry peered around the doorframe as he spoke in English. "Dr. Zheleva?"

"Yes. Do we have an appointment?"

The question came from a far corner of the office. Harry leaned in further, poking his head around a stack of textbooks that threatened to topple over. "I'm looking for Dr. Dessi Zheleva. My name is Harry Fox."

"Harry Fox? What sort of name is that?"

Great. A jokester. Harry stepped farther into the cramped office and finally spotted the speaker. "Are you Dr. Zheleva?"

"Are you a small mammal with red fur?" A mass of dark curly hair shook in Harry's direction at the words. That's all he could see, for the speaker had her head down, hunched over a desk in the room's center.

"May I come in?"

"One moment." The curls shook again, and Harry heard the *scritch* of a pen racing across paper – a red pen, he noted—and then said paper was lifted into the air only to crash down with a resounding smack onto one of the larger piles of paper atop said desk. "Enter."

Harry stepped around a second stack of textbooks, placing himself squarely in the woman's line of sight. He took one more step forward and she looked up at him. He went still.

This woman was barely older than him. The smoky skin tone of a hundred cultures from the mixing pot of Europe told part of her story. The richly dark mass of curls told another. The intensity of her gaze spoke loudest of all. Harry repeated himself. "Are you Dr. Zheleva?"

"Call me Dessi." She stood and pointed at one of the two chairs in front of her desk. "Sit."

Now Harry had to look up to meet her gaze. A long way up. "Hello," he said. "I'm Harry Fox."

"I know." She plopped back down and waited until he did the same. "What is it you want?"

Harry took in the stacks of textbooks fronting walls that were almost completely bare, except for an oil painting of a Newfoundland dog. Piles of paperwork covered the desk. An open laptop sat among the clutter. "Information."

"Americans do not often walk through my door. Tell me who and what you are."

Good question. "I'm an expert in rare antiquities."

Dessi sat bolt upright. "You are with the government."

"I'm a private contractor."

"That is what all government stooges say." She rose to her much-taller-than-Harry height and aimed a finger at the door. "Get out."

"Leave?" Harry sputtered. "You don't even know why I'm here."

"You take the government's money," she fired back. "You are no better than them. Get out."

"You work at a publicly funded university," he said. "So do you."

"I do it to stay close to the enemy." Sparks flew from her words. "What is your excuse?"

This lady was nuts. She was also his best hope right now. "I take it so I don't have to pay taxes on it."

"This is not a joke."

So much for humor. "Give me a second to explain why I'm here. Then, if you want me to leave, I'm gone. I came a long way to see you."

Dessi glared at him a moment longer. "You have one minute." She settled back into her chair. "Begin."

He stared at her, his mind racing. How to wade through all the ideology standing between them and get the answers he needed?

"I found a message from King Cotys that reveals a path to new information about ancient Thrace. I need your help to follow that path."

The clock on her wall ticked. The weak sunlight falling through the office's dingy windows held steady. Harry noticed a framed picture on the desk. A photo of a Newfoundland.

Dessi stood from her chair so fast Harry jumped. She raced around the desk, stuck her head outside the office door, then slammed it shut before rushing back to her chair. "How do I know you speak the truth?"

"Why would I lie?" She couldn't offer a reason. "Listen," Harry said. "This isn't a joke. There are people who wouldn't hesitate to shoot me to get this information."

"I know."

Right. She knew without having to be told. Sara had given him a crazy woman. She was getting an earful after he got home. "I have to keep this quiet."

"Yes." She leaned closer, her entire body practically humming. "Tell me where you found it. No." Her hand shot up. "It was at the dig site. That is the only reason for an American to be in this horrid town."

"I didn't find it at the dig site."

"Then why is your hair dusty? Why do you have a pine needle in it?"

Harry reached up and found said needle. "I found the message in the mountains."

"I do not believe you."

Harry let her words linger in the air. "And I don't know if I can trust you."

"If it is about my country and what you say is true, then you can trust me. I *despise* the government. They have ruined this great land and stolen from its people."

"This stays between us."

The gleam of interest in her eyes said she agreed. "Yes."

"I found the message in Cotys's tomb."

He hesitated, and she sensed it. "Tell me," she said.

That made him pause. Tell her about the aquila? Seemed like a bad idea. *Keep the aquila to yourself.*

Harry described the tomb's layout. "The message was in a hidden passageway," Harry finished. "I believe Cotys hid it in there so the Romans wouldn't see it."

"Thieving Romans."

Harry reached into his pocket. "The message appears to have several layers, pointing to specific locations or cultural references, all tied to ancient Thrace. I have an idea about what the first portion means."

"Do not tell me," Dessi said. "Let me look at it myself."

Harry thought this was an excellent idea. He removed a folded sheet of hotel stationery and laid it on her desk. "This is the inscription."

Dessi set one hand on either side of the folded paper. Her eyes closed and she slowly drew a breath in through her nostrils. Her eyes snapped open, looking at the door. After several seconds' silence she looked down to the sheet, finally reaching for it. "Please, be quiet."

Harry did his best impression of a statue as Dessi unfolded the sheet. Her face remained a mask as she read. The deliberate left-to-right motion of her eyeballs crossing the page was the only movement. Once, twice she read it. Her nostrils flared. "Who else has seen this?"

Harry considered for a moment. "No one."

"Who did you tell about these words?"

Dessi was sharp. "A person I trust with my life." He wasn't giving her Sara's name, not for all the Thracian relics in Bulgaria. "She's the person who recommended I come to you."

"Then she is wise and should be trusted." Dessi set the page down on her desk. "I believe this message is authentic. Thracian warriors understood the need to know the enemy's strengths and weaknesses as well as one's own. Thracians were brave, strong, intelligent. Romans were dumb, slow and powerful. Rome was too big for Thrace to defeat by might, so Thrace used cunning instead. Hiding a message in a secret chamber is how they would defeat Rome."

"What I want to know is why Cotys would hide this message."

"To hide the truth about what path to follow." Dessi grabbed a pencil. "I will translate to English for us." Her pencil scratched across the page for a moment. "Here," she said as she flipped the page around. "In English."

Harry took a second sheet of paper from his pocket and went through the motions of comparing. "Exactly what I had."

"How do you read Latin?"

"One word at a time." He grinned. "Just a joke."

"This is serious."

"I learned in school. Same as you did."

Dessi grumbled something he didn't understand. "I do not meet many people outside of the academic groups who read it."

"What do you think the message means?"

She tapped the first few translated words. "The golden river is difficult. There was no river with this name in Thrace. There were rivers with gold in them, so this must refer to a river that produces gold. Which one?" Now she tapped the second half of the sentence. "*High fortress* tells us. It is the name of a village."

"Gorna krepost."

Dessi slammed her hand on the desk. "Yes!" She immediately looked at the door, then turned her ferocious gaze on Harry. "How did you know this?"

"The person I trust figured it out. That's all she could unravel. Which is why I came to you."

"Your friend is wise."

"You have no idea."

Dessi glanced up from the page, and for the first time since Harry walked in, he felt like she truly saw him. Not as an annoying visitor. As a person. "Good."

Harry turned that one over in his head as she placed a finger on the page. "The second sentence," Dessi continued, "speaks of our religion."

"Which has three main gods," Harry said. "That's where we got stuck. Three gods aren't overwhelming. It's the *false king* part that's tough. How many kings did Thrace have over the centuries?"

"Many," Dessi said. "They fought each other, they fought the Romans, they fought until Thrace became weak. Kings are terrible, but they are better than the government. It is lucky for you I know the false kings as well as the true kings."

Dessi seemed to appreciate the work he and Sara had done up to this point, so Harry risked offering a thought. "A false king isn't necessarily someone who wasn't supposed to be king. It could be someone Cotys's ancestors defeated in battle. Kings steal thrones all the time. Could be what happened here."

"It could. But it is not. That is wrong. Only one temple related to a false king is near a river with gold in it, and also close to Gorna krepost."

The faint hum of warm air moving through overhead ducts faded. The ticking clock on the wall went away. "Which one?"

"The Temple of Dionysus, where Medokos declared himself King of Thrace following the death of King Sitalces. It is not in Gorna krepost, but is nearby. It is the temple that fits every requirement."

Harry had learned long ago not to play with fire. Or sticks of dynamite with lit fuses. And if Dessi were a stick of dynamite, she'd be one with a lit fuse seconds from detonating. Even so, he asked the question. "Is it possible there are other temples you don't know of that fit this description?"

"Anything is possible. Except this. I am certain this is the correct temple."

Her look dared him to disagree. He passed. "Good. Where's the *next triumph*?"

Clouds of discontent crossed Dessi's face. "I do not know. Who is the *Thracian son*? Is it Spartacus, or another?"

"Does Thrace have a most famous son?"

"They are all famous to good Thracians."

Yeesh. "What if you had to pick one?"

"I would be making a mistake." Dessi glowered at the paper as though it were withholding information. "There must be more. I am not missing anything."

Harry leaned back in his chair. His father had taught him a lesson long ago, then Sara had reinforced it. When faced with a question such as this, when he didn't know where to look next, take it one step at a time. Start with what he *did* know, and the rest would eventually come. "We're looking for a person. A man. It has to be someone Cotys knew, a man well regarded either by the king or by the larger Thracian culture."

"A long list."

"It's a place to start," Harry said. "We know we're not looking for an object or a location. We should narrow it down as much as we can first, then use the rest of the message to figure out what Cotys meant." He considered. "Maybe we're translating the Latin incorrectly."

"No. The word is *son*. A male child. We need a son." Lines creased her forehead. "You are missing it."

"Missing what?"

"If I knew, I would tell you. I cannot say." Her hands waved in the air. "There is more. There must be. Think. Tell me what else you know."

A dull ache began in Harry's head. Wearily, he rubbed his temples. "I told you everything. The tomb, the hidden passageway, the message." Everything she needed to know, at least.

"What else is in the tomb?"

"Give me a second." Harry closed his eyes and went back to the tomb, starting at the entrance and working through the entire cave. Maybe Dessi was correct. Something he'd missed, a part he'd forgotten to tell her while withholding parts of the story. "The tomb is a stone coffin. There was rope hanging to one side, a hook on the ceiling. Two images of Cotys on the rear wall." The aching began to recede. Harry opened his eyes, squinting as a shaft of sunlight fell through the window and crossed his face. "There's noth—" His chair flew back as he shot out of it. "It's a sun."

Dessi didn't blink. "I told you that."

"No, you don't understand." Harry pointed out the window. "A *sun*. Big ball of burning gas, gives off light, really hot? That kind of sun. Not a male child."

"The word is for a child."

"There's more in the tomb I didn't tell you about." Harry raised both hands as she opened her mouth to speak. "Hear me out."

Dessi sat back down. Harry took a breath, then the story came tumbling out. Most of it, at least. "There's a message by the coffin. A tribute to Cotys's deeds and to his son."

"How could you not realize this?" Dessi snapped.

"The son's name is Spartacus."

Dessi hesitated. Or did she? "Spartacus was a common Thracian name," she said. "The gladiator was not a prince. It cannot be him. Come." She motioned with her hand. "Tell me. Talk. What did the message say?"

Harry pulled up an image of the message on his phone. "Here. You can read it yourself."

Dessi did so quickly. "There is nothing about a sun here. Only the boy named Spartacus. Which is not helpful. I do not know a prince by that name. It is possible the records do not mention him."

"Did Cotys have several children?"

"Two daughters and two sons, at least." Dessi shook her head. "It is possible another child existed, one named Spartacus. That does not make him the gladiator. Anything is possible. I suspect you know this."

"I do." Harry took his phone back and enlarged the image, homing in on a specific point. "The message doesn't matter. This carving does."

Dessi drew in a quick breath when she took the phone. "A rising sun." His phone clattered as she dropped it on the table.

"What's wrong?" Harry asked.

"I know where you must go. It is obvious." Dessi snatched up the phone again and pointed to the screen. "This is a symbol. This is what you must find."

"The sun?"

"No. *This*. The *carving* of a sun. It is a marker to follow."

Harry snapped his fingers. "When I get to the temple. Of course. It's small enough to go unnoticed, and it can be in plain sight. Nobody would know it meant anything special unless they read this message."

"The boy child is not part of the guide. It comes after. You must go to the city first. Perperikon."

"Where's that?"

"Several hours from here. Follow the Perpereshka River to Perperikon. In ancient times a temple of Dionysius was near Gorna krepost. But without worrying about the son—S-O-N—it makes sense. The answer is Perperikon." She leaned over her desk. "And I know what you must do when you arrive. You must look to Bendis."

"A goddess."

"The goddess of heaven and earth. Seek her to find the sun."

"Is this Perperikon place a tower?"

"No. It is a city. An ancient city whose secrets are still being uncovered."

He liked the sound of that. "Any chance there's a temple for Bendis next to the Dionysius one? Sounds like she's protecting this next triumph."

"No. You should not seek Bendis. You must worship her." Dessi stood from her desk and stepped to one side. "Bendis represents heaven and earth. Anything *below* Bendis can only be in one place." Dessi made an exaggerated motion of looking down. "Below the surface."

"As in dig?"

Dessi shrugged. "The path will tell. Go to Perperikon. Seek the sun. I expect you will find a second image to direct your search."

Logical. Well-reasoned. Dessi would make a decent relic hunter. "Agreed." The clock on the wall ticked. "Thank you. For everything. I need to get moving."

He reached for the paper between them. Dessi grabbed his arm before he took it. "This will be dangerous for you."

"I know." He tried to take the paper. She didn't let go.

"I will help you," she said.

That's the last thing he wanted. "Give me your number," Harry said. "I'll call if I find anything I can't decipher."

"You need more than my knowledge." Now Dessi let go of his arm and pointed to the windows. "Trouble waits out there. You cannot see it yet." She turned her finger on him. "I know it is waiting."

Harry had seen a lot of stuff in his day. The intensity in this woman's eyes was up there with the best of it. "What's waiting?"

"The enemy. You are on a mission from the gods."

"Right." Harry edged his chair back from her desk. "Put in a good word for me."

"The enemy is coming. I can tell." Dessi stood up, then sat down just as quickly. "There is more to this than you know."

Harry tilted his head. "How so?"

"I was not honest with you about Spartacus. Yes, it is a common name, but the actions of this Spartacus are not common. The battles, the victories. It is too close to what the gladiator named Spartacus achieved, close enough to make me wonder." She pointed at him. "You will learn the truth. To do that you will need help."

"Why didn't you tell me the truth at first? About your suspicions?"

"I did not know if I could trust you."

"You do now?"

She shook her head. "No, but I have no choice. It is my sacred duty to help you."

"Mission from the gods—right. How exactly are you going to help me?"

"First, by checking for the enemy." She shot out of her chair again, took hold of his arm, and pulled. "Follow me."

Anything that got him out of here without the crazy lady following sounded good. Harry reached for the translation, then reconsidered. "I'll leave this," he said. "In case you need to check it after I find the next sun."

Dessi tugged his arm. "Up to the top floor."

A steel door outside her office opened to a staircase. Harry let Dessi lead him to the fourth and uppermost floor, the slender scholar flying up the stairs so fast Harry had to run to keep up. Buzzing overhead lights illuminated the interior stairway, a stark contrast to the bright sunlight waiting on the other side of the door at the top. Dessi opened the stairwell door, waited for Harry to follow and then closed the door behind them. She did not move to look out of the nearly floor-to-ceiling windows that lined the hallway of the building's top floor. Closed office doors stretched out on either side. Her hand locked on Harry's bicep to ensure he did not either.

"Stay here." Dessi pushed him back against the stairwell door. "I will look."

"Look for what?"

"The enemy." The way she said it made Harry's chest tighten. Crazy people weren't scary because they were wrong. They were scary because they truly believed they were right. "I will tell you what I see. You tell me if it sounds wrong."

Dessi's words carried unwavering certainty. This wasn't a question of if they were out there, whoever they were. It was a question of where, and now Harry had to confirm it. Funny. Now that they'd come up this far, a flicker of doubt had snaked into his head. Was she truly nuts?

Might as well go along with it. "What do you see?" Harry asked, keeping out of sight.

Dessi stretched her arms overhead as she looked out the windows and down onto the street and sidewalk in front of the building. She rubbed her shoulder, just another employee taking a break from the university desk grind. "People walking. Some sitting or standing."

Harry barely stopped the eye roll. "Anyone watching the front door?"

"Not that I see."

This was useless. And Dessi was a few stops on the wrong side of nutty. "Then I'd better get moving."

"Where is your car?"

"A block away. You can't see it—hang on. Maybe you can from up here." He moved to look out the window. Dessi shoved him back. "Easy. I'm trying to see it."

"I will look. Tell me where." He detailed what his rental looked like and where she'd find it. "I see it," Dessi said. "A white sedan on the corner."

"That's the one."

"There is a man leaning against it."

Harry's head jerked toward her. "Are you certain?"

"Stay here." Dessi pushed past him and through the door. Her footsteps clattered like gunshots on the stairs before a door banged downstairs, and faster than should have been possible the sound repeated in reverse before she was back on the top floor. A pair of binoculars were in her hands. "Use these." Dessi shoved them at him. "I will stand in the window. Lean around the edge beside me and look at your car."

Harry wanted to tell her this was nuts. He wanted to get to Perperikon. He wanted to, yet his gut told him to look outside. "Fine," Harry said. "Cover me."

Dessi stood in front of the window as Harry leaned over her shoulder, her body shielding his from view. He twisted the focus wheel until his car came into sharp definition. "Damn."

"What?" Dessi asked through a feigned yawn.

"I know him." Harry's fingers tightened on the binoculars. "That's the camp electrician." A man he'd seen only this morning as he ran additional electrical lines for lighting into the tomb. "That's not good."

"Look at the man sitting on a bench across the street. He can see your car and the front door at the same time."

Dessi might be strange, but she could also readily identify a strategic vantage point. Harry adjusted the knob, twisting until the fuzzy image of man sitting on a bench came into view. "It's him."

"Who?"

"The guy who tried to shoot me." Harry lowered the binoculars from his face. "You were right."

"I know." Dessi grabbed Harry's shoulder and pulled him through the stairwell door. "You will take my car. Give me your keys."

He trundled down the stairs behind her, nearly falling as she tugged at him. "I'm sorry," Harry said.

"Hurry. Do not be sorry. Be the one who solves this." She stopped so fast he nearly ran her over. Dessi spun around and took him by both shoulders, pulling him close. "Be a *Thracian*."

"I have to get out of here first," Harry said. All of a sudden, this intense, possibly unhinged woman looked like the most intriguing wild-eyed lady in Bulgaria. "You'll really give me your car?"

"What kind of patriot would not?"

No time to argue. "Thanks. When you take my car, I need you to do something for me. Deliver a package to a man."

"What is in the package?"

A solid gold eagle stolen from a vanquished Roman legion, quite possibly by your hero Spartacus. A relic of your beloved Thrace. One of the most valuable pieces I've ever come across.

All of this ran through Harry's mind. All considered, all discarded. Dessi was offering to help him. Was this betrayal masquerading as benevolence? His gut told him no. "Something important," he said, "that will help us both."

"Then I will do it."

They walked back into her office. Harry scribbled Tax's name and the phone number he'd been given on a sheet of paper. "Call this man in three days," Harry said. "No sooner. Tell him you have a package from me. Tell him he can't talk to anyone about it until I get back. I'll explain everything then." Harry could explain how the food guys from camp had likely killed the roommate with ties to the governor. Tax might buy that the fear of those men was what made Harry run. Maybe.

"Understood." Dessi took the intrigue in stride. "Anything else?"

"The package is plenty." He told her it was in the trunk of his car, which she would retrieve after he'd escaped in her vehicle. "You should know those two guys are serious," Harry said. "You sure you want to get involved?"

"It is my duty," she said. "Here are my keys. Look in the glovebox once you are out of town. You will find a useful item in it."

He didn't like the sound of that. "Useful how?"

"It will help if you need to shoot anyone."

"You have a *gun*?"

"For protection."

He sputtered for a beat. "I can't take your gun." His mind whirred.

"What if you need it?"

She leaned down and grasped the bottom of her pant leg. "I have a backup." The pant leg came up to reveal a pistol in an ankle holster. "Take the one in my car. Use it if you are in danger."

One ironclad rule in life: never argue with an armed woman. "Thanks," Harry said. "How do I get out of here?"

Dessi led him through the building, taking a circuitous route that led to a rear parking lot. As they walked, she detailed the roads he should take to get to the main highway without passing the two men out front. "My car is that one."

She indicated a vehicle that appeared to be constructed of dirt and blue paint alone. "Is there gas in it?" Harry asked. What he really wanted to ask was did it run, but one step at a time.

"Full tank. Now go." Dessi shoved him toward the car. "Wait." She pulled him back. "Here is my number. Call me if you need anything. I have friends across the region."

He pocketed the proffered business card. "Even in Turkey?"

"Across all of Thrace's ancient lands. People who still believe. They will help if you need it."

Oddly enough, that brought a feeling of security to him. If Dessi's friends were anything like her, the two guys waiting for him out front were in big trouble. "I will." He meant it. Harry gave Dessi his phone number before he realized the blue car was familiar. "It's a Toyota Corolla," he said.

"What is wrong with a Toyota?" Dessi asked.

"Nothing. Just didn't expect to find one here."

"They are reliable," she said indignantly.

He tossed the shoulder bag, which now held the entirety of his possessions, on the passenger seat. A thought flashed into his head. "What will you do if those men approach you?"

Dessi actually laughed. If there was humor in her reply, however, Harry missed it. "I will make them sorry."

Truer words had never been spoken. "I'll be in touch," Harry said as he ducked into the car. The engine fired to life as much as a Corolla engine could and he was off.

Chapter 13

Perperikon, Bulgaria

Several hours of driving both highways and back roads along the winding Perpereshka River gave Harry time to think. First, about what Tax might do when he realized Harry had stolen an artifact from the tomb. That thought was quickly pushed aside. He then tried to puzzle out who the electrician and gunman could be working for. No way they were acting on their own. Men like that always worked for someone. The problem was figuring out who could be bankrolling the two. A worldwide black market for cultural antiquities existed because it was profitable. Unscrupulous collectors paid top dollar to get their hands on relics. Stolen relics then sold for small fortunes, all of it profit.

Harry gazed at distant mountains dusted with snow as he wound through the southern Bulgarian countryside. A pair of oversized birds floated on the winds overhead, and through the still-green trees on either side of the road he spotted an occasional deer eating grass. Picturesque though it might be, the thought of who could be on his tail kept Harry from appreciating the view. Trouble was close at hand, that much was certain. The smart play in all this remained getting on a plane to New York. Would he do that? No chance.

Harry needed to get away from the dig site, so he'd sent Tax a message that something personal had come up and he'd be gone for a few days. Suspicious? Maybe, but Tax had his hands full. He wouldn't miss Harry. At least until Dessi showed up with the aquila and Harry's deception came to light. Harry would deal with that fallout later. In life he'd found it was much easier to beg for forgiveness than to ask for permission. Figuring out why Cotys had obscured such an incredible story would go a long way toward getting back on Tax's good side.

He couldn't risk losing the lead on this trail now.

Which was why he gripped the wheel a little harder as the red-roofed homes of a small hamlet passed on one side and revealed a hill along the river. White rocks topped the hill, and as he approached, the rocks revealed themselves as not just stones left from the passing of ancient glaciers, but actual man-made structures. It didn't take much imagination to picture the sprawling stone columns and thick walls that once constituted the Thracian city of Perperikon.

He connected with Sara on his drive. Tempted though Harry was to leave out the more perilous details of his meeting with Dessi Zheleva, the entire story spilled out, resurfaced gunman and all. Sara took it mostly in stride.

"You should get rid of that gun," she said. "I just checked. Only Bulgarian residents are allowed to carry firearms."

"You're right. But I need it until I know who's after me. I just can't get caught with it."

Sara dropped the matter. "Perperikon is the largest megalithic archaeological site in Bulgaria," she said. "That means it's made of stone."

"I know what megalithic means."

"People lived there over six thousand years ago. It grew to the size where it had town squares and a dedicated water supply system."

"Any idea where I should start?"

"The first step is to introduce yourself to the head archaeologist. You don't want him to catch you on his site without permission."

Tax would have been useful right now. "I'll do that," Harry lied smoothly.

"You're lying."

The argument caught in his throat. "I am. How am I supposed to get the guy to let me poke around his site without telling him why? If I were you, it would be different. He'll call the cops if I tell him I'm an antiquities dealer."

Harry swerved slightly when she responded. "True."

"You agree?"

"I would do the same in his shoes." Sara fell silent for a few beats. "You can always pretend you're a tourist," she said.

Not a half-bad idea. "A dig site like this would attract visitors. Any advice on where you think the sun carving may be hidden?"

"Start with the church. It's mainly foundations and partial exterior walls now, but it has a well-preserved pulpit. Inscriptions in Greek are on different portions of the remaining structure, along with carvings and other ornamentation. Including, according to my research, an eagle."

"Dr. Zheleva thought I should look for another sun carving."

"Do it. If you don't find one, take a hard look at the eagle. The connection between it and what you recovered in the tomb can't be ignored."

A side road beckoned ahead. It stretched in a looping circle around the bottom of the tall hill on which the site was located. Might as well reconnoiter to find the best route up. Ideally, one that took him through the dense trees so nobody would see his approach. He had to crane his neck to see to the top. This was *steep*. "I'm here," he said to Sara as he followed the curving road. "I see movement near the top of the hill."

"There could be any number of people working. Digs run on funding. If the funds are short for a week or two, people don't come to work."

"Would everybody on a site know each other?"

"Assume they do. Lead archaeologists are fiercely protective of their work. When possible, they employ only people they know. Familiar faces. Expect to stand out."

"I'll keep a low profile."

The sound of a pencil tapping on a desk came through the phone. "There is another option," Sara finally said. "You could come home."

"What?" The dig site far above disappeared as trees closed in on either side of the road. "This morning you were all for it. Now you want me to quit?"

"No. I want you to think this through."

"Too much of that and I'll go home." Harry stopped the car. There had been a clearing in the trees he'd passed. A place big enough to park a Toyota off the road and hope it went unnoticed. "Do I still want to figure out what Cotys went to all this trouble to hide?" He squinted against the afternoon sunlight as he reversed, maneuvered into the opening, and stopped. "Yes. I have people trying to kill me. That says this is worth doing."

"I thought you'd say that."

"Plus, there's the whole thing about Gary being family now. You're right: he is, and that matters."

"Gary's request is no reason to risk your life. Also, admit it. You enjoy the chase."

"More than I should." He cut the engine. "I need to go. I'll call you after."

Sara didn't bother telling him to be careful, only wishing him luck before he clicked off. Harry took Dessi's pistol from the glovebox, popped the trunk and stepped out into the cool shade of the hillside trees. A bird chirped on a barren tree limb as he buried the firearm deep beneath the spare tire. It would have to do. He wasn't ready to toss the gun. He also wasn't ready to trespass with it either. The trunk snapped shut. Harry brushed his fingers over the amulet beneath his shirt, then checked that the ceramic knuckledusters were tucked away in his pocket. One for good luck, the other in case it went bad.

His boots crunched over fallen leaves as he began climbing the steep hill. Doing this in the summer with the full cover of green foliage would have been preferable, but at least the thickly wooded hillside offered some protection against anyone looking up from the roadway or down from the site. He moved quickly, using tree trunks as cover during his ascent.

The sound of voices reached his ears when he was halfway up: a man shouting in what was likely Bulgarian, not that Harry understood it. The shouting stopped. Nobody had spotted an interloping American approaching the site. On he walked, glancing at his watch to find that nightfall was not far off. Darkness fell quickly at this time of year. That meant the dig site would soon be emptying. He didn't want to run into anyone coming down the hill, and he sure didn't want to have to rely on the flashlight in his pocket for light.

Sturdy tree trunks provided cover on all sides as he moved. At last, a low stone wall, marking the perimeter of the site, appeared across a clearing, barely twenty feet ahead. He stood still and looked around. The last tree between him and no cover was wide enough to hide him from view. Any voices or footsteps in the vicinity should be easy to hear. Thirty seconds passed without a sound.

Harry kept low to the ground as he moved from behind the tree, silently covering the twenty feet until his back was pressed against the wall. He listened for another half-minute and then carefully turned to examine the wall. Massive stone blocks laid next to each other created a physical barrier, the lowest level of a much taller wall. To one side, farther down, he could see that the upper rows of the wall were intact, massive chunks of rock stacked with precision and standing taller than Harry. To his other side, the wall broke down and became a series of boulders scattered on the ground.

He twisted to look the other way again. *That's where I'm headed.* The most well-preserved part of the exterior wall lay in that direction. He could see an intact tower, built of much smaller stone blocks, carved and mortared together. Narrow slits of windows had been cut out some two stories overhead. That was the place to start looking.

Harry scrambled along the low wall, hunched over so he was nearly crawling. A voice sounded again in the distance. He went still, then risked a look over the wall. Two men were on the other side, crossing a raised walkway with baskets of what appeared to be dirt and debris in their hands. One spoke, the other laughed, and the men moved on without looking in Harry's direction. He watched them descend a set of stairs and walk out of sight.

The ground sloped steeply down to the woods. Harry reached the rough stone tower and kept one hand on it as he moved, the rocky dirt under his feet threatening to send him sliding down the hill with one wrong step. Stones nearly the size of Harry buttressed the far side of the tower. Fault lines running down each one offered handholds for him to climb up several feet. Far enough to stick his head above the topmost rock for a quick look. Nobody would expect anyone to appear on the other side of the tower wall, so he should be fine. Or so he told himself.

From this angle, he realized it was only half a tower, the round exterior barely half a circle, with the rest having fallen down. A sturdy wooden stand constructed just inside the not-quite-a-tower was how archaeologists accessed the upper portions of the walls. One such archaeologist was standing on it.

Harry froze, his fingers and toes locked into the crevices, not daring to breathe. The archaeologist, standing well above him, was looking down at her cell phone. She hadn't noticed Harry.

A voice called out from across the site in Bulgarian. The woman on the platform turned and waved. She grabbed a toolbox from the platform and descended the stairs. Stairs that ended only feet from Harry's exposed head.

Harry didn't budge as the wooden steps creaked, the woman's boots pounding down until they crunched on gravel; she was close enough for Harry to reach out and touch her. She passed by, looking across the site toward her colleagues, never glancing down as she walked briskly across the site to a pair of co-workers before the trio turned and headed in the opposite direction. Harry had seen a parking area farther down that side of the hill.

Perhaps his luck would hold and everyone would be leaving for the day. Harry waited until the trio were well out of sight before vaulting over the edge of the rock and crouching behind an outcropping. Nobody called out, and he didn't spot any other movement around the site.

Carefully, he looked around. The interior tower walls offered nothing in the way of markings or ornamentation. Why build the platform here? There must be a reason, so Harry darted up the stairs to the platform above, then leaned toward the tower to where a window had been cut from the stone. No inscriptions or engravings on the surface.

Back down to ground level. The dig team had constructed walkways throughout the area. Harry picked the nearest one and headed into the middle of the site, passing crumbling walls and pillars likely used to support original archways or entire roofs. The first off-ramp on the walkway took him to a pile of stones from what used to be a wall. No writing to be found. He turned back to the main walkway.

Three more off-ramps revealed nothing of interest. Looked like they were used to move equipment or tools around the site. On he went until he stood in front of the church and the still-standing pulpit within it. Harry slid under the walkway railing and made his way upwards. The church sat atop the tallest point in the city and was the best-preserved of the buildings.

He passed a toolbox beside a row of shovels, spades and stacked metal rods as he circled the half-wall of the church to find an access point. A crumbling opening marked with fluttering yellow caution tape led him to the interior, where a virtual history of the church unfolded in front of him. The foundation had held up, a rectangle showing the church had been quite large for this hillside town, big enough to pack in a roomful of worshippers. Harry didn't have to read the inscriptions scattered throughout the ruined church walls to know this building honored the Christian God. The layout told him. And it told him this church hadn't always been dedicated to the teachings of Jesus of Nazareth.

He stood in a single-nave basilica that stretched at least fifty feet from end to end. Richly ornamented carvings and engravings on both the pulpit and the surrounding walls told a story of cultural evolution. The names of saints figured prominently, though he found the three Thracian gods listed as well: Artemis, Ares, and most often, Dionysus. This told him that parts of the church had stood since before Christianity had begun to influence Thracian culture.

He froze at the sound of a coughing and sputtering car engine from far down the hill. Perhaps someone on the site team was dawdling down there. The engine rumbled, loud at first, then faded as gears clunked and the vehicle moved on. Harry turned back to the stone wall, which appeared to be the oldest portion of the church.

The stones were worn, the writing faded. He took out his flashlight and used it to examine the shadowed text.

A rising sun was engraved on the stone at ground level. The same image as the one from Cotys's tomb. Harry flattened himself on the ground for a better look. Latin lettering ran across the stones, and he translated the words aloud. *"Seek the sun above Bendis's domain."*

Dessi had told him she'd never seen the image associated with Thrace before, but this was no coincidence. A second rising sun left by Cotys. "Bendis's domain," Harry said to the air. "The goddess of heaven and earth." Harry couldn't very well go above the heavens, but neither could Cotys, so Harry needed to look for a sun image somewhere above ground in Perperikon.

He ran a finger along the inscription again. *"Bendis's domain.* Where did she hold domain in this city?"

His finger stopped moving. The previous message had directed him to a place *safe below Bendis.* Below ground. *Of course.* The messages didn't stand alone. They were meant to be considered together. Cotys wanted him to look below ground, to where Bendis ruled over her domain. "He's talking about a tomb," he said.

He jumped up and ran to the tombs he'd passed without stopping earlier. A series of rectangular burial plots on one side of the ruins, stones placed vertically on the ground, though the bodies inside had been moved at some point. He vaulted over a low wall and up to one of the walkways. The tombs were set well below the main level of the area, but how to get there? The remnants of the stone stairs were now little more than heaped rubble. A large stone block that had fallen from the wall offered a better way to get down to the tomb level.

Harry looked down to ground level from his perch on the walkway.

He counted fifteen tombs laid out below him in five rows. No sign of archaeological excavation in this section. Harry jumped down into the chamber below him and played his flashlight beam over each open burial chamber.

Squatting for a better look, he studied the interior of the first open tomb. Patches of brown moss came off when he rubbed at the weathered stone blocks. No writing. He paused. The shiver running up his spine had little to do with the cold.

The grass beneath his feet was little more than sparse clumps; a few inches of dirt came up with the grass as he pulled it away to reveal stone blocks underneath. Whether it was a natural floor or one the Thracians had laid down, he couldn't tell. There were no markings and no relics. Harry put the grass back as best he could to hide his intrusion before moving to the next tomb.

Same result. Nothing on the walls or the ground. Harry worked onward through seven of the tombs, finding nothing. Seven down, eight to go. He clambered over a low dividing wall into the next open tomb; the sun was now directly at his back, so that his shadow moved across the stone wall in front of him. The tombs were laid out in a grid, with this one sitting in a far corner. His flashlight scanned across the walls to reveal nothing but more blank stone.

Could he be wrong about this? After all, he was out here on just the word of a radical scholar. Sara thought Dessi Zheleva could be relied upon. That didn't mean she was right.

His jaw tightened as he ripped up the next clod of dirt and tossed it over his shoulder; it disintegrated into a dirt cloud that flew up, hung in the air, then rained down on him. Dirt stuck to his neck, fell down his shirt, rolled over his shoulders. Harry didn't notice.

He was too busy staring at a rising sun carved into this tomb's stone floor.

He cleared the dirt and grass, his breath coming faster, fogging in the cool evening air as his mind whirred. Nobody had seen this yet. He looked up, searching the site once again for signs of movement anywhere around him and finding none. Sara had told him this was an active dig site, a sprawling effort that had been going on for years and would continue for quite some time. Judging from the site, these graves were low priority and hadn't been closely investigated yet.

Harry shook his head. *Dessi had figured it out.* "Sorry I ever doubted you," he said aloud. The carving was in a far corner of the tomb. Harry got down on one knee and brushed away dirt that was stuck in a groove. He paused. It wasn't a groove. "It's a cover."

Four grooves lay under the patchy grass, four straight lines forming a square. Definitely man-made. The sharp edges dug into his fingers as he searched for a way to grab hold and pull. A thin line of dirt remained on the stone, which he brushed away, then brushed again. Harry frowned. He leaned over and blew on it. The last of the dirt flew off. His mouth opened.

Two small lines had been cut into the edge of the stone. Why? They served no purpose—except with Cotys there was always a purpose. Harry leaned back, letting his gaze wander over the stone. The two lines didn't fit with anything he could think of. In truth they looked like…*hinges.*

He was looking at a lid. He checked the opposite side of the stone block, running his fingers along the groove, much more slowly this time. *Gotcha.*

Tiny indentations in the groove. So small he'd missed them. Small, and the perfect size for fingertips to grip. "Handles," he said to himself.

He dug his fingertips into the stone and pulled hard. The cold, gritty stone held fast. *Enough of this.* Harry growled and pulled again with everything he had.

The ancient stone ground harshly as the lid lifted, and a rush of dry air whooshed across his face. Swirling dust stung his eyes. He blinked and stared down.

Darkness, the dim outline of a wall, nothing he could clearly see. The lid stayed upright when he released it, and he flicked his flashlight to life.

Another sound of a rattling car engine from the road below made him jump. The engine seemed to hold steady for a moment before, like the first one, moving on and fading from hearing. From so far below it would be nearly impossible for the driver to see any light from his flashlight. Harry pushed any worry aside and aimed his light across the darkness to reveal a staircase. Irregular stone blocks had been mortared together to form a rough set of steps descending to a floor some ten feet below. Kneeling, he swept his light back and forth and saw a wide opening to one side.

Harry stood and took a tentative step onto the first stair. It held, as did the next one. His pocket vibrated before he could take another step. Harry checked the number. One he didn't recognize. It took him a second. A Bulgarian number.

"Dessi?" Harry asked when he connected the call.

"I'm sorry." Her words came fast. "I couldn't say no. They made me tell them and I tried to stop, but it came out because I can't let them hurt—"

"Hold on," Harry said to cut her off. "What are you talking about?"

"Rhesus." Dessi struggled to get the rest out. "They were going to hurt Rhesus."

"Who is they, and who is Jesus?"

"*Rhe*-sus," she snapped. "My Newfoundland."

"Your *dog*?"

"They threatened to kill him."

A hollow pit formed in Harry's gut. "Who threatened to kill your dog?"

"The two men who followed you to my office," Dessi shouted. "So I told them."

Harry's grip threatened to shatter the phone. "Told them what?"

"Where to find you."

When Harry spoke again, it was in a whisper. "Dessi, this is very important. When did you talk to them?"

"I'm so sorry." Tears now, followed by a sniffle. "I'm so sorry."

"I don't care if you told them, but I need to know *when* you did it. When did you talk to the two men?"

"A few hours ago," she said between sniffles. "They locked me in my basement with Rhesus. It took me several hours to break down the door."

"Tell me how it happened."

"The two men ran to your car as I unlocked it. They asked who I was and why I had your keys. I told them it was none of their business. They let me leave, but they must have followed me home and I never saw them. As I walked into my house, the two men came in behind me. They had their guns out before I could get mine. They took my weapon, then threatened to shoot my dog if I didn't say where you were." The shock in her voice disappeared, leaving only a quiet, mournful Dessi. "I'm sorry."

"How much did you tell them?"

"Everything. The message. What it meant. Where to find you. I told them everything except about the aquila and Spartacus. They never asked about those."

"What happened next?"

"They locked me in the basement, then left."

"Did they hurt you?"

"No. When I told them about Perperikon, they ran out."

A fast-moving cloud raced across the reddish sun, now hovering not far above the horizon. "Think clearly," Harry said. "How long ago did this happen? Tell me exactly."

"Three hours."

It was less than two hours to drive from Dessi's university to Perperikon. How long had he been exploring the city? An hour or more. "I have to go," Harry said. "I'll call you. Be alert and don't trust anyone."

"I have my gun. You have one too. Use it."

He clicked off, now uneasily aware of how exposed the top of this hill was. Trees on all sides offered cover for anyone wanting to move up the slope without being seen—just as he had done. The only open side was to the front, looking down onto the parking lot where the dig team had parked. He left the entryway to the newly discovered chamber open and crept across the site. He made it to the far end and looked down the steep hill.

No cars in the lot. The cold hand gripping his stomach loosened a fraction as he turned to head back to the tomb. He could do this. Go into the hidden passage, find what it contained, and get out of here before those two guys showed up. Harry broke into a run.

A bird called from the woods to his left. A strange call, one he didn't recognize. Harry turned to look an instant before a rock bounced off his right leg. He looked to the right. The electrician walked out of the woods, a pistol in his hand, the barrel trained on Harry.

"Don't move," the man said in English.

Harry turned left and ran. *BANG*. A gunshot boomed, and stone shards exploded by his foot. He stopped as a second man walked out of the woods in front of him. The other food guy. The one whose partner had died in Cotys's tomb. The man made a fake bird call and laughed, a humorless grin on his face.

"Stand still," the bird caller shouted. "Next time I do not miss."

The Russian accents again.

Bird caller yelled at his partner. "Yuri, secure him."

Yuri ran up behind Harry and grabbed his arm. He pressed the barrel of his gun against Harry's spine. "Oleg, the rope."

Oleg, he of the terrible bird calls, approached cautiously before removing a thin length of rope from his jacket. "You tie it," Oleg said to his partner.

The men switched to Russian as first Yuri twisted Harry's arm behind his back, then grabbed his other arm and bound them together. Oleg kept his gun trained on Harry's chest all the while, standing just out of arm's reach. Not that Harry had any free arms to reach with.

"What do you want?" Harry struggled against the rope, twisting as Yuri tied a knot.

He never saw Oleg's gun coming until it slammed into his gut. "Be still," Oleg said after Harry finished coughing, having barely kept his feet. "That is better. Tell us. What is here?"

This pair didn't know about the aquila, Harry reminded himself. "I have no idea," he said truthfully. "I was searching when you two showed up."

"Searching where?" Oleg asked. "Take us."

Hard to argue with two armed men and no hands to fight. Harry nodded toward the tombs. "Over there. I found an entrance."

Yuri pushed him that way. "Walk," Yuri said. "To the entrance."

Harry set off slowly in the general direction of the tombs, moving with uncertain steps. All the while he worked his hands stealthily back and forth, trying without success to loosen the ropes. He passed the tombs at a slow pace before finally inclining his head to the still-open passage entrance. "There. Down in the far corner. I found a passage that goes deeper into the hill."

"What is down there?" Yuri asked.

"No idea."

"I saw you on the phone," Yuri said. "Who did you call?"

"Someone called me," he said. "Told me about how you threatened a dog. You're a couple of real tough guys."

Yuri brandished his fist again. Harry didn't move. The fist lowered. "Walk," Yuri said. "Down there."

Moments later all three men stood around the upraised stone. "How did you find it?" Oleg asked.

"The inscription in Cotys's tomb. Though I suspect you already know that."

"I read it," Oleg said. "The words made no sense. Until the woman told us the truth. She said to find the rising sun, then look down."

Right on all counts. "I found it." Harry indicated the engraving. "Looking down is next. You going down first?"

"Do not forget the other tomb," Oleg said. "Where Maksim died."

Maksim. The bruiser who had chased Harry up the false stairs. "I didn't kill him," Harry said. "I had no idea those steps were a trap."

Oleg shrugged. He waved his gun at the open hole. "You go first. Perhaps there is another trap."

This guy didn't seem to care that his buddy had died in Cotys's tomb. Why not? Harry filed that question away and focused on the opening. "I can't climb down there with my hands tied. I'll break my neck."

Oleg offered an identical shrug. "Maybe. Not my problem."

Harry eyed the two men. He played a hunch. "If I die, you two won't know anything. What will your boss say about that?"

The two men looked at each other. *I was right.* These two were killers, yes. But not the brains behind an operation to steal artifacts. No chance. "The boss won't be happy if your best resource breaks his neck."

Oleg spoke in Russian. Yuri grunted. Harry forced himself to keep still when a wicked knife came out of Yuri's belt and made quick work of the restraint. Hopefully it was their only other weapon. Harry shook some life into his arms. "I'll go first, but I'm telling you the truth. I have no idea what's down there."

He pulled out his flashlight. Both Russians produced their own. Harry crouched at the opening's edge. "Aim your lights down here," he said.

The combined beams revealed what Harry had seen earlier. A set of stairs, a dirt floor, and a side opening leading to parts unknown. Harry straightened and moved down the stairs with a confidence he didn't feel. The steps were on a side wall and led to a room that he could see had started as a natural cavern inside the hill before being expanded to a much larger size. Stone supports reinforced the ceiling.

In this larger room openings had been cut into all four walls. Each opening had recessed shelves created for one purpose: to store bodies. There were at least a dozen burial niches on each wall. Harry moved to the nearest one. Dusty, dry remnants of clothing lay atop the dull white bones of a long-dead Thracian. The remnants still retained a deep, rich purple hue. Only the wealthy could have afforded clothes like these. The dead people had been important in Thracian society. A glint of silver hinted at valuables within the tombs, jewelry or other markers of status. One question leapt to his mind. Why bury them down here?

Yuri's voice barged in on Harry's thoughts. "What do you see?"

"Bodies," Harry said. "Lots of them. Come have a look."

Yuri kept his gun on Harry as Oleg descended the ladder; then Oleg trained his gun on Harry as Yuri came down. Both men walked slowly around the chamber.

Harry pointed to the notch in front of him. "These were important people. See this fabric? Only the wealthy could afford purple clothes. I'd guess this was an important burial ground." He aimed his light at the tunnel opening. "You want to know what else is down here? Check the tunnel."

"Not yet," Yuri said. He reached into the nearest burial niche and scattered the bones as fast as he could grab them. A femur clattered over toward Harry. "Nothing," Yuri said. "Keep looking."

Harry stood still in the middle of the room as the two men emptied every shelf of its occupant. Silver and gold jewelry went into a pile by the stairs, along with a set of jeweled daggers and a pair of massive pearl earrings. Only after every burial vault had been ransacked did Yuri look at Harry.

"There must be more," he said.

"What else are you looking for?" Harry asked. He pretended to rub his forehead, covering the look he gave to the daggers on top of their loot pile. Blades that looked to still have an edge.

"The reason for this place." Yuri motioned with his gun toward one of the dark openings. "Go. Find it."

"There may not be anything else down here." He paused. "I don't think you're going to find Roman gold."

Yuri didn't react. *These guys have no idea about the aquila*, Harry reminded himself again. "You go," Yuri said. "Slowly."

Harry aimed his light into the opening. Taller than him and plenty wide, the circular hole in the wall appeared to be a natural tunnel enlarged by Thracian tools, the dirt floor sloping downward as it curved out of sight. Harry moved to the edge, where the room became a tunnel, and stuck his light in as far as he could reach. Nothing but a dirt floor and stone supports for the ceiling.

"Give me one of those leg bones," Harry said as he pointed at the floor. "A long one." Yuri picked up a femur and tossed it Harry's way. "Thanks."

Harry sent out a silent apology to the unlucky soul whose leg he was holding, then used it to probe the ground and walls, finding nothing but dirt and stone. No triggers, no false floors. He tossed the femur halfway down the tunnel. It bounced and rattled along the floor, eventually stopping after it banged into the spot where the wall curved around and out of sight. Nothing happened.

"Good enough." Harry crossed the threshold. His flashlight threw shadows across the rough, rounded walls as he moved. A look over his shoulder confirmed that Yuri and Oleg were not yet willing to follow him. Harry made his way around the curve.

The two men's quick footsteps followed from behind as he walked on. He kept his light moving from left to right, up and down, alert for any threats. The ground sloped downward, and deep tool marks could be seen in places, widening the tunnel here, leveling it there. The stone supports on each side showed no signs of deterioration. His footsteps echoed as he stayed in the middle, leaning forward to look around the turn of the wall to see what lay ahead. Moving faster, forcing the other men to keep up, Harry continued until he stepped around a slightly sharper corner and stopped cold.

"I found something." Harry yelled over his shoulder. Rapid footsteps brought the two others closer. Harry raised his free arm. "Stay back," he said. "Let me look."

Yuri pushed up against Harry's outstretched arm but did not try to pass. "What is it?" he asked.

Harry's voice was low when he answered. "A temple. To a Thracian son."

The tunnel opened up on either side ahead to reveal a wide space. Flat along the back, perhaps twenty feet deep and just as wide. "The tunnel was natural," Harry said. "This isn't. They cut it out of solid rock."

Oleg found his voice. "Why?"

"To honor their gods. And this image is important." Harry indicated the single carving that covered a section of the rear wall. The two had likely seen it before, if they'd been paying attention. "A rising sun."

A flat horizon with half an orb rising above it, lines radiating from the curved line. "There's a marker exactly like this on the tomb we entered," Harry said. "The same as one in Cotys's tomb."

"That is what the woman said." Yuri aimed his light up and down. "There is nothing else here. Where is the treasure?"

Harry responded by turning his light away from the rear wall and aiming it to one side. "I'd start with one of those if I were you."

The two men visibly stiffened. Neither had noticed the burial niches cut into either side wall. "Check the bodies," Yuri barked. "They must have treasure."

As Harry had hoped, the men were so focused on the idea of more loot that they forgot to keep an eye on their hostage. One set of eyes was always coming back to Harry, however, as they men searched. Bones flew, more gold and silver jewelry came out, another bejeweled knife, and soon the niches were empty.

"We came all this way for rings and bracelets?" Yuri said petulantly, then turned to Oleg. "He will be angry."

Must be talking about the boss. Harry waited for more, but the men fell silent and turned to look at him.

Yuri wasn't happy. "There must be more."

"I didn't build this place," Harry said. "But I'll look. You going to shoot me?" He nodded at the upraised gun in Yuri's hand. "Didn't think so. Put that down before it goes off."

Yuri grumbled, but lowered his weapon. Harry made a show of inspecting the rear wall, running his hands over the carving, taking his time. The carving was only a carving, nothing more. A marker the Thracians used to honor a fallen son of Thrace. Harry needed to stretch this out, to put the two men off their guard. He also wanted to slip his hand into one pocket and grab the knuckledusters they had failed to take from him. He succeeded on both counts.

"Nothing here," he said. Harry stood quickly, keeping one hand in a pocket. He pointed to the right side of the room with the flashlight in his other. "Who searched over here?" he asked Oleg. "Which one of the niches didn't have any bones?"

Oleg's mouth puckered up and his eyebrows came together. "I do not know."

"The first rule in ancient tombs is to pay attention." Harry aimed a light at the uppermost niche, which hugged the rear wall. "That one was empty. Care to guess why?" The two men had nothing to say. "I have no idea either," Harry said. "But I bet it's important."

He didn't give them a chance to think about it before moving to the niche in question. The base of it sat at Harry's eye level. He boosted himself up to get a better look at the one that had been empty. He put the flashlight down in the upper carveout, careful to keep his armored hand in the shadows, using it to feel around. The interior appeared to be solid stone. If that were true, why hadn't any bones been in here? It didn't seem right. He couldn't say why, but that alarm in his gut had been ringing ever since he walked in here.

He grabbed his light and aimed it at the other side of the niche. "Oh."

"What?" Yuri asked quickly.

"Hang on." Harry reached into the very back corner, to a discolored patch against the rear wall. "Give me a knife."

Both men laughed. "We are not stupid," Yuri said.

"I think there's an opening here," Harry fired back. "You have guns. What am I going to do, stab you before you shoot me? I want to get out of here alive. Do you want to tell the boss you came up empty-handed?"

Yuri and Oleg conferred momentarily, then separated. Oleg picked up the knife and tossed it inside the niche Harry was investigating before stepping back. Harry grabbed it and scraped the blade over his arm to test the edge. Two thousand years old and the blade could still do some damage.

First, the niche. He pushed the blade tip against the off-colored portion of the niche. It seemed too square, out of place. What would the Thracians hide back here? Images of the path to this hidden chamber ran through his head. Cotys's tomb with a tunnel hidden high above it. Perperikon itself with a concealed vault beneath a marked tombstone. Both used the terrain to obscure a secret. And messages had been left in the open for anyone to see, if only they knew where to look. His eyes snapped open. "They used the cave."

"What?"

Harry ignored Yuri and scraped at the stone with the dagger's edge. Dirt hardened to rocklike consistency gave way. "It's a false wall," Harry said. "They cut out a section of the wall. That's why no bones were here. They didn't want to draw anyone's attention to it. Nobody searches an empty niche when there are other corpses with treasure nearby."

Harry tapped the dagger's hilt against the discolored stone. Again, then harder, and then he smashed the sturdy hilt against a corner and it happened: the square section of stone spun around on an axis to reveal an opening.

"There's a lever here," he said. "Inside this opening." A stone handle jutted out from the wall like an oversized light switch. Harry grabbed hold. "Stand back," he called out. "I don't know what's going to happen here."

Yuri and Oleg quick-stepped back. The lever was in the upward position, so Harry gripped it tightly, gritted his teeth and pulled. The wall rumbled. Nothing moved. "You see anything?" Harry shouted over his shoulder.

"It is a door," Oleg replied.

Harry backed out of the niche so fast he nearly landed face-first. One hand shot out to grab the wall, then he stood straight and stared at the tomb's rear wall. "The carving's gone."

"It lifted into the wall." Yuri pushed past Harry. "That is it." He paused in front of it, awestruck. "It is gold?"

"Yes," Harry said as he looked at the object that had been hidden. "It's an *aquila*. It's the other... It's the symbol of a Roman legion."

Harry let this sink in for a moment. A second eagle. Last week there hadn't been any of them in the world. Now Harry had recovered not just one, but two. The symbols of two vanquished legions that had somehow ended up in Thracian hands. Only one man could be responsible.

As Yuri had said, pulling the lever had caused the entire rising sun carving to retract upward into the wall. A pedestal had been hidden behind it, the aquila resting on top of it.

"Wait." Harry grabbed Yuri as the man reached forward. "It could be a trap."

Yuri went still. "I do not see anything."

"That's the idea." Harry waited until Yuri backed up a few more steps. "The Thracians wouldn't want a Roman to find this." He did not elaborate.

"This is what he wants," Oleg said, meaning their boss.

Yuri shot his partner a glare before speaking in Russian. Harry didn't understand any of it except two words. *Big bird.* Yuri said those two words in English. A name? Harry filed it away as Yuri turned back to Harry. "What are those words?" Yuri asked, pointing to the stone wall behind the aquila.

Harry moved closer. Latin letters were inscribed in the stone.

"It's Latin," Harry said. "Can you read it?" Both men said they couldn't. *Good.*

His lips moved silently as he translated.

Cotys honors the son here. He also looks to honor Victory's wings by kneeling with the Lesser Gods.

"Read it in English," Yuri growled. Harry did. "What does it mean?" Yuri asked.

"I have no idea." Not entirely true. Harry read it again to himself, burning the words into his mind even as he pretended to look for traps around the floor of this hidden shrine. "I don't see anything. This may only be what it looks like. A shrine."

"It looks like money to me." Yuri stepped closer.

"Wait," Harry said. "The pedestal could be rigged. There could be a counterweight we can't see." Harry went through exaggerated motions of care for another few breaths. "I think it's clear. You'd still better stand back."

The cowardly duo again retreated as Harry reached for the aquila. He needed to draw them closer. The Latin writing they couldn't read said a whole lot more than they realized. What did it tell Harry? That he needed to get out of here and to his car. What came next? Harry wasn't certain, not quite. He did know finding the answers required taking a ferry ride.

"I don't see anything," Harry said. "I'm going to lift the aquila off its pedestal."

The men said nothing. Harry's fingers brushed the gold eagle. Yuri and Oleg edged closer. Harry grunted as he lifted the aquila, turning and holding it in front of him, the bird shielding his armored hand from view. "It's real." Harry kept his words low, opening his eyes to appear awestruck. "Nobody's seen one in two thousand years."

The men approached and Harry stepped closer to them. He angled his body, weight on the rear foot.

Yuri's gun was down at his side, greed clouding his eyes. "How much is it—"

Harry smashed the aquila into Yuri's nose. Cartilage shattered, Yuri cried out, and Harry darted around him to loose a rocket of a punch at Oleg's jaw. His knuckleduster crashed off Oleg's face and sent the man spinning. Years of boxing had taught Harry to press his advantage, so he followed his first punch with a jab to the gut. Oleg doubled over right in time for his chin to meet Harry's fist. The uppercut put Oleg down on his back. He didn't get up.

Yuri did, or at least tried to. The big man growled from the ground. Harry twisted, tried to stomp on Yuri's gun arm and missed. Before he could try again, the world flipped and Harry found himself lying on his back, courtesy of Yuri's leg swiping Harry's feet out from under him. The dirt floor had no give when he landed on it. Harry sat up as Yuri gained his feet, the pistol coming around to point at Harry's chest. Harry's foot shot out, catching Yuri in the stomach. The gunman grunted as air flew from his chest, but his gun quickly came back to aim at Harry.

The Roman eagle took flight as Harry launched it at Yuri's face. The bird flew true, sailing at full speed to smash into Yuri's nose. Any intact cartilage disintegrated. Blood poured down Yuri's nose as he grabbed his nose with both hands, the gun clattering to the ground.

Harry scooped up the aquila and took off, his footsteps echoing off the cavern walls as he bolted for the surface; the dim light ahead was like a beacon. Up the stairs, he paused only to drop the tomb's lid back down before racing into the woodlands and down the hillside at a reckless pace. Tree limbs whipped at his face and the thick brush clawed at his clothes as he barreled ahead—until he hit level ground and promptly spilled ass over elbows onto the rocky grass. He got up, only his pride injured, jumped into his car and motored away into the Bulgarian countryside, slowly getting his breathing under control.

Two aquilas. Two symbols of Thracian defiance and victory over Roman legions. A nation unwilling to bend to Roman might. Their resistance had run beneath the feet and behind the walls of their Roman conquerors. The aquilas were beacons of Thracian independence to inspire future generations.

The most intriguing part? He didn't think the defiance had ended here. It had continued, and now he knew where.

His phone vibrated. Harry jumped, nearly swerving into a fence post before he grabbed the device and glanced at the screen. "Rose?"

"Are you busy?" Three words from Rose and he could practically smell the cigarette smoke, taste the martini.

He should have told her 'Yes, I'm pulling back the curtain on a Thracian prince and trying not to get killed in the process.' But no. "Never too busy for you," he said.

"This is about Olivier Lloris. He wants to meet."

Chapter 14

Perperikon

His thoughts of Thrace vanished. "Olivier wants to meet me?"

"He wishes to discuss the bible and its contents in person. I suspect the idea of what may yet be found is at the root of his request."

"Olivier wants to meet the person who can find whatever else tied to Charlemagne is out there."

"Exactly."

"You think it's a bad idea."

"Why would I?"

"You're the broker. You keep both the buyer and the seller safe. The two parties meeting can't help either side, or you."

"Correct. I told Olivier this could never happen."

"Then why tell me about it?" The wheels in his head picked up steam. "Because you think I want to do it," Harry said. "And even though you know it's a bad idea, you'll let me decide."

"It is my responsibility to advise you in these transactions. My advice is to proceed with caution. However, I would be remiss to stand in your way. You feel a debt is owed. Who am I to prevent you from collecting?"

Fair enough. "This isn't about me or even Charlemagne's bible. It's about stopping the man who ruined my father's life." A field of cows passed outside Harry's window. "It's about payback."

Her response carried the weight of an unspoken burden Harry didn't know of. "I understand how the desire for retribution can be consuming."

Harry couldn't guess what Rose wanted vengeance for. All he knew was he felt sorry for the person on the receiving end. "What if I say I want to meet Olivier?"

"I would say I am not surprised."

"Any recommendations for how to not get myself killed?"

"First, Olivier will never meet you. He is too cautious. One of his representatives will come in his stead. The man I spoke with, if I had to predict."

"Not a dealbreaker. Getting close to him will take time."

"Second, disguise your appearance."

"A fake mustache and sunglasses?"

"Use your discretion. Third, meet in a public area of your choosing. Olivier indicated he wishes to meet in France. His business is based in Paris."

A city Harry knew well. "That works. I'll choose a location right before the meeting."

"Giving them no time to prepare any unpleasant surprises. Wise decision. Finally, I would still tell you not to do this, though I have no doubt you will meet as Olivier wishes. Hence my focus on your safety."

"I appreciate it, Rose. Olivier wants to know what else is out there for his collection." Which presented a problem. "He's already purchased the bible. I need more bait to dangle. Another relic to keep him interested."

"Even the possibility of a relic. A description of the writings you found will suffice. I promised Olivier the bible within one week. That week is not nearly over."

"I can't give him the bible yet," Harry said. "I can tell him about what it suggests, what remains to be found." He closed his eyes and pulled the inscription up in his head. "Exquisite gifts, including an elephant. And a water clock with the keys to Jerusalem."

"Olivier will want some evidence those artifacts actually exist."

"I only need to make him *believe* the artifacts exist. He wants it to be true. Charlemagne made peace with the caliphate so that he only had to fight battles on one front, and that peace was symbolized in the exchange of extravagant gifts between the caliph and Charlemagne. I believe Charlemagne ordered Agilulph—who outlived Charlemagne by over a decade—to secure the signs of that peace accord so his heirs would have them."

Rose agreed. "The story will keep Olivier close."

Exactly. "Call Olivier. Say I'll meet him in Paris tomorrow. I can get a flight first thing in the morning." He pulled up directions to the closest major airport as he spoke. "That'll give me time to speak with Sara about the message, maybe make actual progress."

"I will speak with him," Rose said. "What else do you need?"

"Information." The memory of Oleg and Yuri talking in the hidden tombs came to mind. "Do you know anyone referred to as *big bird*? Someone tied to the antiquities trade. A person with the resources to hire men to infiltrate an international dig site and track me across Bulgaria." He briefly recounted his experiences. "Ring any bells?"

The sound of ice shaking in expensive vodka came through the phone. "Perhaps," she said. "I will see what I can find."

"What about the aquila?" Harry looked at the golden eagle on his passenger seat. He was returning the first one to Tax. That was enough do-gooding for one adventure. He deserved to keep this second one. "I need to get it to you."

"Take it on your flight to Paris. Tell security it is an item of personal religious significance."

"It's a massive golden eagle."

"What matters is that it is not an explosive or a weapon. Trust me. I have dealt with a situation like this before. They will not bother you if you are upfront. I will have a man waiting at the Paris airport to collect it."

Harry thanked her, clicked off, then stepped on the gas. Vengeance long overdue was one step closer.

The Parisian morning rush was in full swing as Harry drove a rental car away from Charles de Gaulle Airport toward the City of Light. Had any of those first gaslights that had given Paris its nickname still existed, none would be lit under these clear skies and bright sun. Harry downed his second espresso of the morning as he gripped the wheel, shaking his head at the fact Rose's plan for bringing the aquila to Paris had worked, the handoff going down without a hitch. Another swig of espresso later his head had sufficiently cleared to be ready for what waited.

He dialed Sara's number.

"I assume you made it to the city," she said when she picked up. "I've been thinking."

That was never good. Well, almost never. "About the bible? Or about me?"

"The bible message," Sara said. "Tell me about the meeting arrangement."

"I'm meeting Olivier's guy in front of the Louvre. Plenty of foot traffic and the courtyard is wide open."

"With enough open space to leave if you feel unsafe."

"I'll keep my eyes open." Enough about that. "Any thoughts you want to share?"

"Agilulph's message talks about the symbolic gifts Charlemagne exchanged with the caliph to commemorate their peace accord. Then he gives vague references to a saint and a location. As you said, the locations could be waypoints or markers on a path Agilulph left to ensure Charlemagne's heirs could get to the symbols of peace."

"Any possibilities jump out at you?" Sara didn't answer, but asked him the same question. "No," he replied.

"Then we should read it again." She recited the final portion of the message, the part he believed related to what came next.

The prizes of my Father travel with Columbanus to the Trebbia. Follow the knowledge of that learned servant of God. The true path is marked by the mythical beasts of thunder and fury who dwelled far beyond our lands.

"I have my thoughts in order," Sara said. "Listen closely. The *Father* Agilulph mentions is Charlemagne."

"As in the *Father of Europe*," Harry said.

"Next is another name. *Columbanus*. I suspect Agilulph is referring to a saint. An Irish saint, of all people, known for founding monasteries in his homeland and Italy."

"*Trebbia* is a river," Harry said. "I figured that part out."

"Which makes me think we need to focus on Columbanus's activities in Italy. Unfortunately, he founded several religious institutions in the region."

"The rest of it doesn't make sense," Harry said. "What *knowledge* of Columbanus does Agilulph want us to follow? And what are these *mythical beasts* he's talking about? Odd stuff for a religious man to write."

Sara's voice was so low he had to strain to catch it. "That's why I took so long to share my thoughts," she said. "I am stuck."

Harry frowned. He grumbled. He got past it. "Don't worry. We'll figure it out. Together. Until then, I'll use what we have to reel Olivier in and make the rest up."

Sara seemed to like the idea. "Olivier's man knows less than you. Offer a compelling theory, false or not, and it will be more than enough to serve your purpose."

Harry nodded to himself. Keeping Olivier on the hook was vital. As long as Harry stayed one step ahead, the Frenchman would follow until he was close enough for Harry to slip past his defenses. "I'll call you after the meeting," he said. "How's everything at work?"

"Busy, and don't try to distract me." The tone in her voice spoke of an undercurrent running through her mind, one about to surface. "You know you don't have to do this alone," she said. "I can help."

Harry almost swerved out of his lane. "You want to *help*? I thought you wanted me to forget about Olivier and leave Charlemagne alone."

"I did, and I do. But I also know there's no possibility that you'll do either of those. Also, if you say this is too dangerous or imply in any way that I'm not capable of handling myself, I will find you. And you will be sorry."

"I appreciate the offer," he said. "I also have to deal with Gary's situation."

"Tracking a Thracian prince who defeated Roman legions is not a *situation*."

"I'll let you know if you can help." Which he wouldn't. "I'll call you when it's over." A flash of doubt rose in his gut. "You're at the museum today?"

"Facing endless meetings," she said. "From which I expect you to save me with good news. Don't make me wait."

She clicked off as Harry exited the highway and disappeared into Parisian traffic. Stop lights and car horns accompanied him as he passed the Arc de Triomphe, skirting the Champs-Élysées before he found an exorbitantly priced parking lot. Once he stepped out into the chilly air, he finally sensed the weight of this storied city pressing in all around him. A comforting weight of past and future.

A black fedora went on his head, a pair of sunglasses on his face, and a scarf wrapped around his neck. Feet moving, eyes ahead, Harry touched the amulet around his neck as he approached I.M. Pei's glassy pyramid. Harry circled it, taking care to give the north side a wide berth. That was where Olivier's representative should be waiting, identifiable by a bright green scarf around his neck and a white feather in the band of his hat. A glance at his watch revealed the agreed-upon meeting time had arrived. One full loop and Harry still hadn't spotted the scarf or feather. He began the second circuit, slipping among groups of tourists as he moved.

There. A man sporting a brilliant green scarf stood at the pyramid's edge, hands in his pockets, a white feather in the band of his dress hat. Sunglasses hid his eyes. Harry kept a group of chattering tourists between himself and the man as he watched. The man's three-piece suit was impeccable, his overcoat of the finest quality. The guy didn't set off Harry's internal alarms. Which was cause for concern.

Harry walked on. The man didn't move as Harry approached from the south. The man never turned until Harry stood only a few feet away and spoke.

"Are you waiting for me?" Harry asked in English.

A beat passed. The man turned, smoothly, unhurried. He looked Harry up and down. "I believe I am," he finally said, his French-accented English impeccable. "Shall we walk?"

"I'm good right here." Harry took his phone out. "You want to see the message."

"My client is very interested," the man said. "What is your name?"

"You can call me Pepé." Harry winced as the name left his mouth. *The cartoon skunk. Brilliant.* It had been the first French name that popped into his head.

"Pepé." The man didn't blink. "What do you have to show me?"

"What's your name?" Harry asked. Never let them take the lead.

The man wasn't fazed. "Fortunately, I am not named after a skunk. My name is Benoit Lafont, and I represent the interests of certain clients in their private acquisitions."

"You're familiar with my broker."

Benoit showed a glimpse of polished teeth. "Ms. Leroux is well known. I have the utmost respect for her."

"Then why meet with me?" Harry asked.

"I represent my client's interests," Benoit said. "He wished for me to view the merchandise on his behalf."

"You know I wouldn't bring it with me."

Benoit looked past Harry's shoulder to the crowds around them. Harry resisted the urge to follow suit. "I advised my client as such. I also advised him that if he wished to learn more about the bible"—and here a beat passed—"or any *other* aspects of his newest piece, the prudent course was to ask directly. You are the best source for such answers."

Harry liked this guy. Direct. "I have a clearer image."

Rose had sent it to him this morning. The first image Olivier had received of Agilulph's writing in his bible had been blurred, the entire handwritten message indecipherable; this one revealed part of the message. A part that included the name of a river.

"Trebbia." Benoit studied Harry's face. "A river. What does it mean to you?"

"Taken by itself? Nothing. But with the rest of the message?" The corner of Harry's mouth turned up. "It indicates that Agilulph's purpose was to tell someone where to find something."

"Such as?"

This was what Harry had turned over in his head the entire trip here. How much to reveal. He needed a balance between keeping Olivier's interest and not giving him enough to launch his own expedition. "Symbols of peace," Harry offered. "Symbols to continue the peace that Charlemagne brokered even after he died."

"A way to keep his heirs in power," Benoit said. "Peace brings prosperity."

"Charlemagne did everything he could to secure the future of his line."

"The Carolingian dynasty lasted only a few centuries," Benoit said. "His great-grandchild was the last to rule. Hardly the eternal empire Charlemagne envisioned."

"Their failure to sustain power is the reason we're here today. If they needed the insurance Charlemagne left behind, it wouldn't still be out there, and I wouldn't be able to find it."

"Your confidence is absolute."

You have no idea. "I'm here," Harry said. "Now you've seen Agilulph's writings. What else do you want?"

"An idea of the remaining artifacts my client can expect to purchase from you."

"These artifacts are tied to Charlemagne and the peace he brokered," Harry said. "Artifacts no one since Charlemagne has ever owned." Now *that* was a good story.

Benoit hardly blinked. "My client requires more specific information."

"Then he can wait until I locate the artifacts and offer them to the highest bidder. I don't deal with threats."

Benoit raised a hand. "I meant no threat. I only wish to confirm my client is not wasting his time or his money."

"We have a deal for the bible. You'll have it in a week or so. Until then, this is the best I can do." Harry made a show of looking at the ground. "Unless you want to cancel the arrangement."

"My client wishes no such thing."

"Glad to hear it." Harry looked past Benoit. "You'll receive additional images today. I'm sure your client will be pleased to see the new details." Harry turned away. "Safe travels, Benoit."

He made it one step before Benoit spoke. "There is another matter to discuss."

Harry stopped. He didn't look back. "What's that?"

"A new arrangement."

Harry turned. "I'm not selling anything else today."

"My client has authorized me to offer you a fee for the bible, any additional items it may lead to, and your services to obtain said items for him." Harry said nothing until Benoit spoke again. "He will pay you twice the sales price of the bible for any related artifacts you locate."

Harry's mouth tightened. "I'm not for hire."

"I assure you any fee will be—"

"You're not listening." Harry stepped closer. The brim of his fedora nearly bumped Benoit's hat. "I don't work for anyone. Understood?"

Benoit offered a smile that would have chilled a volcano. "Of course, sir. I look forward to seeing the bible within the week."

Harry tilted his head toward the museum. "Go inside. Enjoy the paintings. Don't follow me."

Benoit turned without another word and walked away. Harry watched until the man vanished into the Louvre, then he moved at full speed in the opposite direction, alert for any sign of surveillance. He found none.

Harry shook his head. *Focus.* Less than a week now until he had to deliver the bible. Was it enough time to unravel the mystery behind Cotys IV and a prince named Spartacus? Harry put his head down and walked faster. No, but now it would have to be.

Harry was back in his car and driving toward the airport when his phone buzzed. He saw Sara's name on the screen. "The meeting just ended," he said, putting her on speaker. "I'm headed back to the airport."

"Tell me everything."

Harry recounted Benoit's questions and eventual offer, as well as the deadline. "I think Olivier's on the hook," Harry said. "He wants exclusivity and access to what I have."

"That's a short timeline."

"It is," he said. "Any insights on the last message from Cotys?"

"How about I come over and tell you in person?"

"No chance. I'm doing this to keep you safe, not put you in danger. Not that you need to be kept safe," he said quickly. "It's my choice."

"I appreciate the concern." There was the sound of papers shuffling. "I reviewed the information you sent from the tombs of Perperikon. Incredible, really. The Thracians hid a temple beneath a temple." A note of concern seemed to enter her voice. "Do you think those two men escaped?"

"Probably. I didn't leave them down there to starve. Which reminds me of something. One of them mentioned a name. *Big Bird.* I think it's their boss's name."

"What kind of criminal is named Big Bird?"

"You'd be surprised. Either way, those guys are working for someone, and I think that's his nickname. Rose is asking around. There's always a chance Joey has connections to the guy. If that's the case, maybe this can all go away with Joey making a phone call. Then I'll have time to worry about what really matters."

"Until that happens you can only focus on what's in front of you," Sara said. "I believe I know what the message in the tombs meant."

"I have a guess." He repeated the phrase etched into his memory. "*Cotys honors the son here. He also looks to honor Victory's wings by kneeling with the Lesser Gods.*" A lot packed into two sentences. "The *son* reference is about Spartacus. An indicator we're on the same path as before."

"Agreed," Sara said.

"Cotys's entire path has been about honoring this son. A path leading to different places of worship. His tomb—the humility is impressive—and then the tombs at Perperikon, where they also had a temple to Dionysius. I think this next reference also points to a place of worship, though not one where you honor the dead."

"Not a graveyard."

"Exactly. A temple dedicated to a god. Or goddess."

Sara agreed. "A Greek temple in ancient Thrace. A temple honoring the goddess Nike. The personification of victory."

"He's talking about a statue," Harry said. On the island of Samothrace."

"Where the temple of Nike still exists," she said softly. "It fits. The temple called the *Temple of the Lesser Gods*. And the statue you're thinking of—now in the Louvre—was taken from Samothrace."

They were talking about a Greek masterpiece. The world-renowned *Winged Victory of Samothrace*.

"Have you ever been to Samothrace?" Harry asked. "I've only read about the statue."

"I have not," Sara said. "I do know there are a number of temples on the island. That should confuse anyone who doesn't fully understand this message."

"The message in Perperikon was in Latin," Harry said. "Those two guys chasing me couldn't read it. That buys us more time while they find someone to translate it." The airport came into view ahead. "I have to go," Harry said. "See what you can dig up about the *Lesser Gods* temple. I'll call when I'm on the island."

Sara's response caught him off guard. "It's not too late."

"For what?"

"To ask for me to come help."

He shook his head. "You *are* helping me. I couldn't do this without you."

"Yes. You could."

Better to leave that one alone. "That's not the point. I'm doing this to protect the people in my life. You want to help? Keep doing what you're doing. There's another mystery to solve."

"Charlemagne."

"You got it." Harry took an exit for the airport as a jet roared overhead. "We're not finished chasing relics yet. You'll have your chance to join the fun. I promise."

Chapter 15

Samothrace, Greece

Harry caught the evening ferry, his rented motorcycle bouncing off the Greek mainland and onto the deck just as the ferry gate closed, tires rolling onto the boat with no time to spare. The ticket-taker was not amused, grabbing Harry's boarding pass as though it offended him, which it likely did. Harry parked his bike and headed for the lounge, where he ordered a beer, slumped in a booth and promptly fell asleep.

Two hours later he leapt up when the waitress shook his shoulder. He paid ten times what the beer was worth to thank her for letting him sleep, then asked for an espresso. The hot Greek coffee warmed him with its pleasant heat as he found his bike and waited to disembark. Last on, first off, so Harry's tires found Samothrace soil before anyone else, and he throttled the bike toward a falling sun. Mount Fengari rose five thousand feet above the city, a towering slope that looked as desolate and forbidding as the city proper was welcoming.

Fuel-efficient cars scooted along and pedestrians turned to watch as Harry weaved through traffic toward his destination beyond the outskirts of Samothrace's current reach, though not very far, for this island resembled Mount Fengari in most areas. Soon he was passing hardy trees, rocky soil, and windswept grounds that only became hospitable closer to the water. The Samothrace Temple Complex had been built not far from the city, a complex that grew from empty land into a site where all Greeks who venerated the pantheon of chthonic deities could come to worship.

Red-roofed homes and small shops interspersed with ancient

defensive walls gave way to clusters of barren trees and bushes. Harry kept looking back as the two-lane road wound across the island. His had been the last ferry of the day. If Oleg and Yuri hadn't come earlier, the only way they could get here now would be on a private boat or plane. For that to happen, they had to get out of the tomb and find someone to translate and decipher the inscription it contained.

This island should be his and his alone for now. It should be, but if that was true, why couldn't he shake the feeling someone was watching?

He nearly missed his turn for the temple complex. The bike skidded as Harry twisted the wheel, cutting between the barren trees standing guard on either side of the road as he shot up a hillside, crested a rise, and jammed on the brakes. A centuries-old religious sanctuary spread out before him. Easily twenty temples and sites of worship dotted the complex, which followed the contours of the land and a curving stream. Tall marble pillars and white stone foundations dotted the grounds. Harry scanned the moonlit ruins.

The ancient Greeks had intended for all followers across the various city-states to come and worship their deities. However, one group had created a secret set of rituals to initiate select members into an exclusive sect called the Cult of the Great Gods. Scholars believed that this group's initiation ritual occurred in one temple. The Temple of the Lesser Gods.

These rituals were administered to only a select few. Kings, princes, and the wealthiest Thracians. Why would they have hidden their actions in a temple where all were welcomed? More importantly, what were they hiding, and was it still in this temple?

Harry parked his bike in a dirt lot, hefted his well-worn pack, and headed on foot for a bridge-like entrance that once sat beneath grand arches. Roughly half of the support pillars remained, the pockmarked marble still stretching to twice Harry's height. He passed fallen walls and newly constructed barriers as he entered the first complex. He checked the map saved on his phone, and it was a good thing he'd saved it, for cell service up here was nonexistent.

An amphitheater carved from the ground passed on one side as he walked, wooden boards now replacing the original stone stage. The seats were cleared and the grass weeded, as though in preparation for a new production. A patch of grass encircled by massive square stones sat on the hillside above him. He passed it without a second look. His destination waited at the far end of the temple complex.

Carved blocks laid horizontally above standing stone columns rose on the path ahead. Harry crested the slope, narrowing his eyes as the breeze stiffened and the empty tree branches swayed. Ahead, a half-circle of pillars still stood on a raised platform about the size of a basketball court. Steps led to a rectangular central area. Stanchions with a single chain surrounded the site to warn visitors from using the steps. Harry stopped in front of the first step. The metal of the chain cooled his fingers when he touched it.

This was the Temple of the Lesser Gods. Where the secret ceremonies took place. A place all could visit, though few realized its importance. Harry nodded to himself. A good place to hide something.

The chain rattled as he stepped over it and went up the steps. He walked to the closest pillar. Its smooth white stone was weathered but sturdy, solid beneath his hands, unadorned by decoration. Cotys wanted him to *kneel* with the Lesser Gods. The platform had no altars and the pillars were unmarked. Only horizontal boulders lay across the top of each pillar, reminiscent of Stonehenge and its mystical formation.

Maybe kneeling was only part of the answer. The first part of Cotys's message referenced the statue of Nike, a statue long since moved to Paris. But it used to be here. He turned to his right, toward the east, to where the mountainside sloped upward and the barren trees stood guard. The statue would have sat in a place of honor. A place from which Nike could watch over the temple complex, the highest point on the grounds. The statue was long gone, and any plinth it rested on had collapsed. At least, most of it had.

He spotted the remnants of a structure between two columns. A structure that used to be a support base for a statue. A statue of the Greek goddess who protected the temple. Evidence of numerous dig sites abounded. Dirt had been turned, though the statue base remained. He walked to stand between the two pillars, his eyes on where Nike used to stand, then he remembered. "Kneel." Harry went to one knee. He looked down. Nothing. He looked up. *That's interesting.*

One long, horizontal block was above him, still supported by a pillar on either side. An image was carved on the underside. A familiar image. "The rising sun," Harry said. His eyes narrowed. "It's different."

The same half-circle above a straight line represented the sun rising over the horizon; the same closed eyes were cut into its upper half. The same straight lines shot out of the sun: the rays of light. In this version, one ray had an additional design on the end. An inverted *V*, which turned the ray into something else entirely. "An arrow," Harry said. "It's pointing the way."

The arrow pointed away from the site, away from where Harry had come, and into the complex, aimed toward woodlands now devoid of leaves. Woodlands with a narrow path leading into the trees.

Pebbles bounced as he descended the steps, circled the platform and headed for the path. The trees were far denser than in other parts of the complex. The area was well maintained, no surprise given the number of visitors who came here. Luck was with him, for on this chilly winter evening Harry found himself alone. He kept to the center of the path, his shadow stretching out on one side in the moonlight. He pushed a low branch out of his way. A *crack* sounded in the distance.

Harry spun around, then went still, his chest tight. There was someone out there. He could feel it. Back pressed against the nearest tree, Harry stared into the woods. No other noise cut the stillness. *Maybe I'm imagining it.* The two guys who had followed him across Bulgaria were in a tomb. They couldn't have made it here so quickly. No one knew where to find him. No, he was alone. Moving with purpose was the best option to keep it that way.

The trail was more dirt than grass. Small tufts of green sprouted from the ground. Harry followed the winding path; darkness was creeping in, and the temperature was dropping with each step. The path veered to one side up ahead, with a white rock at the turn. No, a stone, the same type from which the temple had been built. Why a single stone out here? Harry knelt to inspect it and found a carving on its surface, small and hard to see. The same image as the one from the Lesser Gods temple. A rising sun with an arrow at the end of one of the rays.

Harry spared only a glance over his shoulder as he picked up the pace, the sense of someone watching long gone. The trees narrowed into a veritable forest ahead to block out the sky. Gooseflesh formed on his neck as he pressed on until, without warning, the trees fell away. Harry stopped as a hidden world opened in front of him.

A hidden world containing exactly one thing. A well. Or what resembled a well. Stones piled in a circle and mortared together. It was a big well, two rows of stone thick. The structure was nearly big enough to be a column. His feet crunched on fallen leaves as he walked closer and found it was indeed an abandoned well. The stones held when he leaned on them, though he sure didn't want to get stuck down there. No water could be seen, and given how tall the well's exterior was, chances were good he'd be stuck down there for a long time if he fell in.

Was the altered rising sun pointing him to this well? This area appeared to be partially maintained, with the trees cut back recently. There were no footprints in the dirt, and the well showed little sign of conservation. He ran his hands over the uppermost level of stones and found nothing. This well wall was *thick*. As if it was intended to stand for centuries. The hair on his neck rose again, and this time not from the cold. This well meant something. He could feel it. But what?

Cotys's message said to kneel. He had knelt at the Lesser Gods temple; perhaps he was meant to do so here as well. Harry dropped to one knee and saw that tufts of dry grass sprouted from the base of the well. Might as well leave the place nicer than he'd found it. He bent down, pulling at the clumps of grass and dirt, tossing each aside until the bottom row of stone came into view. He cleared several more rows only to find he'd dug below ground level, and stopped when his fingers smashed into solid stone. How the Thracians had sunk a well here was beyond him.

Harry ripped more grass aside, and suddenly his arm stopped in mid-throw. Chunks of dirt lay on his shirt, a few sneaking down his collar. Harry didn't notice. He couldn't move. "The rising sun."

There was another rising sun carving on the lowest row of stones. No arrow this time, no other markings. Dirt and grass flew again as he cleared the adjacent stones, with no result. Only a single carving, cut into the well's base, just above the layer of solid stone.

Harry sat back. What did it mean? This was the right place, that much was clear, where Cotys was pointing. But to dive down a well? That made no sense. The correct answer had to be right in front of him. Darned if he could see it, though. He leaned back, hands splayed behind him, and breathed deeply of the cold air. His fingers ached; he stretched them out, digging into the soft dirt.

Soft dirt. Harry shot up as though bitten. The ground beneath him was soft, dirt he could stick his fingers in. Unlike the stone ground mere feet away, ground that had nearly broken his fingers when he dug. It shouldn't change composition so quickly, from dirt to hard stone.

He did not have a shovel, so he ran back to the complex and grabbed the first sharp rock he spotted. Suitably armed, he retraced his steps and stopped just short of the well, where he'd been sitting. The rock went up above his head, and with both hands he smashed it down, the rock sinking into the earth. He inched forward and tried it again, with the same result. Another shuffle forward, and this time when the rock crashed down shrapnel flew and his molars rattled.

So that was where the rocky ground started. Harry shook his head until his vision cleared, then used the rock edge to dig where the ground turned from stone to dirt. It took him only seconds to notice. Something wasn't right. Normal bedrock displayed an irregular pattern or shape. This rock ended smoothly.

"This isn't natural." He stopped digging, his hands still in the dirt. "Cotys dug out the ground and put this stone down." He reached out and ripped more dirt from the ground. *It has to be here.* Moments later, he found it. Lines in the stone. "These are man-made blocks. There's something down there."

Cotys had dug into the ground and placed cut stone blocks beneath a layer of soil. Blocks that had been mortared together. "There must be a way to get below the stones," Harry said to himself. He left the next question unasked, at least aloud, though it rattled through his head. What lay beneath the stones?

The moon rose above the tallest trees as he tore more dirt from the ground. The cut stones were only on the side of the well with the rising sun carving. The other side of the well had nothing but normal dirt. Harry leaned over the well as far as he dared, using his headlamp to study its interior. No water as far down as he could see. No bottom either. The inside stones offered no clues as to why Cotys would put a layer of stones down and then cover them with dirt.

Harry stood back, momentarily stymied. There were no obvious next steps. His father had taught Harry, however, that the answers might not be obvious, but they were usually in front of him, if only he would look. Cotys had hidden whatever awaited Harry under a layer of dirt and stone. He hadn't wanted to keep his secrets hidden from everyone, though; only from those who shouldn't find them. Which meant he'd have left a way for the people who *should* find them to do just that.

All the earlier locations holding clues were sites meant to be visited by Thracians. Places to honor their forebears, to remember their past and chart a course for the future. Places Thracians could access. Thracians who likely couldn't rappel down a well or scale a wall. There had to be an easier way to pull the shroud of mystery back from around this well. A way Harry could use, if only he could see it.

His gaze went back to the one familiar aspect of this well. The rising sun carving. An inspection of the stone it was carved on compared to the other stones didn't find anything odd. He scratched the stubble on his chin. The dirt and debris from so many years outside could be in the way. Using smaller rocks as tools, he scraped at the mortar, to little effect. His back shouted at the abuse; his hands were raw and dry. Harry cursed as he threw the small stones away, grabbed the bigger rock and, in a fit of anger, slammed it against the carving.

The stone disappeared. It moved into the other stones, sliding beneath the layer above it as a grinding noise rose from the well. Harry fell back, scrambling away from the rumbling stone, an image of himself falling into a dark abyss filling his head. Back he went, hands scrabbling at the dirt as the noise intensified and the ground vibrated and the well itself seemed to split in half.

He stopped. The well wasn't breaking. It was *opening.*

As abruptly as it had begun, the noise ceased. Harry stood up and moved forward. A man-sized section of the well had opened. The first layer of thick stones was hinged on the inside. It was a door. That's why the well was so thick: to accommodate this entrance.

A dark emptiness beckoned to him. Dry, warm air snaked up his pantleg when he stepped in front of the opening. A set of steps descended into the darkness.

The opening was hardly wide enough for a man to walk down. Even Harry, slender as he was, felt cramped when he looked in. Harry tested the first step. It held. He grabbed a rock from outside and propped the door open before starting down the stairs. He made it two steps before he stopped, then ran back up and outside. Why couldn't he shake the sense somebody else was here? He shook his head and went back into the entrance.

The steps descended perhaps ten feet to a landing. A wall of the same stone blocks stood in front of him, forcing Harry to turn left. His headlamp washed over a chamber. The entire chamber was less than twenty feet long and wide, an underground box cut out of the earth and built with that familiar stone. Harry took all this in with a glance, then forgot it. He couldn't focus on anything other than the object in front of him.

A sarcophagus. The rectangular stone grave resembled Cotys's from the Bulgarian cave. Symbols adorned the sides. Harry lifted his foot to walk into the chamber. He looked up, touched the wall, and held still.

"Writing." The sound of his voice filled the small space. There was

Latin writing above the tomb. Latin letters, and a familiar image. "The rising sun again," he said. He tilted his head. No, not exactly. This sun image was different. It took him a second. "Eyes. The eyes are closed." A pair of closed eyes had been cut into the upper half of the sun. What it meant, he had no idea, but he kept still. Cotys didn't do anything without purpose.

Perhaps the inscription would tell. Harry checked the words once, then once more. Only then did he read aloud.

"Here the son of Thrace has set forever. The memory of his remains serves to inspire us all. A son and hero whose valor captured Mars, who carries the hero's name. Mars sits with Cassander's muse and see the place in her city."

Son of Thrace. That had to be Spartacus. His remains? Harry laid a hand on the tomb. What Cotys meant by *the memory* of his remains was beyond Harry, but that answer might lie under the tomb lid. Harry snapped a photo of the message with his phone and put it out of mind. There would be time for that later. The feeling he wasn't alone here was getting stronger now, and again he tried to shrug it off.

Harry knelt to inspect the tomb and noticed a line in one stone on the floor. *Hold on.* He reached down to brush away the dust and dirt. It looked like not one but two lines had been cut into the stone. The lines crossed in the middle, almost like an *X*. Or the Roman numeral ten. A move to wipe the last of the debris off made him lose his grip on the tomb, and he slapped a palm on the floor for balance, hitting the *X*.

Stone ground on stone and a spear flew out of the wall, zipping past just inches from his head with a wicked hiss before it slammed off the wall. Sparks exploded as it shot back, hit the floor and rolled toward him until it bumped against his leg. Shaking light from his headlamp glinted off the metal head.

Harry looked up to find a hole in the wall directly across from the tomb. The spear had shot out of it and would have sliced through his chest if he'd been standing in front of the tomb when he activated the trigger. A trigger marked with an *X*.

He inspected the chamber floor for any other signs of danger and found none. Harry stood and moved slowly to the tomb, keeping his head down until he stood in front of it. Various depictions of a Thracian warrior covered one side. An armored man on horseback, spear in one hand and reins in the other, his armored charger racing ahead. Another of the man on foot carrying a raised spear and shield, ready for battle. A third of the warrior holding a bow and arrow at the ready. No writing, only depictions of what this man had been. Harry reached for the sarcophagus lid, keeping his head low, and he pushed.

Stone ground on stone again as the lid moved a fraction. He pushed harder, trying to stay out of unknown harm's way, putting his back into it. More grinding, then the lid shifted and he lifted it on stone hinges until it stood straight up. Harry's light filled the grave for several short moments. Words carved into the underside of the tomb's lid caught his eye. Latin. It was all he needed to see. He snapped another photo on his phone before closing the lid, then bent down to pick up the spear meant to impale him and laid it on top of the closed tomb. His hand lingered on the wooden shaft for a second before Harry turned and headed for the exit.

Where Cotys's path led next, Harry wasn't certain, but he had an idea. He climbed the hidden stairs and walked out into the cold embrace of the Greek night, his steps slow and measured. Real people had lived and died to create this path, one that was now his. It wasn't often he came face to face with such compelling evidence of the human story behind his relic hunts. A reminder of who had gone before him, and the prices they had paid.

Harry's footsteps crunched on gravel as he walked out from the trees and headed for the parking lot. The moon was already high overhead, far above the sprawling temple complex. What he'd seen hidden inside that well would stay with him for a long time.

Harry's shadow chased him as he exited the temple complex and walked to his motorcycle. The image of Spartacus's tomb filled his head. The tomb contained nothing. King Cotys had ruled over an entire nation, but at the end, he was a father who had lost his son and who had mourned him by standing in front of an empty tomb.

Chapter 16

Brooklyn

Joey Morello's espresso had gone cold. He muttered an Italian curse, stood from behind his desk and headed for the machine in his office that appeared to have come straight out of a mad scientist's lab. Why it was so complicated was beyond him, but he had learned how to make this overpriced hunk of metal churn out espresso worthy of his father's homeland, so it was money well spent. Besides, because he used it in his home office, he could write off the expense.

Buttons beeped, water burbled, and the machine went to work. Joey went back to his desk while he waited, pulling up yet another spreadsheet on his computer and narrowing his eyes at the numbers. Thank goodness he'd studied finance. Vincent Morello had been strong enough to consolidate power in New York with his iron will and even stronger fists, but his true genius had been to understand that their world always changed. Past *capos dei capi* had learned their trade on streets and in dimly lit back rooms. Joey had experienced those conflicts, yes, but his real advantage came from earning his stripes in classrooms ruled by demanding professors.

"Green energy is looking up," Joey said to himself. More government subsidies were being offered, boosting his bottom line as new consumers shifted toward wind-produced electricity. He made a note to review which politicians should be earmarked for donations during the upcoming quarter. Anybody opposing expanding government investments in wind and solar power would get an earful, along with a reminder of how large a check Joey Morello's people could write.

Wind profits were trending up, but those returns were nothing compared to his new holdings in an online casino. So far this year he was earning double-digit returns on the venture, with no end in sight. Of course, that's when the bottom tended to drop out, but it hadn't yet and he was padding his accounts.

Less promising news was coming from his efforts to start a boutique bank. Do that and he could control the money flow from start to finish. Why worry about interest rates when you could loan yourself money? One of his fronts needed to be refurbished? Take a loan from the bank he'd started, hire the contracting business he owned, then reap both the fiscal and tax rewards. On paper it was perfect, but right now the damned paperwork was the problem. It never ended. The legal bills and consultant fees to get this bank operational were ridiculous.

The espresso machine beeped. Joey grabbed his cup, closed his eyes, and inhaled. *Perfect.*

He got one sip in before his phone buzzed. An international number. It took him a second. *Italy.* He set the hot drink down and connected the call. "*Pronto,*" Joey said.

"*Buongiorno.*" A man's voice Joey knew but couldn't place. The man continued in Italian. "It is good to hear your voice, Joey. How are you?"

"*Sto bene.*" *I'm fine.* Joey struggled to place the voice. "Who's calling?"

"Forgive me," the man said. "I forgot it has been so long. It's Franco. Franco Licata."

Joey almost slapped his head. "Franco? My friend, forgive me."

"Do not worry, my friend. We are both busy men. I hope you received the card and flowers I sent for your father's service, may he rest in peace."

Franco Licata was head of one of the biggest Sicilian clans. A man of influence on the island. A man whose family had held a position of prestige in the Cosa Nostra for over a century. A man whose father had been extremely close with Vincent Morello, and someone Joey could trust.

Franco wasn't the sort to make social calls. "Is anything wrong?" he asked.

"I have not spoken with an old friend in years," Franco said. "Is that not enough?"

"If that's the case, then consider me grateful." Joey sipped his drink. "Is that the case?"

Franco's sigh gave Joey his answer. "Do you remember Carmelo Piazza?"

"A man whose influence nearly rivals your own. Beyond that, I know little of him."

"He is tough, perhaps fair, and a man of business. I would never go so far as to say he is without honor, for that would be sacrilege."

The mere fact Franco said it out loud meant Carmelo was anything but honorable. "I see," Joey said.

"We are not associates," Franco said. "When our business aligns, we work together. At other times, we stay away. Respectfully, of course."

"Of course." Joey fell silent. Franco had something on his mind, and he would get to it in his own time.

"You are a busy man," Franco said.

Joey sat straighter. "Never too busy for an old friend."

"The world is hard, Joey. Men like us must stick together." A long silence filled Joey's ear. "Are you alone?" Franco finally asked.

"You may speak freely," Joey assured him.

"Certain inquiries are being made on my island. Inquiries that may be of interest to you."

Joey frowned. He had no active business in Sicily. Managing the families in New York and keeping his Brooklyn operations humming were business enough these days. That wasn't to say he'd never worked with the Sicilians before. His father had come over in the turbulent years of World War II, when Italian immigrants were often treated like Mussolini's cousins. He had arrived with little, though he had connections in the old country, and he had gone to great lengths to keep those connections.

"I have no business in Sicily at the moment," Joey said. "What has your ear?"

"Whispers. The sort of words that often travel too far."

Joey's knuckles whitened as he gripped his desk. "This is about me?"

"Not about you, my friend. About a woman you know. One whose business interests align with your own. A fence."

Only one person he knew fit that description. A woman whose name carried weight both here and in Sicily. "Rose Leroux," Joey said.

Franco confirmed it. "Whispers have reached my ears about artifacts trafficking, and about a man who does this for you. *Allegedly* does this for you. I did not mean to give offense."

"None taken," Joey said. "We are friends. I do not employ anyone who fits this description." He was hedging in case anyone heard. "However, if I did, one name comes to mind. A man I trust with my life."

A closer bond could not be found in their world, and Franco couldn't have missed the meaning. "I see," Franco said. "Men such as that are to be treasured. Protected from anyone who may not have their interests at heart."

"Who might this be?"

"A man who is not honorable."

Carmelo Piazza. That's who was asking about Rose Leroux and Harry Fox. "Agreed," Joey said. "I wonder why a dishonorable man would ask such questions. It can serve no good purpose."

"A dishonorable man would do it for one reason. Money."

"Someone is paying this man to ask these questions."

"Questions that may not be beneficial to your friend's health," Franco said. "If he existed."

Carmelo Piazza's questions were an intrusion, and an insult to Joey Morello. "I would think any man would take pains to avoid insulting me in this way."

In Sicily, insults often ended in violence. Conflicts spanning generations had been started from less than this insult. Few Sicilians would begrudge Joey seeking retribution. However, Joey's father had taught him better.

"I have one question," Joey said.

"Before you ask, there is more information I must share. When I learned such questions were being asked, I asked a few of my own and I learned the name of the other party."

"The one paying Carmelo Piazza."

"Correct. His name is Olivier Lloris."

Of course. Olivier wasn't a man who liked to wait. Harry was making him wait for Charlemagne's bible, dangling the possibility of additional relics to keep Olivier close until Harry could make his move. A dangerous ploy had just gotten even more dicey.

"Thank you," Joey said. "I won't forget this."

"I am here if you need anything."

Joey assured Franco he would call if necessary and hung up. He immediately called Harry.

The sound of whistling wind filled the phone when Harry answered. "Hey, Joey."

"Where are you?" Joey asked. "I can't keep track of what country you're in each day." Not to mention Harry didn't work for him any longer. It wasn't Joey's business to know where Harry went.

"On a Greek island called Samothrace," Harry said. He offered a story of hidden carvings, a secret tomb and one near miss with a spear. "It's close to midnight here," Harry said. "I'm headed to a hotel. I rented a motorcycle and should be back on the mainland tomorrow."

A heck of a story, but this was Harry Fox. "You sure those two guys didn't follow you to Samothrace?" Joey asked.

"Almost certain," Harry said. "Why? Sounds like you have something on your mind."

That was what came from growing up with a guy. At times you hardly had to speak to carry on a conversation. "I just got off the phone with an old friend from Sicily." Harry knew all about how Sicilian clans worked. "Another clan leader has been asking questions about me," Joey said. "And about anyone who might locate cultural relics on my behalf."

Harry picked up the gist immediately. "What clan leader would do that?"

"The man asking questions is Carmelo Piazza. He's influential. One of the top clan leaders."

"That's not good. What sort of questions?"

"Who you are, mostly." Joey finished his drink. "Guess who's paying Carmelo Piazza to ask these questions. I'll give you a hint. He's French."

Harry groaned. "Olivier Lloris."

"You got it."

"Why can't that guy wait for his relics?" Harry asked. "He'll get them if he just plays by the rules."

"What you mean is he'll get what's coming to him," Joey said.

"I've been careful," Harry said. "He's a rich guy who doesn't like to wait."

"That's my guess. Regardless, I can't have Carmelo Piazza asking questions about our business. If others find out he barged into my affairs and I let it go, I look bad."

"Does anyone know you've been told about this?"

"Only my Sicilian friend, and he won't tell anyone. Franco Licata and I go way back. My father and his father were tight. He called to warn me."

"Will Franco keep his ears open?"

"Yes, until I decide how to handle this. Which is secondary to making sure you're safe. You said two guys are on your tail? Could be Olivier sent them after you."

"I doubt it," Harry said. "He knows he's getting his relics. No reason to send men after me right now. I'm already doing his dirty work. I think this is someone else." Harry paused. "Someone I need your help finding. I have a name."

"Tell me. I'll find him."

"The two guys chasing me mentioned his name in Perperikon. 'Big Bird.' Mean anything to you?"

Joey knew a lot of questionable people with odd nicknames. It was practically a rite of passage in his business. He knew a Sticky Fingers, a Maserati Mike, Eyebrows, Bananas, even a Cement Dave—whom Joey avoided at all costs; Dave was insane—but Big Bird was a new one and Joey told Harry so. "It doesn't matter if I don't know him," Joey said. "I expect I know someone who does. If he exists, I'll find him."

"I already asked Rose to look for the guy," Harry said. "I don't believe it's Olivier Lloris. These two guys have heavy Russian accents."

"There's another guy searching for this relic?" Joey shook his head. "How's that possible? I thought you had the only lead on Spartacus."

"It's the only lead I know of. That doesn't mean there's not another starting point on his trail somewhere out there."

A fan circled overhead as Joey's elbows found the desk, his hands folding over each other. Now for the sticky part. "This trail is getting crowded. You worried?"

"No. I'm in the lead. I'll be fine as long as I stay ahead."

"And if you don't?"

"I'll figure it out."

Joey knew better than to argue. But Harry deserved to be told the truth. "I have to be straight with you," Joey said. "I should have a talk with Carmelo Piazza. He's been disrespectful."

"Is it worth the trouble?"

Harry had a knack for cutting straight to the heart of things, even if he sometimes kept his insights to himself. "You mean is it worth risking bad blood with Carmelo over a slight no one knows about." Joey considered. "It's worth the trouble if it will help you."

"I can handle this."

"You always say that."

"I'm still here, aren't I?"

"It only takes one time being unlucky."

Harry grumbled. "Enough about that. You're really going to start trouble with this Sicilian over a few questions?"

"The fact that Carmelo is asking those questions drags my name through the dirt. Do I go onto his turf and act as though it's mine? No. Because I offer him the respect a clan leader deserves."

"That's one reason. The second is you're the boss now. The *capo dei capi*. Your decisions impact every New York family. Crossing Carmelo Piazza will likely bring consequences. Could be he ignores you, pretends it didn't happen and everyone forgets about it. Or it could be much worse. If he's anything like the Sicilians I know, my money's on the latter. Stick your finger in Carmelo Piazza's face and there's no telling what happens next."

"Let him get away with this and I lose face."

"Not necessarily. I think you're saying that because standing up to him is your way of looking out for me. I appreciate it. I also know I can handle myself. If that changes, I'll tell you, and then maybe you reconsider. Don't start trouble on my behalf."

Joey stared at the framed picture of Vincent Morello on his desk. What would his father do? Unfortunately, Joey knew the answer. "Maybe you're right," Joey said. "Which upsets me. What kind of guy lets his friend go it alone?"

"A guy who's the right leader for New York. I'll call you if this gets too hot. Then you can start all the trouble you want to get me out of it."

"If I find out it's getting too dangerous and you didn't tell me, those guys on your tail will be the least of your problems."

"You going to come to Europe and whip my butt?"

"It's a promise."

"It'll be good to see you then." Harry kept talking as Joey chuckled. "I gotta get moving. It's freezing out here and I don't want any cops to stop and ask what I'm doing on a bike in the countryside this late at night."

"One more thing," Joey said. "Tell me the truth. You don't sound like yourself."

"How's that?"

"Hunting relics lights a fire under you. It's easy to see. What I'm hearing now is a guy who sounds like he's had enough."

"You're smarter than you look." Harry sighed. "You're right. It's not the relic, though. It's a grave I found here."

"Spartacus's grave?"

"His empty coffin. It's dumb, I know, but that box made me think of my dad. Of everyone we've lost." He didn't have to say Vincent's name out loud. "King Cotys felt the same way. All the money in the world couldn't save his kid. I don't know." Joey could picture Harry running a hand through his hair. "I'll snap out of it. That's another thing my dad taught me. All the skeletons we find along the way are people who lost their focus."

"You certainly don't forget it," Joey said. "I know how you feel. We're not forgetting them. We have to move ahead."

"They'd be disappointed in us if we didn't," Harry said. "It's a good thing Sara is around. I'm just confident enough in what I found in Spartacus's tomb that it worries me."

"Nothing like being almost certain."

"The only thing I'm certain of is I need to run this past Sara."

"Care to tell me what you did find in the empty coffin?"

"A message," Harry said. "Engraved on the underside of the lid. About Spartacus and how he inspired Thracians. It described Spartacus as *A son and hero whose valor captured Mars, who carries the hero's name. Mars sits with Cassander's muse and see the place in her city.*"

"His valor captured Mars?"

"Mars can be a planet or a god. You can't truly capture either one. Then there's the next line. *Mars sits with Cassander's muse and see the place in her city.* Not plural, 'sees.' Singular. It has to be intentional."

"I'm guessing you have an idea about why?"

"I do. I need to ask Sara before I get back to the mainland. If I'm correct, the Mars he captured isn't far away. In fact, I won't even have to leave the country."

Chapter 17

Manhattan

An ancient temple sat in the middle of Manhattan. An Egyptian temple, a place of secrets and knowledge. A place born of a mother's love for her children. The hidden temple of Antony and Cleopatra, where they stored the greatest treasure of their time. All the knowledge contained in the Library of Alexandria, exactly as Harry and Sara had found it.

Row after row of statues filled the room. Gods, mostly. Egyptian, Roman, Greek, Persian, a few Mesopotamians. Cleopatra and Antony were there as well. Each statue opened with the press of a button to reveal the true treasures of this room. The scrolls left by Antony and Cleopatra, copies of what had been inside the Great Library. It was a place of wonder, of mystery. A vision of a vanished world and the mysteries it contained. Mysteries that were still being revealed even today.

At least that was what Sara Hamed hoped her display did. She'd spent months creating the American Museum of Natural History's latest display, *The Great Library*. Sara and her team had painstakingly recreated what she and Harry had found when they uncovered a massive temple hidden beneath the Egyptian desert sands. Each detailed statue could be opened, which triggered a recording to explain to visitors what scrolls had been found inside. The stories in each statue were meant not only to inspire, but to leave guests wanting to learn more. And if they sent their friends to the museum to see this exhibit, friends who paid another entrance fee? All the better.

A soft chime sounded from Sara's laptop and disturbed her from her review of the exhibit's promotional materials. She looked over the rim of her coffee mug and caught sight of the time. Sara swore softly, pocketing her phone and grabbing her laptop before rushing into the hallway. Never a good start to the day, being late to your own meeting.

Sara walked as fast as decorum allowed her, as the curator-in-charge of Asian and African ethnology, to move through the hall. As luck had it, her team was only settling in when she walked into the conference room and greeted each person in turn. She still couldn't entirely shake a deep suspicion the men on her team resented having her—a woman— lead them. Part of her feeling came from growing up in Egypt and seeing so many of her childhood friends never receiving encouragement from their parents to chase their dreams; hers had thankfully encouraged Sara to follow them at every step.

"Let's get started," Sara said. Her team included a half-dozen accomplished Egyptologists, all at her service. "Any announcements for the group?"

The interminable minutiae of an academic institution slogged on for about ninety seconds before Sara raised a hand. "Alright, thank you. Let's move on. Who has the trafficking report?"

One of her team was assigned to track the ongoing rumblings of New York's underground black market for cultural antiquities. Dylan Nocita was a former expert at a prominent auction house, and Dylan was New York through and through. He also came from old money, which bought him full access to said auction house and others like it. He was a godsend, with a nose for finding the truth hidden in an artifact's murky past.

"Nothing new today," Dylan said. "Though I did get a note from the boss." His eyes moved from the computer in front of him to the windowed door to their room. "Speaking of which."

Sara turned to find a face in the window. Laurel de Voogt, the curator of the anthropology division and her direct supervisor. It was like looking in a magical funhouse mirror offering the complete opposite version of yourself. Sara's smoky hue and honey-tinted eyes couldn't be more unlike the Nordic features of her supervisor, though Laurel stood the same height.

Dr. de Voogt opened the door and walked in.

"Excuse the interruption," she said before turning to Sara. "I need to speak with you for a moment."

Sara turned to her team. "Let's stop here. I'll circle back to each of you later this morning for updates."

"This will only take a few minutes," Laurel said as they walked to her office down the hallway. Sara didn't speak as Laurel closed the door and indicated a seat at her office table. A single folder lay on top of it. "This information came to me this morning from a contact of mine in Greece. She works for the Department Against Smuggling of Antiquities."

"Dylan had no updates on any current illegal activity," Sara said. "Though he did say he had a note from you."

"I sent him a text immediately before your meeting," Laurel said. "Then I received additional information. That is why I brought you here. It's a matter you should know about first."

Sara leaned forward. "Does it involve one of our pieces?"

Laurel shook her head. "This alert is somewhat speculative. You may choose how and when to share it with your team."

Sara understood. "Sharing less than concrete information with a group tends to send speculation into overdrive."

Laurel nodded. "Exactly."

A framed picture on the wall caught Sara's eye as Laurel opened the folder. A small windmill standing over rows and rows of brilliantly colored plants, a riotous rainbow on the ground beneath a lightly clouded sky.

"Pretty, isn't it?"

Sara turned to find Laurel looking at her. "It is," Sara said.

"That is a field in my hometown."

"It's beautiful."

"It's a reminder for me."

Sara lifted an eyebrow. "Of?"

"The need to maintain perspective. Are you familiar with the 'tulip mania' that occurred in the Dutch Republic during the seventeenth century?"

"The first recorded speculative bubble."

"A moment that showed how incredibly shortsighted humans can be when money is involved." Laurel pointed to another image on her wall, this one a painted flower. "That is the *Semper Augustus*. The single most expensive tulip sold during the craze. Contracts for future tulip deliveries were purchased for outrageous sums. A single tulip sold for five thousand guilders, or more than the price of a house." Laurel laid the sheet of paper on the table in front of her. "The images are beautiful. They are also instructive. If I ever feel as though I require perspective, two examples hang on my walls."

"Useful." A quote on Laurel's desk calendar caught her eye. *Well-behaved women rarely make history*. Sara grinned. Indeed.

"My point is to maintain perspective." Laurel tapped the page on the table. "Including when I receive information such as this. My Greek contact has learned of rumors that a private expedition to uncover a Frankish artifact may recently have been launched."

Sara did an excellent job of not reacting. "What sort of artifact?"

"The details are unclear, but it allegedly involves a well-known Frank." Laurel paused. Sara's stomach tightened a fraction as the silence stretched on. "Charlemagne," Laurel said quietly.

The heating system humming softly in the background seemed to fall silent. Sara's hands tightened on themselves. It took her a moment to find her voice. "Interesting."

"Far more than that," Laurel said, "if it's true. Which I suspect will not prove to be the case."

Sara slowly pulled her hands off the desk and leaned back. The support of her chair did wonders. "Why did this catch your eye?"

"The source has provided accurate information in the past, so I am inclined to believe them."

"I'll tell my team to keep their eyes and ears open for anything related to Charlemagne," Sara said. "Is there any indication of what to look for?"

"No. If I learn more, I'll share it." Now Laurel flipped the page around so Sara could see it. "Most of these alerts are measured in sentences, not paragraphs. This one is no different."

Sara noted a handful of lines on the paper. She couldn't quite read it, but there was hardly enough to bother with. "Makes it hard to know what to do with it."

"That's the truth. The only time we can work with certainty is after the artifacts are already being bought and sold." The paper flipped back around and returned to her folder.

Sara's brain caught up with her ears and her stomach twisted again. "You said an expedition was being launched. You mean a private effort?" Laurel said she did. "Who would do that?"

"Some meddling rich person with more money than morals. All I know is that my contact in Greece heard through unnamed channels that a Frankish artifact hunt is now underway. Who is financing the operation and what they're after is a mystery."

Not if you know the right people. Sara kept this thought to herself.

Laurel gained steam. "One outcome I can predict is this will not end well. Amateurs in the field chasing items they do not respect and cannot fully understand only leads to disaster."

Sara sat up in her chair again. Her stomach was no longer twisting. "Why do you say that?" she asked, cool as ever.

"Because of the damage they will undoubtedly cause." Laurel shook her head. "If there is even a remote chance such an artifact can be recovered, the search should be conducted by experts, not money-driven thrill seekers."

Sara chose not to point out what drove their museum. "We shouldn't assume their motives are so base. And it's a bit unfair to assume whoever may be searching is incapable of doing it properly." Various images of Harry in foreign lands surrounded by carnage came to mind. She banished them.

Laurel's eyes narrowed. "I'm surprised you feel that way. I suspect care for the proper processing and handling of artifacts is not foremost on their list."

Sara didn't back down. "I do have some experience in the matter."

"I recall. Half the journals I subscribe to still mention it."

"An amateur found the Library of Alexandria."

"He had you to help him." Laurel tilted her head. "You truly believe the matter would have turned out as neatly as it did had you not been involved?"

"Harry Fox didn't need me to find the library."

"Then he is a very skilled grave robber."

Sara clenched her jaw hard enough to crack a tooth. "Grave robbers don't give their finds to the world."

Laurel shrugged. "Fair point. Do you still speak with him?"

"On occasion."

A brief wait ensued, Laurel allowing Sara a chance to fill the silence. She declined. Her private life would remain that way. "Should he undertake another venture to locate cultural artifacts," Laurel finally continued, "I hope you will accompany him. Your knowledge will certainly result in a more positive outcome."

"Perhaps," Sara said. "Perhaps not. Harry Fox is quite capable. He was capable before our time together. I'm certain he will be so in the future. I see his interest in preserving history as a positive, not a negative."

Laurel wasn't buying it. "Noble though their intentions may be, and I truly question that, are they properly trained? My fear is that destruction accompanies their enthusiasm."

"Harry and those like him are better than thieves and terrorists."

"Fair point, though I still maintain that this is better left to professionals. Such as yourself."

As though their museum were a shining tower atop the hill. Several wings in this very building were named after donors who had more than a passing acquaintance with the wrong side of the law. Not that Sara could complain. If rich people wanted to donate to a museum in order to get their name on it, who was she to turn down their offer? Even if everyone suspected that the money wasn't entirely clean.

"I do agree," Sara said. Laurel's eyes narrowed. "That someone such as myself should be involved," she went on. "Or you. A person with the proper training. Provided these independent operators act properly and with due respect for what they seek, I still welcome their assistance."

Did Harry Fox operate "properly"? Often, he did. Occasionally he also stretched the rules. Either way, it was impossible to argue with his results.

Laurel kept her gaze level. "An interesting perspective."

This time Sara jumped into a tiny gap of silence. "The world is often gray," she said.

"Gray?"

"Not black and white." Sara pointed first at herself, then at Laurel. "We spend our time in this safe, secure environment. The world outside"—and here she moved her finger in a circular motion—"is not always safe. Nor are many of the people. Cultural relics require our protection. In order to do that, we should use every resource at our disposal."

"Including outside contractors," Laurel said. "For lack of a better term." She tapped her chin. "You make a solid point. I do not necessarily agree with it."

Sara wasn't backing down. "Why not?"

"I disagree that those outside parties are beneficial. Some of them, some of the time, yes. However, their activity comes with inherent risk. Risk of destroying rather than preserving history, whether in part or in whole. Of alienating international partnerships. Of someone being injured. Or worse."

Sara was talking to herself when she responded. "The field can be dangerous."

"In and of itself, and because of others who may be on the same path. Others with less wholesome motives."

The nerves in Sara's fingers and toes came alive, cold and tight. She didn't react as Laurel's phone vibrated on the table. Her boss looked at the screen, frowned, and picked it up. "A message from my Greek contact," Laurel said.

That caught Sara's ear. "Related to the Frankish artifact?"

"It appears so." Laurel scrolled through the message for a few moments longer. "What do you know of Perperikon?"

Sara's breath froze in her chest. She couldn't find her voice. Laurel looked expectantly up from the phone. "An ancient Thracian city," Sara said, "noted for a temple dedicated to Dionysus that sits near the Perpereshka River."

Laurel's eyebrows went up and she leaned back a fraction. "You are well informed, as usual. Several members of a dig team at Perperikon were assaulted yesterday. It appears one team member left their tools on site. When the team returned to retrieve the tools, they heard noises underground. The noises were two men trapped in a previously undiscovered subterranean cavern. Once they were freed, they assaulted the dig team and ran away."

Sara did her best to act surprised. "How did those two men get underground? More importantly, what did they find?"

Laurel's gaze went back to her phone. "Somehow, they stumbled onto an underground cavern with tombs. Quite a number of them, from what I gather. They found writing on the wall."

"Where in Perperikon did the dig team find these men? The city is known for its temple. That could be what drew the men. Could they have had information the research team on site did not?"

Laurel's fingers tapped her phone rapidly. "I will find out shortly. This happened within the past twenty-four hours. My contact is still gathering information."

So, Harry was safe and he hadn't killed those two men. Even if they'd been willing to kill him. Sara needed to warn Harry the men were likely on his trail, though they would need someone to decipher the message from inside those tombs. That should buy Harry a few days. Hopefully.

"I expect your contact will have news on what's beneath the surface," Sara said. "Thracians wouldn't hide simple drainage systems beneath their temple floors. If this happened at the temple," she said quickly.

Laurel agreed with her. "I will share anything I learn. In the interim, please be alert for information regarding Frankish relics."

Sara said she would and rose from her chair. She had one foot out the door when Laurel called her name. Sara looked back. "Yes?"

"Nicely reasoned," Laurel said. "On both the relic recovery and Perperikon topics. I always appreciate your input. Even if I don't agree with it."

Sara left the office with more energy than she had when she'd entered. Laurel was tough to read. Stern, stoic, supportive. All good qualities in a boss if work needed to be done, and done well. She made it exactly three steps down the hall before her phone buzzed. The screen revealed a message from Nora Doyle. Sara opened it, read through it once, then once more.

Sara forced herself not to run as she accelerated down the hall, on a direct line for the privacy of her office. This couldn't wait.

Chapter 18

Manhattan

The phone on Nora Doyle's desk was under permanent threat of destruction. Were its current danger of destruction measured the way the threat of nuclear war was tracked, it would be at two minutes to midnight. The past four days had not been kind to the phone's survival chances. Nora's boss and father had gone behind her back in recruiting Harry Fox to unravel a Thracian mystery involving a prince named Spartacus. Then Harry had gone radio silent. No calls, no emails, nothing telling her of his success or failure. Or that he was still alive. She'd been forced to go to Sara to learn more, which put a bad taste in her mouth. Harry worked for Nora, not Sara, and certainly not for Gary Doyle. So what if her anti-trafficking team's workload seemed to grow every week? She could handle it.

What she couldn't handle was people overstepping their boundaries. Her father, for one. What business did he have handling the Thracian assignment? None, that's what. And Harry. His lack of communication with his boss irked her no end. Reporting structures existed for a reason. A part of her also worried for his safety. Her phone needed to ring with updates, not more problems. Every call coming through that didn't fit that bill was one call closer to the phone's demise.

The truth of the matter was she wanted to help him. Harry had lucked out, in many ways, over a long period, but right now he'd landed a plum assignment in the field tracking down the truth behind King Cotys IV while Nora sat chained to her desk shuffling paper and handling endless calls. None of it interesting, at least not like it used to be, back when she was fighting to make a name for herself, trying to show that her father wasn't the reason Nora Doyle had a job here.

Funny how things changed.

The phone rang. Nora stabbed a button. "Doyle."

"I got your message." Sara Hamed sounded slightly out of breath. "Is anything wrong?"

"You tell me," Nora said. "Harry isn't calling me back. All I know is an alert came across my desk about an ancient Thracian temple."

"Perperikon," Sara said.

"That's the one." Nora frowned. "Do you get the same newsflashes?"

"No. My supervisor has a connection in Greece. He keeps her informed of any artifacts-related activity. What else do you know? Your message said there may be trouble."

Nora leaned back in her chair, looking out her office window at the thousands of other office windows on just this single block in Manhattan. "I have a friend who works for Interpol. Detective Inspector Guro Mjelde. She works out of their Oslo office, and we've coordinated on a few cases in the past. I helped her with an Incan statue. She helped me with Magnus Dahl."

"Thor's hammer." Sara had nearly died retrieving the artifact. "What does D.I. Mjelde have to do with Harry's search?"

"Your last update mentioned a nickname."

"Big Bird," Sara said. "Harry thought it might refer to the man those two in Perperikon are working for. The person behind all this."

"Does Harry know you're keeping me updated?"

"It's none of his business who I speak with."

Nora liked Sara Hamed more and more each day. "Despite Harry's best efforts to keep me in the dark and otherwise piss me off, I care about him, and about finishing this mission successfully. That's why I put a feeler out to several contacts, Guro being one of them, about this Big Bird person. She can access Interpol's database. Guess what she found?"

"That Big Bird is the name of an international criminal and Harry is in serious danger?"

"That's three-quarters accurate. Harry is in danger, and the nickname Big Bird is a real thing." Nora pulled a file up on her monitor. "Kiryl Korzun is a Bulgarian national with an extensive criminal record. He's alleged to be the leader of an outfit based in the capital city of Minsk, involved with a laundry list of repulsive crimes. Prostitution, arms dealing, drugs, human trafficking. Recently his operation expanded to include international smuggling, including cultural artifacts. His body shape is unfortunate in that it has an uncanny resemblance to the shape of a popular character from children's television."

"He's tall and skinny except for a massive middle section."

"He looks like Big Bird. You got it. There's just one problem. Kiryl Korzun is missing. No one's seen him for weeks."

"Do the Belarussian authorities keep him under surveillance?"

"No need," Nora said. "He's from the Al Capone school of gangsters. Flashy suits, fancy cars, always showing his face around town. Korzun is a big soccer fan and he never misses a home game for his favorite team. Until a few weeks ago. Now no one seems to know where he is."

Sara saw a connection she didn't like. "You said Korzun recently became involved with artifacts trafficking. Could that be the reason he disappeared—to follow the Thracian trail?"

"It's possible. Which is the problem. Anything's possible. Korzun could be with those two Russian guys right now."

"Why join them only to abandon them underground?"

"Good point."

Sara didn't hesitate. "We need to help Harry."

"He may not like that."

"I don't care. This is more resistance than he expected. Harry thought he was facing two men. Now we know there could be more. He's in the field." Here Sara's voice dropped. "At your father's request."

"It wasn't my idea."

"Then it's lucky for Harry you can help make certain he survives. I expect Gary would approve you taking action. Harry is on your team, after all."

Damn Sara Hamed and her guilt trip. She was right. "I'll call you back," Nora said. "I have to talk to my contact again."

"We have to help Harry even if he doesn't think he needs it."

"I know."

"Harry told me the two men tried to kill him." Sara's voice went low. "I think this has gone too far. You realize Harry wanted to say no so he could focus on his other work."

"You mean reeling in Olivier Lloris."

"Yes."

"Which is probably even more dangerous."

"At least it's here in New York. Now he's across an ocean by himself." Sara was as close to pleading as Nora had ever heard her. "Help me get him back here. I have a very bad feeling about this."

Nora had never heard Sara speak this way. "What do you want me to do?"

"Make him realize this is beyond what Gary wanted. At least one group of criminals is on Harry's tail, men who will kill him. Harry shouldn't risk his life because someone connected to the governor died. That had nothing to do with Harry."

Nora opened her mouth to argue. She closed it. "My dad is incredible in many ways," Nora said. "He can also be shortsighted." The part where Nora harbored more than a little resentment against Gary Doyle for not assigning her to handle the search went unsaid. "I'll get Harry back here if I can."

Nora agreed to update Sara shortly and clicked off. She immediately called Guro Mjelde. Her racing mind was making too many connections she didn't like.

The Norwegian answered on the first ring. "D.I. Melde speaking." Nora identified herself. "Is this about Perperikon?"

"It's about Korzun."

"The Big Bird," Guro said. An edge of mirth crept into her voice. "Who has flown away."

Nora was having none of it. "Yeah, that one. Found him yet?" Guro said they had not. "Where do you think he might be?" Nora asked.

"I cannot say. Kiryl Korzun is a thriving criminal in a former Soviet state. A man who can succeed in that challenging environment is more than capable of disappearing if he chooses. It may be some time before we find him."

"If you ever find him," Nora said. Guro did not disagree. "Listen, I just had a thought. How did you find out there was an artifacts trafficker in Perperikon?"

"We heard it from two sources," Guro said. "Most recently when the report came in of the dig team at Perperikon being attacked. We can only assume those men were traffickers."

"You said *the most recent one*. You heard it from another source before the attack?"

"Several hours before," Guro said. "A tip called in to the Interpol artifacts-trafficking hotline. Occasionally anonymous calls prove worthwhile, including this one about Perperikon. This tip gave the exact location and a range of only a few days when the unidentified traffickers would be at the site."

Nora's knuckles whitened as she made a fist. "Why didn't you notify anyone at the site?"

"The tip came in too late," Guro said. "Then we learned of the attack."

"And that confirmed the tip." A bad taste started to form in Nora's mouth. "What else can you tell me about Korzun? I know he likes the spotlight, enjoys attention. Not the brightest move if you're into arms dealing and human smuggling and whatever else he does in his spare time."

"Prostitution, cultural artifacts, and one more. Murder."

Nora jerked in her chair. "What?"

"Korzun is rumored to be the reason several of his rivals have vanished in recent years. People who stand in his way often go missing." Guro sighed. "It did not take long for Korzun to gain control of a crime syndicate in which he used to be a nobody. His ascent was made easier due to a number of deaths."

Nora's mind worked furiously as an idea took shape. A way to keep her promise to Sara Hamed and protect Harry. And a way, if she were being totally honest, to show her father the error of his ways. "Korzan may be deadly," Nora said. "But he's out of his league this time." Nora paused. "Guro, I have an anonymous tip for you."

Silence filled the phone. "What?" Guro finally asked.

"Just listen to what I say and write down the anonymous tip I give you." This line had better not be recorded, she thought. "Do you have local people in Greece you trust? And I mean really trust."

Hesitation tinged Guro's response. "Yes. Why?"

Nora took a breath. "Write this down."

It took only a minute. One minute that could potentially unravel years of her work. When she finished, Nora still didn't know if it was the right move or not. She did know the sour taste in her mouth was gone. "You get all of it?" Nora asked.

"I need more information to take action."

"You'll get it," Nora said.

"Then I will handle it."

"Guro, I'm counting on you."

The Norwegian assured Nora again, then Nora said she would be in touch shortly with the additional information. It could work. And if it failed? *Too late to stop now.*

She called Sara again. The clock was ticking.

Chapter 19

Thessaloniki, Greece

Harry stepped out of his rental car and arched his back. Joints cracked in protest at six hours in the car without a break. Once his tendons and muscles stopped shouting, he shielded his eyes against the sun, now directly overhead.

The drive from Samothrace to Thessaloniki should have taken just over eight hours. Harry had made it in six. Brilliant light sparkled off the rippling Aegean in the distance as the Greek port city came into view, the modern buildings and ancient structures a testament to its endurance.

Over a million people lived here on the Thermaic Gulf. The second-largest city in Greece, Thessaloniki dated to 315 B.C. when it was founded by a Macedonian king, who named it after his wife. Queen Thessaloniki was the daughter of King Philip II of Macedon, and half-sister to a man who was arguably history's most successful conqueror: Alexander the Great. Her brother had conquered much of the known world in his day, giving his name to many cities, though his sister had also managed quite well; the city named for her had thrived for over two thousand years. For all that it offered, however, Harry had eyes for only one specific property in the city. It now lay in front of him.

A crumbling and abandoned open-air theater.

Ancient rows of stone seating spread out before him, crumbling in some spots, sturdy and ready for patrons in others. Theater had held a place of honor in ancient Greece, and had been a vital part of their culture. Tragedies and comedies were distinct genres, never merged, both revered. Many of the theaters in Greece had been left to nature for centuries, reclaimed by the forests and wilderness. Only in recent decades had archaeologists begun excavating these formerly vibrant social centers, restoring some to their former glory so that the plays performed in the time of Cotys could once again be enjoyed by patrons on the very stages where they had first been produced. So many theaters had been found that the restorations were backlogged and sites were forced to wait for their chance at reclaiming lost glory. One of these was the Ancient Theater of the Queen, the theater in front of Harry.

He stood atop a hill looking down on lower ground, not quite a valley, but a smooth and sloping descent opening to a flat patch of woods. The hillside produced a natural viewing area overlooking the circular orchestra, a word whose original meaning translated as "dancing place." The performers' voices were able to reach the most distant seats because of the site's natural acoustics.

Harry took all this in with one look. Why was he here? Because Cotys IV had told him to come, in the last line of his message in Spartacus's empty tomb: *Mars sits with Cassander's muse and see the place in her city.*

The linguistic error of leaving *see* as singular was no mistake. *See the place* was a literal translation. Originally Greek, translated to Latin, it was a message hidden by the words themselves. Harry had seen through it. Sara had too. He had spoken with her on the drive there, told her his suspicions, and she had agreed. *See the place* translated into Greek as *theater.* Cotys was telling Harry to go to a *theater.* But which theater?

Mars sits with Cassander's muse and see the place in her city. Her city referred to *Cassander's muse.* Cassander referred to King Cassander, ruler of Macedonia, contemporary of Alexander the Great and husband of Alexander's half-sister.

Thessaloniki. Cassander's muse, was his wife. The woman he'd named this city for. The queen had been a devoted patron of the arts who funded the construction of numerous theaters around Greece. Only one, however, bore her title. The Ancient Theater of the Queen.

There was just one issue: the entire theater sat in plain view before him, but Mars was nowhere to be seen. No matter. Mars was here, he knew, waiting for him. Harry just had to figure out where to look.

Harry slipped back into the driver's seat and pulled far off the road, stopping in an open area that allowed access to the theater's upper rows. He slipped a pack filled with tools over his shoulder before he locked the car and started walking. No gates blocked his entry to the theater area. Stone seats embedded in the hillside sat as they had for centuries as he hopped onto the rear wall, jumped down to the uppermost row of seats, and started walking down the aisle. The stone had disintegrated in places, forcing him to hop around to keep moving, and in other areas small bushes had forced their way through the rock to stake their claim. This theater would eventually reopen, but that day was not here yet. For this Harry was grateful.

The upper section ended abruptly at a perpendicular walkway, forcing him to hop down to continue. Halfway down the thirty-odd rows he began to lose cell service. The seating was steeper than he realized. Harry checked again; his cell reception was spotty at best, nonexistent father down the hill. No matter. Find a sign of Mars or the rising sun and he was in business.

Success required him to keep moving and stay ahead of the two guys from Perperikon. Learning from Sara that they'd escaped from the tomb didn't worry him much, not with his head start. Those guys couldn't figure out what Cotys's messages meant. He'd be fine. At least that's what Harry had told Sara.

The remains of an arched backdrop stood behind the circular orchestra where the play would have taken place. Four pillars still stood, two on each side; two more on either side had collapsed over time to leave only their bases and jagged pieces, sticking up from the ground like the fists of an angry god. Halfway down the central aisle he passed another walkway running perpendicular to the one he was descending, a walkway for spectators to get out of the lower half-bowl. Once he walked down this far, he could see that the lower rows extended farther out on either side, following the hill's natural contours to provide additional seats. Deep shadows shrouded the walkway to either side as he passed. The last row of seats above the perpendicular walkway would have made for interesting viewing; lean forward too far and a patron would topple ten feet to hard stone below. Harry pressed onward.

The lower bowl showed nothing of note, and at the bottom in the orchestra, he paused and turned, craning his neck to look up and up to the very last row. From down here the world shrank to only the stage and the seats. A perfect place to create a new world and explore the unknown, to offer laughter or tragedy. Or, Harry suspected, a place to hide the truth.

He turned to the orchestra backdrop. Originally the three columns that had stood on either side of the actors supported a stone archway that would have been an integral part of the production, whether for backdrop curtains or props hanging from above. That archway now lay in chunks behind the orchestra. The stone columns were intact, rising twenty feet into the air, while the remnants of the collapsed outer columns on both sides were barely taller than Harry, with shrubbery encroaching closely on where the stone had fallen.

Sara had done a quick background review of the theater, relaying to him during the drive that two statues had once been part of the orchestra stage. One statue on each outer edge, hard alongside the now-broken columns. Neither was of Mars; rather, they depicted the two monarchs whose patronage had built this theater. Queen Thessaloniki to one side, King Cassander to the other.

Stage left called to him first. Grooves of carved fluting ran the length of these Doric columns. A quick circle around all three on this side found nothing remarkable about the decoration. He moved to stage right and found nothing again. This theater had plenty of places to hide a message. Unless, of course, that message was on a piece of fallen stone. Harry narrowed his gaze. He'd check every rock he could find. The thought that Cotys's message could be on a piece of stone the locals had removed was summarily dismissed.

The winter sun warmed his face as he stepped back from the columns, tilting his head to look up to where the archway used to be. Nothing.

He sucked in a lungful of the bracing air. Tiny streams of vapor flew from his lips. A chunk of rock at his feet received a solid kick, which he immediately regretted. The vapor turned to a curse. Now not only did his toe hurt, there was a chunk of moss on his boot. A good shake failed to dislodge it, so Harry bent down and pulled it loose. The moss stayed put, his fingers hovering an inch above it. The breath stayed in his lungs. Sometimes hunting relics in the field made him rise to the challenge, show he had the skills to find them. Other times he simply got lucky.

An image had been carved into the base of the column. Harry knelt. Accumulated dirt and debris fell away under his thumb. The rising sun. Proof he was still on the trail. Harry scrubbed more dirt away. His theory took a hit.

"Where are the eyes?" he asked himself. "They're missing."

The prior rising sun images all had eyes. This one did not. "It's intentional," he said. "To tell me what to do next." But what? Close his eyes? That made no sense.

Okay, think logically. Assuming this sun had eyes, they had to be somewhere. The rays had no unusual markings. Where did the eyes go? Harry rubbed the back of his head. It dawned on him. "The eyes aren't missing. This sun is facing the other way."

Harry spun on a heel and looked in the other direction. Rows and rows of seating, along with an exit ramp. A ramp that began directly in front of Harry and went all the way to the top of the amphitheater.

He put his head down and headed forward, eyes on the ground, walking without haste to be sure he didn't miss it. Whatever *it* was.

He crossed the orchestra and began climbing the stairway between rows of seats. Each seat on either side of him was solid stone, each one part of a long, continuous row stretching to another aisle, and so on. He inspected each one in turn, but flat stone was all he found; the seats were unremarkable in every way. Up and up he went, taking his time. Harry was kneeling to inspect another end seat when his ears perked up at the sound of a distant rumbling on the cold wind. It grew louder: a vehicle with a diesel engine was chugging along the road above him. Harry ducked into the row beside him and lay flat. The noise peaked before slowly fading as the car moved on. It happened again as he reached the perpendicular walkway—an engine growing louder before moving away. Or at least it seemed to be moving on. He couldn't say for certain, not with his heart pounding so loudly.

Harry stepped back onto the central walkway, then stopped. The first row of seats in the upper area were accessible only by climbing down from the top. Patrons exiting from the lower bowl would go left or right down here, filing out onto the hillside and using one of the end ramps to continue up and out. The wall separating the upper and lower bowls stood in front of him. He'd have to haul himself over it if he wanted to keep walking in the same direction. He needed to walk *away* from the rising sun. One arm went up and he grabbed hold of the wall's edge, tensing to leap.

Harry blinked. A rising sun carving stared back at him from the wall, inches from his nose. Eyes, sunbeams, the half-circle. All of it. *Wait.*

Grime and moss covered this wall, as had been the case with many of the others. He scrubbed and scraped at the moss, not on the carving, but below it. Under it was a horizontal line, and below it a vertical line. They were attached. "Is that a *T*?"

It was indeed. Harry kept scrubbing. Directly below the *T* he found a faint circle cut into the stone, a circle slightly wider than his fist. He paused. Something was off here. He tapped the circle, then tapped it again, harder this time. A hollow knocking sound filled the air. He stepped back. "It's a cover. This wall isn't solid."

Harry stepped back. *Think, Harry.* Cotys had hidden a message in these symbols. The backward rising sun, the letter *T,* and a hollow circle. Together, they meant something.

He looked around at the two levels of seating, the orchestra, the standing columns and the crumbled remnants of the two statues.

Statues. Thessaloniki and Cassander. Sara had told him about the statues and sent pictures. Each monarch had carried an accessory.

Cassander had a sword. Thessaloniki, a scepter. The bottom of Thessaloniki's scepter had reached the base of her statue. It was at an angle, held in one hand, with a small cross decoration at the top.

A cross that couldn't be a cross. Christianity hadn't taken hold in the Western world for more than two hundred years after Cotys ruled. Nor did the cross symbol have ties to Greek religion.

Harry tilted his head to one side. Then he tilted further. He stood there, his torso nearly parallel to the ground. "That's it."

The pack on his back came off, and he knelt and opened it, digging until he found the items he needed. "Now for the other part." Harry stood, ran up the aisle to his car, grabbed an object out of the glovebox and then hurried back to where his pack lay open on the ground in front of the three symbols. He had a roll of electrical tape. A tire pressure gauge. And a collapsible metal rod meant for probing the ground.

The metal rod extended. Harry tore lengths of electrical tape from the roll. It took only a minute to attach the slim metal tire pressure gauge across the end of the extended rod. Once taped, it formed an awfully good impression of the scepter Thessaloniki's statue held. Which, if he was correct, was more than a scepter.

Harry tapped the hollow-sounding circle. He put his hand on it and pushed. Nothing. He pushed again with both hands. Still nothing. A nearby rock called out to him. Harry picked it up and bashed it against one side of the stone circle. The circle spun, fell out of the wall and clattered to the ground, spinning round and round before rattling to a stop.

Harry knew better than to put his fingers in the wall. There could be spikes, blades, any manner of horrid devices inside. He did lean down to peer inside, his phone's light revealing nothing nefarious lurking within. Not that he expected to find anything. If he was correct, this hole wasn't meant to injure.

Harry put his phone down. He picked up the extendable metal probe, held it straight so the tire pressure gauge was away from him, and put it in front of the hole. The gauge almost touched either side of the circle.

Almost, but not quite. His improvised scepter fit inside the circular carving, and as Harry pushed it farther in, he convinced himself it was the same size. Which mattered a lot.

The metal rod was long enough. He ran out of room to push with less than a foot to spare. Holding steady, Harry gritted his teeth and twisted the rod slowly. It caught, unable to move. He pulled back and kept twisting until the pressure vanished and he was able to twist the rod around, encountering resistance that slowly, painfully slowly, gave way under his continued pushing. He almost let out a shout. *I was right.*

The electrical tape held. He'd used half the roll to secure his gauge to the rod, enough to keep it attached as he twisted the rod, and stone ground on stone inside the wall. Then, without warning, something deep inside smacked into place and he could turn no more.

Rock grated on rock. The floor rumbled. Harry jumped back as dust poured from the wall in front of him and part of it slid aside to reveal a passage. A retracting doorway rolled into the wall and disappeared, leaving only a dark opening large enough for two men to walk through side by side.

The opening called to him, seeming to pull him toward it. He resisted for the moment. Anyone near the site could have heard the noise. Or the ground could collapse from beneath him. Anything at all could go wrong. Harry's lip turned up at the corner. *I'd better get moving.*

Harry left the metal rod in the circular opening, pushing it in just far enough to allow the stone cover to slide back in place and hide his impromptu key. He couldn't do anything to camouflage the open door. Harry shouldered his pack, reached into his pocket, and loosed a choice word. He'd left his headlamp in the car. He dropped the pack and ran back up the rows, head down and arms swinging as he jogged up the hillside, cresting the rise to where his car was parked. Only then did he look up.

Directly at a policeman standing beside his car. A policeman holding a radio in his hand, his beret-like hat angled to one side. And a gun on his hip. Harry took all this in with one glance.

"*Poios eísai?*"

Harry's Greek was abysmal. He kept his hands in plain view as he responded. In Italian. "*Non capisco.*" I don't understand.

Many Greeks spoke Italian as well. Including this cop. "*Chi sei?*" Who are you?

Harry dodged that one. "I'm visiting the theater," he replied in Italian. "Is that okay?"

"Is this your car?" the cop asked.

"Yes, it's my car." Harry gestured to the theater behind him. "Am I not allowed?"

The cop stared at Harry for a few seconds. "Is anyone with you?"

"I'm alone. I didn't know this was closed." A beat passed. "Is it closed?"

"This area is not safe," the cop said. "When did you get here?"

Harry made a show of looking at his watch. "An hour ago. Maybe less."

"What are you doing?"

Harry shrugged. "Looking around."

The officer kept looking at Harry. His radio squawked. He didn't take his eyes off Harry as he answered the call, the device close to his mouth and his voice low enough Harry couldn't catch anything. He did get a look at the guy's name badge. *Mavropanos.*

Officer Mavropanos tucked the radio onto his belt. He looked over his shoulder, only for an instant, then back at Harry. The hand near his gun didn't get any closer.

Harry tried again. "I didn't mean to do anything wrong."

"The sites must be inspected for safety," Mavropanos said. "You are the first person I have seen here."

"You're an inspector?"

Mavropanos shrugged. "Money is tight." A thick finger aimed toward the theater behind Harry. "Why did you run up here? Did you see anything dangerous?"

Harry's hands clenched. "No," he said after a moment. "I forgot my phone in the car. Came back to get it."

Mavropanos grunted. "We do not want anyone to be injured."

"Am I allowed to go back down?" Harry asked. "I'm excited to see it all."

"One minute." The cop hitched a finger on his belt. "Where did you come from?"

"I came here from Bulgaria." Harry left it at that.

Another grunt. The radio came to life. Mavropanos turned down the volume, instead reaching for his cell phone. Whatever he saw pleased him. "He is here."

The icy cold filling Harry's veins went subzero when a second police car appeared on the road. It slowed and pulled to a stop beside the first car, and a few breaths later a second uniformed cop stood in front of Harry, studying him.

"Hello, officer," Harry said, managing to read his name tag before the guy turned away. *Gekas*.

The two kept Harry in view as they conferred, their voices low and words quick. Gekas walked over to Harry's car and laid a hand on the hood, palm up. Harry shifted his weight from one foot to the other when Gekas's head shook once.

"How long have you been here?" Mavropanos asked again.

"Not long," Harry said. "I drove from town." Thessaloniki wasn't far. Close enough his engine could realistically have cooled. Maybe.

Mavropanos eyed his partner. "We must inspect the site."

"Should I leave?" Harry asked.

Mavropanos showed his teeth. "No. You came from Bulgaria. You can stay." Now one of those big fingers wagged in the air. "But walk with us until we finish the inspection."

The frigid air chilled another degree. Harry forced a response out. "Okay."

Mavropanos took a few steps past Harry, his head down, eyes moving back and forth as he walked. His gaze locked on Harry's recent footprints in the dirt. Mavropanos followed Harry's path to the closest row of seats, stepped over and began descending. Gekas gestured for Harry to follow and then fell in behind him, penning Harry in.

I'm faster than these guys. Harry looked left and right as he followed the first cop, feeling the second close behind him. He could make a run for it. Or he could beat them back up the stairs to his car. Keys in his pocket, speed on his side… He might be able to escape. Unless they shot him.

Mavropanos continued down the central aisle, looking left and right. He kept moving until he saw the open passage door. The cop stepped back from it, arms at his side, a frown on his face. Greek words poured from his mouth. His partner responded in kind. They kept talking, Harry stuck between them.

"What is this?"

The question in Italian from Mavropanos caught Harry by surprise. "I don't know," Harry said. "Looks like a door."

"Was this open when you got here?"

"I think so."

Mavropanos clearly didn't believe him. "I have never seen this."

"It looks like it just opened," Harry said.

The cop ignored him, spouting more indecipherable Greek to his partner. They exchanged one last short phrase and then, without warning, Gekas clamped a powerful hand on Harry's shoulder.

"Hey," Harry said as he twisted against the grip. "What's going on?"

Gekas said nothing, keeping a tight hold on Harry. Mavropanos turned around.

"How did you find this?"

"What are you talking about? I just got here."

Gekas spoke for the first time. "Your car hood was cold, and I have been here before. You did it."

"Stop that," Harry said as Gekas tightened his grip. "You guys can't do this."

"Tell us how you found it," Gekas said.

"I didn't—"

A knee to his back sent Harry sprawling to the ground. He rolled, right into the path of Mavropanos's boot swinging into Harry's midsection. Harry lay still, gasping for breath.

"Get up," Mavropanos said. "Talk."

These guys might be cops. But someone besides the city was paying them for this. Harry stood and tried his luck one more time. "Look, I don't know what you want, but I'm telling you—okay, okay." Mavropanos drew back his clenched fist. "Fine. I knew the door was open. But I didn't do it." He kept his eyes from going to the circular plug now back in the wall. "I found it like this. I was going to get a headlamp when you showed up."

"You lie," Mavropanos said. "You found other messages. They brought you here."

Harry went still. He played a hunch. "Did Olivier tell you everything?"

Lines creased the foreheads of both men. "Who is Olivier?" Mavropanos asked.

Not Olivier. "Big Bird," Harry said. Mavropanos flinched. Gekas did not. "Thought so," Harry said. "He's the one in charge."

This time Mavropanos gave no warning. The words had barely left Harry's mouth before a fist crashed into his midsection and he stumbled back. Directly into Gekas. The second cop gave him a shot to the kidneys and Harry was down on the ground again. It took him a bit longer to get up this time.

"Glad we settled that," Harry said through gritted teeth.

Mavropanos wasn't amused. "Show us what you found."

"You're looking at it."

"Tell us what is inside."

Inside the passage lay his only hope. "I need a flashlight," Harry said. One was shoved into his hand. One heavy enough to do some damage. That thought vanished when Gekas unholstered his weapon. "Yeah, I get it. Try anything and you shoot me." Gekas growled something in Greek. "Follow me," Harry said. "And stay back. I have no idea what's in here."

A powerful beam shot out from the flashlight when he flicked it on.

Spiderwebs hung in the corners of the passage ahead. A few cracks ran across the plain walls and ceiling, but nothing worrying. Dust on the floor had been undisturbed for millennia. The ceiling was barely above Harry's head. Although the path was wide enough for the two burly cops to walk side by side, he made it a good ten feet into the darkness before realizing they weren't behind him.

"You guys coming?" Harry called over his shoulder.

That got them moving. The closer those two stayed to him, the better.

"Keep up," Harry said. "There could be traps in here. Sometimes they're on a delay."

Boots pounded stone as the two cops moved closer. Harry could almost feel them breathing down his neck. They couldn't see him smirk.

"I don't see anything that worries me," Harry said. "Yet."

"What do you know about all of this?" Gekas's words carried an edge that hadn't been there before. An edge not of threat, but of fear.

"Enough to know this may be deadly." Harry stopped walking. "Didn't your boss warn you?" he asked, turning his head to look at them.

It took a few seconds. "About what?" Mavropanos asked.

Harry raised an eyebrow. "A king's wrath."

The two cops exchanged a look. Harry kept walking, pushing the two from his mind. Part of what he said was meant to scare them. Part of it was true. "This hallway is empty," he said to himself. "No markings, no messages. Just bare stone. Odd."

The cops faded into the background, Harry's entire world now the stone hallway and any clues it offered. Harry stopped walking and closed his eyes. The cops had enough sense to keep quiet. The second half of Cotys's last message flashed through Harry's mind.

A son and hero whose valor captured Mars, who carries the hero's name. Mars sits with Cassander's muse and see the place in her city.

Spartacus had captured Mars. Hard to say what that meant. Mars was a god. No one could physically capture a god. *Mars* could be an idea, a goal. Or it could be a physical object, one waiting to be found. How did all of this carry Spartacus's name? No idea. Only that rising sun image was left to guide him, and it had led him to this hidden door.

"Look for carvings anywhere," Harry said.

"Why?" Mavropanos asked as a burst of noise came from the radio on his belt.

"Just do it." Either these guys already knew the connection between rising sun carvings and the path, or they had no idea—and Harry wouldn't be giving away such a valuable piece of leverage. Pieces in short supply at the moment. "The people who left it would also leave a message saying why they did. The trick is knowing how to read it."

On Harry walked. More noise sounded from the radio, this time from the one Gekas carried. Was that one of their names he heard? Harry turned to find the two men looking at each other. Both lowered the volume on their devices. Neither turned them off. Interesting.

The hallway beckoned and Harry walked on. By now he must be halfway toward the end of the seating. Given that, why wasn't this hallway curving as the rows of seats did? It carried on in a straight line, with no descent or rise, only a low passageway leading deep into the hillside. Harry played his light over the man-made walls. Perfectly cut walls. The precision was incredible. A message in and of itself.

"Look at the craftsmanship," Harry said.

Mavropanos wasn't impressed. "There is nothing here."

Harry's light flashed across the hall ahead. He stopped so fast Mavropanos bumped into his back and sent him stumbling forward. "Wrong," Harry said. "Look."

His flashlight beam revealed an opening ahead. A doorway cut into one side of the passage, at so sharp an angle he couldn't see inside. "Stay here." Harry played his light over the floor. "This is when things usually go sideways."

He heard their tight breaths. Harry moved into the doorway, each step measured, his head moving all the while to check for danger. Cotys had left security measures at all the prior locations save one. But here, the stone walls to either side were bare. Same with the ceiling. Only the rectangular opening ahead stood out. No door. Nothing but the promising dark.

Harry aimed his light into the room and leaned around the doorframe. He remained still for several long seconds.

"What is there?" Mavropanos asked.

Harry didn't look back when he motioned for the two men to join him. "Come see for yourself."

The men were beside him in seconds. Two sharp breaths later their jaws hung open. Harry held out an arm. "Don't step inside until I know it's safe."

"You will take it," Mavropanos said.

Harry laughed. "You think I'm gonna carry that out of here past you? Gold is heavy."

His flashlight lit up the room as Harry walked in, checking the floor all the while. It took every ounce of self-control to look away from what stood against the rear wall. First, he needed to make sure nothing in here would kill him. Then he'd worry about the prize. Only after he was satisfied the room was safe did Harry aim his light ahead. He had to lean back to take it all in.

Eight feet of solid Roman fury stood in front of him. A message for any who dared to stand against the empire. A promise of destruction to some; a promise of protection to others. An image stolen from the Greeks, repurposed for Roman use.

Mavropanos called from his post by the entrance. "It is gold."

"And his name is Mars." Harry lifted a hand again. "Wait."

He moved on before the men could respond. A golden spear reached from floor to ceiling, clasped in one hand at the end of a thickly muscled arm, while the other held a circular shield wholly unlike those of the Roman legions. A helmet protected his head, topped by an extravagant plume; no cheekpieces hid the clean-shaven face. A breastplate on his chest and scaled armor reaching to his knees completed the warrior's uniform.

"It's Roman," Harry said. "I think Spartacus captured this in battle." It was all coming together now. Two Roman *aquilas* at each of the prior sites. Two symbols of Spartacus defeating Roman legions on the field. This must be the third. "He sacked a provincial city for supplies after the second battle."

"What did you say?" Mavropanos asked.

"Nothing." How Spartacus had led his forces to victory against an entire city garrison was irrelevant now. All that mattered was Harry getting out of here without these two crooked cops on his tail. "Your boss will love this," Harry said.

Gekas turned out to be sharper than Harry realized. "How can you know this came from Spartacus?"

Harry pointed at the shield. "His name is on it."

Letters etched into the shield spelled out the Thracian's name. A show of strength and defiance. That was what Cotys had referred to in his last message: how Mars carried the hero's name. A brave yet ultimately futile effort. Harry looked left. He looked right. "I'm missing something."

Both cops responded together, fear tinging their voices. "What?"

"If I knew, I wouldn't be missing it." Harry turned around. *Bingo*. "Found it."

An inscription on the wall behind him, akin to a plaque. The Latin letters stood at eye level and were large enough to read from here. "Move," Harry said as he brushed past Mavropanos. "This is what I'm here for."

"The statue is up there," the cop said.

"This is the real prize." He ignored them and translated the inscription silently.

So ends the mortal victories of the great Spartacus. Honor his courage. Take strength from his bravery. His body is gone, yet his spirit lives forever. A burning beacon to all Thracians. We must remember.

Should any heart waver, the protection of the Thracian icon will inspire. Stand before where the king who built our capital sleeps. Travel five stadions beyond his bed.

Follow Helios to his destination for one stadion. The protection and truth lie behind the shield of the gods.

Harry read it again, burning the words into his memory. Only when he stepped back did Mavropanos speak.

"Tell me what it says."

You don't read Latin. Good. Harry made noncommittal noises. "I'm not sure," he eventually said. "My Latin is a little rusty." Harry glanced over his shoulder. The two men were far enough back. He looked ahead, feigning interest in the plaque, his legs tensed.

A sharp phrase in Greek met his response. Again, strong hands clamped on his shoulders. He tried to twist out of them and got nowhere.

"Now you walk." Gekas shoved him forward. "Outside."

Damn. He'd been about to run for it. The gold statue should have been enough to keep them in here, buy him time to run outside. Now he had a gorilla latched onto his shoulder as he was pushed and shoved toward the bright light outside.

"You're leaving that behind?" Harry asked as they marched. No response. "I didn't get to finish checking the chamber," he continued. "There could be more."

"We will check later." Mavropanos had again assumed command. "Now go." His radio erupted once more with Greek words Harry didn't understand.

Then it hit him. "You guys are worried other cops will show up. They've been calling and you're not answering." He got a shot to the kidney for his trouble that nearly sent him down.

"Stop talking." Mavropanos grabbed the flashlight from Harry's grasp. "Move."

Winter sunlight assaulted Harry's eyes as he stumbled into the chilled air. He blinked rapidly. Mavropanos pushed him up the steps toward the cars. Harry turned to hide his arm and reached into his pocket, where he slid his fingers through the ceramic knuckledusters. Both men were edgy now. Edgy people made rash decisions. Harry couldn't let them dictate what happened next.

Gekas maintained his grip on Harry's shoulder as they climbed. When they reached the top of the hillside Harry pretended to stumble, kicking at the ground and dropping to one knee. He rolled, got to his feet and made a fist. Gekas moved toward him, his chin exposed. Mavropanos was still behind.

Sirens blared and tires screeched. Harry twisted as a slew of police cars roared up the road and pulled off to encircle the three men and their vehicles. The look of fear on the faces of both wayward cops was impossible to miss. Harry quick-stepped away from them.

Cops jumped from the cars. Greek shouting filled the air and guns were drawn. Harry didn't need to speak the language to know what they wanted. He dropped the dusters back into his pocket and raised his hands.

Mavropanos and Gekas took hold of Harry's arms. The former lifted a hand, shouting in Greek to be heard over the ruckus. Two men in suits barged through the assembled uniforms and came right at them.

One man jabbed a finger in the captive's chest. "Harry Fox?"

Three pairs of eyes went wide. Three mouths opened. No one could speak.

"Are you Harry Fox?" the finger-jabber shouted again. He spoke English.

"Yes," Harry said. He was too shocked to lie.

"You are under arrest."

Mavropanos and Gekas didn't say a word as Harry was pulled from their grasp and cuffs slapped on his wrists. He was marched rapidly to a police car without so much as another word and tossed in the back. The door slammed shut behind him.

Chapter 20

Thessaloniki

This police station was nothing like in the movies. No emotional victims telling their stories to bored detectives. No benches filled with handcuffed criminals. The Thessaloniki precinct was practically empty and sparkling clean, and as Harry was escorted through the main area by a pair of silent officers, the scent of freshly brewed espresso filled the air. It was almost *nice*.

He walked into a room containing only a scuffed table, two metal chairs and bad lighting. The manacles on Harry's wrists were looped into a metal circle bolted to the table before the two silent men turned and left, closing the door with a *click* that pushed the last bit of warmth from his veins.

Minutes passed. Not many, for it wasn't long before raised voices filtered through the air ducts and under the door. Somebody wasn't happy. And that somebody sounded like Mavropanos.

Harry flinched when the door flew open. The woman who entered was a stranger to him, though her manner was not. The way she flung what could only be Greek curses at the door sounded familiar. The glint in her eye that promised destruction to any who crossed her rang a bell. And the set of her jaw, the squaring of her shoulders as she studied him? All reminded Harry of his half-sister, Nora Doyle.

The woman stood to her not-very-tall full height and walked up to Harry, looking down her nose at the seated and restrained man. "What is your name?" she asked in English.

"Harry Fox."

"Why are you in my country?"

"I like history."

"Lie to me again and you go to jail. One week from now I will ask you the same question."

He stalled. "Who are you?" he asked.

"The woman who may have saved your life." She put a finger to her lips before he could respond. "Don't say it."

His voice dropped to almost a whisper. "Say what?"

"What you were about to say about the two officers," she replied in kind. "Mavropanos and Gekas."

Harry motioned for her to lean over. "They're corrupt," he said in low tones.

She didn't blink. "I know."

She straightened, walked to the door and opened it to stick her hand outside. She didn't say a word. Metal clinked before she closed the door and came back to his side. "Do not try to escape."

"I won't."

Seemingly less than satisfied, she nonetheless used the key she'd been given to unlock his cuffs. Harry rubbed his wrists even though they didn't ache. It seemed the thing to do. "Thanks," he said. "Care to tell me what's going on?"

"I am Chara Markou. I am not a police officer."

"Who are you?"

"I already told you."

"The woman who may have saved my life. Got it." Harry crossed his arms. "Any reason I should think I'm better off with you than those other two?"

Her glare would have turned sand to glass. "You are not in the back of a police car being held hostage by two men who work for an antiquities smuggler. That should be enough." Harry conceded the point. "Where to begin?" Chara asked. She gave him a chance to talk. He declined to fill the silence. "First, here." Now Chara tapped a folder lying on the desk, one she'd carried in with her. "You are Harry Fox. American citizen, born in Brooklyn. Recently you uncovered what may be the most important archaeological discovery since Tutankhamun's tomb."

"I had help."

Chara's icy demeanor warmed by a degree at most, though she hardly looked at him. "Yes. You did. Prior to this you were in the employ of a New York gangster and his father."

"Don't believe everything you read."

"You were led to a career on the wrong side of the law by your father, Fred Fox."

Harry's face tightened. He managed to keep quiet.

"Your father was murdered in Rome. My apologies. Your mother drowned when you were a child."

Until now, Chara's gaze had roamed across the room, flitting over Harry now and then but never staying put. As the next words came out of her mouth, she stared him full in the face, unflinching and unblinking. "This proved to be a lie. She is alive and well. Remarried, and the mother of a very capable woman. Nora Doyle."

That about knocked him over. The feeling drained from his body, his arms hanging loose, his mouth no longer working. All he could do was blink.

"Now I have your attention." Chara sat on the edge of the table and leaned close. "I saved your life, Harry Fox. As a favor."

"A favor?" he managed to ask.

"I work for Interpol. My office is in Athens, and I assist national law enforcement agencies around the world to prevent antiquities theft and trafficking. Our organization has an office in Norway. A colleague of mine, Guro Mjelde, called me this morning. She had quite the story to tell. A tip about a possible theft at the Ancient Theater of the Queen. I immediately drove here. Lucky for you I drive fast."

Harry's head spun. "Someone gave you a tip about me?"

"Try to keep up. I heard of your detention on my drive here. Now you're under arrest. And, for the moment, safe."

A tip about him to Interpol? Nobody knew where he was, at least not anybody that would call Interpol. The two men who chased him from Bulgaria wouldn't call the police, not when they intended to steal anything Harry recovered. The only other people who knew were—*no way*.

Harry blurted her name without thinking. "Nora?"

"A better sister than you deserve," Chara said.

"She turned me in?"

"She *saved your life*." Chara frowned, reaching into her pocket. "Lucky for you. I suggest you thank her." With that, Chara held out the phone. "Take it," she said when Harry only stared at her. "It's Nora."

Harry felt as though the world were spinning faster than normal when he took the phone from Chara and connected the call. "Hello?"

"Where are you?"

"Nora?"

"Who else would have this number?" The impatience in her tone came with a new flavor. One he'd rarely heard before. Concern. "Tell me where you are."

"A police station in Thessaloniki," Harry said. "With a woman named—"

"—Chara Markou. Good." Nora blew out a long sigh. "That was a close one."

"What was?"

"You nearly getting kidnapped and killed at the theater. Why—did you almost die somewhere else?"

He may have been floundering to gain his footing, but Nora coming at him provided the boost he needed. His temper flared. "Tell me what's going on right now."

"Ever hear of a man named Kiryl Korzun?"

Harry wracked his brain. "No."

"He's a Belarussian gangster. A real piece of work. You know the type."

Harry let that one go. "What does he have to do with me?"

"Korzun's enemies have a tendency to go missing." Nora gave a brief summary of the man. Flashy, deadly. "He's not a man to cross," Nora finished. "Which is why you're under arrest."

"You think Korzun was coming after me because of the artifacts?"

"There's one more thing," Nora said. "He's tall and skinny, except for in the middle. Stick legs, long arms and neck, a huge midsection. Sound like anybody you know?"

"Cut the nonsense."

"Think about it, Harry. Who looks like that?" She didn't give him a chance. "A children's character. He looks like a big bird. But he's deadly."

"Korzun is Big Bird?"

"My Interpol contact in Norway confirmed it." Now Nora's voice dropped a few decibels. "She also told me Korzun is missing. I'd say he's up to something."

"Like chasing an ancient Thracian trail."

"And eliminating anyone in his way. I can't prove it, but a man died with you in Cotys's tomb—however that happened..." She left the thought unfinished. "I wouldn't want to be the person Korzun blames for it. Remember the two men you trapped in that tomb?"

"In Perperikon. Yes."

"They assaulted a dig team member," Nora said. "They probably only missed you by a few minutes. Those guys are lethal, and they're after you."

"Do you know about the two Greek cops?"

"Chara told me. Korzun's influence extends even further than I realized. We can't prove those cops are dirty, but real cops don't act the way they did. You just dodged a bullet, Harry."

"Thanks to you."

"We're a team. That's what teammates do."

And he was darned glad about it right now. "Does Gary know?"

"I'm putting you on speaker." A second later her voice sounded again with an echo. "You still there?" she asked, and Harry said he was. "Gary's here."

Gary Doyle's voice came through. "I'm glad you're safe. Apologies for not giving you notice of our contact with Interpol. It was a last-second decision."

"Yours or hers?" Harry asked.

"Both," Gary said. "Nora told me how this Korzun fellow handles anyone who opposes him. It made the decision for us. We can't risk putting you in harm's way."

"Why now?"

"Part of what I do is evaluate risk. As I said before you left, your skills and past success outweighed my concerns you might be overmatched. That has since changed."

Nora, never one to stay quiet for long, cut in. "We know who's after you. Korzun isn't someone to let bygones be bygones. If he got his hands on you and thought you were between him and whatever he thinks is at the end of this, he'd either kill you immediately or keep you close until you weren't useful. Then, same result."

Harry couldn't stop himself. "What about the governor?"

"You have done more than enough for the governor," Gary said. "And for me. I will not forget it."

Nora and Gary exchanged muffled words, as though someone had put a hand over the speaker. "Nora will explain what happens next," Gary said. "Harry, you have a business to oversee, and your own safety to worry about. Perhaps it's best to leave Cotys and his trail in the history books. I'll see you when you return."

Gary must have departed, for Nora took him off speaker and her voice rang clearly in his ear again. "Interpol is taking you into custody on my behalf. Chara is taking you to the airport and putting you on a flight back home. She will eventually report this entire situation as a misunderstanding. You were a tourist and noticed a hidden doorway in the theater. Now, listen closely. You don't know how that doorway opened. All you did was walk inside. The first two officers understandingly were confused about your intent, regardless of what their report may say, and this will be forgotten. Any questions?"

"What about the message I found inside?"

That caught her off guard. "What message?"

Harry looked at Chara. She pointedly did not look away. Harry suppressed a smirk. *She'll like this.* "A message from Cotys." Chara's eyebrows rose. "One I understand."

"How so?"

"I read Latin."

"That's not what I mean."

"I need to speak with Sara first. I *think* I know what it means, but I want to double-check with a real expert."

Nora sighed. "Sara knows about what we did. The passageway. The two cops. The Interpol tip and your arrest."

"How?"

"I told her."

Well, that changed the matter. "You told her everything?"

"Everything."

"My progress with Charlemagne was between us." Chara visibly started at the name.

"She did it to protect you," Nora said. "And because I asked for her help. Think about it, Harry. You're doing something to protect your mom. She's my mom too. That's what you need to focus on. Protecting yourself and your family."

Harry could hardly find the words. "Seriously? You're supporting me now?"

"I've always supported you," she fired back. "Almost always. Cotys and this Spartacus path are too risky with Korzun in play. Come home. Focus on what you were doing before."

Harry closed his eyes. *If only it were that easy.* If it were, he'd be somebody else. "I appreciate you saving my butt," he said. "Now I need you to do one more thing for me."

"You're not in a position to make demands."

"Probably not. I'm doing it anyway. You need to tell Chara to let me go."

There was a long, incredulous pause. "Do you have any idea how much trouble went into saving you?"

"I need a head start," he said. "Let me go. That'll buy me enough time to finish this. I'm close, Nora. Very close."

"Close to what?"

"I have to talk to Sara first. She'll tell you. *After* I'm on my way."

"Put me on speaker." Harry did as ordered. "Chara, how many favors did I call in to make this happen?"

"All of them," Chara said.

"You hear that, Harry? I don't have any more strings to pull."

Harry looked Chara square in the face. "What if I could offer you the truth behind King Cotys's path?" He waved away her question. "You don't know what that is. I get it. Trust me when I say it'll be one of the biggest stories of the year." Harry tapped his chest. "We found the Library of Alexandria, remember? I know a big find when I see it."

"I am in the business of protecting artifacts," Chara said. "Not exploiting them."

"Then protect a part of history no one's seen for two thousand years. Let me find it for you, hand it to you on a silver platter. The traffickers don't get it and your team looks good."

Chara Markou frowned. Then her face softened a tad. She crossed her arms, her gaze moving across the walls and ceiling before turning back to Harry. "I'm listening."

Harry noted that Nora didn't interrupt as he relayed a summary of his adventure so far, leaving out only the golden *aquila* discoveries and how this had all started because Gary Doyle was a secretly ambitious man. "Take credit for the Mars statue. You also get credit for anything I find next."

"How do I know you will not disappear?"

Harry did his best to look offended. "I would never." Chara wasn't interested. "For two reasons," Harry said after she didn't budge. "And they're the same. One, Nora Doyle is my sister. Her reputation is at stake. Ask the other Interpol agent, the one who told you to come here. I may take risks in my life, I may push the envelope, but I'm not dense. Nora is the last person I'm messing with, because when she's boiling mad, Kiryl Korzun has nothing on her." Chara almost stopped the look of appreciation from crossing her face. Almost. "Second," Harry continued, "Nora is my sister. I won't tell you why, so don't ask, but what I'm doing helps her. I won't let you down because that would let her down as well."

Nora finally piped up. "You don't have to do it, Harry."

"My finishing this helps you and lets me get back to the other project without this hanging over my head. That means it helps our mom. You going to stop me from helping her?"

Nora grumbled and offered a few choice words. "You're not giving me a choice."

"Darn right I'm not. We're not only family. We're a team."

"Use my own words against me again and you'll be sorry."

"Glad it's settled." Harry looked at Chara. "I assume Nora can serve as your contact for my progress?"

"That is acceptable."

"May I have my stuff back?"

He'd been frisked upon entering the police station. All his belongings, including the amulet taken from around his neck, were last seen in a brown paper bag. A brown paper bag Chara retrieved by opening the door and sticking her hand out to grab it. "I expected you would ask for it," she said. "Everything is there."

Including his trusty ceramic knuckledusters. Those went into a pocket along with his wallet. His phone flashed to life and revealed a text message. "I have to make two calls," he said.

"Who?" Nora asked. "I can help."

"Appreciate it, but I got this. Sara first. A friend after that."

Chara was only interested in one thing. "Tell me what you know about the message at the theater. And what you are doing next."

"Making sure I'm on the right track. Sara's forgotten more about history than I know. I need to talk to her."

"I'll leave you to it," Nora said. "Stay in touch. Don't do anything stupid."

"I never do." Harry clicked off and handed the phone back to Chara. "Give me five minutes," he said. "May I have some privacy?"

"You may not." Chara pulled out a chair and sat beside him. "Make your calls."

Harry shrugged. "Worth a shot." He dialed Sara's number. She answered at once. "I'm fine," Harry told her before she could ask. "Thanks to Nora. Now listen to me and don't say anything," Harry told her. "I need to tell you about what I found and what I think it means. Tell me if you agree."

"I'm listening."

He detailed the message and his thoughts. By the time Sara told him she agreed with him, down to the final warning, Chara was on the edge of her seat, close enough for Harry to smell the fresh, minty scent of her chewing gum. Harry promised to call when he arrived at his destination before clicking off.

"I need a pen and paper," Harry said. Chara obliged, and after Harry scratched a short phrase on the sheet, she accepted it with both hands. "That's the place," Harry said. "I'm sure of it. Well, pretty sure."

"Mr. Fox, you are quite impressive."

Harry shrugged. "It's what I do."

"In that case, may I suggest you get to it?"

Harry looked at the single exit door. "How am I getting out of here?"

"With me." She stood. "I will take you back to your car. When the police ask what happened…" She shrugged. "I will tell them it is none of their business."

Harry grabbed his things and stood. "I appreciate this."

"Do not make a fool of your sister or of me." Chara turned to the door. "And do not get yourself killed. I am counting on you to hold up your side of the agreement."

He could always count on doing business with these law enforcement people. The business of what can Harry do to make them look good.

Well, so be it. Olivier Lloris was the real target. Harry just had to deal with a Thracian prince first.

Chara stuck her head out the door and looked both ways. "Follow me. Try not to look like a prisoner."

Harry walked briskly down the hall with his head up, right on Chara's tail, moving through a back hallway past uniformed officers who didn't give them a second look. A side door banged open, cold air bit Harry's cheeks, and he was free. His phone came out when he dropped into the passenger seat of Chara's unmarked car and they drove off. Harry read the message a second time, then a third. Joey Morello wasn't a man to exaggerate. That was why Harry's grip tightened on the phone, why his breath came short and quick. Joey Morello needed to talk to Harry, and he needed to talk now.

Harry sent a message saying he'd call Joey shortly. Right after he got away from Chara Markou and the Thessaloniki police. Harry had at least five hours in the car ahead of him and an international border to cross. Sara had agreed: whatever Cotys IV had secreted at the end of his path honoring Prince Spartacus, it would be found in Bulgaria. Harry looked toward the northeast. Toward the Valley of the Thracian Rulers, where dozens of royal tombs from Thracian society stood. Where he believed another tomb lay undiscovered. A tomb with an incredible secret.

Chapter 21

Thessaloniki

"Can you run me through that again?" Joey Morello had seen a lot of things in his life. Apparently, this wasn't one of them. "I may be getting confused about which set of cops is corrupt and which wants you to survive."

"It changes constantly," Harry said. The Greek countryside flew past outside. Harry's foot may not have been on the floor, but it was darned close. The speed limit signs flashing by didn't even warrant a second look. It wasn't a question of whether he was breaking them. It was by how much. "The Interpol lady is on my side at the moment. The locals were the ones up to no good."

"Because they're working for this Big Bird character."

"Kiryl Korzun. I'm not trying to start a beef with a guy like him."

"Wise decision. In more ways than you realize."

Joey's tone caught his ear. "Why's that?" Harry asked.

"That's why I needed to speak with you," Joey said. "There have been developments."

"Not good ones."

"No, they are less than positive."

"Did I step on the wrong toes somehow?"

"No," Joey said with force. "Not at all. Olivier Lloris is the one walking where he shouldn't. I'd be within my rights to cause a problem about this. To demand satisfaction."

Harry knew all about the mysterious Italian ways of settling scores.

Which is to say he had no idea how it really worked. "What would that look like?"

"In my father's day? Very ugly. However, times have changed. I can't accuse Carmelo Piazza of offending my honor without concrete proof. I don't have any, and even if I did, now I have to consider whether it's worth the trouble. It doesn't matter if I'm right and everyone knows it. Carmelo won't forget if I make him look bad." Joey laughed without humor. "Men like Carmelo would rather lose a couple of their men than their good name. Even if it's all a lie."

"Remember what I said," Harry told him. "Don't start trouble on my account. I agreed to chase this Thracian trail. Not you. It's my responsibility."

"You listen to me, Harry. Right now." Harry assured Joey that he was listening. "I'll buy your argument this time. Yes, I know you're good. The best, if you ask me. That doesn't mean you can't lose. If you get in trouble with these guys, and I mean any sort, you call me. I say you still work for me and this Big Bird goes away. I don't care how tough he thinks he is; the guy can't be stupid enough to pick a fight with me. He does that and half the families in Italy are lining up to exact retribution on my behalf."

"Because every organized family in Italy wants Joey Morello in their corner," Harry said. It was true. "I appreciate it, Joey. You're sticking your neck out for me."

"I wouldn't be here if it weren't for you."

Harry maneuvered around a slow-moving van. "You still keeping an eye on Sara?"

"Two-man teams rotating out every twelve hours."

"Thanks. Does she have any idea?"

"Not that anyone can see. My guys are good at blending in."

"I assume Mack isn't involved?"

Mack was Joey's personal bodyguard. He'd been one of the first Italians in the crew to embrace Harry, accept him for who he was, even before Joey and Harry got through their differences. He also resembled in height and width the vehicle with which he shared a name. Mack could seamlessly blend in at a professional wrestling event. Anywhere else would be tough.

"He's sitting this one out," Joey said. "She's safe. We'll keep her that way. Speaking of, how close are you? To being done, I mean."

Good question. Harry almost asked which quest Joey was asking about. "Two days at the most." Optimistic? Sure, but he hadn't gotten this far by not believing in himself. "Then I'll be back to take care of business at home."

"Good. I hear rich folks who collect your artifacts are getting antsy. They're worried about missing out on the next world-class collectible from Fox and Son."

Harry shook his head. "Running a business is harder than I thought."

Joey laughed. "You don't say."

"Yeah, yeah, I know. Maybe I'll take a management class from Morello University."

"You couldn't afford the tuition."

Joey hung up, leaving Harry shaking his head. Harry put both hands on the wheel and pressed the gas pedal, and five hours turned to four by the time he arrived at his destination. His tires rattled over loose rock alongside the road when Harry finally pulled over and shut off the engine. He stepped out of the vehicle to find an eerily familiar sight stretching before him.

Verdant fields spread out ahead of him with mountains in the distance, their peaks shrouded in haze. The shimmering surface of a reservoir sparkled. Flat green lands were punctuated by rich green mounds dotted with evergreens and lush trees: the burial mounds of many Thracian rulers, only a fraction of what experts suspected the area held. Roughly three hundred burial mounds had been located and researched. The prevailing theory was that there were four times that many still to find. Harry shut the door and shielded his eyes against the glare. Time to cut that estimate down by one.

His pocket vibrated. Harry's eyes narrowed at the name on screen. *Rose Leroux.*

"I'm glad you called," Harry said when he answered. "The situation is evolving rapidly."

"As is often the case, dear boy." Rose's cigarette lighter fired. "Tell me."

Rose didn't do social calls. "Is something wrong?" Harry asked.

"Perhaps. Tell me what has changed."

Harry brought her up to speed on events from Perperikon to Samothrace and then Thessaloniki. One seemed to strike Rose the most. "The police are not your friends," Rose said. "That pair in Thessaloniki nearly ended this search." A beat passed. "As well as you."

"It's about Big Bird," Harry said. "Kiryl Korzun. He's behind it. I'm ahead of him now. Those guys won't be able to catch up."

"The valley is only five hours away from their police station," Rose reminded him. "Do not underestimate their reach."

"Even if Korzun has an antiquities expert on his payroll, I doubt they can decipher the last message from Thessaloniki. That's the only way they can figure out where to go next."

"Korzun was able to track you to Thessaloniki."

He had, but that wasn't the point. "Even if they figure out where I'm going, I have a head start. I'll be out of here before they arrive."

Rose didn't seem to share his optimism. "Perhaps," she said. "Tell me why you believe the valley is where your search ends."

"It's not only me. Sara believes it too."

"Humor me."

Harry recited the second half of the message from Cotys's hidden chamber in Thessaloniki.

Should any heart waver, the protection of the Thracian icon will inspire. Stand before where the king who built our capital sleeps. Travel five stadions beyond his bed. Follow Helios to his destination for one stadion. The protection and truth lie behind the shield of the gods.

"Prince Spartacus is the Thracian icon," Harry said. "Is he the same

Spartacus who led a rebellion? Maybe. It was a common enough name. Would a prince ever become a gladiator? Probably not, but who knows."

"How is that relevant?"

"It's not. What is relevant begins with the second sentence. The *king who built our capital* refers to the capital of ancient Thrace. That's the city of Seuthopolis. Which sits at the bottom of a reservoir I am looking at right now. I don't need to get to the city. The message only uses Seuthopolis as a reference. King Seuthes the third built the city. His tomb is here, not underwater."

"You begin in front of his tomb and move several thousand feet."

Over two decades working with Rose in one fashion or another and she still surprised him. "That's right," Harry said. "A *stadion* is around six hundred feet."

"Yes. A standard Roman unit of measurement."

"Which means I have to go about six-tenths of a mile beyond the tomb entrance. Then another six hundred or so feet to the west."

"Where Helios ended his daily journey across the sky."

"Is there anything you don't know?"

"If there was, I certainly would not tell you."

Harry chuckled dryly. "Helios was the sun god," he continued, "so I agree about heading west." He studied the landscape. "Which should put me near the base of a small mountain." The hazy sky obscured his vision to a degree, but if he squinted, Harry could make out a plateau-like rise, one with sloped sides and a slightly rounded top. "As for the *shield of the gods*, no idea. I'll figure it out when I get there."

"Your analysis appears sound." Metal scraped on metal. Harry pictured the lighter flaring, the end of a cigarette catching fire. He waited for the familiar sound of tobacco crackling. "In which case," Rose continued, "move quickly. Because of the corrupt police, and because of Kiryl Korzun."

"Who may have gone into hiding. That makes me nervous."

"It should not."

"Why's that?"

"Because you have bigger problems."

Harry rubbed a hand on his chin. "You're losing me. This Korzun guy apparently wants what I'm after. People who get in his way disappear. What's a bigger problem?"

"The man who confirmed Kiryl Korzun's identity is a person with whom I have done business in the past. He is a man to be trusted. As far as trusting goes in our line of work."

"You never trust anyone."

"Correct, though on occasion I believe people tell me the truth." Tobacco crackled as it burned. "My source is Russian, and he operates not far from the Belarussian border. He recently experienced conflict with Korzun, conflict that necessitated resolution."

"Korzun's in hiding to avoid your source? He doesn't seem like the sort of guy to run from anyone."

"My source is a very serious individual. Even more so than Kiryl Korzun. My source could confirm Korzun's identity because he physically saw Korzun recently." Burning tobacco crackled now. "My source shot Kiryl Korzun two weeks ago, tied an anchor around his body and dropped it in a Russian lake."

"Korzun is dead?" Rose assured Harry this was the case. "Then who are those guys working for? The two cops and the fake dig employees all said they work for Big Bird."

"They may believe they do. The fact is they do not. I confirmed my source did not co-opt Korzun's ongoing operations."

Harry's mind churned. "Two weeks ago is too long for those guys to still think Korzun is alive. Unless someone is making them believe he is." Memories flashed to life. "Maybe someone is pretending to be Korzun and running this operation. Not your source. Someone else." The wind nearly carried his next words away without a trace. "Who?"

"There are many options," Rose said. "None appealing. Whoever it is has no qualms about killing you. Which is why you must move quickly, Harry. Before the shadows chasing you arrive."

Chapter 22

Kazanlak Valley, Bulgaria

A small town of white-walled buildings topped with red roofs stood on one side as Harry jumped back in his car and fired the engine. The village was quiet, sleepy, even during the day; only a handful of cows stood out in the fields. Grassy hills rose gently in all directions.

Harry punched it, zipping closer to the tomb of Seuthes III, passing the burial mounds dotting the fields. Harry took a hard turn on a dirt road. He needed a different tomb now. For a different reason.

That will do. A small mound perhaps five hundred yards ahead had his eye. The car sliced through waist-high grass, the uneven ground putting his suspension to the test until he came to a stop at the tomb's base. A tomb that now stood between his car and the town of Kazanlak, shielding Harry and his vehicle from view and perhaps buying him a little extra time. Time that could save his life.

Who was impersonating Kiryl Korzun? The guy had enemies, that was for sure, but his enemies didn't want to *be* Korzun; they wanted to *be rid* of him. And now at least four people were being paid to beat Harry Fox in this search, paid by a person they believed to be Korzun. And if it wasn't Korzun, then who was it?

Was it a private collector wealthy enough to fund their own recovery effort? Was it another gangster like Korzun, someone out to make a profit in any way possible, no matter who got hurt in the process? Or was it someone else entirely?

Harry shouldered his pack and locked the car. He stashed the keys under a rock, checked that his knuckledusters were in one pocket, then started walking. In truth he didn't care who was after him or why. His goal was to get to the end of Cotys's trail before anyone else showed up. Do that and nothing else mattered.

The distant thrum of a boat engine rattled the air as Harry marched ahead. Harry squinted at the lake in the distance. A small craft buzzed across the water, throwing plumes of spray up behind it. Why anyone would be out on the water in this sort of cold was beyond Harry. The weather seemed to be keeping visitors away from the valley.

He didn't bother keeping low or trying to hide himself in the grass as he walked. First rule of getting up to no good? Act like you belonged. Most of the unstudied burial mounds and ancient tombs were small, hardly taller than a man. A few were bigger. Much bigger. Harry rounded a copse of trees on a gentle slope and minutes later came face-to-door with the most magnificent tomb of them all.

The tomb of Seuthes III. Founder of Seuthopolis. Ruler of ancient Thrace. This was Harry's first marker on the final step of the journey.

The hillside had been cut away, two stone walls holding back the earth and forming a corridor leading to glass doors fifteen feet high. Beyond them lay Seuthes' tomb. On any other day he'd have stopped for a visit. Today, he checked the sky, then the compass on his phone. What lay three thousand feet beyond the entrance? He couldn't see that far with this hill in front of him, so he ran around the entrance and stood on a ledge above the glass doors. Harry checked his compass once more and continued walking.

One thousand feet brought him well beyond the rear side of Seuthes's tomb, into an open field with the town far to his right and low mountains ahead. Two thousand feet and what he would describe as tall hills rather than mountains were close. Three thousand and Harry stopped. He turned. The compass said he now faced west, where Helios ended each day. The grass rippled. Thin clouds hung in the sky. And Harry Fox understood what King Cotys was saying.

"The shield of the gods."

A cliffside rose before him. Part of the low mountain range, this wasn't a rising slope like the other peaks, but a nearly sheer wall that plateaued at the top in a flat expanse looking down on the fields below. Or, more accurately, it *nearly* formed a flat expanse at the top. Nearly, because this geologic feature wasn't quite flat on top, but curved along either edge. With the flat face and curved top, it resembled nothing so much as a shield. A massive shield fit for a god.

He craned his neck. The shield formation was ten stories high from base to top, one hundred feet of solid rock. Harry frowned. He'd made it here. What next?

Whatever waited on Cotys's trail wouldn't be found in the middle of this field. Harry marched ahead, on a direct path for the shield's center. Cracks and crevices ran across the rock face: natural surface wearing, what anyone would expect to see on it. Which made him wonder what he wasn't seeing. He jogged the last few steps to reach the sheer face, then looked straight up.

Small ledges jutted out above him here and there. The face was mostly flat, though anyone wanting to climb it would need the proper gear, unless they were an exceptional free climber or just crazy. Harry had a little experience with climbing, all of it indoors or close to the city. Nothing he'd ever done compared to this.

Harry bent over and pulled at the tufts of grass, tossing aside clods of dirt to reveal the rock face at its lowest level. Nothing caught his eye as he covered the two hundred feet to the left. He walked back to the center, this time scanning everything from the grass line to above his head. A marker would have been visible, yet he made it back to where he'd started in the middle without finding a thing. Grass and dirt flew as he moved.

He found it with ten feet to spare. A clump of grass came out of the ground and Harry stopped. He blinked, rubbed furiously at the stone and revealed an old friend.

"The rising sun," Harry said. "Good to see you." It was the same as the original, a half-circle above the horizon with rays shooting out. *Hold on.* It wasn't identical to the original. This sun also had an extra mark on one beam. The beam pointing straight up to the stone above. Harry looked up. There was a small stone outcropping, large enough to use as a foothold. "No way."

Harry stepped back. He looked up again. No additional carvings on the rock face. He walked to the center and then back again. Only this one sun with an arrow pointing up. To what?

Cotys mixed both the symbolical and the literal in his messages, which were meant to obscure as much as guide. This arrow pointed up. Nothing Harry could see tied to the arrow, but chances were Cotys was using it as a literal message. Except nothing above the arrow related to Cotys or Thrace at all. Unless he was looking too hard.

Harry rubbed his chin. He eyed the rock face again, this time as a climber. That made a difference. "It could be," he said. His foot went on the small outcropping above the arrow. He tested it. The step held. When he stood on it, he could reach a higher outcropping with ease. A perfect handhold, with another one beside it. Harry jumped back down to the ground and looked up. At a shadow halfway up the rock wall, not quite in the center, maybe fifty feet off the ground. A shadow, he now thought, that might not be a shadow at all.

"It's a crack. A big one." A long, vertical crack in the rock he could probably fit through if he went sideways. A crack he could reach if he followed the path of handholds leading from one corner of the shield to a spot near the center.

"This is crazy." He shook his head. A king, climbing this rock face? It was nuts. Unless, of course, there was another way in. A way Harry couldn't see. Only one way to find out. He stepped on the small outcropping and moved as quickly as safety allowed, securing each hold before moving to the next. From up here he could tell specific handholds had been gouged into the rock, cut discreetly so it wasn't obvious unless you were looking for it.

Ten feet up and the belief grew. Twenty feet up, fear snuck in. He buried it, his nose scraping over the rock as he climbed, ill-used muscles starting to protest. Reach, grip, pull, step, repeat. At thirty feet he remembered that a fall from forty feet killed you half the time. Higher than that and the odds worsened dramatically.

The wind tore across his face, pulling at his hands and feet; the frigid stone sliced at his fingers. The ledges were half-steps, really, intended as handholds. Harry kept his face close to the rock, moving until he was nearly at the shadow's height. Now he stood barely five feet away from getting his foot on the larger outcropping in front of the open gash in the rock.

His arm went out in search of the next hold, the last one before he could reach the final ledge, far above the ground. The risk so far had paid off. He gripped the next handhold, stepping off the miniature foothold and swinging his foot out. His foot found nothing but air. Harry took a breath. *I missed it.* He tried again. Same result. Holding tight, he leaned back a fraction to look.

The hold had broken off the rock face.

Where there should have been the next opening for Harry's foot, he found only broken stone. The ledge had cracked off.

Harry kept still. Patience kept you alive up here, for the rock was an unforgiving opponent: one slip meant disaster. He was now nearly fifty feet up. Going back down didn't appeal. Another breath fogged the air for an instant before the wind blew it away. An old climbing adage came to mind. *Stop. Assess. Act.*

He'd stopped. Time to assess. Two good handholds, one foothold. He was safe for the moment, though the wind was quickly robbing his raw hands of feeling. The next foothold would have been up and over, putting him close enough to step on the small ledge fronting the opening. Without that step, however, he had more than five feet to go and no way to get there. The stone scraped his forehead as he leaned against it. *Act.* He knew what came next.

A leap of faith. No other way to get there than to jump for it. He could jump, or he could descend. His jaw muscles tightened. *I didn't come all this way for nothing.*

His current footholds were too far apart. To jump the gap he needed force, the sort of force generated with both feet close together. That meant putting both feet on the same foothold. A tight fit, both boots smashed together on a perch meant for one. He crouched to jump. One boot slipped off. A few seconds' scrambling for grip got him back to rights. He didn't have room for his legs to bend, not with both feet on the ledge and his body smashed up against the rocky face.

He turned until his chest was perpendicular to the cliff, one foot dangling in the air, the other on the outcropping. One hand hung loose as well. This way he could bend down to jump without knocking himself off the ledge. Would it be enough to get across? It would have to be.

Bend. Jump. Grab hold and don't let go. That's all he needed. The outcropping ahead stuck out enough he could get two hands on it. Landing on his feet was out of the question. He needed to grab hold, pull himself up and then roll over to safety. Miss and the odds weren't good.

A string of abuse for Gary Doyle, Nora and King Cotys IV filled his mind. He shouldn't be here, freezing his tail off, hanging from a cliff face about to do something only a fool would attempt. But here he was, and people were counting on him. He couldn't suppress a wry grin. *It's what I do.*

The last image in Harry's mind before he crouched and wiped it clean was of a person who didn't want him to be here, because she only wanted him to stay safe. Sara Hamed had only his best interests in mind, but if he listened to her, he would be living a lie. Time to show he really was the right man for the job. Or the only one foolish enough to take it, at least.

He crouched. The wind kicked up. He waited for it to die down. It did not. Harry cursed as tears blurred his sight. He wiped a hand across his eyes, crouched on one leg and locked his gaze on the outcropping. He jumped.

Harry turned into a sail flying against the wind, his arms out, feet hanging, the gusts pushing back as he reached for the outcropping hanging too far ahead. Gravity took hold and he started to drop.

Got it. One hand caught hold of the stone ledge as he fell. His abused fingers latched on as his body kept moving, swinging forward like a pendulum, his weight threatening to rip his hand from the rock. He kicked at the wall, dragging his feet to slow the swing, and reached up to grab the outcropping with his other hand. He missed. His body flew out, fingers clutching at the edge, nearly horizontal to the ground far below as he slowed, stopped—and his left hand slipped off.

Harry threw it back toward the rock and caught hold again. His right hand came up and grabbed hold of the outcropping. He pulled, lifting his torso with screaming muscles to throw first one arm and then the other over the edge and onto the outcropping. Boots scraped on stone as he pulled and kicked until one last heave sent him up and over before he flopped forward and twisted onto his back.

His chest heaved. His hands bled. Harry had never felt better.

He lay still for a moment longer. He looked to one side. His eyes narrowed. *Holy smokes.*

A closed door was set back in the shadows. The slash of an opening in the rockface hid it from view, the perfect camouflage. Harry got to his feet, staying low beneath the strong wind until he reached the vertical opening and peered inside. What looked like a narrow slit from outside was much wider once Harry stepped through. The entrance was wide enough for two men to walk through together before opening into a larger entranceway where a wooden door stood twice Harry's height. A doorway made not of stone, but of iron and wood. A door sporting a prominent carving of the rising sun.

A lever stole his attention. A vertical stone pole, contained in a recessed panel in the stone wall. Harry reached out with a hesitant hand to touch it. Nothing happened. Nor did anything happen when he wrapped his hand around it. He almost pulled it. Almost. Then any number of outcomes sprang to mind, so he let go and circled the entranceway. No holes in the walls, no seams in the floor, nothing that looked like a trapdoor in the ceiling ready to rain fury down on him. Not ideal, but it would have to do. Harry grabbed the lever with both hands and pulled.

Stone ground on stone as the pole jiggled an inch. He redoubled his efforts, leaning on the lever to try and move it another inch, rocks grinding as Harry grunted and tried to push it through the wall. The lever jerked, held, then gave way and fell back with a deep grinding sound. Harry stood back. A long breath later the floor rumbled, the vibrations running down the stone until they seemed to hit something solid far below.

The door opened. Ancient hinges protested as the wood and steel contraption pivoted, swinging wide until it stopped with a *thud* against the stone. Harry took one step toward it, and then the rumbling began again, more distant this time. He flattened himself against the ground in case the wall cracked. It did not, and the rumbling again faded. He turned to look behind him. A single car moved slowly along one of the roads crisscrossing the empty plain, too far away for its driver to see Harry. He rose cautiously as the last of the rumbling faded, then moved into the unknown.

The shrill whistle of wind vanished as he stepped through the door. Harry pulled his flashlight out and flicked it on. The floor ahead extended for only a few steps. Beyond that, stairs descended into the darkness. Sconces lined one side of the staircase. Rushes wrapped in twine and dark with accelerant filled each one. Harry aimed his flashlight to one side and spotted what he was looking for.

Two engravings of King Cotys. One depicting him as a warrior, the other as a statesman. The same engravings Harry had studied in the Bulgarian cave at the beginning of this journey. The hair on his arms rose. He couldn't say why, not exactly, but his gut told him to pay attention. Harry aimed his light down the stairs. He knelt, leaning over the first step, but he didn't move down.

A landing waited about twenty steps below. Unlit sconces lined the wall on one side. No other carvings or markings were visible on the walls. Harry tried the first step. It held. So did the second one. Air blew between his lips. What did the engravings of Cotys mean? Everything he'd done so far had been with a purpose. The two images carried a message. One he did not comprehend.

Harry's flashlight beam flickered. He smacked it. The light went out. He pulled out his cell phone and stuck it between his teeth, using the screen's light to dig through his pack for more batteries. A silent thanks went out to his father for drilling into Harry the need to be prepared. The light restored, he slipped an arm through one strap on his pack and forged ahead.

In the Bulgarian cave Cotys had left a message on the wall warning him to avoid every fourth step. These engravings were the same as what he'd seen in Bulgaria. They didn't represent a new idea or message. Harry tried to shrug the second strap over his other shoulder and missed, distracted by his thoughts. Why repeat the same carvings here? It didn't make—*oh no*.

Harry tried to stop and failed, stumbling forward. His foot landed hard on the fourth step and went straight through. Harry threw one arm up as he fell and his fingers scraped over flat stone without finding purchase. He shouted through a closed throat as he plummeted toward what only the gods knew waited below.

He jerked to a stop.

The strap on his backpack had caught on the wall sconce now above him. For the moment, anyway. He twisted in the air, the strap making alarming noises as he spun slowly in a circle, doing his best to not even breathe. Only his eyes moved as he searched in every direction for a handhold. Nothing. He lifted his other hand, stretching for the edge of the broken step above. He came up a foot short.

The wall sconce groaned as he swayed. A crack snaked down the wall. Harry grabbed onto the strap around his shoulder. Swinging invited disaster, as did staying in place. He looked down and confirmed his fears. Stone spikes, dozens of them. At least Cotys was consistent.

He clasped the pack tightly, reached up for the single strap looped over the sconce and did a pull-up. One-handed, shoulder screaming, he rose in the air until he could go no further, then reached his other hand up and did it again. *Crack*. The crevice on the wall widened with a noise like a gunshot. Harry went still. Another pull took him higher, enough to reach out and grab the lip of the false step. He used both arms and lifted, with one hand on the pack and the other on the broken stone step.

The sconce broke. He swung wildly above the deadly spikes as he threw the pack up and over the lip, then held on with one hand as the pack flew out of sight. He grabbed the lip with both hands, pulling and kicking against the wall until he went up and over the ledge and flopped onto solid ground.

A section of the stone wall by the fallen sconce broke free and crashed with a noise like thunder onto the rows of spikes below. Harry didn't even look. He lay on his back, chest heaving, heart pounding, happy to be alive.

He got to one foot, shook his head, then stood. A section of the wall had collapsed to reveal more stone underneath. The step behind him no longer existed. The stone spikes below waited for the next interloper. Harry set his jaw and turned away. Not him. *Not today.*

The pack went over his shoulder and down the steps he went, leaping over each fourth step until he reached another landing. It stretched ahead; more sconces with rushes hung on the wall, ready to light his way. Harry aimed his flashlight at the floor for a long while before proceeding. The weight in his gut dissipated with each step until he looked ahead and spotted them.

*X*s on the floor. The hallway widened at the same point the stone floor became covered with engravings. Or rather, one design, repeated again and again. "Roman numeral ten," Harry said. "The same as Samothrace."

An *X* engraved on the floor in front of Spartacus's empty tomb had nearly killed Harry when he touched it. The *X* engraving had marked a trap, and if Harry had been standing in front of the tomb a spear would have rocketed out of a hole and sliced through him. No such holes existed in these walls or on the ceiling.

The floor was a grid-like pattern of stones, laid out like a chess board. Stones marked with an *X* alternated with unmarked stones. A safe stone, then a deadly one, the pattern repeated. His foot hovered over the closest unmarked stone.

Something's wrong. He stepped back. The floor seemed off somehow. He tilted his head and crouched down, looking at the stones. It hit him. "That's not an X. It's the mark of Dionysus."

The Thracians had worshipped three deities: Artemis, Ares and Dionysus. The latter was the widely revered god of wine, fertility and festivity, the saint of celebration whose symbols included one borrowed from the ancient Egyptians. The *ankh*. This t-shaped hieroglyph topped with a drop-shaped loop represented life to the Egyptians. To the Thracians, the symbol represented the same, but with more of a festive edge. The Egyptian *ankh* stood upright like the modern Christian cross. The Thracian version, for Dionysus, turned to forty-five degrees and tilted. Tilted so it resembled an X, the Roman symbol for the numeral ten.

The loop at the top was the only difference. Each of these floor markings had a loop in the upper left corner of each stone, small and easy to miss. It was as though Cotys IV intended for it to be misread.

Harry crouched down, reached out a hand and pressed on the closest symbol of Dionysus before jerking his hand back to safety. Nothing happened. He tried it again with no effect.

A noise sounded behind him. Harry spun, hands balled into fists. Nothing. He aimed his light back toward the stairs. No movement. Probably a last piece of the stone falling loose.

The clock running in his head ticked on. Big Bird was still on his tail, so he took a cautious step onto the closest stone marked for Dionysus. It held. Same with his second step, a diagonal move. On he went until he made it the roughly thirty feet across and stepped onto unmarked ground.

He'd been so focused on keeping his balance as he moved across the grid that he didn't notice what waited ahead: stairs that descended into darkness, sloping down like a big-city subway entrance. Harry shone his flashlight down toward the bottom of the staircase, revealing another

The Thracian Idol

hallway below. He took a deep breath, and then began a walk of faith, one stair at a time, until he reached the bottom. At this point the walls widened and the curved ceiling soared above him. What was this place?

The stairs he'd descended and the marked floor he'd crossed were but a prelude to this grand room. The ceiling rose several stories overhead, while the wall to his right was at least twenty feet away, with a set of stairs to his left. This massive room had been cut into the mountain. It no longer felt like a cave or even a hidden room. This was a sanctuary. A place where a grieving father could honor his lost son and inspire a nation.

"This is Spartacus's real tomb."

Harry played his light over the walls he could see. They were plain, unmarked. The set of stairs to his left descended to parts unknown. He looked again and realized there were markings in this sanctuary after all. If Harry moved a few steps ahead and faced left, he would face what resembled a pair of empty picture frames cut into the wall, frames as tall as a man. One row of letters had been carved above the rectangles.

Harry's gaze dropped to what he could only call an island on the floor in front of the empty frames. Oblong, it stood in front of the marked wall. A deep pit had been cut into the ground all around the island, with only a narrow walkway connecting the main floor area to the raised island, which was close enough to the front wall that a person could reach out and touch said wall. The island had a vertical stone lever on it. The bottom of the pit was shrouded in darkness. Harry turned to look at the second set of stairs descending into the darkness beside him. He aimed his light down the stairs. There was another flat landing below; these stairs were a mirror image of the ones he'd just come down. He could see decorative imagery on the floor. It was a grid, and every other square on the grid had a mark.

"The symbol of Dionysus." Harry took a halting step back. "The same as the last tunnel." He aimed his light around the lower tunnel, sweeping from one side to the other. Another grid, just like—

Gunfire flashed from below. Harry ducked as a bullet zipped well overhead, sending rock shards raining down. A voice shouted from the bottom of the lower stairs. Harry jumped up and ran back the way he'd come, racing halfway up the staircase before stopping cold.

A man stood waiting, with a pistol leveled at Harry's chest.

Chapter 23

"Don't move."

The man held his gun steady as the sound of feet running on stone came from behind Harry. He turned. His gaze narrowed. "You two again."

Oleg and Yuri. The men who had chased him into Perperikon, last seen locked underground. "You were lucky at the ruins." Yuri spoke in English. "No more."

The man on the steps aimed a flashlight beam down at Harry. "I should shoot you now. For Maksim."

Harry squinted through the light. He knew that voice. "You're the food delivery guy from camp."

"Shut your mouth."

"I didn't kill your buddy," Harry said. "He fell into a trap."

The guy above him started to wave his gun until Oleg shouted. "Stop," he said. "Do not be a fool, Anton. We need him."

Anton put his gun down. He left his scowl on full display.

"Do not move," Oleg said. "I am coming to you. Yuri, shoot him in the leg if he moves."

Harry followed orders as Oleg approached and checked him for weapons. These three men had followed him across Europe. All had Russian accents or names. All were connected to a man named Big Bird. It made sense, but Kiryl Korzun was dead and these guys didn't seem to know.

Oleg took Harry's pack and was about to turn his pants pockets inside out when Harry blurted out, "Where is Korzun?"

Oleg stopped searching. He didn't look surprised, only puzzled as he leaned back to look up at Harry's face. "Who is Korzun?" He hadn't found the knuckledusters.

"Big Bird," Harry said.

"That is not—you know nothing."

"Big Bird is dead."

A moment later all three men laughed in a way that made Harry's heart race. "He is not dead. I talked to him a minute ago." A look Harry didn't like crossed Oleg's face. "He is pleased with your progress."

Either these guys were all good actors, or they truly believed Kiryl Korzun was alive when he'd been dead for over a week. Harry had no idea what that meant, but knowing Korzun was dead gave him a card to play. How to use it was hard to say.

"Check his neck," Anton said. "He has treasure."

Harry jerked back as Oleg reached for the visible chain around his neck. "That belonged to my father," Harry said.

Oleg paused. Harry held his gaze, which is why he never saw Oleg's fist smash into his stomach. Harry was too busy being doubled over gasping for breath to stop Oleg from taking the amulet from around his neck. Oleg tossed it to Yuri. "Hold it," Oleg said.

Yuri grunted as he held Fred Fox's amulet up to his flashlight beam. Harry bit his tongue. He'd get it back. No matter what.

Oleg shoved Harry back toward the stairs. "Move."

Harry used some nifty footwork to stay upright as he stumbled down and stopped beside Anton, who was still admiring his temporary new amulet. Harry looked down the staircase from which Oleg and Yuri had emerged. The floor was marked with a grid of alternating squares that were either blank or had the symbol of Dionysus etched on them. He turned to the pair of Russians. "How did you know where to walk?"

"Anton knew," Oleg said as he walked down the stairs and stood beside Harry. "He watched you cross the other floor."

Harry looked at the man holding his amulet. "You were behind me?"

Anton shrugged. "I can climb fast."

The car he'd seen before walking into Cotys's hidden door must have been these three. "You saw me on the staircase too." Another shrug. "How did you get in?"

That wicked smile on Oleg's face again. "You let us in. Whatever you did at the high door opened a door at the ground."

The lever. That's what the noise had been, that rumbling below his feet. Harry pulling the lever had activated a hidden door at ground level. King Cotys would have wanted access there as well.

"What's your plan?" Harry asked. "I have no idea what's here."

"You have survived this long," Oleg said. "You will know." He inclined his head to the darkness. "Go."

Harry forged ahead without waiting for a response. Missing the amulet's familiar weight made him clutch his fists in anger, a feeling he immediately pushed away. Now was no time to lose focus. Unravel Cotys's trail first. Then focus on revenge.

Harry stepped further into the sanctuary and finally had a clear look at the wall ahead. The two empty rectangles cut into the wall in front of the island, standing vertically, with nothing inside the lines. The flat, unmarked floor in front of him, stretching from the empty rear wall to the front. The room was big, but it didn't feel right. Harry couldn't say exactly why, couldn't explain it, but his gut said the room was, well, *incomplete*.

"What is this place?" Oleg asked from several steps back.

"I think it's a sanctuary," Harry said. "A place for Cotys to honor his son." He pointed to the lettering running above the empty rectangles, letters he was now close enough to read. "That's Latin. It says *Thrace*." He took a step closer and froze.

Oleg came to his side. "What is it?"

"The rising sun." Harry pointed at the wall. "It has finally risen."

Harry moved closer to the wall, close enough to see the image carved beneath the Latin letters. An evolution of the image that had guided him on this entire journey. "I've seen this in every location so far," Harry said. "A rising sun representing Spartacus."

Oleg said he recalled the image. "Cotys's son."

Harry nodded. "The son has finally risen."

What had always been a half-circle with rays beaming out as it rose above the flat horizon was now a circle above the flat horizon line, rays extending all around it, a full sun in the sky. "This is the end," Harry said. "Cotys's son. He's risen."

Oleg aimed his light around the room. "Where is he?"

Harry's instincts kicked in. "They didn't build that island just for show. You guys better stay back. I'm going up there." He walked up to the edge of the pit and aimed his light down. He sighed. "How original."

Stone spikes lay at the pit's bottom some ten feet down. Five-foot spikes that promised a grisly end for anyone who fell in. "Want to join me?" Harry asked.

"I do not," Anton said.

"Give me my pack." Harry grabbed it before Oleg could argue. "I have no idea what's up there. Don't get jumpy and shoot me." He shook his head at the gun in Anton's hand. "That won't do you much good down here anyway. Cotys doesn't need weapons to kill us."

He turned and headed for the narrow walkway. It was only a few feet wide; one good stumble and he'd be over the edge and have several new holes in his body for the trouble. No skeletons were visible below, which was a good sign. So why did his stomach tighten more with each step? Cotys hadn't meant for this place to kill Thracians. He'd meant it to protect them and the memory of his son. The ideal of a Thracian. To Cotys, this was akin to a holy place.

The narrow path brought him to the oblong island, perhaps three steps deep, but easily fifteen feet wide. It was surrounded by the pit on all sides, with that odd stone lever standing in the middle. Circular lines were engraved beneath his feet. Harry aimed his light at the Latin word in front of him, close enough to touch. "Thrace," he read. "Why put it there?"

Oleg was clearly the leader of the trio. "Is it a code?" he asked.

"Could be," Harry said. "But if it's a message, I don't know what it tells us."

The risen sun image likely meant Spartacus was nearby. Harry's light moved down from the carving to the closest rectangle in front of him. He stood very still for a long while. Long enough that Oleg asked what was going on. "Quiet," Harry said. "I'm thinking."

He tilted his head. "*That's* what's wrong." He snapped his fingers. "It's a *frame*." He turned around. "Look. I think these are openings."

He reached one hand out and touched inside the closest edge of the rectangle. He pushed. Nothing happened. He pushed hard. That was all it took. Dust flew, rock groaned, and the wall moved.

Not just moved. Revolved. The rectangle twisted on an unseen hinge.

"It's a carving of Cotys." Harry pointed to the royal figure clad in robes and holding a scroll. "You can tell by his crown."

"Who is the other man?" Oleg asked.

It took Harry a second. "He's holding the Constitution."

"The what?"

"The scroll in his hand. It represents the Constitution of Thrace. The document that detailed the rights of Thracian citizens. In Thracian assemblies, it was held by the person whose turn it was to speak." Harry took his hand from the wall. "This isn't a picture. It's an *idea*. The idea of Thracian democratic governance. Cotys is showing us their democracy."

Harry pushed on the image and it continued to rotate. Another picture emerged on the third panel of this rotating canvas. "This isn't Thracian," Harry said. "It's Roman."

The scene showed a man seated on a raised platform, his chin resting on one hand, leaning down to listen to others standing below him. His sharp nose and wide eyes looked on with dispassion, while a strand of leaves encircled his head. Oak leaves. The purple garment he wore was more than enough to tell the story.

Harry pointed to the seated man, the central figure in this busy scene. "That is Julius Caesar."

"How can you tell?" Oleg asked. "It could be any Roman."

"He's wearing a purple toga."

Oleg's shrewdness resurfaced. "A symbol of wealth."

"Fair point. The truth of it is here and here." Harry tapped first the man's head, then the seat under his backside. "That's a *curule* seat, a symbol of power in ancient Rome. Used by kings across Europe. But the robe and the seat are secondary to what's on his head."

"Leaves."

"*Oak* leaves," Harry said. "It's called the Civic Crown, and it was one of the highest military decorations Rome awarded. Julius Caesar had one. And if all this isn't enough evidence, you're telling me that doesn't look like Julius Caesar?" Surely at some point in his life Oleg had seen an image of Caesar.

"It does," Oleg admitted. "What does Caesar have to do with Thrace?"

"I think Caesar represents Rome," Harry said. The idea made sense. "A picture, but more than that. A contrast with Cotys. The idea of Thracian democratic governance. The antithesis of Rome and Roman dictators."

Two opposing ideas from two nations that were first allies, then enemies. His gaze moved to the other rectangle. He reached out and pushed it. The three-sided panel turned, and an image appeared. "It's a map," Harry said. "Of Thrace."

As he studied it, he saw more than Thrace. The coastlines of modern-day Greece, Bulgaria and Turkey around the Aegean Sea were also depicted. The huge landmass was marked into dozens of different areas like states, but these weren't states. They were Thracian tribes. Harry explained to the others. "Thracians came from many different tribes, united under one leader. It was a melting pot of cultures united for mutual protection. Warriors, farmers, sailors. Stronger together. That's the kingdom Cotys ruled over when this was carved." A pause. "I don't know what it all means." He did have an idea, but he wasn't showing his cards yet. "This rectangle has three sides, same as the first panel. One blank, one with this map on it." He reached out and pushed. "And a third with this."

The final side flipped into view. Unlike the first three carvings, this panel had two distinct images, one on top, another below it. A horizontal line ran through the middle to separate them. Harry pointed to the image on the top half. "That's a Roman legion." The carving showed several rows of soldiers facing Harry. "Roman legions carried rectangular shields, like these. They marched in formations identical to this." He tapped the shields and outlined the geometrical precision with which the men stood. "They're carrying spears in their other hands, and each man has a gladius on his belt." Harry tapped a soldier's short sword, then pointed to the man's head. "The plumed helmets are correct for the period."

Oleg spoke up. "The bottom is a map of Rome."

Harry agreed. "Around the turn of the millennium." The map on the lower half showed the coastlines of Europe, Northern Africa and Eastern Asia along with the Black Sea, the Mediterranean and the western Atlantic. "This is Rome at the height of its power." His finger moved from the map back up to the legion. "A power claimed by force."

Harry snapped his fingers. "Rome conquered territory. It took what it wanted by force. Exactly the opposite of Thrace. Thrace negotiated. It didn't conquer, and that's how it survived." Although history told how that had worked out in the end.

"Tell us what the pictures mean."

Harry didn't respond. His gaze lingered on the vertical stone lever beside him as he rubbed the stubble on his chin. Two panels. Depictions of Thrace and Rome and their dramatic differences.

"These panels are Cotys speaking to his people about what his son represents: the *idea* of Thrace and his hope for the future. The path ahead if Thrace is going to stay Thracian and not be consumed by Rome."

Oleg, as always, led the pack. "Rome defeated Thrace."

"It did, but Cotys didn't give up. He held on throughout his lifetime. He lost his son. He couldn't accept losing his country as well. This is all meant to inspire his people and remind them of what Thrace stood for.

Why Thrace was worth fighting for. I think I know what's behind these images."

Oleg wasn't buying it. "It is a wall. It does not hide anything."

"Let's bet. I show you it isn't just a wall, and you let me go. You keep whatever you find behind it." He meant it. Harry had recovered enough treasure for one hunt. He didn't need more. "And tell your boss I'm done helping him."

Oleg's face hardened. "Show me what is behind the wall."

"Or what? You're gonna shoot me?"

"No. I will shoot the dog. The one your friend likes so much."

Shoot the dog? Harry couldn't have that. Besides, he suspected Cotys had a few more tricks up his sleeve. "Stand back," Harry said. "And don't move until I say."

Oleg had sense enough to follow orders, barking at the other two in Russian until they gave Harry space. Harry pointed at each Thracian image in turn and spoke softly. "Thrace or Rome."

He put both hands on the stone lever, took a breath, then leaned on it. Not hard at first, for if it snapped, he was out of luck. He needn't have worried. The pole slid forward, caught for a moment, then plunged ahead.

He looked down, found it had more space to go forward. Now he shoved, and rock grated over rock as the pole slid forward and locked into place hard enough to rattle his teeth.

His vision blurred. The air vibrated. Harry clutched the stone pole to keep from falling over as jets of dust shot from the ground and a cloud encircled him. He coughed. The ground rattled, and Harry held tight. Several beats later the room stopped shaking. He waved a hand at the cloud around him to clear it away, keeping his other hand locked on the pole. His flashlight beam reflected millions of tiny dust specks and created a blinding curtain of light that slowly dissipated to reveal what he'd done.

A section of the wall had retracted into the ceiling to reveal a small room.

"It isn't a tomb," Harry said once the dust cleared. His flashlight beam played over the newly exposed room. "It's a memorial."

The room in front of them contained five items.

Oleg shouted from behind. "What is there?"

Harry turned to find the dust cloud behind him hadn't dissipated. The three men were all waving their flashlight beams around, creating a shining curtain that blocked their view. Harry told them to be still for a second and wait. The dust settled and the men craned their necks to see what was in the room.

Five objects were on display. A waist-high pillar in the center, with Latin writing on the top. A pair of wooden chests bound with iron on either side of the pillar, and beside those, two symbols for the hope and future of Thrace. A man made of stone stood beside one chest, holding a weapon in one hand.

Harry knew. How, he couldn't say. But he knew. "That's Spartacus's spear," Harry said. He turned to face the second stone man on the far side of the hidden room. "And that's his shield. Both of these belonged to Spartacus."

Oleg asked how he knew. "Cotys placed them here as symbols," Harry said. "Of the ideals King Cotys wanted Thrace to remember. Those are the weapons of a man whom others idolized for what he accomplished with his spear and his shield."

"He defied Rome."

Harry looked back at Oleg. "*If* we're talking about Spartacus the gladiator. Nothing in the history books suggests Spartacus was a prince."

"Do your books say he was not?"

Oleg was too sharp by half. "Keep back," Harry said. "I'm going across."

The only way to access the new area was over the ramp. He made it one step forward before Anton interjected. "No," the man shouted. "Those are treasure chests. I will go first."

"Can you disable the traps?" Harry asked.

"Traps?"

The ones I just made up. "Didn't think you were ready," Harry said. "I'll go first." He took another step, then hesitated. "I don't mind letting you go ahead. Better your neck than mine."

Anton offered his ugliest glare. "Thought so," Harry said. "Now stay back. Don't come across until I tell you."

Yuri had been quiet so far. "Why is there so much dust?" he asked as Harry stepped into the opened room.

A good question. Dust shooting up from cracks in the floor suggested a mechanism below their feet. Perhaps it moved the wall, but why had the mortar between the floor stones cracked so much? He pushed the question aside as he walked toward the central pillar. Four-sided, made of stone, it rose to his waist and ended in a flat surface, with Latin lettering covering the top.

"More writing on here," Harry said.

"Open the chests." Anton again.

Harry didn't respond. He was reading King Cotys' final message.

Here we honor the fallen idol of Thrace. Prince Spartacus fell in his battle against Rome, but his spear and shield were recovered. Each chest holds a piece of his final glory. So vital is his message that worthy Thracians must view it in turn. Reflect on what the prince lost so we may live. Glory to Spartacus forever.

"It *was* him," Harry said. "Prince Spartacus. The slave who led a revolt against Rome. He wasn't only a gladiator. He was a future king."

Oleg shouted through Harry's thoughts. "What does it say?"

Anton followed with a growl. "I am coming over."

"Hold on," Harry said. "Listen to this."

He read the inscription aloud in English. The three men across from him stayed put.

"He is a prince?" Oleg asked.

"The son of King Cotys," Harry said. "But he somehow ended up a gladiator and led a revolution."

Harry turned toward the stone man holding a spear. He moved to it, passing the wood and iron chest without pausing.

"Open the chest," Anton yelled.

"It's not going anywhere," Harry said. "I need to check the weapons." He had no idea what the *final glory* might be, but Anton probably wasn't far off the mark about it being treasure. Not all treasure glittered, and there were more valuable objects than gold.

Harry stopped in front of the spear. He reached out but didn't touch it. Wooden shaft, metal head, leather bindings wrapped around the shaft for grip and support. The wicked head had writing across it. Harry aimed his light up and leaned closer. *SPARTACUS*.

"His name is here," Harry called out.

More Russian grumbling, a bit softer, all of which Harry ignored. They could protest all they wanted if they did it from back there. Harry didn't see any traps, but that didn't mean he needed to tell those three goons. He turned and moved to the stone man holding a shield. The grumbling picked up as he passed the other chest.

"Open it," Anton yelled.

"Yes," Yuri said. "Do it."

Harry still ignored them. His gaze fell to the inscription on the stone pillar as he passed. One line stuck out. *Worthy Thracians must view it in turn.* Worthy Thracians. Those loyal to Cotys and a future Thrace built on the ideals of Spartacus. But why *in turn*? Sharing it with only one person at a time didn't make sense.

"Open the chest."

"Patience," Harry said. He looked at the second chest. "These chests haven't moved in two thousand years. They can wait. The shield is more important."

Heated Russian chatter sounded from across the pit. Anton didn't sound happy. Neither did Yuri. Harry couldn't care less. He cast his light around the hidden room's back wall. It appeared to be very solid. No exits, no escape routes. He'd trade these relics for a way out of here without thinking twice. There would be more relics to find. If he got out of here alive.

Harry's voice rose above the rabble behind him. "The shield and spear belonged to Spartacus. Are they valuable? Yes. Incredibly valuable. That doesn't matter."

"It *does* matter. This is about money," Oleg said stubbornly.

"No." Harry stopped walking. He turned to face them. "It's about the truth." He pointed at the pillar. "That proves Spartacus was a prince. Do you understand what that means? A man who was born to be king became a gladiator and came closer to toppling the Roman empire than anyone had or would for centuries."

"But he lost."

Harry looked at Oleg. "Yes. He lost. But that's not the point. Billions of people are going to learn what we discovered, and it's going to change everything they thought they knew about Spartacus." Harry turned back to the pillar. The cave didn't seem so dark right now. "And we found it."

These guys were mercenaries, nothing more. What if they knew Korzun was dead? What if they killed him? If that was the case, chances were Harry Fox would never leave this tomb.

He now stood before the stone man holding a shield, a shield without decorations of any sort. This was uniquely Thracian, a round piece of metal with a crescent-shaped piece cut out of one edge, the shield of a Thracian infantryman, another clear sign of Spartacus's heritage. It didn't have a name on it, didn't have anything indicating the man holding it had royal blood. The only marks were from sword cuts blocked and spear thrusts parried. A particularly vicious gash across one edge suggested not all the attacks had been dodged.

The voices behind him grew more insistent. "I'm almost done," Harry said without looking back.

His gaze turned to the central pillar. *Must view it in turn.* Harry closed his eyes. What did it mean? He replayed everything he'd seen since he'd walked into this chamber. The spiked pit. The central island. Picture frames showing Thracian ideals. The wall lifting and a storm cloud of dust encircling them. Dust billowing from the floor.

The floor.

The Thracian Idol

He opened his eyes as Anton's shouting rang out. "I am coming," the man yelled. "We must look inside."

"No!" Harry turned, his arms out and palms up. "Don't move," he yelled.

Too late. Anton was halfway across the narrow walkway when he tripped, flying forward, arms flailing as he crashed to the ground. Anton got to one knee and looked back at the section of floor that had dropped. Dust spouted into the air. The walkway vibrated and the chamber rumbled.

Harry shouted over the noise. "The walkway is rigged so only one person can cross at a time. That's what the message says." Cotys's message had warned them. Only one person at a time could visit the hidden room. He had tried to tell them.

"Get back," Harry shouted. His words were lost as the ground shook violently, and he grabbed the stone man for support. The vibrating chamber threatened to push Harry over the edge of the floor and onto the spikes before he wrapped both arms around the statue and looked across the pit.

Anton was on one knee, trying desperately to rise and continue crossing the walkway. He rose, then fell, then staggered up again. Oleg and Yuri shouted, their mouths moving silently as Anton scrambled in slow motion to turn and get back across the walkway to his companions. All too late, he realized what he'd done.

A loud *snap* ripped the air and the rumbling faded. Harry looked up in alarm.

Anton never had a chance. Even as he tried to hurry back across the shaking walkway, a massive stone block swung down from the ceiling, knocking him over the edge and into the spiked pit.

That's when the walls started moving.

Harry's mouth fell open and he did a double-take as the front and back walls began closing in. Closing fast, too fast for any of them to make a break for either staircase. Harry noted carved-out areas in the front wall as it moved, slots into which the chests and statues could fit so they weren't pushed into the spiked pit. That's when he realized the two men across from him were rooted to the ground, their eyes wide, legs frozen.

"Hang over the edge," Harry shouted as the walls continued moving. Frozen with terror, Oleg and Yuri didn't budge. He shouted again, and this time they jumped into action, grabbing the edge of the floor, swinging their bodies over, and hanging by their fingertips as the walls rumbled toward the pit.

Yuri yelled as one of his hands slid loose. Oleg reached over and caught Yuri's hand, helping him regain a grip on the ledge.

The spear. Harry ran to the other stone statue before it vanished into the moving wall, grabbed the spear and ran to retrieve the shield before going back toward the dangling men. "Watch out," he shouted.

The whites of Oleg's eyes were visible now as Harry took aim with the spear, pulled his arm back and let it fly. The spear *thunked* into the wall beside Yuri, vibrated, and held tight.

"Stand on it," Harry yelled back.

Yuri got a foot on the spear and reached up to try and pull himself out as Oleg hung tight.

The wall was right behind Harry now, pushing him inch by inch toward the pit. *Only one chance.*

Harry leapt into the pit, pulled his feet up and stood on the shield as he fell toward certain death, the spikes rushing up to meet him.

He crashed to a halt.

Harry now stood on top of the upturned shield, balanced between four spikes. His heart thudded hard enough to upend him. He didn't move an inch as the rumbling intensified, then softened.

"Grab it!"

Oleg's voice startled him. Harry moved only his eyes as he looked up to find his captor kneeling at the edge of the pit above him, holding Spartacus's spear out, point first. "Grab the spear," Oleg said. "I will pull you out."

That's when he realized the walls had retracted, just far enough that the other two men could pull themselves up to safety. Now Harry was ten feet below the lip. Oleg was on his stomach, holding the spear out as far as it would go. The bottom of the pit was another ten feet down, with smaller spikes in between the larger ones that the shield was balanced on. He couldn't drop down. He couldn't jump off. He couldn't do anything.

"I'll die if you drop me," Harry said.

"You will die if you stay. Grab the spear."

Harry had no other options: lose his balance before falling onto the lower spikes, or grab the spear and hope this man who had pursued him across a continent didn't decide to let him die.

Harry fired off a colorful phrase that would have made Nora Doyle proud and grabbed the spear.

"Hold on," Oleg said.

Harry didn't have a chance to think before Oleg pulled him up and off the shield. Harry's foot caught in the shield's strap as he fell toward the pit wall—too fast. He collided hard with it, arm muscles screaming as one hand lost its grip on the spear. His body swung around and he crashed against the wall again, the shield still latched to his foot by the strap. He gave a shout of dismay as his other hand opened and the spear slipped from his grasp.

He fell.

"Got you!"

The pit wall was racing past inches from his face when a strong hand closed around his wrist. Harry grabbed back, looking up to find Yuri straining to catch Harry's hand before he fell out of reach.

"Pull up," Yuri said. "I cannot hold you."

Harry hauled himself up, took Yuri's other hand with his own, then helped drag his savior up over the lip of the pit. They lay side by side, sprawled on the ground, gasping for air. After a time, Harry raised his head and looked down. The shield's strap was still looped around his foot. He laughed.

A crash rang throughout the chamber. Harry stopped laughing. "What's that?" he asked, scrambling to his feet.

Oleg's head twisted every which way. "I do not know."

"The chests are still there," said Yuri, who was standing by one of them. "They were not pushed in." He opened its lid and looked inside. "This is it?" Yuri scowled. "It is a book."

"Don't drop it," Harry said. Another crash sounded, and a low rumble shook the ground, getting louder by the second. "This isn't right."

Oleg was at the other chest, and now he raised its lid and peered in. "It is the same. Only a book. No gold."

"Hold on to them. They're valuable." The floor rattled under his feet as a massive piece of the ceiling crashed down to block the upper tunnel. Harry grabbed Spartacus's spear. "We have to go," he said. "Right now."

He grabbed Yuri's arm and shoved him toward the lower exit tunnel. Oleg had the good sense to follow the two as they ran. "Look behind you," Harry shouted over a shoulder at him.

The walls behind them were collapsing, crashing down on each other like dominos and heading their way. Harry sprinted past Yuri toward the lower tunnel. "It's coming for us," he said. "We have to outrun the collapse. Use the marked stones," Harry reminded the two as he crossed the grid pattern. He looked back to find Yuri and Oleg following his path to safety.

Harry raced down the staircase and found a landing, the same as on the other side, leading to another staircase going down. Harry opened his mouth to warn the other two about each fourth step. He got two words out before Yuri bolted past him and kept accelerating. As he sprinted, something fell out of his pocket, shining under Harry's light.

My amulet. Harry skidded to a stop and turned back.

Oleg smashed into him at full speed. The tunnel spun, the ground smacked him in the face and Spartacus's relics went flying. Harry reached for them, and was promptly bowled over as Oleg shoved him aside and headed for safety, yelling at Harry to keep moving as he raced down the hallway.

"Not yet." Harry clambered to his feet, slung the shield over his back and ran back toward the collapsing walls. The sound of the destruction rattled his brain and shook the world as Harry hurtled toward the fallen amulet.

The amulet lay against the wall. Harry grabbed it, slid the chain over his neck and turned for the exit as the walls crashed down five feet behind him. Legs churning, lungs burning, Harry went full speed down the hallway toward the staircase. Every fourth stair offered death, he knew, but the math was too much with his life in the balance, so Harry hit the top step and launched himself over the edge, arms swinging and legs bicycling as he flew down, down in the dark, chasing his flashlight beam until he crashed in a heap on the landing below.

Harry grabbed his light from the floor and aimed it up. The avalanche of collapsing walls poured over the top step.

He shot up, feet churning on the slick stone floor, a square of bright light calling from up ahead. Oleg's head poked in and the man shouted in Russian, words Harry couldn't comprehend as the ground beneath him shook and the walls rattled. Oleg waved Harry on as the walls smashed together with a series of pulsating booms that shook the ground and sent him stumbling.

Harry righted himself, turned and found the destruction almost on top of him. A voice broke through the noise.

"Jump!"

Harry turned toward the voice. Oleg shouted again. Harry leapt, time slowing as he flew, the last of the walls crashing into him, sending him soaring into a blinding light before the world exploded and everything turned to night.

Epilogue

Somewhere in Bulgaria

"Wake up."

A harsh voice cut through the cloudy softness filling Harry's world. He blinked and tried to open his eyes. He had a brief glimpse of something hazy for an instant before he closed his eyes again and returned to the safe darkness where no one was trying to kill him. A ghost of a smile flitted across his face as he fell back into sweet nothingness.

"Get up."

The same voice, this time accompanied by a slap to his face.

Harry started, mumbling a curse. It took several tries to open his eyes again. They didn't want to cooperate.

"Sit up." A rough hand grabbed his shoulder and pulled.

Harry blinked away the fog to find himself lying flat in the back seat of a sport utility vehicle. A moving vehicle. He tried to sit up. "Oh, that hurts." Harry reached up and touched his face, finding it tender. A voice in the back of his head pointed out his hands weren't bound. That was one good sign. "What happened? Where are we?"

"In a car." The same rough voice, which Harry discovered was Oleg, sitting in the passenger seat as Yuri drove. "You are lucky."

Harry touched his face again. One side ached like he'd been in a prizefight. The other only hurt. "How's that? I'm in a car with you?"

"You are alive." Oleg offered what passed for a smile in his world. "You are hard to kill."

"Why, are you trying to kill me?"

"I would have left you in the pit if I wanted to kill you." Oleg pointed at Harry's face. "And I will not kill you now."

"Why not?"

"You saved Yuri's life. You saved my life."

"Right." It had been spur-of-the-moment. "Don't make me regret it."

Oleg chuckled. "It is not me who will decide if you do."

Harry's internal alarm clanged. "What's that mean?"

"You will see. We are almost there."

It all came back at once. The boulder. The spear and shield. His father's amulet. Harry reached to his neck and found the amulet in place. He looked up to find Oleg's eyes on his in the rearview mirror. "Almost where?"

Oleg ignored his question. "We will not take the amulet," Oleg said. "It is yours."

"What about the relics?"

"They are not yours."

Harry opened his mouth to protest. *Pick your battles.* "What about the books in each chest? Did you look at them?"

"They are in Latin," Oleg said.

"Are they here?" Harry asked. Oleg nodded. "Let me see them."

"No."

"Why not?"

The car stopped "We are here." Oleg opened his door. "Do not get out or they will shoot you."

They? Harry kept his mouth closed. The sun had fallen close to the horizon but was not yet out of sight. It was late afternoon and darkness would soon fall. Harry Fox was with at least two killers in the middle of nowhere. He was alive, but overall, his situation had not improved.

Yuri remained quiet behind the wheel. "Who's *they*?" Harry asked.

Yuri looked in the rearview mirror. "Them." He pointed at the sky.

Harry craned his neck to look up through the small rear window. That's when he heard the *thump-thump-thump* of rotating blades. Two sets of them. Twisting around, he spotted two dark blots on the sky, coming in fast. Not a minute later, both helicopters were circling the car, one setting down on each side as downdraft buffeted the parked vehicle. Oleg stepped out of the car and stood beside the door, shielding his eyes. These were *big* helicopters, massive birds with no markings on their exteriors. Not even tail numbers. He was pretty sure you had to have those.

The engines on both choppers kept running as a door on one of them opened and three men hopped out. Two of the men carried submachine guns. They stood on either side of a third man who approached Oleg. The third man did the talking, Oleg nodding a few times.

Oleg pointed at the rear window where Harry sat. The unknown man glared at the car, though with the sun at an angle he likely couldn't see in. Even so, Harry almost flinched. The hooded eyes and deep creases across his forehead spoke of a hard life. The fact that this guy looked capable of ripping Harry's arms off made Harry keep still. Then he noticed the knife the man had on his belt. A knife Daniel Boone would have envied.

Both men abruptly turned and walked toward the car. Oleg opened Harry's door and pulled him out. Rapid Russian ensued. The man with the knife studied Harry.

"Wait here," Oleg said.

Harry decided this was a time to listen. Oleg and knife guy walked around back, opened the trunk and inspected Spartacus's relics. Knife guy barked an order, which sent one of the armed men running back to the helicopter, where he retrieved two metal cases. One large and square, the other long and slender. A case for the shield and a case for the spear. Both books went into the large case with the shield before the armed man carried them to the second helicopter and placed them inside.

Knife guy handed Oleg a thick envelope. Oleg did not look inside it. Instead, he came to Harry's door and opened it.

"We are even," Oleg said, his words nearly lost in the whirring noise of the helicopter blades. "You are to be set free."

"Thanks." Harry looked around. "How am I supposed to get home?"

Oleg handed him a cell phone. "Wait until everyone is gone. You will forget everything you see here today."

"Will you give me a ride?"

Oleg shook his head. "I am told to leave." He inclined his head toward the as-yet-unopened chopper. "He wants to see you."

"Who is *he*?"

Oleg smiled humorlessly. "Big Bird."

With that, Oleg turned and got back into the car. He did not look back at Harry as Yuri started the engine and they pulled away, driving into the grassy expanse until they were lost from sight.

"Come with me."

Harsh words once more, this time in English, with a familiar Russian accent. Knife guy did not smile when Harry turned to face him. "What do you want with me?" Harry asked.

Knife guy pointed to the second chopper. "You will go in there."

As if he had a choice. Harry started toward the chopper. He made it one step before knife guy grabbed his shoulder. "Stop."

Harry stopped. Knife guy reached into his coat pocket and pulled out a large black velvet bag. "Do not move," he said.

It took every bit of willpower to stay still as knife guy slipped the bag over Harry's head and then checked him for weapons. He confiscated Harry's ceramic knuckledusters. Harry couldn't see a thing as knife guy clapped a hand on Harry's shoulder and led him toward the chopper. A push on the top of his head told Harry to duck low as the rotors buzzed overhead. A heavy door slid open. Harry was told to step up, and knife guy pushed him into a seat. The door slammed shut behind him. The bag over his head rustled as he turned his head from side to side, ears searching for any noise, hands on his lap. Nothing.

"*Ya unichtozhu yego!*" roared a voice directly across from him.

Harry jumped in his seat.

"I will destroy him! Do you hear me? He is done. With the fish."

The Russian accent to those English words bowled him over. Or was this a different accent, from Eastern Europe? Bulgarian, perhaps. The home of gangster Kiryl Korzun. A man who now slept with the fishes.

This thought froze Harry's bones as more animated Russian filled the cabin. The bag made his heartbeat sound like drums banging in his ears.

The tirade ended with one final shout. Harry sensed movement in front of him, and then he caught the rustle of fabric and an electronic noise, as though someone were tapping a phone screen very quickly. He angled an ear toward the noise and waited.

"You speak English."

The statement seemed directed at Harry. "Yes," he said.

"Why are you in Bulgaria?"

Now seemed like a good time to tell the truth. "To find the end of a Thracian trail."

"Explain."

How to summarize his search? "King Cotys the Fourth of Thrace left the spoils of victories over Rome and a trail of relics for his people to follow. He meant for Thracians to never forget what their country stood for, and to never forget one man who exemplified their ideals. His son, Spartacus."

"Spartacus?"

"The enslaved gladiator. Who was also a prince."

"Speak up. I cannot understand you through the bag."

Harry almost suggested taking it off his head. Instead, he repeated himself.

"Good. A prince's relics are more valuable." The sound of rustling fabric moved closer to Harry. He could sense more than feel someone directly across from him. As though they were leaning in close. "How did you learn of this treasure?"

"From a friend."

The man grumbled. "I will ask you once more. How did you learn about the treasure?"

"An earthquake opened Cotys's tomb and someone I work with learned about a message in there. They asked me to investigate. I started at the tomb and followed the trail."

"Are you a policeman?"

Harry shook his head. "Not even close."

"Then you are a thief."

"Not really." Harry considered it. "Depends on who you ask."

That elicited a rumbling laugh, so Harry risked a question. "You're not Kiryl Korzun, are you?"

The response came in leaden tones. "I do not know that name."

"That's who those guys said they worked for." Silence. Harry took the bait and filled it. "Big Bird is what they call Korzun."

"What do you know about him?"

"I know Korzun was murdered two weeks ago. Shot and dumped in a lake."

"You know a lot. Knowing too much can be deadly."

"I only know what I was told. And I'm very good at keeping my mouth shut." *Should have kept my mouth shut.*

The Russian voice mirrored his thoughts. "Then you should keep it shut more often. If you say what you know to the wrong man, he might shoot you. I am not the wrong man. I am no tsar."

He practically spat the last word out. It stuck in Harry's ear. More than a word. An insult, a curse as filled with hate as anything Harry had ever heard. Not only that. Harry heard a promise in that single word. A promise for revenge. The word sent an image hurtling into Harry's head, along with a sense of absolute certainty. The face of a man Harry had once met. A man for whom the word *tsar* held great meaning. A man who could change the world.

"No," Harry said. "You're not a tsar." He plunged ahead. "May I take this bag off my head?"

A slight pause, and when the response came, the man giving it was no more than six inches from Harry's face. "No."

And Harry knew. "Is this any way to treat an old friend?" Harry asked. "I know you. And you know me. You don't want to hurt me. Who else is going to find your relics? I hope you're taking care of Achilles's helmet." Harry stuck his hand out. "It's good to see you again, Evgeny."

"Who..." The words trailed off for a moment. "Who—who are you?"

Harry reached slowly for the bag over his head. He never got a chance to touch it. One instant he was reaching up, shrouded in darkness, and the next an oversized hand grabbed the black bag and tore it loose. Harry scrunched up his eyes in the sudden light. "Darn, that's bright. Give me a warning next time."

"*Harry Fox?*"

"In the flesh," Harry said as he blinked rapidly. "You didn't know it was me?"

The man across from him sputtered. A rare sight, indeed. The world's press would have paid handsomely to see Evgeny Smolov at a loss for words. It wasn't often you saw a surprised oligarch. Exiled oligarch, that is. One with a price placed on his head by the current Russian president. Or tsar, as Evgeny called him.

Evgeny had collected himself by now. "You," he said.

"Me," Harry replied. "You're looking well."

The last time Harry and Evgeny were face to face had been on a Greek mountainside. Harry had recovered armor and weapons belonging to the man who inspired the legend of Achilles, relics that Evgeny Smolov wanted to possess. To that end, Evgeny had recruited a team of mercenaries to retrieve the relics, pitting Harry in a race against his hired guns to recover the prize.

Evgeny patted his formerly generous stomach. "I am exercising now." A scowl darkened his expensively tanned face. "I hate it."

"I like the longer hair. Looks good on you."

Evgeny had once worn his silvering hair like a disease. Now he sported a longer style, casually cut as only overpriced stylists could manage. "My girlfriend likes it." The scowl remained. "I am starting to think she is more trouble than she is worth."

Harry lifted a hand to cover his mouth. Evgeny Smolov was many things. Obscenely rich. Argumentative. Terrifying. He was also not a man to be laughed at. "She has good taste," Harry said after he controlled himself. "And she's a lucky lady."

Evgeny waved his hand. A hand far too large for the man who stood not much taller than Harry. "Enough," Evgeny said. He stuck one finger in Harry's face. "Now tell me the whole truth. How did you get here?"

"I told you the truth. The mayor of New York leaned on the district attorney to look into the find at Cotys's tomb. I have connections to the D.A., which is how I got roped in."

"I hate politicians more than I hate exercise." Evgeny touched the silk handkerchief tucked into his suit jacket pocket as he grumbled. "I only trust the ones I can buy."

"You still sure you aren't going to shoot me?"

Evgeny looked offended. "Why would I shoot you?"

"I'm in the way of you getting an artifact." Harry lifted a shoulder. "And I remember how everything went last time."

"Last time?" Lines creased Evgeny's forehead before understanding dawned. "Oh. The men who tried to kill you."

"Men you hired."

Another wave of the big hand. "They were not my men. They wanted to shoot your friend. Real men do not hurt women."

The mercenaries had threatened to kill Sara. Harry had been standing there with no weapons, no friends, no way to save her. Then Evgeny Smolov had shown his true colors. He'd shot the mercenaries and let Harry go. Sort of.

"You are with the Italians in New York," Evgeny said. "How can you also be with the district attorney?"

"It's complicated."

"It usually is. Tell me."

Harry shrugged. "I still work with Joey Morello from time to time. He set me up with my own antiquities business."

"A front."

"Sometimes. Sometimes not. I sell relics to rich people."

"Perhaps I will buy some."

"My half-sister's father is an assistant district attorney. And she runs the Anti-Trafficking Unit. We occasionally work together."

Evgeny's face lit up. "You work on both sides!" His roaring laughter filled the helicopter. "You are always safe. You are a smart man, my friend. It is a good thing you also work for me or I might worry about you." He jokingly wagged a finger in Harry's face. "A smart man like you should never be fully trusted."

"I was worried you forgot about me."

"Forget about the man who found my Achilles helmet? I could never forget you. It is the pride of my home in Windsor. The relics from Spartacus will look very nice beside them."

By *home* Evgeny meant a palatial estate rivaling the nearby one belonging to a man named Charles. The third of his name.

"I thought you might let me keep them," Harry said.

"No. They belong in my museum." Evgeny reached into a compartment beside him. A bottle of champagne and two glasses came out. "Here." He handed the glasses to Harry an instant before the cork exploded from the bottle, whizzing within inches of Harry's shoulder as it flew. "We drink to our success."

Evgeny filled the glasses. Harry accepted one. May as well have a drink. "To our success," Harry said. "And friendship."

"*Bóo-deem zda-ró-vye!*" Evgeny tapped Harry's glass, threw back his champagne, and immediately poured another. "I am happy to see you again," he said after polishing off the second glass. "Now I must go."

"I'm surprised you came this close to the homeland."

"I admit it makes me nervous." Evgeny craned his neck to look out the window. "That tyrant has eyes everywhere. Where do you need to go?"

"New York."

"Maxim will take you to the airport." Evgeny inclined his head to indicate the man who had frisked Harry outside.

"Do you know about the two books?" Harry asked.

"Yes."

"The books were diaries?"

"One belonged to Spartacus. The other to Cotys."

Harry's head spun. "You have to let me see them. Those are firsthand accounts of what happened during the Servile Wars." The battles Spartacus had waged during his uprising. "Sara will kill me if I don't let her read them."

"The girl from Mount Olympus?" Evgeny asked. Harry said it was her. "You cannot have them. They are mine."

"Will you send us pictures?"

Evgeny considered. "For you, yes. Pictures."

Harry knew when to stop pressing his luck. "Thanks."

"For a price."

"A price? I just found you an incredible artifact. And I didn't get paid."

"I could shoot you instead."

"I'd be happy to pay a fair price," Harry said without pause.

"The price is you must help me again."

Harry's heart sank. "Help you?" Inspiration struck. "On two conditions. First, pictures of the entire diaries. Every page."

"Agreed," Evgeny said. "What else?"

"Your help."

"With what?"

"Revenge."

Evgeny leaned forward. "I am listening."

Harry opened his mouth. A thought occurred. "What happened to Korzun? Everyone after me on this search thought they worked for him, not you."

"I had him killed. He backed out of a deal to sell me an artifact."

"You killed him because he sold it to someone else?"

"I killed him when I learned that he ordered his men to kill a rival. The rival was shot while in his car." Evgeny's face hardened. "The rival's wife and child were also killed. That is why I had Korzun shot."

"Then you used his identity to cover your involvement in the Spartacus relic search."

"I did."

"Shrewd," Harry said. "My second condition is about a man who is threatening my family."

"Who is he?"

"Ever heard of Olivier Lloris?" Evgeny started swearing in Russian. "I'll take that as a yes," Harry said.

"He is a thieving French bastard who sold me a counterfeit painting."

"He tried to swindle *you*?"

"A man working on my behalf. But it was my money he took."

Bad move, Olivier. "Don't worry," Harry said. "We'll both have our revenge."

"How?"

"By finding a relic Olivier Lloris can't refuse to come after. A relic tied to Charlemagne."

"Which you will sell to me when it is over."

There were problems for now, and problems for later. This was a for-later problem. "We can negotiate," Harry said noncommittally. "First, I have to find it. For that, I could use your help."

"I will help you. At the same time, you help me."

Nothing in this life was free. "I'm a simple antiquities dealer," Harry said. "How could I possibly help a man worth eleven billion dollars?"

"Fifteen billion," Evgeny replied. "It has been a good year." He took a drink straight from the champagne bottle. "You will help me because you are the best in the world at what you do. Finding relics."

Harry sighed. "What are we after?"

The handmade suit on Evgeny's frame stretched as he leaned forward. A smile to chill the blood of a madman appeared on his face. "Have you ever heard of the Antikythera?"

Author's Note

Few leaders in history impacted the world to the degree which Charlemagne did. King of the Franks, the Lombards (who later became Franks) and the Holy Roman Emperor. Commonly known as The Father of Europe. Charlemagne's conquests shaped Europe in countless ways, implementing whole-scale religious, societal and political changes across a wide swath of the continent and which shaped the Middle Ages.

Charlemagne was born into power. The eldest son of the interestingly named Pepin the Short, he became King of the Franks in 771 A.D. and quickly proceeded to expand his territory, leading conquests of Bavaria and Saxony (parts of modern-day Germany) and northern Spain. In addition to conquering, Charlemagne also sought to broker strategic alliances with other powerful nations, which had the impact of shoring up his grip on power at home. Much of the legwork upon which these arrangements were built was done by emissaries of each leader. Given the vast geographic distances between the powers involved, it would be impractical for a leader such as Charlemagne to conduct much of the negotiating in person. Trusted associates and confidants would be dispatched in his stead to handle the bulk of the work. Men such as the abbot Agilulph *(Chapter 1)*. Though he is fictional, countless men and women much like him existed in Charlemagne's time and were vital to successfully brokering peace and protection accords between rulers. It is possible one or more of Charlemagne's wives *(Chapter 1)* also played a role in strengthening diplomatic ties, though the tomb in which Harry found their names is from my imagination.

One alliance which truly occurred was the Abbasid–Carolingian alliance *(Chapter 2)*. This accord began under Charlemagne's father in the eighth century to establish "friendship", collaborate on a military level with each other and to eventually increase commerce between Pepin the Short's Frankish empire and the Abbasid caliphate, which was founded by a dynasty descended from the prophet Muhammad's uncle. Pepin the Short initiated this accord for the above reasons as well as to strengthen both sides' positions in their respective areas of the world. Charlemagne sought to strengthen the alliance to further protect his empire from potential attack of disruption, and one way in which he did so was by exchanging diplomatic gifts with the caliphate. Charlemagne was given an array of exotic valuables, including exquisite chess pieces, perfume, a candelabra and a water clock *(Chapter 2)*. The water clock is real and is described in the 807 Royal Frankish Annals as having spherical decorations which would strike cymbals below to create a chiming sound for each hour. There were also twelve figurines of horsemen that would animate at the end of each hour. It is also reported the caliphate offered custody of the holy places in Jerusalem to Charlemagne. As to if the keys to the holy city of Jerusalem were inside the clock, the historical record is silent.

The search for and acquiring of historical relics attracts all manner of people. Some of them are incredibly wealthy and will go to incredible lengths in their quest to obtain rare artifacts. The magazine article in this story detailing concerns for Olivier Lloris *(Chapter 3)* is based on the real-life American billionaire and disgraced collector Michael Steinhardt, who received a lifetime ban on owning cultural artifacts due to his flagrant disregard for international law and lack of care regarding researching provenance when acquiring artifacts. One of the many missteps which led to his fall from grace include an expose in which Steinhardt was photographed in his home. The photographs showed various pieces in the background, including a piece which had been stolen from a European museum years ago. As it turns out, an employee of the museum read this article and spotted the stolen piece. The authorities were notified. Jump ahead several years, and Steinhardt was ordered to return nearly 200 items valued at more than $70 million following an investigation by the New York District Attorney's office in 2021. No word on if Nora Doyle handled the case. The New York District Attorney's office collaborated with law enforcement from around the globe in a multinational effort, possibly including the Greek government's Department Against Smuggling of Antiquities *(Chapter 7)*, which is a real organization working with INTERPOL to stop international arts crimes.

The Sanctuary of the Great Gods on Samothrace *(Chapter 7)* exists. Open to all who wished to worship in ancient times, it nonetheless reserved certain aspects of religion for only the chosen few. This Mystery Religion—which is the true name for such practices—was reserved for select initiates and little is known of the inner workings. My research indicates a good way to have been part of the inner circle was to have been rich or famous, so in some ways, the world changes little. Though I'm sure their ways are interesting and full of wonder, any underground chambers containing exotic riches have yet to be discovered.

Spartacus's battles against the Roman Empires during the Third Servile War included a brief period when one Roman legion lost its aquila *(Chapter 9)*, though the aquila was later recovered after Rome's overwhelming and ruthless victory. Such a loss would have been unthinkable to Roman soldiers and they would have gone to any length to recover their standard, aware that the shame which accompanied such a loss could only be dealt with in two ways. Recover the aquila, or perish in the attempt.

Perperikon *(Chapter 13)* was a vibrant city in Ancient Thrace, located near the Perpereshka River and a small outpost called Gorna krepost, which translates as *Upper Fortress*. The river contains gold deposits, and in the time of Thrace these deposits were mined and proved quite productive. Ongoing archaeological excavations continue to this day, and the layout of the site is much as described in this story, including the church site and the open-air tombs in which members of the ruling class were buried. The church on this site was not built until the fourth or fifth century, placing it several hundred years after Spartacus would have lived, and any inscriptions in the area are in Greek, not Latin. I chose to use Latin as Harry speaks this in the stories. However, Greek or Latin, no inscriptions or carvings have yet been found which may lead to a series of subterranean rooms containing treasure. Which, of course, doesn't mean none exist.

Charlemagne envisioned his Carolingian dynasty lasting for millennia. A grand vision, though the truth of the matter is that the dynasty barely lasted four generations *(Chapter 14)* in which war and discontent proved more powerful than blood. Charlemagne's empire was eventually split into three parts, one for each of his grandsons. A civil war erupted and because of this only two of the regions survived for long, the precursors of what today we call Germany and France. The last member of the Carolingian dynasty died in 1122 A.D., barely three centuries after Charlemagne.

The Winged Victory of Samothrace statue *(Chapter 14)* is real and has been displayed at the top of the main staircase in the Louvre in Paris since 1884. Discovered in various pieces on the island in 1863 by a member of the French consulate in Turkey, this image of the goddess Nike was immediately sent to the Louvre, where it was reassembled and placed on display in the same prominent location where it stands today. Though the statue does not have a known association to King Cotys, it is the subject of a dispute between the French and Greek governments, with Greece officially considering the statue—as it does many artifacts of Greek origin—to be illegally plundered. Greece has demanded the statue be repatriated to Greek soil. To date, the French government has refused this request.

Also tied to the statue are the secret rituals and initiation process described in this story *(Chapter 15)* as part of the mystery religion are real, though little is truly known about what happened during this process. And while the secret ordeals did occur on Samothrace, these events would only have taken place at the Sanctuary of the Great Gods, not the Temple of the Lesser Gods, which I created for this story.

Harry Fox visits more than his fair share of ancient sites, including several theaters. In Ancient Greece the theater held a special place in a community, and so many were constructed before being left to time that more and more are discovered in Greece every year. The theater Harry visits near Thessaloniki *(Chapter 19)* is, however, not one of these. I created it for this story, though it is based in fact in that theaters much like the fictional one I describe have been not only found, but revived, with productions occurring in these marvels every year.

The Roman god Mars is closely tied to—if not outright stolen from—the Greek god Ares. Both are gods of war, both represent masculine ideals in a time when strength was valued, yet only one could come first. Rome was notorious for (shrewdly, many would say) allowing conquered peoples to continue worshipping their original gods alongside the Roman gods, provided they paid their taxes. That Ares inspired Mars is not surprising. Also unsurprising would be if a Roman wealthy enough to fund a personal army paid for a solid golden statue of Mars, eight feet of bluster and bravado and conspicuous consumption. Though this is all true, what is not true is that Spartacus captured such a statue during his rebellion. I made up the statue because it seemed like a neat prize for Harry to find—and it distracted the bad guys!

Seuthopolis was not the only capital of Ancient Thrace, merely one of several. It does exist today, but if you wish to visit, you'll need to bring scuba gear, as the ruins of this capital city are located at the bottom of the Koprinka Reservoir in central Bulgaria *(Chapter 22)*. The tomb of King Seuthes III exists as described and can be visited in the Valley of the Thracian Rulers not far from the reservoir, though you will be hard-pressed to find any hidden hillside tombs requiring a daredevil climb to enter. If you do, let me know. There may be treasure inside.

Harry survives his adventure in the hidden cliffside tomb near Seuthopolis by identifying the mark of Dionysus *(Chapter 22)*. The mark is fictional. I based my description of it on the *ankh* symbol, a wholly factual symbol which is as described and is a precursor of the Christian cross. However, the ankh has nothing to do with Dionysus other than making for an interesting part of the story. And for keeping Harry alive, of course.

Harry must decipher the series of rotating panels *(Chapter 22)* to reveal the spear and shield of Spartacus hidden inside the mountain near Seuthopolis. The chamber and what Harry finds are from my imagination, but the ideals Cotys depicts to show the contrast between Rome and Thrace are based in fact. Thrace existed under a loose coalition of tribes, utilizing a form of democratic governance in which member tribes had a voice. As Harry notes, this is the antithesis of Rome and Roman dictators. The other set of contrasting ideals Cotys depicts tie to the philosophy behind each empire's existence. During Cotys's time, Rome was the most powerful nation in the world. It ruled by force, by its strength of arms. Rome conquered by force. Thrace did not. Now, it must be noted Thrace did not possess the same military and numerical superiority as Rome, so it didn't have the same options at its disposal. Had it, it's hard to say if Thrace would have adopted the Roman method of expansion by brute force, or if it would have existed in a more peaceful manner. As it was, Thrace took a different tact toward maintaining its independence—which didn't exactly work out. Thrace negotiated. It didn't conquer, It didn't wage war without cause, and through this approach, it survived. Not forever, but for some time, and in a better situation than it would have otherwise. As for the historicity of my imaginary panels, Caesar is depicted as a dictator, though that title wasn't conferred upon him until three decades after Spartacus died. Caesar was awarded the Civic Crown, the second highest decoration awarded to Romans. The curule seat in the panels is real and symbolized power in Rome. A final note is that Spartacus would likely have used a pilum, not a spear *(Chapter 22)*. Roman legions typically carried the pilum, which was like a javelin in that it was nearly seven feet long and constructed of both metal and wood. Typical spears weren't quite so long, but for the purposes of this story I chose to call the weapon a spear.

I hope you enjoyed this exploration of who Spartacus may have been. In truth, little is known about Spartacus outside the events of the Third

Servile War, the title given to the slave uprising in which Sp... central figure. Historical evidence indicates he was a former ... an accomplished military leader. Of note, the major sources for this information were all written over a century after his death and none were from eyewitnesses, so it is not a far leap to assume some (or most) of what we view as fact today is not in fact true. Spartacus was Thracian, we know that, but how did he become such an adept military strategist who orchestrated one of the most unlikely uprisings in history? Common men and women did not have access to the type of training through which such knowledge was imparted. Could Spartacus have grown up in a privileged background? If so, how did he end up an enslaved gladiator, one with not only a thirst for vengeance, but the ability to both inspire his fellow slaves to revolt and lead them to success on the battlefield? It's hard to comprehend just how unlikely his victories over Roman legions were. And he did it *twice*. Perhaps Spartacus was more than the product of a privileged upbringing, or even a noble one. Perhaps Spartacus was the son of a king with something to prove. Perhaps he was not. We'll likely never know for certain, but writing a story about it sure was fun.

This is Harry's first adventure in a new world. The mystery of his father's amulet has been solved, Sara is now in New York, and Dani Doyle is becoming part of his life. Harry's world is evolving, and the challenges he'll soon face are as well. Enemies as-yet-unknown will appear from far beyond his former borders. Relics he can't imagine are yet to come. There is much more to Harry's story, and while it's uncertain what will come—or how he will fare—I do know that we must evolve to survive, and Harry Fox is no exception.

I hope you enjoyed this story. I promise the fun is only getting started and there are more adventures on the horizon.

Andrew Clawson
February 2024

Excerpt from
THE ANTIKYTHERA CODE

You can get your copy of THE ANTIKYTHERA CODE at Amazon

Chapter 1

The first punch knocked the guard down. The second kept him there. Harry Fox shook his numb hand and looked around. Nobody came running.

Punching people was no fun. Not even for the one doing the punching. Moonlight glinted off the unconscious guard's holstered sidearm as Harry manhandled him into the back of the delivery truck and dumped the unconscious man beside an oversized metal container. One with airholes in it. He wasn't here to kill anyone. Harry only wanted the book. Nobody had to get hurt. Well, not badly, at least. The guard didn't move as Harry stripped off his uniform, opened the container lid and tossed the man in wearing nothing but his underwear. The container lid closed with a click. Harry tossed a blanket over it and buttoned his newly-acquired shirt. Someone would find the guard. Eventually. After Harry was long gone.

He took a breath and turned, casting an eye over the other containers in his truck. Two rows of short tubes pointing up. Twenty tubes in all, each a few feet long and a foot in diameter. A breeze rustled the canvas roof covering the box truck bed as he stepped out and onto the dry ground. He checked the canvas roof again. The truck had been repurposed from an old army cargo truck, one with no solid roof. Exactly to make the spotlights shining from the building next to him that much brighter. Harry looked up at the monstrosity. It was a long way up. German castles built five hundred years ago tended to be large. This one fit the bill perfectly. Dark stone brooded over what during the day was a picturesque estate of wide green fields and thick woodlands. The water of a nearby lake sparkled. Towers rose at each corner of the rectangular castle. One in rear corner stood taller than the others, the chapel tower with a massive bell inside. His gaze lingered on that tallest tower for a moment. *It can work.*

Static crackled and startled him. Harry grabbed at the stolen radio clipped to his belt. He listened to another guard speak in German, then turned the volume down. Harry's German was atrocious. As long as he didn't have to speak directly to any other guards, he could get by with a few phrases over the radio, but anything beyond that was pushing it. Get in, get the book, get out.

The anonymous blue guard uniform should buy him cover. He lifted the collar, confirmed the guard's keycard was clipped to his belt loop, and headed for the side door, patting his pocket to confirm the small electronic device was inside. It was, and his plan depended on it. His truck was parked at a corner of the massive castle, the corner diagonal from the tall belltower. That would matter greatly in a few minutes if all went according to plan. Get in, get the book, get out. Nothing to it.

The pack strapped to Harry's back was the same dark blue as the guard uniform. Hard to believe such a slim backpack held the key to his escape. He pushed that worry from his head and walked to the front door, a massive wooden affair Harry would need a tank to blast through. Fortunately, he had a keycard. He waved the stolen card in front of a reader, which flashed from red to green. Harry pushed on a handle bolted to one of the ten-foot planks and the entire door opened without a sound. Harry slipped through, closing the door behind him and moving quickly to a shadowy alcove nearby.

A staircase wide enough to drive said tank up looked over the front entrance. Hallways on either side of the stairs led deeper into the castle, while open doors and entrances dotted walls on both sides. Harry pulled up a map of the castle's interior in his mind's eye. He'd come here for one reason. A reason sitting inside a locked display case in a viewing hall on the second level. Harry lowered his chin, hunched his shoulders, and marched out like a guard on patrol.

His footsteps echoed off the stone walls as he moved at a steady pace past the giant staircase and down the left hallway. What centuries ago would have been a dreary and smoke-filled passage now had recessed lighting in the ceiling to guide him. Harry kept his head low in case another guard happened past, never looking up at the surveillance cameras along the wall. The owner of this castle took security seriously. A private company had the contract for this castle, with nearly the same personnel on staff every day. One thing going for him was the guards weren't supposed to chit-chat. There was no water-cooler talk on duty. Not when Leon Havertz was paying the bills.

He passed three entranceways as he walked. The fourth, he took, turning on a heel and continuing his fake patrol until he found a staircase leading up to the second level. Electric sconces lined the walls as Harry kept going up the stairs toward the landing, above which the moon gleamed through a window of thick glass. His feet had barely touched the landing when a sound grabbed his ear.

Footsteps. Coming from above. He forced himself to keep his eyes down and feet moving as another guard came around the corner above him and walked down the stairs. Harry hugged the wall.

"*Alles klar?*" Everything all right?

The other guard's rough greeting sounded as they passed. Harry didn't think. He reacted.

"*Alles klar.*" It's alright.

His chest tightened as he kept climbing. The other guard's footsteps stopped. Harry didn't turn, but slipped a hand into his pocket, his fingers sliding into the ceramic knuckleduster in it. He could turn and jump down at the guard, take him out before anyone else showed up. But then what?

Harry risked a glance over his shoulder. The guard stood on the landing, his back to Harry as he looked out the window. The breath escaped from Harry's lungs. He quickened his pace to the second level hallway and turned a corner, pausing a moment until his heart slowed. Thank goodness he'd researched a few common phrases the guards may use. His guttural response had fooled the man. One chance meeting was enough.

Harry straightened his back and walked straight ahead, into the heart of the castle. Suits of armor stood guard on one side as he walked, polished to shine under the electric chandeliers above. The suits were smaller than most people would imagine, only the largest of them big enough for a man Harry's size to wear, and he wasn't tall. The other side of this passage was a thick stone railing, beyond which Harry could see down into a hall of some sort. The castle blueprints he'd studied told him to expect this. They did not tell him to expect it would be occupied. Raised voices suddenly filled the air and Harry went still. Voices coming from the hall downstairs.

Keep going. The best way to stick out in this guard's uniform was to act as though he didn't belong. Harry forced himself to keep moving, slowing his pace as he moved closer to the railing to get a view of the lower level. A small group of men sat in high-backed chairs around a blazing fire. One man stood, his booming voice reaching to the darkened rafters as he shouted at the men in German. Not shouted. Sang. The man was singing and though Harry only understood a few words he didn't need to speak the language to know this guy was butchering some ancient German tune. Not that Harry wanted to understand. He was much more interested in the man singing.

Leon Havertz came from old German money. Around two hundred years ago the Havertz family had a title conferred upon them by Emperor Bismarck. That had vanished under the Reich, though Havertz didn't seem to have received the message. Leon Havertz was a man in need of ceremony to stand on, and not only because he needed a stepping-stool to stand on if he wanted to reach the top shelf. Harry kept one eye on the balding, diminutive man from whom this roaring voice emitted. Nobody that size should be able to blow the windows out with his singing, yet Havertz's tortured song was rattling the walls.

Harry didn't see the chair until it was too late. One moment he was looking at Havertz over the railing, the next he tumbled ass-over-elbows to the floor. He froze. The singing continued unabated. Harry checked fore and aft, found no other guards watching, and jumped to his feet. He kept going as though the tumble didn't happen, and Havertz sang as though no one could hear. Another stairway beckoned ahead, and as Harry turned to go up the stairs, he passed the final suit of armor standing watch in the hall. He angled his head. *There's a mannequin in there.* So that's how they kept the suits standing.

No guards came down as Harry ascended this set of stairs. A tapestry hung on the wall. One from a family not named Havertz. It seemed Leon's ancestors had purchased both the castle and everything that came with it when they received their empty title, purchasing the grandeur at a cut-rate price from a noble name fallen on hard times. Unfortunately, Leon wasn't as cheap when it came to buying and selling artifacts. That's why Harry was skulking around this castle and risking his neck to avoid armed guards. Leon Havertz wouldn't sell a book, which meant Harry Fox had to steal it.

It all started when Harry found a note scrawled inside a bible. Not just any bible. One owned by Charlemagne's personal abbot. A note suggesting a storied treasure tied to the Father of Europe had been hidden long ago. Hidden, and never found. That's why Harry was in this German castle on a moonlit night. He needed a specific book to continue following Charlemagne's trail. An illuminated manuscript Leon Havertz kept in this castle and refused to sell.

The third floor was much darker than the first two, the only lights dim bulbs along the ceiling. The glass chandeliers up here were unlit. Harry glanced around the corner and found the hallway empty. No promise it would remain that way for long, as the guards had randomized patrol patterns, their movements seemingly haphazard and varying every time. Supposedly ten of the guards were always on patrol to keep Havertz's castle secure. Harry thought it was overkill until he learned of what else Havertz kept in his home. A collection of relics and cultural artifacts to rival a museum. All for his personal enjoyment.

Harry pushed any thoughts of pilfering other relics from his head as he walked down the hallway, alert for the sound of other guards. This was the third and highest level, where Havertz's private quarters took up most of the real estate and the level where his relic collection was housed. An elevator door glowed in the wall as Harry kept moving at a steady pace toward one side of the castle, his footsteps snapping on the stone floor. Fewer doors led off to either side in this hallway, the air noticeably colder, which was saying something in this hunk of stone. Keycard readers glowed red outside of each door.

He needed the third door. This was the display room where Havertz kept his smaller treasures, the ones closest to him. Also the closest room to his personal quarters. Harry could imagine the little guy peering through his round glasses at the treasures inside, watching as someone else cleaned the cases and cared for the artifacts. Leon Havertz was the kind of guy who gave relic collectors a bad name. Harry shrugged. Same as most of his customers. Except they hadn't refused to sell him a relic he needed.

Harry waved his keycard in front of the reader. It beeped as he twisted the doorknob. The light stayed red. The door stayed shut. He frowned and tried it again. Same result. What the heck? A look over his shoulder found the hallway still empty, though that could change any second. He darted back to the last door he'd passed and waved the keycard in front of its reader. The red light turned green and he pushed the door open with no issue. Why couldn't he open the relic room door? The guards were supposed to have access to all castle areas.

The door swung silently shut as he stared at the keycard reader, silently cursing it for not working. A flash of light caught his eye and Harry stuck a hand out to stop the door from closing. He looked up. A flash of light he could see through the window in this room. Harry walked into the darkness, closing the door behind him before heading to the window. He leaned over and peered out to the ground three levels below. Not three stories, like modern buildings. Three levels of a castle with twenty-foot ceilings on every floor. Sixty feet down from this window to the gravel drive out front. His canvas-topped box truck was still down there not attracting attention. That wouldn't last forever.

The relic room holding the book he needed was beside this one. Harry looked around and found himself in a sitting room, chairs in front of an unlit fireplace, book-filled shelving on one wall and a table in the corner. Ivory-colored chess pieces sat on a thick board. He took all this in with a glance before turning back to the window. A simple latch secured it. Harry reached out and lifted the metal latch, pulled on a small handle and opened the window. He instinctively leaned back as a gentle breeze blew in. Nobody would climb this high to break into the castle, so no need for an intricate lock. No screens or protection of any sort kept people from falling out. All it would take was one wrong move, leaning over too far, and it was all over.

Harry leaned out. He looked straight down. *Perfect.*

A ledge ran along the castle wall directly below this window. A decorative ledge, and calling it a ledge was generous. Half his foot could fit on the outcropping if he were lucky. A single row of stone leading to the adjacent window, and beyond it a small turret at the corner of the castle. Nobody would go out there for any reason. Nobody except Harry Fox, that is.

It stood to reason the windows of every room at this level would be equally unsecured. All Harry need do is get on the ledge, make the short trip over to the next window, slide his pocket knife between the window panes to lift the latch and he was set. Get into the relic room, retrieve the book and be on his way. Nothing to it.

As long as he didn't fall off the ledge. Harry grinned. *No need to think that way.* He pushed the worry aside and stepped out onto the ledge. One foot first, which he had to turn sideways to fit onto the stone, then the next. Both hands stayed glued to the window frame. The next window was twenty feet away. Not far when he was inside the castle. A veritable chasm from out here. Harry took a breath, put his backside against the wall and started shifting. One foot, then another, his heels scraped over the outcropping until he could no longer hold the window frame. He didn't stop, sliding over at a steady clip, his fingers digging into the mortar lines in a desperate attempt to find any sort of support.

Bang. A gust of wind threw the window inward so it smashed off something inside. Harry winced. No breaking glass, but another gust came and the window crashed inside once more. He picked up the pace. A guard might hear that and come to inspect the noise. Unless Havertz's dreadful singing covered his tracks. Harry almost laughed.

His foot slipped. An old bird's nest on the ledge got beneath his boot and sent his foot skidding ahead. Harry froze, mortar cutting into his fingertips as he gripped the wall. The thundering of his heart would draw the guards if the banging window didn't. The birds nest fluttered down into the darkness as Harry slowly pulled his foot back and paused for a moment, cold air harsh in his throat with each gasp. Easy does it, Harry. You're almost there.

He pushed on, never looking up, only at his feet until one fingertip banged against the windowsill and he was there. Out came his pocketknife, the blade flipped up and Harry slid it between the panes, wiggling up and down until it caught the latch and the window fell inward. A distant scent hit his nose as he stepped up and over the sill with exaggerated care. The scent of smoke. Probably from Havertz's fireplace downstairs.

Harry closed the window and opened the curtain. Better to work by moonlight than risk having someone spot his penlight under the door. The moon's reflection would block anyone outside from seeing in, giving him the privacy he required. Harry kept still as his eyes adjusted to the dark room. They did, yet he didn't move, his feet rooted to the ground. None of his research had prepared him for this.

A golden man stood nearby. Harry's penlight went to what at first was the dark outline of a man, nothing more than shadow. His light turned the man to gold and sent waves of flashing light over the walls and ceiling. A suit of gold-plated armor stood at eye level with Harry. Gilded panels interspersed with polished metal gleamed. A gaudy plume of red feathers decorated the helmet, while gemstones dotted the breastplate. Harry particularly admired the golden beard carved into the face protector. How anyone could move in that stuff was beyond him. Probably the armor a king who drank wine and sat on his horse while the battle raged.

Display cases lined the wall on either side, dark spotlights above them to better showcase this collection of private treasures. A pair of gold-and-silver pistols sat on the next display stand. Pistols which appeared to be the earliest version of a six-shooter Harry had ever seen. He didn't bother to read the informational placard on the stand as he walked past. Same with the pair of swords on the next stand, one a curved samurai blade and the other likely a Viking sword, the latter with a ruby in the pommel that could have ransomed a king.

Harry paused for only a second to look up at the marble statue which came next. Bearded, muscled beyond measure and holding a jagged thunderbolt, Zues stood seven feet tall and had likely been carved in Greece at least two thousand years ago. Harry's light moved to the final artifact in this row, held in the place of honor in a corner of the room, a protective glass case covering it. An illuminated manuscript commissioned by Charlemagne, thicker than a phone book, previously owned by Charlemagne's personal abbot Agilulph. The man whose scrawled note had set Harry on this journey.

He stood over the case. Colors of a richness those living in the ancient world could scarcely imagine leapt off the page. Harry drew in a short breath. "Elephants," he whispered to himself. "Sara was right."

Even the gray ink seemed to glow, lustrous and vibrant unlike any he'd seen before. Harry shook his head. There would be time to admire it later while he uncovered the truth within. He put the penlight between his teeth and reached for the glass cover. The only upside of Havertz keeping his prizes in a castle with a squadron of guards was it seemed like enough. That's why the only thing holding this glass cover in place was a latch. Harry lifted it, the same as he'd done with the window. It flipped open. No passcodes, no keys. He lifted the hinged glass top, grabbed hold of the open book on either side and closed it with care.

Time to go. Harry tucked the book under his arm like a football, closed the glass cover and headed for the exit. He cast a long look at the Viking sword, specifically the ruby as big as a golf ball in its pommel. *Maybe next time.*

He unlocked the room's door and slipped into the hallway, re-securing the lock before closing the door behind him. Across the castle, up to the corner tower. Then he'd give Havertz a real show right before he left. The German could have avoided all this if he'd been reasonable. Except Leon Havertz didn't listen to reason. He didn't sell his book. Too bad for him. Harry smirked as he tested the door handle and found it locked. A scent of smoke hung in the hall as he turned. Havertz was in for a surp—

Two stood in the hallway. The acrid scent of smoke hung on their clothes. Two guards with a look of shock on their face, the look of men who snuck a cigarette in a far corner room of the castle when they were supposed to be on their rounds, two guards who never expected to find a man coming out of the relic display room. Two men with pistols holstered on their belts. Both men stood as stiff and still as Harry.

One of them blinked. He leaned closer, peering at Harry through the shadows. *"Jurgen?"*

Harry ducked his chin even lower. He grunted a monosyllabic response and turned his back on the two. The guys were sneaking a smoke. They probably wanted as little to do with him as he with them. Harry shielded the book with his torso and started walking. One step, two steps, forcing himself not to move fast. The two guards said nothing and Harry let out the breath he'd been holding. It worked.

"Jurgen." Harry ignored the name and kept walking. The guard repeated himself, louder this time. Harry waved a hand without turning

around and grunted again.

A flashlight beam came to life behind him. Harry's shadow stretched out in front of him. The guard's raised voice followed. "*Halt.*"

Harry didn't need to speak the language to understand. The stairwell was too far ahead. Even if he ran for it, these guys would have every guard in the castle on his tail in seconds. He only had one play. He stopped.

He turned and marched back toward the pair before they could respond. The light was in his face, so Harry lifted his own penlight and aimed it right in their eyes. A protest formed in one guard's throat as Harry came at them, feet pounding as he reached into his pocket, slipped his fingers into the knuckledusters and started yelling at the two guards. "*Guten morgen! Wo befindet sich die bilbiothek? Kaffee wit milch!*"

The first three German phrases that popped into his head. Wishing them good morning, asking where to find the library and ordering coffee with milk confused them just enough so Harry could get within arm's reach. The guard who had been speaking still had his mouth hanging open when Harry clocked him flush in the jaw with his knuckledusters on. The guy dropped. The other guard stared with wide eyes as his friend collapsed, looking up in time for Harry to send him down for the count alongside his partner.

The second guy barely hit the ground before Harry was running for the stairwell. Everything depended on him getting across the castle and to the far tower before those guards raised the alarm. He stopped on the stairwell landing and looked out the window. Nothing seemed amiss. His truck was still parked there. A flashlight beam snapped on an instant before he turned and lit up the truck's side. Harry lingered long enough to see a guard approach the vehicle and stop. Harry turned the volume on his radio up and beat feet down to the second level, slowing as he rounded the corner and marched along the walkway overlooking Havertz's still-raucous gathering below. The fire crackled, mugs crashed together, and an abomination of German folk song filled the air.

A new guard walked out of the stairwell moments before Harry walked past. Harry nodded and grunted first. The other guy did the same and kept going. Harry turned the corner, ignoring the stairwell in favor of a hallway that kept him on this level and put him closer to the tower he needed. He was halfway through when his radio burst to life.

"*Eindringling! Eindringling!*"

He didn't have a clue what that meant. He didn't have to, not with how the man was shouting and the radio came alive with responses. Harry started jogging, head on a swivel as he cruised toward the turn ahead. Hang a left, head down that hallway until he found the last stairwell, then straight up to the tower. Two minutes, tops. Avoid the other guards for that long and he was out of here.

A guard appeared from a doorway ahead. Make that two guards. Harry kept jogging toward them as they watched him go. He raised a hand and pointed past them, shouting as he picked up speed. "*Augen! Augen!*"

The guards rightfully hesitated. Why was their comrade yelling eyes as he ran at them? They couldn't have realized it was because Harry didn't know to say look in German and this was the best he could do. They did understand something was wrong. One drew his sidearm as Harry raced at them. The second tried to as well.

They were too close. Elbows smashed together and each howled in pain. Harry kicked one gun loose and punched at the other. Both went flying away. He jabbed the closest guard in the gut, doubling him over so the knee Harry brought up caught him square on the chin and sent him down. Harry turned to take care of the second guard.

Who was faster than he looked. The standing guard's fist landed smack on Harry's nose, knocking him back as light exploded in his vision. Harry stumbled, head shaking to clear his vision as the guard closed in. Harry saw a fist coming and threw his arm up, catching enough of it to send the blow glancing off his chin. He didn't catch the next shot, which caught him on the cheek and knocked him back another step. Harry twisted, a punch whizzed past, and he threw an elbow at the guard's nose. Cartlidge broke. Harry head-butted the guard's nose and the guy fell back, barely catching himself before Harry threw a hook that caught the guard square and dropped him.

The radios erupted with frenzied German. Harry ran for the stairwell which led upstairs. He made it halfway before the sound of pounding feet and shouting guards came from the stairwell, the noise sending him running back the way he'd come. His breath came fast after lugging the heavy book around on top of the pack on his back. He turned the corner and passed a suit of armor. By now Havertz and his companions were huddled together in front of the fire, one of them watching Harry race around upstairs while the rest listened to Havertz shout into a radio. The man had no idea Harry wasn't a guard, looking on as Harry kept running.

The armor. Harry stopped and went back to the armor, set his book down in a dark shadow and went to work. Off came the arms, the helmet and chest plate, Harry keeping the noise down as he worked. The legs were next, and before any of the guards he'd heard in the stairwell appeared, Harry had the mannequin underneath in his arms. He used his stolen keycard to open the closest door, ran in and went straight at the window, hefting the mannequin back and hurling it through the thick window. Glass shattered, Harry doubled back to grab his book, and as the noise of onrushing guards sounded in the hallway Harry disappeared behind a thick tapestry on the wall and stood still.

The guards ran past. Harry poked his head out as shouting came from near the broken window. He ducked back as a number of guards came running out of the room and headed downstairs. They were in for a surprise when they discovered the body on the ground was mostly plastic. The noise of their departure quieted and Harry slipped from behind the tapestry, hugging the wall as he made it down the hallway and turned toward the stairwell heading upstairs.

"*Halt!*"

The shouted order came from below. He looked down to find a guard pointing at Harry. "*Buch! Das Buch!*"

The book. He'd spotted the book under Harry's arm. Out came a pistol and Harry ducked as the guard fired and a bullet pinged off the stone railing. Another shot did the same. So much for sneaking around.

Harry lowered his head and took off at full speed. Two more guards joined the one firing below to fill the air around Harry with bullets. Shards of rock erupted off the wall at every step, dust stinging his eyes as the roar of gunfire punctuated each step. One shot buzzed so close he felt it pass. Harry lifted the book up to cover his head as he dove the last few feet toward the stairwell door, rolling as he hit the ground and crashed off the wall before skidding to a halt in the stairwell.

The book was clasped to his chest. He got up, tucked it under his arm, and ran off to the sound of a single round clattering on the ground. A bullet that fell out of the book.

His footsteps echoed off the stone walls as Harry took the stairs two at a time up to the third level. He paused, leaned around the corner and kept still. Noise intensified from below. Loud and getting louder, but not enough to mask the sound of a radio crackling softly around the corner. Harry leaned further so he could see. A man stood not ten feet away, his back to the wall and a bottle at his lips. A mostly-empty bottle. Maybe these guards weren't as reliable as Harry had believed. Even so, this guard stood between Harry and the bell tower. He needed to be dealt with.

Harry slipped his knuckledusters on. He set the book down. Better to do this with both hands free. He took a breath and stepped into the hallway.

The boozy guard stood in front of him. Harry gaped. The guard punched him.

Harry stepped back as the too-sober guard smashed the glass bottle off Harry's head. Blinding light flashed across his vision as Harry lifted his hands and desperately backed up, warding off a heavy fist before his vision cleared and he could fight back. Harry swung, connected with nothing, then the air vanished from his lungs when the guard socked him in the gut. Harry doubled over, went to one knee and tasted blood on his tongue. *Enough of this.*

Harry threw an uppercut and hit the guard where the sun doesn't shine. The guard let out a high-pitched squeal before Harry smashed a fist into his gut, landed a hook to the head and grabbed the man by the shoulders as he stumbled and smashed him bodily into the stone wall The guard collapsed and didn't move. Harry grabbed his book, looked down to find flashlight beams crazily painting the steps below and booked it into the third level hallway, following the route he'd memorized until he arrived at the narrow stairway leading up to the bell tower. His keycard opened the heavy wooden door, cold air greeting him as he raced up the winding stairs to an open landing on top.

The giant metal bell was suspended below a conical tower roof. A brisk wind blew this high up. Harry ran over to the stone wall and looked down to where a group of guards stood around the dummy he'd thrown from the window. They stood only a few feet from his cargo truck with its canvas roof. Harry grinned. *Get ready.*

He took of his pack and set it down, unzipping the top before removing a folded piece of fabric with straps attached to it. Harry secured the illuminated book in his backpack, cinched it tightly around his torso, then shrugged into the straps attached to the fabric. He tucked the fabric into a strap to secure it, stepped up and onto the stone wall which kept people from falling out of the tower and reached up. A gutter running around the roof was within reach. Harry pulled himself up to the roof as the first banging sounded on the wooden door below.

The guards were coming up. Time for the grand finale. Harry pulled a small electronic device from his pocket, a device no bigger than a deck of cards with a single button on it. Harry powered it on and a solid red light illuminated. He walked with care up to the peak of the pointed roof, leaning low so he didn't slide off, and when he reached the very top he stood and turned. The shouting from below was getting louder. They were nearly on him. Harry grabbed the folded fabric from his strap and looked at the dark horizon, then to the cargo truck below. He pushed the button on his device. The light turned from red to green and Harry started running.

The edge of the roof rushed up too fast. Harry ran at the darkness, took one last step on the roof and leapt into the void as the cargo truck erupted in an explosion as rockets tore through the canvas roof and screamed for the sky.

Harry didn't see them explode as he careened into the night. He pulled a handle on his pack and flinched as the engine on his back came to life and the fan concealed in his backpack went to work. Harry threw the folded fabric skyward. The air caught it and the paraglider chute filled to stop Harry from plummeting seventy feet to the ground. The parajet engine on his back shoved him forward as light filled the sky, brilliant red, blue and yellow painting the night as fireworks from the back of Harry's truck tore through the canvas, flew skyward and exploded in a wondrous display.

No bullets tore through the dark fabric of Harry's chute. None punched holes in him. He kept his eyes ahead, the fan on his back churning to push him up and on into the night, gliding in near-silence to the north. A compass strapped to his wrist glowed green and told Harry he was on the proper heading. Two minutes from now he'd touch down in a field beside a river, leave his pack and get into the boat he'd docked there. A boat to take Harry – and his new book – one step further on Charlemagne's path.

You can get your copy of THE ANTIKYTHERA CODE at Amazon

GET YOUR COPY OF THE HARRY FOX STORY
THE NAPOLEON CIPHER,
AVAILABLE EXCLUSIVELY FOR MY VIP READER LIST

Sharing the writing journey with my readers is a special privilege. I love connecting with anyone who reads my stories, and one way I accomplish that is through my mailing list. I only send notices of new releases or the occasional special offer related to my novels.

If you sign up for my VIP reader mailing list, I'll send you a copy of *The Napoleon Cipher*, the Harry Fox adventure that's not sold in any store. You can get your copy of this exclusive novel by signing up on my website.

Did you enjoy this story? Let people know

Reviews are the most effective way to get my books noticed. I'm one guy, a small fish in a massive pond. Over time, I hope to change that, and I would love your help. The best thing you could do to help spread the word is leave a review on your platform of choice.

Honest reviews are like gold. If you've enjoyed this book I would be so grateful if you could take a few minutes leaving a review, short or long.

Thank you very much.

Also by Andrew Clawson

The Parker Chase Series
A Patriot's Betrayal
The Crowns Vengeance
Dark Tides Rising
A Republic of Shadows
A Hollow Throne
A Tsar's Gold

The TURN Series
TURN: The Conflict Lands
TURN: A New Dawn
TURN: Endangered

Harry Fox Adventures
The Arthurian Relic
The Emerald Tablet
The Celtic Quest
The Achilles Legend
The Pagan Hammer
The Pharaoh's Amulet
The Thracian Idol
The Antikythera Code

About the Author

Andrew Clawson is the author of multiple series, including the Parker Chase and TURN thrillers, as well as the Harry Fox adventures.

You can find him at his website, AndrewClawson.com

or you can connect with him on Instagram at andrew.clawson

on Twitter at @clawsonbooks

on Facebook at facebook.com/AndrewClawsonnovels

and you can always send him an email at:
andrew@andrewclawson.com.

Made in the USA
Columbia, SC
05 October 2024